VANISHED

VANISHED

A Maggie McKenzie Mystery

LYNN GARDNER

Covenant

Cover image *Woman Walking Down the Stairs in an Old Church* by Spike Mafford © Photodisc Green/Getty Images

Cover design copyrighted 2004 by Covenant Communications, Inc.

Published by Covenant Communications, Inc.
American Fork, Utah

Printed in the United States
First Printing: October 2004

16 15 14 13 12 11 10 09   12 11 10 9 8 7 6 5 4 3

ISBN-13 978-1-59811-798-1
ISBN-10 1-59811-798-X

Dedication

No writer is an entity unto themselves. In the course of the creation of a book, many contribute to its final success. Thanks to my writer's group that keeps me focused on the elements of the story the reader needs to know. I frequently race through the adventure without stopping to provide the sights, sounds, smells, and motivation that make a story come alive to the reader. My writer's group reminds me to stop and let my characters smell the roses—and other things.

Then there are the evaluators who ask endless *why* questions and catch any blips in the story. And the proof-readers and editors who make sure my well-researched facts are just that—well-researched and factual. My thanks to them all.

But mostly, my heartfelt gratitude to editor Shauna Humphreys, who has the patience and vision to shepherd a project through rocky areas with tact and a sense of humor. Thank you.

And to my readers. Thank you for embracing the characters born of a lifetime of experience with people all over the country, and a wild and fertile imagination. Your letters are the only thing that keep me at the computer instead of on the golf course with my husband.

CHAPTER 1

Mary Margaret McKenzie took a deep breath, squared her shoulders, put on her most professional face, and swung open the heavy glass door of the newspaper office. She paused momentarily to take in the desks scattered throughout the large room, the glassed partition in the center and private office doors that rimmed the big central office, then strode straight to the reception desk with no hint of hesitation or uncertainty.

She flashed a smile at the woman behind the desk. "Good morning. I'm M. M. McKenzie. I think Mr. Lawson is expecting me."

As the woman glanced up from her work, her mouth fell open and the phone she held cradled on her shoulder dropped to the desk.

Maggie immediately lifted her hand to her long auburn hair, then smoothed her royal blue suit jacket, wondering if something was wrong with her appearance. She had carefully checked the mirror before leaving her motel, making sure the outfit she had chosen for this important day was appropriately sophisticated to prove she was not just off the farm, but not too dressy for a small-town newspaper.

Normally cool, competent, and completely unflappable, Lily Noble, general office manager of the San Buenaventura Press, suddenly was none of the above. Never taking her gaze from the penetrating deep blue eyes in front of her, Lily placed the phone back on the cradle and pressed a button with three quick clicks of a long crimson nail, a signal to the recipient to come unobserved to the front office. At this early hour, the rest of the staff had not yet arrived, and Lily wanted Dorothea to see what she was seeing. Regaining her composure, she smiled up at the young woman standing in front of her.

"Good morning, M. M. McKenzie. Do you have another name or are you called M. M.? Or M&M maybe?" Lily's mind raced, trying to match this face to one she'd last seen more than seven years ago. Was this the face, changed by those passing years?

Relief flooded through Maggie at the amusement in the woman's voice, and the smile that quickly appeared to replace that first shocked expression.

Maggie laughed. "M. M. McKenzie is my professional name. I sign my articles and pictures that way. That was the name on the contract Mr. Randolph sent me, so I assumed that was the name Mr. Lawson would recognize as his new reporter. But I go by just plain Maggie."

"Well, just plain Maggie, I'm Lily, and you're going to have to bring me up to date. Mr. Lawson didn't mention he hired a new reporter, and he's in a breakfast meeting now, so fill me in. Then I'll relay the good news to him when he arrives."

"Oh. I thought . . . Mr. Randolph said . . . he would let Mr. Lawson know . . . I won the contest and he said the job was mine." Maggie's stammered explanation accompanied a flaming face almost the color of her hair.

"It's okay, sweetie. Just tell me from the beginning. In fact, let's do better than that." Lily placed the phone on the high reception counter between them and clicked another button with the crimson nail that perfectly matched her crimson lips. "Now just tell me about the contest and the job while I record the whole thing, and I'll play it back for Mr. Lawson. That's much easier than taking notes."

Maggie placed her manila envelope on the counter, took a deep breath, and plunged into her tale. "Just before graduation last semester, my journalism professor gave me an entry form for a contest sponsored by the famous publisher, William H. Randolph. The prize was a job with one of the newspapers he owned. My entry won. Mr. Randolph sent a contract and a letter . . ." Maggie's torrent of words ceased while she rifled through the envelope, found the contract and the letter, and handed them to Lily.

"He said to come to this office, at this address, today, and I'd start work." She paused to give Lily time to read the papers. "This is my first job since graduation . . ." Maggie stopped as a frown creased

Lily's forehead. This wasn't going as she'd envisioned on that fifteen-hour drive from Idaho yesterday. Something was wrong.

Lily tapped the phone recorder with the fingernail and turned it off. "Well, M. M. McKenzie, this all looks legal and proper, but I think you need to know one little thing before you see Mr. Lawson." That bright crimson fingernail pushed Lily's glasses back in place on the bridge of her nose, then traced a path from there to the tip of her nose where it paused while she decided how to phrase what she had to say. "Mr. Randolph and Mr. Lawson have been good friends for years, in a competitive sort of way. They're always playing practical jokes on each other, and through the years that has sort of gotten out of hand."

"Oh." That took the wind out of Maggie's sails. "Is this . . . just a practical joke then?" Her stomach did a distressing flip-flop.

"No," Lily hurried to explain. "Neither of them would ever hurt anyone else in their pranks. It's my guess that Mr. Randolph didn't tell Mr. Lawson he'd hired a new reporter. You may be a complete surprise to our illustrious editor." She looked up into those deep blue eyes, gauging how this young woman would receive the news. Would she cry? Get mad? That would be a major factor in how Lionel Lawson took this unexpected bit of news.

Maggie drew herself up to her full five feet, eight inches, squared her shoulders, and beamed a charming smile. "Then I guess we'd better break the news so I can get to work. I didn't drive all the way from Idaho to stand around the office all day."

Lily liked that. In fact, she liked everything about this girl. She liked her friendly, enthusiastic approach. No timidity there. And no stilted sophistication. Maggie seemed totally genuine. A painful memory pierced Lily's heart, and she had to compose herself again, hiding her disquiet in a flurry of shuffling desk papers and using her crimson nail to activate the recording.

"Okay, let's get the whole story on here so I can give it to Mr. Lawson. He'll be in meetings most of the morning, but he left an assignment." She paused to find the right words so she wouldn't actually be lying. "For the first available reporter, and I'll give you that so you won't have to 'stand around the office' all morning waiting for him."

"What do you want to know?" Maggie's brother had warned her things were different in California, but she hadn't expected anything like this. In fact, she thought Steve was pulling her leg. Apparently this was the one time he'd leveled with her—it was turning out to be the strangest introductory interview she'd ever encountered.

"Tell me about yourself, what you do, why you like to do it, your background. Just whatever makes you who you are." Lily leaned back and watched the young woman with hair the color of a strawberry roan. *Who was she, really?*

"What makes me who I am?" Maggie smiled and relaxed. "I have five older brothers and I'm the only girl in my family. We live on a ranch on the Utah-Idaho border where I grew up. I've always loved to write and take pictures, so I combined my two loves with a double major in political science and criminal investigation and a minor in photography. My dream is to be an investigative reporter. I finished my degree a couple of months ago and freelanced while I waited for the results of the writing contest."

"Were you that sure you'd win, or couldn't you find a job?" Lily interrupted, curious about Maggie's delay in seeking immediate permanent employment.

"My family's very close and we try to spend time together every year," Maggie explained, "and this was our only opportunity to be together before I left." She flashed that infectious smile again.

Lily relaxed a little. With a story like that, this girl couldn't have any connection to the other, could she? But the resemblance . . .

"Okay, Maggie. Are you familiar with the area?"

"No, I just arrived last night. But I bought a map of San Buenaventura so I'll have no problem finding my way around."

Lily liked the confidence in Maggie's voice. "Where are you staying, child? Do you have an apartment already?"

"No. I checked into the first motel I found. Well, not the first," Maggie admitted with an impish smile. "I mean, this *is* California, so I found one on the beach. I thought I could look for apartments after I get to know the town and decide where I'd like to live. Although it may boil down to where I can afford to live."

"Are you sure you don't want to take the rest of the day and find an apartment and get settled in?" Lily asked.

"No thanks. You just get the information to Mr. Lawson, and I'll get started on the assignment." Maggie held out her hand. "May I have it?"

Lily rifled through her stack of papers and found the sheet with the printed heading, From the Desk of the Editor. "Let me decipher this for you. Lion Lawson isn't known for his penmanship."

"Lion Lawson? Is that what they call him?"

Lily laughed. "His name is Lionel, but when he yells out that office door, it's like the roar of a lion. And if you're called into his office for doing something wrong, it's like being sent into the lion's den. The assignment is to write a story on the new road going through an old cemetery. A little investigative snooping should give him what he wants." Lily smiled up at Maggie. "Just what you wanted to do. Find out why they're taking that route. What will they do with the graves that have to be moved? Does anybody care that it's an historic area? Nobody's writing letters to the editor. He's curious there has been no public outcry. All assignments have a deadline of 5:00 P.M. unless otherwise noted. Questions?"

Maggie examined the scribbles Lily handed her, making a few notes of her own. "Nope. No questions. I'll see what I can dig up." She flashed that brilliant smile again. "No pun intended. Thanks. You will see that Mr. Lawson gets the word on me?" She pointed at the manila folder and the phone still sitting on the high counter.

Lily tapped the button with a bright fingernail, ending the recording, and leaned back in her seat. "I'll see that he gets this information. Good luck, M. M. McKenzie." She watched Maggie stride confidently from the office and wave her remote opener on her car keys toward the sapphire-blue Mustang convertible that almost matched the young woman's eyes.

Dorothea quickly crossed the outer office from the corner where she'd watched the interaction. "I couldn't hear what you said, but I simply couldn't believe my eyes. That can't possibly be who I thought it was."

"Not unless she ended up with amnesia and began another life. And if these papers are as authentic as they look, she's our new reporter."

Dorothea plopped into the chair beside Lily. "Has Lion seen her?"

"No. I'm afraid it was another of Mr. Randolph's little pranks. Do you suppose he doesn't remember what she looked like, or maybe he never saw Maggie? Wait, maybe we can find out from this letter." Lily snatched the letter from atop the manila envelope. "'Lion: This will introduce your newest reporter, M. M. McKenzie. You probably won't remember the contest I sponsored to find some fresh blood for the newspapers, but I think I found a winner twice over: once for the contest and once for my papers. After winning a full scholarship to some college in New York, McKenzie apparently won all sorts of prizes in writing all over the East Coast, edited the college newspaper, and earned extra money freelancing while maintaining excellent grades. You seem to have the only opening, so you're the big winner. I think Mr. McKenzie . . .' Oh, dear." Lily looked up wide-eyed from the letter. "He didn't know McKenzie was a woman."

"Read the rest," Dorothea urged.

"'I think Mr. McKenzie will be just what you're looking for. You can tell that 'star reporter' of yours he'd better sharpen his pencil, because this writer is going to give him a run for his money. My congratulations on getting a brilliant and energetic new talent. You owe me one for him. And by the way, he's only on loan until I need him somewhere else. Regards, WHR.'"

Lily slumped back in her seat. The two women sat dumbfounded for a few seconds. Then Lily leaned forward. "Dorothea, pull the files and put them in my office. Let's see how close the resemblance really is. I've sent Maggie out of the office on that cemetery thing Hatfield was supposed to do. He keeps ignoring it—says there's no story there and it's beneath him. Won't he be surprised if our little newcomer digs up some real dirt out there? But it will keep her out of the office most of the day and give us time to figure out how to break the news to Lionel."

"Lily, you can't be thinking of keeping her on." Dorothea looked aghast. "Can you imagine what that would do to the old man to have to see her day in and day out and have to work with her face-to-face?"

"Mr. Randolph hired her. She works for him. And just because you look like somebody else isn't a crime, you know. You find the files. I'm going to take the phone off the hook and do some brainstorming."

"You'd better be really creative. I couldn't handle that kind of trauma. I'm sure Mr. Lawson can't either." Dorothea untangled her long legs from the office chair and headed back to her office in the archives, shaking her head all the way.

Lily's creative thought process was interrupted five times by people walking into the newspaper office with ads for the classified section or business with someone in the office. She took care of the business by rote until the receptionist arrived, thinking all the time how grateful she was that Maggie had come in at seven forty-five instead of eight o'clock when everyone else arrived. No one had seen her except Dorothea.

Lily had a hard time concentrating on tasks at hand, haunted by Maggie's face. How could she possibly work with her every day, looking at that familiar face? How could Lionel?

* * *

Maggie sat in the car jotting some quick notes before she located the cemetery on the map, started the engine, and drove out of the parking lot onto the busy street. She had plenty of experience writing for the high school newspaper, then the college press, and had held down a part-time job at the local newspaper while working on her degree. But she didn't have to prove herself on any of those. She'd gone into each previous job with a portfolio of articles to prove she had a nose for news and the talent to write about it.

That was then; this was now. This was a real job. A career. She hadn't even taken any of her articles with her, supposing that Mr. Lawson would only read the one that won the contest and know she could write. This assignment was her chance to prove she could not only do the job, but be worth every cent of her salary, which she had thought was considerable until she encountered California prices.

San Buenaventura nestled between the Sierra Madre mountains and the Pacific Ocean, a town of some ninety thousand lucky inhabitants, spreading partway up the mountain and along the sun-drenched coast. Maggie followed the street that wound through town and dead-ended one-fourth of the way up a green hillside at the wrought-iron gates of a small cemetery. She parked beside the lone car in the gravel parking lot, tucked her camera in her navy canvas tote along with her notebook, and slipped through the gates.

Huge Spanish oak trees stretched ancient branches across the width of the little cemetery, giving the impression they were protecting the carved stone monuments below their canopy.

Dates on the nearest tombstones ranged from 1796 through the 1900s, all carved with the same few family names: Ortega, Olivas, and Castenada. The farther Maggie progressed into the little family cemetery, the more recent the dates became. The newest tombstone she could see as she walked the winding, red cinder road was October 1971. A small, red white and blue flag, stuck in the lush green grass covering the grave, waved in the morning breeze.

In the far corner of the well-kept cemetery, an old man with white hair and sun-bronzed skin trimmed rose bushes, glancing up only momentarily to see who approached before he went quietly back to work.

Nestled under an ancient oak, a beautiful carved stone bench sat beside a tall, ornate monument engraved with the name Castenada. Kneeling beside the recent grave, a tiny woman with a perfectly coiffed head of pure white hair arranged flowers in a crystal vase. Maggie stopped, careful not to disturb her, and snapped a picture just as the woman brushed a tear from her cheek. Then she moved quietly forward, but as her footsteps crunched on the cinder path, the woman looked up, startled.

"I'm sorry," Maggie apologized. "Please forgive me for intruding."

"Are you lost, child?" The woman, hardly five feet tall, rose gracefully from her knees and sat on the bench, patting the space next to her. "Come, sit. What brings you to this little plot of sad memories?"

"Are you sure I'm not intruding?"

"Not at all. I'm Marisa Castenada. This is my husband, Ramon." She waved her hand toward the monument that would have towered over her had she stood next to it. "Or about all I have left of him. Today would have been our sixtieth wedding anniversary, if he'd lived another few weeks, so I brought some bubbly to celebrate with him." Marisa smiled at Maggie. "Does that sound macabre?"

That explained the woman's lovely black dress and single strand of pearls, which otherwise would have seemed strangely out of place this time of morning.

"I think it's charming. I'm Maggie McKenzie. I'm very pleased to meet you, Mrs. Castenada, but I don't want to interfere with your celebration."

"Actually, we're through. Since he didn't drink his portion," Marisa winked mischievously at Maggie, "I'll take it home and finish it tomorrow, unless my girls join me tonight."

"Your girls?"

"My daughter-in-law and granddaughter. They're all I have left of family. My son was killed in Vietnam and Kristina never remarried, so I only have one grandchild. She's a jewel, but unless she gets on the ball, I'll die without seeing my great-grandchildren." The two women sat quietly for a moment with the magnificent view spread out before them, then Marisa reached for Maggie's hand. "But you didn't tell me what you are doing here. No one ever comes . . ." She stopped and her lips pressed together in a firm, straight line.

"You started to say?" Maggie prompted.

"This land has been in our family for generations, since San Buenaventura was settled by Father Serra in1782. It was a land grant from the Spanish kings before the Mexicans ever came to California, and our rancho was reapproved by Mexican Governor Juan Alvarado in 1847. I started to say no one ever comes here but family, but that isn't true anymore." Marisa stood and walked out from under the tree, to point up the hill, above and beyond the cemetery. Maggie followed to see where she pointed.

Her finger stabbed at an outcropping of rocks about halfway up. "After all these centuries of ownership, now some highfalutin' Easterner wants to build a house up there and says the only access to it is through this cemetery. Over my dead body."

The energy suddenly evaporated from the tiny woman. Maggie grabbed Marisa's arm to keep her from falling. "Come, Marisa, let's sit for a minute."

The older woman leaned on Maggie's arm and allowed herself to be assisted back to the bench. "Maybe it *will* be over my dead body. I get so angry my heart just pounds. They'll drive me to an early grave and laugh as they bulldoze this beautiful spot."

"Who are they?" Maggie asked.

"*They* are the city council, herded by Wild Bill Wilcox wherever he desires to drive them. He's entered into a compact with the devil himself—big money from New York—and swears the city council's authority of eminent domain takes precedence over everything else.

The sad thing is, there is a more scenic and probably far safer route than through here. But Wilcox is ramming this through for the money he's getting. If they claim eminent domain, they have the legal right to take my property, pay me a paltry fee, and I have to accept what they're doing. But it's not about the money. It's about our family—they've been buried here since 1784."

Marisa was interrupted by a large SUV that roared up the hill and screeched to a stop in the gravel, kicking up a dust cloud that almost obscured the petite driver as she jumped from the vehicle. She ran up the red cinder path as if ready to confront evil personified, her long, straight black hair flying behind her.

"Kristina, I'm okay. No hurry," Marisa called. She turned to Maggie. "Kristina is my daughter-in-law. More like a daughter. Very devoted and loving. Watches over me like a mother bear over her cub."

Kristina stopped directly in front of the two seated on the bench and stared at Marisa as if to determine everything really was okay, then turned to Maggie. "Good morning. What brings you up the mountain to this private family cemetery so early in the morning?" Her tone was barely civil and filled with suspicion.

Before Maggie could answer, Kristina's cell phone rang. She dug it out of the pocket of her tight-fitting jeans, and with a glance at the name in the display answered without saying hello. "Let me get back to you in a minute, Tony," and she terminated the conversation.

"I suppose Antonia called to tell you I had company." Marisa turned to look over the hills behind them, then pointed. "There she is. That's where we're all supposed to be this morning, rounding up the cattle before the rains begin bringing the possibility of mud slides in the mountains. But I played hooky to celebrate our anniversary."

A single rider on a magnificent Appaloosa horse just across the small valley waved and headed at a dead run for the cemetery.

"You didn't say what you're doing here." Kristina immediately returned to business.

Maggie looked up into the flashing dark eyes of the woman in front of her. She had a single white stripe at her left temple in otherwise gleaming black hair that fell straight to her waist. She might have weighed one hundred pounds, all poured nicely into her working clothes: expensive but well-worn boots and jeans, a blue cotton chambray shirt with embroidered collar, and a Stetson that hung on a cord from her neck. Her beautiful, well-proportioned face with high cheekbones reminiscent of other Spanish beauties Maggie had photographed, was tanned from the sun, but surprisingly unlined. Maggie did some quick calculations. Marisa would be about eighty, Kristina between fifty-five and sixty. If the newest tombstone belonged to her husband and he had died in 1971 in Vietnam, then they were about the same age, and their daughter would be thirty-something.

Before Maggie could answer Kristina's repeated inquiry, a silver limousine pulled into the parking lot. A middle-aged man jumped out, frowned at the blue convertible and Kristina's SUV, and strode up the red cinder road toward the three women.

Maggie and Marisa stood at the same time, tension now palpable in what had been a serene setting. That the other two women knew him was obvious, but Maggie was surprised to discover she also recognized him. No one spoke, no one moved, until he stood facing the three.

With a cocky expression on his face, he opened his mouth to greet Marisa and Kristina, then saw Maggie. Surprise and recognition forced him to step back and regroup. "Well, well, well. M. M. McKenzie. What are you doing here? I thought I'd seen the last of you."

CHAPTER 2

"Good morning, Mr. Purcell. Let me guess what you're doing here. In addition to fleecing grieving widows out of insurance money and property while in a state of mourning, you're now involved in some nefarious scheme to seize the rightful property of these women."

Houston Purcell's face turned purple. He clenched his fists and spoke through gritted teeth. "It's a lie. They're lying to you. I'm not trying to do anything of the kind. I offered them fair market value for the land, but they're driving the price up higher than I can afford to pay, so I'm having to pursue legal means . . ."

"Purcell, they didn't tell me anything," Maggie interrupted. "Your name has never come up, but knowing your modus operandi, it appears to me what you're doing is not only unethical, but illegal. Be assured I'll not only pursue this, but if I find what I think I'm going to find, I'll call the judge and report the violation of your parole." While she confronted Purcell, Maggie palmed the little digital camera from her bag and turned it on. "So I suggest you take your big car back to the rental agency, get on an airplane, and hightail it out of town ASAP."

"McKenzie, you can't . . ." Purcell protested.

"Oh, but I can. You aren't planning to build a house on that hill. If anything, you're buying the land for speculation. That makes your actions even more despicable. This is not your kind of country. This is not your lifestyle. Crawl back under your rock and quit picking on old ladies."

The thunder of hoofbeats shattered the tension as Antonia rode full bore to the gate of the cemetery, vaulted from the saddle, and raced up the red cinder path to where the four awaited her dramatic arrival.

While everyone's attention was on Antonia, Maggie stepped back and quietly captured on camera several pictures of Houston Purcell, the women, and the surroundings.

Antonia was dressed much as her mother in working chic: worn but expensive boots and jeans, plaid cotton shirt, and a wide-brimmed Stetson. But unlike her mother, Antonia had a holster strapped to her slender waist and tied with a leather strap around her leg. The weapon in it made a powerful statement that this young woman was not to be messed with.

Houston Purcell's purple face drained of all blood when he saw the gun. He backed away stuttering, "I'm leaving . . . I'm going. Leave that thing where it is." He turned and fled to the car where the chauffeur opened the door and waited for him.

"I'll check on you, Mr. Purcell, to make sure this whole thing is dropped and you're out of town for good," Maggie called after him, "or the judge will hear from me."

Before the limousine was out of sight down the hill, Kristina whirled and faced Maggie. "Okay, Miss McKenzie. Once more. Who are you and what are you doing here? And how do you know Purcell?"

"Oh, dear. All of this has my heart beating wildly again. I must sit down for a minute." Marisa's hand fluttered to her heart, and Antonia immediately helped her grandmother to the stone bench, then sat holding her hand with her arm around her.

Maggie drew in a deep breath and began unfolding the story of her acquaintance with Houston Purcell. Every time she thought of him, it made her mad all over again. "While I worked on my degree, I also worked on the school paper. One assignment was to identify an example of criminal behavior as reported in the papers, investigate, and write about it. I read that several widows had been fleeced out of a great deal of money by a man who read obituaries, went immediately to the bereaved, and offered sympathy and consolation while he pried into their financial affairs. He either had them sign over property to him, give him jewels to put into safekeeping, or give him money for services he never rendered. His crimes were as diverse as the women's circumstances. He had an incredible imagination and apparently was quite convincing in his act."

Antonia leaned forward. "What about their relatives? Surely they didn't just stand by and watch this happen?"

Maggie shook her head. "He was too smart for that. He only targeted women who had no family—or none living close by. The obituary contained a wealth of information for him, and what he found there determined whom he targeted. I discovered his MO by reading past issues of newspapers and comparing the obits that appeared at the same time. It was easy to see how he'd chosen his victims. So I watched the daily obituaries, chose people I thought he would target, and tried to get there first. I missed on a couple, but finally was with one woman when a man knocked on the door and said he was a friend of her daughter who was listed as living on the West Coast. While he was in town, he wanted to offer his condolences. I slipped into the other room so he didn't see me, listening from there. I filmed the entire conversation and when he left, warned the woman not to ever see him again. I took my story first to my editor who was also my journalism professor, then to the police."

"How did you get in to see her in the first place? I would never let a stranger into my house, especially when I was in such a state," Marisa said, shaking her head.

"I told her I was a college student writing an article for my school paper and wanted to interview her. If you don't have close family, sometimes you're so lonely you'll welcome any human contact, and that was what Purcell counted on—knowing human behavior and preying on the weak and lonely."

Kristina relaxed and shoved her hands into her back pockets. "What happened to him when you went to the police?"

"He appeared before a liberal judge who ordered him to make restitution to his victims and placed him on probation with the stipulation that he refrain from all such activities in the future." Maggie clenched her fists and stamped her foot. "How could that judge be so blind? Purcell is an habitual criminal. That little slap on the wrist did no more than delay the pursuit of his livelihood a few days, and he went back to his old tricks. Makes you wish the judge's mother had been one of his victims."

"Does this mean he'll go back east and leave us alone now?" Marisa asked, allowing Antonia to help her to her feet.

"Yes. I'm sure he's no longer a threat," Maggie assured them. "But what about the city council? Who did you say—Wilcox—was trying to ram through a resolution that would allow the road to go through here? Will that still happen?"

Kristina took Marisa's other arm. "Without Purcell's financial backing, I don't think he'll get anywhere. He'll just keep the hundred thousand dollars Purcell gave him to get the council to declare eminent domain and that will be the last of it. After hearing your story, I'm sure Purcell saw my father's obituary in the paper and made my mother a target."

Apparently the interview had concluded. The three women slowly made their way to the gate.

"You didn't tell me what you were doing up here this morning," Kristina reminded Maggie.

"I went to work for the San Buenaventura newspaper this morning. This was my first assignment. The editor wanted to know why there was no outcry about the new road going through an historic cemetery." Maggie paused and directed her question at Kristina. "Can you tell me why no one seemed to be objecting?"

"Wild Bill Wilcox is the driving force in town. When he wants something done, he applies a little pressure here and a few bribes there, and everyone capitulates out of fear that he will expose their transgressions or worry that he won't help them when they need something from the city council." Kristina shook her head in frustration. "The average citizen has just about given up on anything happening that benefits the community as a whole."

"Whoever coined the phrase 'trouble in paradise' could have been talking about this fair little city," Antonia said. "What could be nicer than a lovely spot on the coast with a great climate and good neighbors? It's a paradise of sorts, until you have to deal with the city council."

"Then I guess that's the approach I need to take on this story. We'll see if the power of the press can help straighten out the city council, or at least get something going to clean up the apparent graft and corruption that seems to grease the wheels of your city government."

As they reached the gate, the old man silently appeared to pull it open for them. Maggie let the three Castenada women precede her, then followed behind, snapping one final picture of the ornate old wrought iron gate, catching the intriguing face of the man in her photo.

"Manuel, will you drive the car back to the ranch, please? I'm taking Mom with me." Kristina turned to Maggie and offered her hand. "I'm glad you were here this morning. Thanks."

Marisa stepped toward Maggie and reached up to kiss her cheek. "I can't think your being here at this time was a coincidence. I think you were sent to be our guardian angel. Thank you so much."

Maggie took Marisa's hands in hers and squeezed them. "I don't think it was coincidence either. I believe God uses us as His instruments to help others. I'm so glad I was able to help, and I'll do what I can to see that Mr. Purcell and Mr. Wilcox don't give you any more grief."

Maggie kissed Marisa's cheek and helped her into the SUV. Kristina strode quickly to the driver's side, jumped behind the wheel, and started the engine. They waved as they drove away with the old man right behind them in Marisa's car.

Antonia silently stroked the forehead of her magnificent horse until the noise of the cars faded. The only sounds remaining on the mountain were the twittering of the birds flitting through the trees and the busy hum of bees as they darted from rose bush to sagebrush to dandelion. She mounted the horse with the easy grace of one who spends a great deal of time in the saddle and stared down at Maggie for a minute before she spoke. "Will you really take on the city council, or was that just an empty promise to make an old woman feel good?"

"I'm going to ask my editor for that assignment. I intend to pursue this." Maggie stepped forward and rubbed the horse's chin, looking steadily up into Antonia's big dark eyes. "But today is my first day on this job, and I have yet to meet Mr. Lawson so I'm not sure how he feels about what's going on. If I get the go-ahead, I'll give it everything I've got. If not, then I'll see what I can do behind the scenes and on my own time. I promise you that Mr. Wilcox will not be forgotten."

"That's good enough for me. Thanks, Miss McKenzie. Hope to see you around." Antonia wheeled the roan and thundered down the mountain the same way she had come up—with the horse at a full gallop.

It made Maggie ache to be on her own horse, reliving those last idyllic weeks before she left for California. It had been good being home with her parents again, and with Steve, her unmarried brother. Two of her other brothers, Rick and Taylor, lived close enough with their families that they got together at least once a week. She loved being a doting aunt and spoiling her nieces and nephews. She didn't get to see her two oldest brothers as often: Jeff and his family lived in Colorado, and Alan and his bride lived in New York, but everyone came home for Christmas. As she walked to her car, she wondered if she'd make it home for Christmas this year. It was only a fifteen-hour drive, but as the newest staff member, she was sure she wouldn't have enough seniority to warrant the privilege of Christmas vacation.

Maggie dug her cell phone from her bag, punched the newspaper's number on her speed dial, and leaned against her car while she waited for someone to answer, drinking in the incredible scenery that spread below for miles in all directions.

"San Buenaventura Press. How may I direct your call?"

"Lily, please." Maggie breathed deeply of pure mountain air tinged with a smell of the sea that carried up the hill on the breeze from the ocean. *Paradise*, she thought happily. *I've stumbled into paradise. Dream job. Dream location. What could be better?*

"Lily Noble."

"Lily, this is Maggie. I've finished the investigation of the first part of my assignment. Do you want me to come to the office and file the story or start investigating the second part?"

There was a pause on the other end. "Maggie, it's barely nine o'clock. What have you accomplished in a single hour?"

"I discovered who was trying to put the road through, and why, and he's now headed out of town to crawl back under his slimy rock. But it seems there is also the matter of someone on the city council taking bribes. I can write the first part of the story in the next hour or two, with pictures. Do you want me to do that or begin working on the city council angle?"

"By all means," Lily said, "write the first part. But rather than coming in to this zoo and not being able to get anything done, do you have a laptop?"

"Of course. I'll be happy to go back to my motel and write the story—on my balcony above the ocean. Much nicer than an office. When I'm finished, I'll bring it in and download the pictures that go with it, if Mr. Lawson wants them."

"I have a better idea. Why don't I meet you for lunch? I'll give you two and a half hours to finish the story, get it on disk with the pictures, then I'll meet you at the Busy Bee Café on Main Street at eleven-thirty. We can get acquainted, and I'll either give you approval to start on the rest of the story, or another assignment to begin after lunch. How does that sound?"

"Wonderful. Thanks, Lily. See you at the Busy Bee."

Maggie took one last look at the brilliant blue sky and white waves rimming the silver beach below. Definitely a topless day, she thought, dropping the convertible top. The little blue Mustang had been a graduation present from her family—everyone had pitched in for the down payment, and it was up to her to make the monthly payments.

The wind whipped through her hair as she descended the winding road, and she looked forward with growing excitement to composing the story that would expose Houston Purcell and his latest scheme. Life was good.

* * *

Lily disconnected and sat absently holding the phone, wondering how she would ever get through this nightmare of a day. She hadn't figured out yet how to break the news to Lionel Lawson that, first of all, he'd acquired a new reporter; second, that reporter was female; and third, that every time he looked at her, a dagger would be thrust through his heart. Not to mention her own. Until she figured out how to perform that miracle, she had to keep M. M. McKenzie out of sight. One of Lily's self-assigned responsibilities was protecting her boss, for personal reasons as well as professional.

Then she had another thought. That was a pretty fast wrap-up, especially for someone who'd just hit town, knew no one, and was a cub reporter with not much experience. Just how good was Maggie, or had this been beginner's luck?

The files Dorothea placed on her desk had confirmed the incredible likeness to Lionel Lawson's daughter, who would be about Maggie's age now. The girl had disappeared without a trace on her sixteenth birthday, seven years before. The case remained high profile for three years, then other cases took the limelight, and Alyssa Lawson disappeared from the public mind but not from Lily's or Lion Lawson's. Alyssa, his only child and the delight of his life, had been talented, smart, beautiful, and full of potential. Then she'd vanished like smoke in the wind.

Lily's thoughts were interrupted by the man himself. "Do we have any word on that cemetery? I have a couple of spaces to fill, and that subject would fit nicely with another article. By the way, where's our 'star' reporter today? I haven't seen him."

"He's working on another story, but your publisher sent you a new reporter—the winner of one of his literary contests—so I sent M. M. McKenzie to cover the cemetery. I'm meeting the cub for lunch to pick up the article before I make another assignment. You were in meetings this morning, so I thought I'd just see what kind of writing Mr. Randolph thought was good enough to win his contest and his job offer." Lily held her breath, hoping there wouldn't be questions she'd be required to answer before she figured out how to handle this delicate problem. She handed Lawson the envelope with Maggie's information, purposely neglecting to give him Maggie's recorded explanation.

"Hmph. Up to his old tricks." Lawson scanned the note from Mr. Randolph. "Now I'll have to come up with something to get back at the old codger. Hope this McKenzie is worth his salt." He gave only a quick perusal to Maggie's article, but a slight smile crossed his lips. "This doesn't look too bad, for an amateur."

He turned and strode toward his office, then barked over his shoulder, "Make sure I get that article when it comes in, and I should meet McKenzie today. Have him wait around till I get back from downtown. I'm lunching with the mayor at the Busy Bee at noon and won't be back in the office until two o'clock."

Panic hit Lily like a punch in the stomach at the thought of Lawson seeing McKenzie at the Busy Bee with her. She couldn't keep deceiving him, but neither could she just present the newcomer without some preparation. If she marched Maggie into the office, or even if Lion Lawson saw her sitting on the bench outside of his office, the shock could be too much for him. She'd simply have to make sure Lionel and Maggie did not meet until she'd safely paved the way.

* * *

Maggie threw open the sliding glass doors that led to her small personal balcony, shifted the table and chair to get the right light, and brought her laptop outside to enjoy the sun overhead and the sand and the sea beneath. It wasn't that she'd never been to the beach before, but being born and raised inland where it was a long day's journey to the sea, family vacations or special trips to the beach were few and far between and much too short.

The word *paradise* again escaped her smiling lips as she settled at the table to compose her story. To Maggie, this was pure pleasure: finding just the right words to convey the information she'd discovered in just the right way so her readers would understand what happened. She had a simple system that worked for her. Review the notes, put priority symbols next to them, then enter the information into the computer in the proper sequence, filling in details as she went, discarding information that wasn't pertinent or relevant. Then the editing began. Write, rewrite, and rewrite again so the article was concise and to the point. It was always helpful to know how many column-inches the editor wanted, but since Maggie hadn't been told, she put the additional information at the bottom of the article where it could be cut easily without affecting the body of the work.

She downloaded her story on a disc, with the pictures from her digital camera. Technology was wonderful. How much easier it was now than when she first began writing articles for her high school paper and had to develop the pictures before she could turn them in with her work.

Not sure if it was required, she connected her little portable Citizen printer to her laptop and printed a copy of the article, just in case someone wanted to look it over before it went to the copy editor and have her answer questions while she was right there.

Maggie glanced at her watch, surprised to see that her morning had evaporated. In fifteen minutes she was supposed to meet Lily. Fortunately, San Buenaventura wasn't a large city and, according to the tourist map left in her room, she was only a few blocks from Main Street. She slipped the disc and the hard copy into her bag, ran a brush through her hair, and replenished her lipstick before heading out the door on a run, nearly colliding with the chamber maid's cleaning cart in the hall.

At precisely 11:30, Maggie parked her car two doors from the Busy Bee and hurried toward the restaurant the advertisements had called a popular '50s-era eatery, but Lily intercepted her before she could go through the door.

"They're terribly busy today. Let's go somewhere else that isn't quite so noisy and we can hear each other. I think the entire high school is in there." Lily took Maggie's arm and steered her back toward her car. "I walked over so we'll have to take your car. Is that alright?"

"Of course. Just tell me where to go. I'm still not totally familiar with this beautiful little city yet, but before the week's out, I promise I will be."

As Lily reached out for the door handle, she spotted Lion Lawson's car whipping around the corner. Her heart nearly stopped beating. A disaster was in the making.

CHAPTER 3

Lily ducked behind the car. "Maggie, look under your side of the car. I thought I heard something drop."

Maggie knelt beside the car and peered underneath. "I can't see anything."

"I can't either." Lily smiled at her under the car. "I was sure I heard something. Oh, well. Let's go."

Lily directed Maggie around the corner toward the beach, watching anxiously in the side mirror to make sure they hadn't been seen by Lionel. This town wasn't big enough for both of them right now, and until she could figure out a way to present Maggie to Lion, one of them had to leave.

As Lily guided Maggie along the route she wanted her to drive, she pointed out various city landmarks. "Did you bring a hard copy of your article? I'm anxious to see what you discovered this morning in such a short time."

"Matter of fact, I did." Without taking her eyes off the road, Maggie dipped into her oversize bag and retrieved the pages, passing them to Lily. "I assumed you used the same style most newspapers use today. If not, I'll need a quick course on techniques Mr. Lawson prefers."

Lily didn't answer, intent on the printed pages.

"Do I turn here or go straight?" Maggie asked as they stopped for a red light. "I'm not sure where we're going."

Lily looked up. "Straight through the light and continue toward the beach. Are you a light-salad-for-lunch person or do you like a hamburger and fries?"

"I eat anything but anchovies or smelly fish. Pizza is a favorite, Mexican, Italian, and I usually prefer onion rings to French fries, simply because most places now use processed potatoes instead of making their fries from scratch. I'm from Idaho, you know, and we like our potatoes straight from the field, not the factory."

"Then park wherever you can find a place in that next block. One of my favorite lunch places is there. We can either eat in or take out and eat on the beach." Lily pointed ahead. "Which is straight in front of you."

"I haven't been down here yet. This is nice." Maggie maneuvered the convertible into an available slot while Lily finished reading the article. Maggie waited for her evaluation, not really worried about the article's content or her writing style, but a little apprehensive this wouldn't be the slant her new editor wanted on the story.

"Maggie, this is good!" Lily waved the article toward Maggie and stabbed it with her crimson fingernail. "This is great writing and an amazing story. I can't believe you got to the bottom of this so fast." She narrowed her eyes and stared at the young woman sitting in the driver's seat. "Why did you go to the cemetery first? Why not go to the courthouse to see if the proper notices had been filed and check the legal angle?"

"I've always been taught that you go to the source first—whether you're studying the scriptures or writing a story. You don't go to commentaries, or to neighbors to get their opinion. You go directly to the source to find out how things really are. I just happened to be there at the right time when it all came together." Maggie shrugged and smiled. "My lucky day, huh?"

"I'll say! If you'll give me the disc, I'll take it back to Lionel. He hoped to use this article alongside a related piece. He'll be pleased you finished so quickly—and surprised at your results."

Maggie dug into her seemingly bottomless bag and produced the CD. "There are pictures on here, too. I'm not sure he'll want to use any of them, although I'd recommend the one with Marissa Castenada kneeling at her husband's recent grave. It will give the piece more impact. The others are just character shots. It's a hobby, capturing interesting faces on film. I usually end up with a story from it. Everyone has a story, some more intriguing than others, of course, but behind every fascinating face, there seems to be an equally novel narrative."

Lily smiled at Maggie. "If your photos are as good as your writing, you'll be worth your weight in gold." She slid the paper and disc into her purse and opened the door. "I'm hungry. Let's eat."

They hurried across the street to a hole-in-the-wall-looking place painted rusty orange that proclaimed the world's best hamburgers. The lunch crowd had already taken most of the tables, but Lily spotted an empty one in the corner, tossed her jacket across it, waved to a couple of friends, and hurried to place their orders.

"Is it safe to do that?" Maggie asked. "Just leave your jacket and walk away?"

Lily laughed. "Probably not most places, but I know a lot of these people. Not many out-of-towners today. In the summer, I wouldn't do it. California's like most everywhere else—you just have to know who's around before you do something like that."

Maggie ordered the vegetarian garden burger Lily recommended, though she was skeptical that it could possibly be as good as an all-beef hamburger. She passed on the French fries and the onion rings when she saw the size of another customer's veggie burger. They certainly didn't believe in small servings here. As it turned out, the burger was delicious, and so was her chocolate-banana milk shake.

Surfing paraphernalia hanging from the ceiling and adorning the walls fascinated Maggie. This was a whole new world to her, one she looked forward not only to exploring but immersing herself in when time permitted. In the back, behind another dining area, game machines clanged and beeped noisily, competing with surfing music blasting from the jukebox.

Maggie caught Lily studying her, actually staring at her a couple of times during lunch, but the older woman quickly filled the conversational void when that happened. "This place is a favorite of mine," Lily said, waving her last French fry at the room. "It's not chic, but the people who run it work their buns off to make a living. They keep a spotless kitchen and serve only the best quality food, and try to keep the price down so we common folk can afford it." She smiled. "It works. We just keep coming back. And speaking of back, guess I'd better move in that direction."

Maggie dug into her bag for her car keys but couldn't find them. She pulled out a couple of books, her wallet, sunglasses, and brochures she'd picked up on San Buenaventura and placed them on the table, finally locating the wayward keys in a corner in the bottom of the voluminous bag.

Lily reached for the books as Maggie began replacing the items in her purse and read the titles aloud. "*The Journals of Lewis and Clark. National Geographic's Guide to the Lewis and Clark Trail.* You appear to have a thing about Lewis and Clark. And do you make it a practice to carry heavy books around all the time in that bag? What else do you have in there?"

Maggie laughed. "My life. A bag of toiletries including toothbrush, hair brush, and shampoo, a change of underclothes, camera, notebook, and you will note it is big enough for my laptop. In short, everything I need in case I get stuck on a story." Maggie nodded emphatically, "And yes, that has happened. My journalism professor, who was also the college paper editor, had a habit of sending me off at a moment's notice every time I had a free day. I never knew how long I'd be gone, so I began carrying my necessities with me."

"And the books?" Lily's brows knit together in a puzzled expression.

Maggie reached for the books. "America is celebrating the bicentennial of Lewis and Clark's monumental Voyage of Discovery. I'm fascinated by them and what they accomplished. I've traveled some parts of their trail, and it was an incredible experience. I always carry reading material with me, and when I'm planning some long-term project, it's usually my research material I keep handy."

Lily leaned forward, her elbows on the table and her hands clasped under her chin. "Are you planning such a project now?"

Maggie blushed. "I know this sounds slightly ridiculous—and you have to understand how grateful and happy I am to have this job." She averted her eyes, not sure how to continue without sounding like an ungrateful wretch.

Lily waited a minute, then prompted, "But?"

Maggie looked down at her hands. "The contest mentioned several of the papers Mr. Randolph owned. Some of them were located along the route of Lewis and Clark's journey." She finally looked up and met Lily's intent gaze. "I guess I hoped to get on with one of those so I could do a series of articles during the next few months on the bicentennial."

"What were you planning to write about?"

At Lily's seemingly genuine interest, Maggie forgot her embarrassment and uncertainty, and her dreams poured forth. "I want to tell people about the different celebrations cities are planning and the official state commemorations. I hate reading about something in the paper after it's already happened. People need to know months ahead of time to plan vacations around these things. This is a wonderful opportunity for people to teach history to their children, to focus on true American heroes, to remember all that these brave men, and one incredible woman, did. I want to tell the stories of what happened as they pushed into totally unknown territory. This is real. This is better than Indiana Jones or Harry Potter or Tolkien. When you think what's been accomplished in the last two hundred years in this country because of the accomplishments of that little band of people, it's amazing."

Maggie didn't stop for breath. She leaned forward, both hands clutching the books that aroused such passion in her. "I want to make this story live for people all over the country. I hope they'll get out of their easy chairs and take their families to see these sights, to visit the spots William Clark wrote about in his journals, to experience the majestic powers of the rivers, hike the trails, and smell the flowers Meriwether Lewis found and preserved to show President Jefferson. I wish every child could imagine him or herself a member of that Corps of Discovery. Think what that would do for a child, what dreams it would inspire, what ambitions it could fire in his heart."

Maggie stopped short, realizing she'd gotten totally carried away again. She felt her face flush bright red and bowed her head to recover her equilibrium, letting her hair fall over her face to cover her embarrassment. She clenched her hands in her lap to hide their trembling. She hadn't meant to get on her soapbox, hadn't meant to pour out this secret dream that obsessed her, especially on the very first day of her new job. She took a deep breath and looked up at Lily. What must this woman think of her and her idiotic rambling?

Lily's wide smile surprised Maggie, but not nearly as much as her words. "Maggie, was this article you wrote this morning beginner's luck or is this the kind of thing you've been turning out for your articles?"

Maggie tilted her head. "What do you mean?"

"I read your winning essay. It was great. But you could have spent weeks polishing it. You spent less than two hours this morning on this piece, and it's every bit as good." Lily leaned forward. "I have to know if this was a fluke, or if you're as good as you seem."

Maggie's mouth opened, but she didn't quite know how to answer. Lily shook her head and hurried to explain, "This isn't about your job. You have the job. This is about an assignment that just came to me."

Maggie finally found her voice, looked Lily in the eye and said carefully, "I know how to write. I love the process. I love the inter-action with the people and the story." She paused. "My fault is that I sometimes get too involved and have a hard time leaving the story when the article is finished. I often find it difficult remaining simply an observer, although I can discipline myself to *write* as an impartial observer." She stared at her hands, still clenched in her lap. "I do have a hard time leaving a problem that I might be able to help solve, or make better."

"Like the Castenadas this morning?" Lily asked softly.

Maggie looked up and met Lily's eyes. She nodded. "Yes. I'd like to pursue that story and see what can be done about the city council."

"Would you object if I gave that story to another reporter?"

Maggie sighed softly in disappointment, then took a deep breath and sat up straighter. "I'll be glad to give my notes to whoever gets the assignment."

Lily studied her for a minute. She watched Maggie square her shoulders, and a peaceful expression settled across her features. "You're sure you'd want to do that?"

"The sooner the story gets written, the sooner things begin to happen, and the sooner changes can take place." Maggie slapped the table. "The important thing is that somebody investigates and writes about what's going on and the problem gets solved."

"Good girl. You just passed the first test." Lily leaned back and folded her hands in front of her, like a judge on the bench waiting for the defense and prosecution attorneys to present their cases. "Now, tell me how you feel about traveling alone. Long distances."

"I've been driving long distances by myself for years. To and from college, on assignments, and just yesterday, from Idaho to here." This had to be the strangest interview ever conducted, Maggie thought, wondering where this line of questioning led.

"Does it bother you to stay alone in a motel?" Lily pressed.

"Of course not. I have no trouble being alone, and often it's a blessing. I use the time to either research the assignment or write about it." She smiled. "After being raised with five brothers, any minute I could be alone was golden. I cherish peace and quiet. I have no problem with my own companionship for even long periods of time, and I don't get lonely or homesick."

Lily didn't respond, just leaned slowly forward to rest her elbows on the table, steepled her fingers, and touched them against her lips in a thoughtful manner.

Maggie waited for her to speak, almost holding her breath in anticipation. Her cup of curiosity could not be contained; it brimmed over, almost drowning her. What was this all about? She wanted to grab those crimson-tipped fingers and shake the information out of Lily. But instead, Maggie sat quietly, disciplining herself to appear cool, nonchalant, and patient, when she felt none of those things.

"How would you like to make that dream happen?" Lily watched Maggie.

"What do you mean?"

"How would you like to leave—today—and travel for the next month to those places, write a daily column and send it in?"

Maggie couldn't believe what she was hearing. She leaned back against the padded bench unable to speak, feeling like someone had just double-whammied her in a pillow fight.

"No comment?" Lily asked. When there was no answer, Lily laughed and stretched her hand across the table to grasp Maggie's. "Some friendly advice, dear. Don't ever play poker. I can see every emotion on your face as you experience it."

Maggie leaned forward and almost whispered, "Are you serious?"

"Yes."

There was total silence for several seconds while a million thoughts raced through Maggie's head. "When did you get this idea?"

"Just now."

"Mr. Lawson doesn't know about it?"

"No."

Maggie took a deep breath. "Can you do that? Can you make an assignment like that without checking with him? Or was this just a feeler to see if I'd be willing to go if he approves it?" Now that the initial shock was over and she could think straight, the possibility of actually doing this thing she'd dreamed of for four years seemed unlikely. Lily could offer it, but Mr. Lawson would probably deny it. How could he send someone out he had never even met, to where he didn't know, to write about whatever she wanted? Not feasible.

"I've been with Lion Lawson longer than I like to remember. I handle all employee complaints, all hiring and most firing, oversee budget and finances, and make a lot of the daily reporter assignments. He runs the paper. I run the office and the personnel and whatever else comes up."

Maggie wondered if that included some of his private life, too. "How would the trip be funded? Would I have an expense account?"

"Mr. Randolph has an account for monies above and beyond the normal expenses of each of his newspapers set aside for special reports such as this. Since you're an employee of Mr. Randolph, you qualify to use that special fund. I'll give you a cash advance and a credit card to which you can charge your expenses. You'll keep track of every penny you spend and will have to justify every expenditure. And you will have to justify to Mr. Randolph my faith in you by doing superb work. Any more questions?"

Maggie sat quietly for a minute, overwhelmed at the whole prospect. There had to be a catch somewhere. This was too good to be true; therefore, it must not be—or there must be something she hadn't thought of yet, some problem that at the last minute would interfere with this dazzling, unbelievable opportunity. "When would I leave?"

"Today. You can go pack your belongings and check out of your motel while I go back to the office and get the finances ready. Then I'll meet you with all the paperwork and money you need and you can be a couple of hundred miles down the road before dark."

"What about Mr. Lawson? Shouldn't I at least meet him before I leave?" Maggie dared to believe this actually could happen.

Lily didn't answer. A horrified expression flashed across her face as she stared out the front window. Maggie started to turn when Lily grabbed her hand.

"Maggie. Follow these instructions immediately. Don't turn around. Slide quickly out of your seat, walk as fast as you can out the back door, and wait for me to come. Do it now."

Without hesitation, Maggie scooped up her bag and books, stood, walked swiftly to the rear of the café and into the alley. Lily had been frightened by whatever she saw. *What was that all about?* Maggie thought. *Should I have stayed to help her? What if it was someone she was afraid of, someone who would hurt her? Should I go back?*

Maggie vacillated, torn between needing to know what was happening with Lily and going to her assistance, and being obedient. After all, Lily had said she passed the first test. Maybe this was another test. Maybe Lily wanted to know how well she followed directions. It wasn't every day you met someone for the first time, then immediately had the opportunity to take off across the country, traveling thousands of miles with an expense account.

Maggie paced between the back door and the garbage cans, ignoring the cats and seagulls vying for the remains of customers' meals; ignoring the smell arising from the sun-warmed bins; ignoring the kitchen help that watched her through the window.

She glanced at her watch. How long had she been out here? How long would she have to stay? What if Lily didn't come back? What would she do then?

CHAPTER 4

Lily burst through the door and stopped, wrinkling her nose at the smell. "Whew! Let's get out of here and talk somewhere that smells better." She grabbed Maggie's hand and led her quickly through the alley toward the beach, apologizing as they went. "I'm sorry, Maggie. I know you must think I'm out of my mind."

"Actually, that thought didn't occur to me, though now that you mention it, it seems a distinct possibility. What on earth was that all about?" Maggie concentrated on dodging cats, cars, garbage bins, and boxes cluttering the alley. In a short block, it opened onto a narrow lane serving as a buffer between the buildings and the beach.

Lily glanced down the street, apparently checking to make sure they could not be seen from the café, then motioned to a concrete bench vacated at their arrival by a couple of squawking seagulls. She brushed the sand from the bench, plopped herself down, and patted the seat beside her. "Sit. I know I owe you an explanation after that." Lily paused. "I'd hoped not to have to tell you this for awhile, but guess you might as well know the whole story right from the beginning."

Maggie sat. She would rather have stood. She was wired, infused with nervous energy she could barely contain. First, to have that unbelievable prize dangled in front of her was more than she could ever hope for, but Lily's strange behavior coupled with that exciting opportunity required an immediate explanation—before something else bizarre happened.

"I'm not quite sure where to start," Lily began, then stopped.

"Try the beginning."

"There are too many beginnings. And no endings."

"Okay," Maggie said. "How about starting with what just happened? What did you see that frightened you so and sent me out the back door?"

Lily took a deep breath and closed her eyes. "Lion Lawson," she breathed softly.

That was the last thing Maggie expected hear. "Why would Mr. Lawson . . . ?"

"Okay, we'll try it this way." Lily leaned back on the bench and looked toward the beach.

Maggie followed her gaze out over the horizon, above the sand and the waves, above couples walking on the beach and dogs chasing Frisbees into the water and joggers concentrating on their headsets and paces.

"Lionel lost his wife to cancer about ten years ago and was raising their only daughter by himself. I helped when I could. Alyssa was a gangly, klutzy, metal-mouthed mess for a couple of years, but Lion loved her through their mutual loss, through her awkward years, and she turned out to be a beautiful, poised, self-confident, lovely person."

When Lily's narrative suddenly stopped, Maggie glanced at her and saw tears glistening in the older woman's eyes. She sat quietly while Lily composed herself enough to continue.

"On her sixteenth birthday, Lion threw his daughter a coming-out party fit for a princess. It was a wonderful affair with half the town invited to the bash on their estate. When the main party ended, several of her friends had been invited to stay for a slumber party. The girls were up most of the night, laughing and talking, and finally fell asleep just before dawn. When they awoke, Alyssa had disappeared. No one saw or heard anything. There was no sign of forced entry into the house. No sign of a struggle if she had been kidnapped. None of her clothes were missing, except the pajamas she had on when they went to bed."

Lily bowed her head and stopped speaking for so long, Maggie finally broke the silence. "Did they ever find her? Is she still missing?"

Lily put her hands together between her knees and leaned forward, her shoulders trembling. She shook her head. "No, they never found her. It was high profile for a couple of years, and every agency you can imagine searched for her. Lion sent pictures to every newspaper in the country, and we had a few phone calls from people in the Midwest spotting someone who matched her description, but they never panned out. He hired private investigators who all finally gave up. There were just no concrete clues to follow."

Maggie waited for the rest of the story. It didn't come. She asked quietly, "And what does this have to do with me?"

Lily turned and looked at her. "You're a dead ringer for Alyssa Lawson."

"What?"

"You look just like Alyssa. Same color hair, same facial structure, same blue eyes. You could almost be twins. In fact, when you walked in the office this morning, I thought you were Alyssa."

"That explains that surprised look on your face when you dropped the phone. I thought I must have spinach on my teeth or something. And it also explains why you don't want Mr. Lawson to see me. But how can I work for him if we can't meet?" Then the light dawned. Maggie turned to Lily. "You're sending me out of town until you can discover a way to break the news of our resemblance."

Lily nodded.

Unable to contain herself a minute longer, Maggie jumped to her feet and paced back and forth in the sand. She stopped in front of Lily. "Is this the only way?"

Lily looked puzzled. "Don't you want to go?"

Maggie threw her arms in the air and whirled around in the sand. "Of course I want to go. I want this more than you can possibly know." She stopped, folded her arms, hugging herself as if to ward off the cold, and shook her head. "But it seems . . . dishonest, or something. I don't want to start this job under false pretenses." Maggie paused only a moment, then resumed her nervous pacing.

"There is nothing false about it," Lily countered. "You'll be working your tail off writing a major article every day and traveling to the next location so you can file that story. I'll expect them on my e-mail by five o'clock every afternoon. I leave the office at five-thirty, so if it isn't in my hands before then, you'll answer to the Lion himself, or worse, to Mr. Randolph, since he's paying your salary." Lily stood in the path Maggie had blazed in the sand. "Do we have a deal?"

Maggie stopped, studied Lily's face for a long minute, found the sincerity in her eyes she needed for confirmation, and thrust out her hand. "We have a deal."

Lily grasped Maggie's hand with both of hers, then kissed her on the cheek. "Thank you. Now let's get this show on the road."

As she turned to go, Maggie heard herself say. "Lily, I want the files—or at least copies of everything in Alyssa's files."

Lily whirled around and stared at Maggie as though she couldn't believe what she heard. "Files? Why do you want the files?"

Maggie swallowed hard. Why *did* she want the files? She hadn't known she was going to say that, hadn't even thought about it before the sentence escaped her lips. Those words came out of nowhere. She scrambled for a logical answer. "You said there had been some calls from the Midwest. That's where I'm going. As long as I'm in the area, I might as well see if I can come up with anything."

Lily reached for the bench and lowered herself slowly to the seat. Her mouth opened, then shut again, as though the words she'd planned to speak got lost before they reached her lips and her brain couldn't retrieve them. Her eyes were wide and vacant, unfocused, and her breathing quick and shallow.

Maggie knelt in the sand in front of Lily and took both of her hands. "Lily, talk to me. What's the matter?" There was no answer, no change in Lily's expression. Maggie groaned and stood, pulling the woman to her feet. *That's all I need. Give this poor woman a stroke. Why did I say that?*

"Say something. Talk to me!" Maggie grasped her by the shoulders and shook the older woman.

Finally Lily focused on Maggie's face, but immediately looked away. Maggie recognized the anguish in her eyes and understood. "I'm so very sorry. I can't help the way I look. I'm sorry it hurts you. I imagine you've just relived those horrible days and months. But if I could find something, anything, wouldn't that be better than all the unanswered questions? Wouldn't that be better than the erosion of hope year after year? I'm not promising that I will find anything, but if I did, wouldn't it be better than what you're living with now?"

Lily nodded, but the life, the spark seemed to have gone out of her. Finally she found her voice. "You're young. Ambitious.

Invincible. You haven't been hurt in this immeasurable way. I'll give you the files, Maggie, but you will not mention this to any living soul and you will not report to me anything about it. I don't want to hear that you *think* you've found a lead. I don't want to hear a single word about this until, and unless, you find concrete evidence—evidence that would stand up in a court of law—one way or the other. Otherwise, I promise you it will cost you your job."

Maggie nodded in agreement. "This will be our secret. You'll have your feature story every day by five o'clock with pictures. You'll have my expense report—daily or weekly, as you wish, also by e-mail. I'll do any investigating on my own time, after each story has been filed, and will not mention a word of this to you again unless I discover something definite, something concrete. I promise."

"I will hold you to that promise." Lily turned and walked off the beach toward the car. Maggie followed a few steps behind, wondering what had possessed her to even conceive of such a request. It had suddenly escaped from her lips before she knew it was coming. What was she thinking? If professionally trained detectives couldn't locate Alyssa, couldn't find a single clue after her disappearance, what made her think she could do any better years later?

Maggie followed Lily, berating herself all the way to her car for such an impetuous outburst. It had definitely affected their relationship–a relationship that had formed so quickly, and Maggie had felt it was a wonderful way to begin a new job. Now she feared her friendly mentor would no longer be either friendly or a mentor.

The ride back to the newspaper office was tension filled and silent, and, for Maggie, blessedly brief. As they turned in to the office parking lot, Lily looked at her watch. "You have thirty minutes to pack and check out of your room. Be here by two o'clock. Don't come in. Park over there in front of the real estate office. I'll watch for you and bring everything out."

Maggie nodded, not knowing what she could say that would bridge the icy chasm that stretched between them. What could possibly heal this fracture of a friendship Maggie had felt begin to bloom immediately after meeting Lily? She drove back to her motel under a black cloud of depression and spent only a minute on the balcony gazing at the incredible blue sky and silver sparkles on the water below. It had been too good to be true, this paradise she'd found herself in just hours before.

Packing took only ten minutes, since she hadn't had time to unpack after her late arrival the night before or before leaving for work that morning. Check-out was just as fast. As she began driving the short distance to the office, she barely noticed the swaying palm trees, charming Spanish architecture, refreshing ocean breeze, or the wonderful warm December sun glistening off the waves—everything that had excited and delighted her a few hours ago. Her world now appeared gray and distorted. The drive was short, and she parked in one of the many empty stalls in front of the real estate office. As she waited at the appointed hour for Lily, she still had not discovered a single thing to say to offer comfort or apology or excuse for her impetuous and unexpected outburst.

Then she began to question Lily's motives for offering the dream job. Why would she send her out of town, spending all the money Maggie knew it would cost for a cross-country trip, to do stories she could do from Internet research? Articles written this way wouldn't have nearly the same quality and depth, as far as Maggie was concerned, but they wouldn't have been so costly to produce. She could just have stayed out of sight for a few days while Lily came up with some way to introduce her to Lionel. Was there more to this than met the eye? Because she wanted this so very much, could she just not see the real reason behind Lily's offer?

Lily hurried across the parking lot with a bulging manila folder, slid into Maggie's car, and began speaking without even looking up. "Here's some of the info on Alyssa. I picked out what I thought you'd be interested in seeing—what seemed to me to be most helpful. We have files and files of newspaper clippings, but these are the pertinent ones." She pulled another smaller envelope from the large one. "Here are the copies of sightings when people called or wrote in response to the missing-person notice in the paper. There are some in the Midwest, in the area where I imagine you'll be traveling. The detectives found nothing. A few are only a year or so old."

Lily looked at Maggie for the first time. "I'm sorry I went wacky on you. It stunned me to relive those horrible memories and realize Lion might have to face the outcome. We've both been up and down so many times with little threads of hope that were dashed to pieces when leads didn't pan out. I simply can't endure that terrible pain again. I can't hear anymore about it until she's found, either dead or alive. Do you understand?"

Maggie reached for Lily's hand and covered it with her own. "I understand," she said softly.

Lily hurried on, digging into the manila envelope again. "Here's a thousand dollars—probably will cover gas, room, and food expenses for about a week, but here's an ATM/credit card on Mr. Randolph's special account. Send an expense report weekly. I'll forward them to both Lion and Mr. Randolph, along with your articles, so I'm expecting great things from you. You'll have to prove yourself by doing incredible articles out there on your own and justify spending Mr. Randolph's money like this. We'll leave your return date open-ended."

She turned to Maggie. "Now get out of here quick before I cry. I had a feeling you were a special kind of person when I first met you this morning, a different breed than we usually see. Don't let me down, okay?"

Maggie leaned over and hugged Lily. "I promise I'll do my very best. Thank you—more than I can tell you—for giving me this opportunity. I won't let you down. And good luck with the explanations."

Lily touched Maggie's face in a tender gesture, then turned and ran back across the parking lot to the office. Maggie sat motionless for a minute, wondering if what she experienced was a mirror of Lily's feelings. She definitely felt a kinship to this good woman, and, after Lily's apology, an immense lightness of mood. Life was good again. As she wheeled out of the parking lot, Maggie found herself happily humming "Count Your Blessings." Yes, she did have a lot of blessings to count, but as she pulled onto Highway 126, the realization of exactly what she was embarking on tempered that happy glow.

How could she possibly find a girl who had been missing for seven years? The trail would be cold. Professionals hadn't found anything. How could she? But that was not the item of greatest concern at the moment. Where was she going? She was on the highway, but heading where? She needed a plan.

Maggie did some quick calculations. It was well into December. Winter across the United States had been mild so far. Should she go

north first, then backtrack Lewis and Clark's journey and avoid the
winter that was sure to come, or head straight for St. Louis and travel
north following their route and probably head right into winter?

This was not a good time of year to be working this prized assignment, but since she had it, she certainly wasn't going to let a little
thing like bad winter weather stop her. Then she had another
thought. Lily said she'd provided a list of places where supposed sightings of Alyssa occurred. That could alter her plans if they didn't corre-
spond to the Lewis and Clark Trail.

Heavy traffic prevented Maggie from pulling over to open the
envelope with that information, but she remembered there were some
fruit stands along the road. She could stop, buy a bag of delicious-
looking Valencia oranges she'd seen in the stands, and plot her course
of action. In the meantime, her mind flew through the information
she'd been digesting for months in case she ever had the chance to
write about the Voyage of Discovery.

She stopped at the first fruit stand she found and bought a bag of
oranges, avocados, and almonds to munch to keep her alert on the
long drive. Then she peeled a juicy orange and ate it in the parking
lot while she read the accounts of people who believed they'd seen the
missing girl.

There were five sightings: Rapid City, South Dakota; St. Joseph,
Missouri; Pine Bluff, Arkansas; Texarkana, Texas, and New Iberia,
Louisiana. Interesting. Maggie opened her road atlas and traced the
route—southeast from Rapid City, then straight south into Lewis and
Clark country. And beyond.

Included with the information was a color photo of Alyssa
Lawson. Maggie did a double-take when she saw it. The resemblance
was amazing, uncanny. No wonder Lily had almost gone into shock
when she saw her. That may even have accounted for some of the
strange questions Lily asked her. Well, they say everyone has a twin
somewhere in the world. This certainly appeared to be hers. Wouldn't
it be interesting to find her?

Her heart beat a little faster as a plan began taking shape in her
mind. She glanced at her watch: two-thirty. The drive to Las Vegas
was approximately five and a half hours, which would put her there
about eight o'clock. She could grab a motel room, sleep a few hours,

and spend the next night with her parents in Idaho, using that as a jumping-off point for the rest of her trip. Rapid City would be her first destination.

Maggie eased back onto the busy highway, her mood over the top. She couldn't believe her good fortune at having immediately received the assignment of her dreams. To have a mystery to solve, some good hard investigative reporting to do, was just icing on the cake. How had she ever lucked into this?

She had no doubt about her ability to send back stories that would please Lily and her editor. She'd been blessed with a natural talent to see what many other people never saw and to string together the right words in just the right way to tell an informative and interesting story. Aunt Hattie had once called her a busybody when she began asking her usual endless questions, but her mother had defended her daughter, saying Maggie just had a natural curiosity about everything under the sun. It was true. Her natural curiosity led her to ask questions many others never thought to ask, which was how she ended up in journalism in the first place.

Maggie spent the long hours driving across the brown desert composing her first column on her little tape recorder. She gave background on the story of Lewis and Clark: how President Thomas Jefferson, even before, but especially after the 1803 Louisiana Purchase, felt the urgent necessity of exploring and mapping the great expanse of newly acquired territory and how he chose his two explorers. But Captains Meriwether Lewis and William Clark were charged with much more than the challenge of exploring and mapping the uncharted wilderness; they were to meet with the native peoples and record all they encountered along the way, how those people lived, who inhabited the area, as well as detailing the flora and fauna, soil and minerals.

Finally satisfied that she'd included all the essentials in the introductory article, Maggie's thoughts turned to the missing girl. She couldn't wait to get to Barstow, the midpoint on this beginning portion of her journey, so she could stop for a bite to eat and read the articles Lily gave her. The mystery of Alyssa Lawson grew with each passing mile. Maggie's curiosity became almost more than she could control, even tempting her to just pull over at a rest stop and read about the kidnapping.

Then she had a new thought. Alyssa had been sixteen. Lily said there was no sign of forced entry. Maybe Alyssa walked quietly away in the night to begin a new life. Maybe there was no crime involved at all. Well, Maggie amended, if she did just walk away, it would have been a crime to leave her father in such a state and break his heart.

Or maybe the teenager slipped out to meet someone, meaning to return. Had something prevented her from doing that? An accident? A boyfriend who convinced her to run away with him? Or had Alyssa been kidnapped after having left the house of her own will, and not been allowed to return?

Maggie was all too familiar with the horror stories of someone stealing through a window and taking children to use, abuse, and then throw away. When she reached Barstow, she was happy to pull off I-15 and stop. Her thoughts had become dark and depressed with the possibilities of what could have happened to Alyssa.

She chose the fast-food restaurant with the fewest cars in the parking lot so she could more readily concentrate on the articles on Alyssa's disappearance. What she ate at this point was incidental, but once she began reading, she couldn't stop. Maggie glanced at her watch, horrified to discover she'd been poring over the newspaper clippings for an hour and still had the bulk of them to go.

Time for a change of plans. She scooped the papers back into the manila folder and dumped her food tray into the garbage receptacle. She'd spend tonight in Barstow getting familiar with the case, reading and making notes. That would increase tomorrow's drive by two hours, but she could spend that time thinking, planning, mulling over the clues—or lack of them. She would never be able to sleep until she'd read everything Lily had given her, and the two-hour drive to Las Vegas would be excruciatingly long with her curiosity growing by the minute until she could finally read what Lily thought were the most important items in the files.

Maggie checked into the motel across the street, requested a room with two queen-sized beds, and immediately spread the articles in chronological order on both beds before she settled down to begin her study of what she feared had already become an obsession: the quest to know, then find Alyssa Lawson.

CHAPTER 5

The girl with a face hauntingly similar to her own interrupted Maggie's sleep so often she finally gave up, dressed, and checked out of her motel long before the sun appeared on the horizon. During the two-hour drive to Las Vegas, she listened to the notes she'd dictated to her tape recorder the night before as she read the interviews with Alyssa's friends, father, and teachers, marking them with red pencil so she could quickly locate the source again when she needed it.

The interviews were informative, revealing much about Alyssa's character and personality. None of the girl's friends ever heard her mention any problems at home; she was usually very upbeat and positive. She had no special boyfriend, just a group of friends that hung out together, guys and girls who rarely paired up but enjoyed associating as a group.

Alyssa had a close relationship with her live-in housekeeper. *Had there been a name of the housekeeper?* Maggie didn't remember reading it. She made a mental note to follow up on that. The teenager also had a noteworthy relationship with her P. E. teacher who encouraged her, after her mother died, to either try out for the cheerleading squad or participate in track and field. Alyssa had decided against both, saying they would take too much time from her home, family, and her horse.

The young woman spent a lot of time grooming and riding the Arabian stallion her parents had given her for her tenth birthday. She never minded being alone and spent long hours riding in the hills behind the estate. A shiver ran down Maggie's spine. Alyssa Lawson not only looked like her, but the missing girl's life eerily paralleled Maggie's own teen years.

Alyssa had never gone off on her own without telling her father or her housekeeper where she was going. An obedient child who exhibited, at least outwardly, no rebellious attitudes, her peers said she always appeared happy and in good spirits and allowed no fighting among her friends. She was a peacemaker who often repeated her motto: "Life is too short and uncertain to fight or have hard feelings. Get over it."

A good student, Alyssa loved science and biology and planned to become a marine biologist. That made Maggie feel a little better. Finally a marked difference in their interests. Maggie tried to shake off the mental and psychological webs that seemed to bind her to this girl she had never met, but to whom she now felt very close. Frighteningly close.

As she listened to the items she had recorded, she wondered why Alyssa was an only child. Was she the only child Mr. and Mrs. Lawson had wanted? Or could have?

How was she affected by her mother's death? Had she turned even more to the live-in housekeeper after her mother died, or had she been very close with the woman all the time? Had Alyssa's mother been a career woman who was absent from the home, requiring the house-keeper to be there when Alyssa came home from school? Maggie made a second mental note to find out about the housekeeper. She was defi-nitely a key player in Alyssa's life. It would have been helpful to have interviewed her before leaving San Buenaventura, but then her investi-gation would no longer have been secret.

How long had Alyssa's mother been ill? The articles had not said. Just "died after a lengthy illness," which could have been anywhere from six months to six years. So many things would leave a lasting effect on an impressionable teenager. Did she resent her mother's illness and then feel terrible about it when her mother died? So many questions—to which there may never be any answers.

Then another question jolted Maggie: had anyone ever done a DNA work-up on Alyssa? Maybe her body had been discovered somewhere and was never identified. DNA had really come into its own in the last few years and was now being used to identify badly decomposed bodies or even skeletal remains. Maggie stopped the tape to think about that. Bodies are usually found in the local area, not transported long distances, but the paper stated that thousands of volunteers had searched the area several times, covering the mountains and the beaches. Nothing had turned up that could be connected to Alyssa.

Maggie watched the sun rise over the mountains as she approached Las Vegas. This broad, barren desert would be a perfect place to hide a body, but it seemed unlikely a killer would take a chance on transporting a corpse so far from the scene of the crime. She continued to listen to the notes she'd taped as she threaded her way through pre-rush-hour traffic on I-15 in Las Vegas, stopping only long enough to fill the gas tank.

Instead of listening further to her taped notes as she headed north for St. George, Maggie changed tapes and began recording the article she'd need to have ready to type and e-mail as soon as she reached home in several hours.

She began by paraphrasing the foreword historian Stephen Ambrose had written in Bernard DeVoto's edited version of *The Journals of Lewis and Clark*. Maggie hoped this great introduction to the story would motivate millions to actually read the eight volumes of the journals themselves—or at least, DeVoto's acclaimed one-volume synopsis. She began with Ambrose's lyrical prose: "These journals are a national literary treasure. Lewis and Clark's exploration of the western two-thirds of the continent was our epic voyage, their account of it is our epic poem." Even after reading them so many times, those words thrilled and stirred something deep in Maggie's soul.

The summer when her family followed a portion of the trail, they'd gathered around the campfire to read the emotional account of what the explorers had encountered that day. Lewis and Clark recorded their anger, joy, indignation, worries and fears, and their triumphs. They recorded snapshots in prose of those in their company so Maggie felt she knew each of them intimately when she finished reading their journals.

It wasn't until she saw a sign for the Garden of Eat'n Café in Fillmore, Utah, that Maggie realized she'd had nothing to eat all day but a couple of pieces of fruit and some almonds. She pulled off I-15 and ordered a bowl of hot homemade soup and freshly made bread. While she waited to be served, she stepped to the entrance to walk around to loosen her stiff limbs while she called home on her cell phone.

"Hi, Mom. It's Maggie."

"Maggie, where are you?"

"In Fillmore, heading for home. Just giving you a heads-up; I'll be there for dinner. Set an extra plate and tell Steve he better not be sleeping in my room. I know he likes my mattress better than his, but I want to sleep in my own bed tonight."

"What happened, hon? Didn't you get the job?"

"I got it, and even more! But I think I'll just leave you in suspense until I see you tonight." Maggie almost laughed out loud, knowing exactly what her mother would do all afternoon with a mystery like this to fret over.

"No, you won't, young lady. I want to know right now what's going on!"

"Remember that big secret you and Dad tormented me with for weeks before my birthday? It's payback time, Mom. See you tonight about four o'clock. Then I'll have a story to file immediately, so don't plan dinner until five o'clock."

"Maggie . . ."

"My lunch is here. Bye, Mom. Love you. See you tonight."

The country vegetable soup and hot bread hit the spot, exactly what Maggie needed. She frequently forgot to eat well when she was on assignment, too often grabbing whatever was handy to appease her hunger, while neglecting the nutrition angle. Then it was back on the road again.

Maggie finished taping her story, adding a little colorful background about the French and Spanish passing the title to the Louisiana lands back and forth, which actually included the right to access and navigate the Mississippi River. Neither nation appreciated the value or extent of the land, thinking of it simply as a worthless swamp peopled with a few uneducated savages. She stressed Thomas Jefferson's farsightedness in pressing to purchase the Louisiana Island, which included the all-important port of New Orleans. That was an essential area, along with the Mississippi River, if the United States was to ever expand its trade routes.

Then she spent the next couple of hours trying to get inside Alyssa's head, trying to figure out what might have caused her to leave the slumber party: whether she left voluntarily, or how someone could have gotten into the locked house and abducted her without anyone knowing and without leaving any sign of entry.

Traffic had thinned considerably after she left Fillmore. Maggie did shoulder-rotating exercises to stay alert. As she passed one gruesome accident site that tow trucks were just cleaning up, she could see the flashing lights of the ambulance on the highway ahead of her. Normally an aggressive but careful driver, she checked her cruise control to make sure it was set on the speed limit, not over.

She listened to her taped notes on the interviews again. Alyssa sounded a lot like Maggie; they had several things in common, but where Alyssa's interests were concentrated on sea animals, Maggie's interests were far more grounded. Where Alyssa had her own aquarium, Maggie had her own mini-zoo. It began with hamsters and gerbils, but expanded with the arrival of stray cats she secretly fed and that stayed around the barn, producing a new litter of kittens every season. Then McTavish, her border collie, found a snowy-white barn owl with a broken wing. She helped her brother repair the wing, and the owl became a pet. She'd spent her allowance for months buying white mice to feed it. Next came an orphaned lamb, which she bottle fed several times a day.

Maggie had even raised her own horse from the moment she helped to deliver it. She'd begged for a horse since she was eight years old, not one that belonged to her father, but one of her very own. Finally her father agreed the next time Sultana was bred, Maggie could have the foal. Thrilled beyond measure, she had taken excellent care of the colt she named Pegasus, never once forgetting to feed, water, or brush him down.

The two were inseparable. Maggie even slept in the barn on occasion, slipping outside to stay with the horse when her mother thought she was asleep, and especially on those nights when the thunder and lightning frightened Pegasus. When she left for college, she'd missed her horse almost as much as her family.

The hours and miles flew by as Maggie alternately relaxed listening to Bizet's *Carmen* and Michela Petri playing the recorder in her favorite version of Vivaldi's *Four Seasons*. Then, her mind refreshed, she returned to catalog more and more questions regarding Alyssa. When she tired of that, she worked on the next column for the San Buenaventura paper. *Her paper.* What a great feeling that thought gave her.

* * *

Wiping her hands on her apron as she ran down the front steps, Maggie's mother met her daughter as she pulled into the driveway. "You've kept me waiting long enough. What's your big surprise?" she asked, giving her daughter a hug and helping her with her bags.

"I have the job of my dreams and the assignment to die for. But I'll give you all the details at dinner so I only have to tell everyone once." Maggie grabbed her laptop and tape recorder and hurried with her mother back into the house, shivering. Idaho was much colder than California in December, and it looked like snow any minute. "Right now, I've got to get my article written and sent to my editor."

"How long do you need? You said dinner about five o'clock and that's what I told your dad."

"Dinner at five will be fine, as long as I don't have any interruptions. Tell Steven I really need this time alone, so not to bug me."

Maggie's mother laughed. "You know Steven would only bug you more if I told him that, but he's helping Rick build a new addition to his veterinary clinic and won't be home until dinner. Go on up to your room. I'll try to make sure no one interrupts you."

Maggie's fingers flew over the keys on her laptop, almost keeping pace with the recorded column she'd written in the car, needing to stop and rewind the tape recorder only occasionally. She finished at four-fifty, hooked the computer to the phone line, and e-mailed the article to Lily in San Buenaventura, adding a note that she would check her e-mail every morning before she left her hotel room and every night when she checked in. That way Lily could contact her if she couldn't reach her on her cell phone.

As she clicked the Send button, she heard her brother Steven on the stairs. Just in time.

"Mom said dinner is ready. What are you doing home, Sis?" Steve kissed her cheek and ruffled her hair playfully, but Maggie noted he watched her closely. "Those Californians not want your extraordinary talents?"

"Nope." Maggie stood and stretched. "They sent me packing as soon as they heard I was your little sister."

"Low blow, Magpie."

"Not as low as that." Maggie caught him in the stomach with a well-placed elbow and darted for the stairs. "You know I hate that name."

Steve caught up with her halfway down the stairs. "Sorry. Old habits die hard."

Maggie had everyone's undivided attention as she told them about her dream location on the coast of California. "You can't believe how beautiful it is, so warm and sunny, definitely not like Idaho right now. I love the Old Spanish architecture and the palm trees and the ocean . . . and it's so relaxing and refreshing watching waves rush up on the sand, then ebb away."

Steven waved his fork at her. "Alright, already. We've been to the coast. We know what it's like. But what are you back doing here? You just left two days ago."

"That's the incredible part. I wanted to win that writing contest because William H. Randolph had newspapers scattered throughout the Midwest. I hoped to get a job with one of them so I could write articles on Lewis and Clark. You remember how disappointed I was at first when he sent me to California instead of Missouri or Montana or North Dakota."

Well acquainted with Maggie's big dream, everyone nodded.

"I get to do it anyway! I'm on my way to Rapid City, South Dakota, to write the articles, and I'm backtracking from there on the Lewis and Clark Trail. I get to write an article a day!"

Scott McKenzie stopped buttering his hot roll and looked at his daughter. "And how much are they charging you to do this for them?"

"Oh, Dad," Maggie laughed. "Stop teasing me. I'm not paying them. They're paying me, plus I have an expense account to pay for all my expenses."

Silence fell on the group. Steve, for once, didn't have a wisecrack.

Maggie stared around the table at her family. "What's the matter? Aren't you excited for me?"

Steve spoke first. "What's the catch, Sis?"

"Catch?" Maggie shook her head. "Why does there have to be a catch?"

"Anything that sounds too good to be true usually is," Maggie's father explained quietly. "They didn't even give you one day on the job. Doesn't that strike you as unusual?"

Maggie sat back in her chair. "Not really. I was given an assignment at eight o'clock in the morning, finished it at nine, wrote the article, and turned it in to the office manager at eleven-thirty when we met for lunch. She liked it. She saw my Lewis and Clark books and asked about them. I told her what I wanted to do and she loved the idea." Maggie stopped.

This was not the reception she expected to receive as she shared her delightful news. Had she been blinded by the dazzling carrot Lily dangled before her eyes and hadn't thought through all the implications of the unbelievable offer?

But if she told them about her amazing likeness to her editor's missing daughter, which was the real reason she was here, would she then end up telling more than she ought to? Or because they knew her so well would they guess how involved she had already become? How much of the story should she tell her family? How much *could* she tell without also revealing her search for Alyssa? It was so hard not to just let the whole story pour out. She had never kept secrets from her family before, especially not from Steve who could usually finagle every last detail out of her.

Rose reached over to squeeze her daughter's hand reassuringly. "We don't want you to get hurt, sweetheart. If this is legitimate, the job and the assignment, we're as excited as you are. We just need to make sure no one is taking advantage of you."

Maggie took a deep breath. "Okay. Someone play devil's advocate. How they could be taking advantage of me? Point out the flaws I obviously can't see." She leaned forward, elbows on the table, and propped her chin on her hand. "I thought it was too good to be true when Lily offered it, but she seemed so sincere, and I couldn't think of a single reason why I shouldn't leap at the chance."

Not surprisingly, Steve jumped in first. "What *is* your assignment?"

"To go wherever I want to go and send a story on the Lewis and Clark expedition to Lily by five o'clock every night."

"No restrictions on what you write?" Maggie's father asked.

"None. Although I'm sure Lily is expecting to receive what I told her I'd do—report the celebrations cities and states on the route that are planning for the bicentennial of their journey and get people excited about becoming involved. I want to motivate them to read the journals. I want them to catch the vision of those courageous explorers. I want them to travel part of the route, or all of it. Go where it happened. Be aware of the great things these heroes did. I want to inspire young people to read about them, then go out and do great things of their own."

Rose laughed. "Well, if you got this fired up talking to her, I can certainly see why she'd grant you this opportunity. It makes me excited to read what you'd have to say."

"But you're her mother," Steve pointed out. "That doesn't count."

"Can't mothers be objective?" Rose countered.

"No offense, Mother dear," Steve winked at her, "but I don't think you could possibly be objective, knowing how you feel about your daughter's talent." He turned back to Maggie. "What are the financial arrangements?"

Maggie shrugged. "She gave me a thousand dollars to get started and an ATM/credit card on a separate account of Mr. Randolph's, which he keeps for special assignments. I'm to send an expense report once a week."

Scott had given up all pretense of eating. "How long is this dream assignment to last?"

Maggie spread her arms exuberantly. "She mentioned a month but left it left it open-ended. Can you believe it? Supposedly until I've either written as much as they want to hear or I've run out of things to write. It'll probably depend a lot on how well the stories are received by the public. If the paper gets good feedback, I imagine I could be doing this for a couple of months. If not, I'm sure they'll tug on the leash and reel me back to the office."

Silence again. Apparently she had satisfactorily answered all their questions.

"I don't know about you, but I'm starving. This will be my last chance to eat a home-cooked meal for awhile, and I'm not going to let it get cold." Maggie dug into her meat loaf and baked potato with gusto. The appetite that dissipated when her family voiced their doubts and began their interrogation returned as she answered their questions. Now she felt excited—over-the-top excited—maybe more so since her harshest critics and greatest supporters now seemed satis-fied the offer was legitimate.

"And you're planning on doing this all by yourself?" Her dad's quiet but pointed question made her choke on her last bite. "You'll be on the road for weeks alone, staying at motels alone, eating alone, stopping to research—alone?"

"Dad, I've been doing this for years and you've never objected. Why is this different?"

"Because the assignments you had in college involved much shorter travel than this. You're planning a long-term, cross-country trip with what goals in mind? Besides producing an article a day, which, if I'm not mistaken, you usually crank out in an hour or two with very little Internet research."

"But that's not the same as being there. I can't include the sights and sounds and smells and impressions if I'm a thousand miles from the scene. You can't diagnose a sick calf over the phone and recommend the proper medication and treatment any more than I can incite millions of people to get excited about this subject just by sitting behind a desk. I've got to be there, to see what differences have occurred since they traveled the route; to see what preparations the cities and states have made; to tell people how to get to those places to experience it best. You simply can't do that long distance sitting at a computer."

"She has a very good point, Scott," Maggie's mother noted.

Scott McKenzie sat silently for a minute toying with the food on his plate.

"It's hard to let go, huh, Dad?" Steve said quietly. "Hard to believe your baby girl is ready to spread her wings and fly away and be all on her own."

The elder McKenzie shot a look of acknowledgment at Steve. "Sure is." Then he turned to Maggie. "It was one thing to let you go to California. At least you'd be in an office every day and account to someone. I felt a measure of security in that. This seems too . . ."

"Unfettered?" Steve offered as his father searched for the right word. "Emancipated? Independent?"

"Enough." Steve's father pointed his fork at his son. "I may have second thoughts about letting you finish college if you're going to be such a smart aleck."

"Steve, a smart aleck?" Maggie declared in mock surprise. "Never."

Scott reached for his daughter's hand and squeezed it. "Guess I wasn't ready to acknowledge that you're all grown up, hon, and you're ready to do greater things than I was prepared to turn you loose to do."

"I promise I'll be very careful, Dad." Maggie couldn't hide her immense relief and joy, knowing her family was finally behind her in this unprecedented opportunity. They spent the rest of the dinner hour discussing her plans for the articles, where she'd travel, and how she'd stay in touch with them.

The phone rang as they finished Maggie's favorite dessert, her Mom's lemon meringue pie, and Scott had to rush off to help his son, Rick, deliver a breech foal. "See you before you leave in the morning, hon." He blew his daughter a kiss as he raced out the door.

"Mom, I know you're teaching a class tonight at Church. Maggie and I can do the dishes," Steve volunteered. "Go ahead and get ready."

"Thanks. I'll have to start right now or I'll never make it out of here on time. I'll be home by about nine-thirty. If you're in bed already, I'll see you in the morning." Rose hurried up the stairs, leaving Maggie and Steve with the aftermath of dinner.

"What's buggin' you, Sis?" Steve asked as they cleared the table.

"What do you mean?"

"I see a little storm cloud on your usually sunny horizon."

"No, I'm just tired from that long drive." Maggie busied herself tucking leftovers in the refrigerator so Steve couldn't see her face.

"You're not holding back on your big brother, are you?"

"What's to hold back?" She smiled and motioned for the catsup and butter he held in his hands. "I told you all my plans."

"Sure you're not keeping secrets?"

Maggie laughed. "Have I ever had any secrets from you? You pester them out of me."

"Worried about something?"

"No!"

"Want a little company on your trip?"

"Absolutely not!"

"I could drive while you write."

"Thanks, but no thanks, Steve. When I'm doing research, I don't need to worry about anything but the job at hand. If I don't want to eat, I don't have to. If I want ice cream for dinner, I have it. If I want to detour from my planned route because I sense a story, I don't want to have to worry about what you want—or whether you're bored or not. I love you dearly, big brother, but I don't want your company on this trip, or anyone's for that matter."

"Maggie, that's a long trip you're looking at—something in the area of five or six thousand miles." The teasing disappeared from Steve's tone and his voice filled with concern.

"Steve, I can handle it. Your baby sister grew up, remember?" Maggie finished loading the dishwasher and filled the sink with soapy water to wash the pots and pans. She turned to Steve and pointed at the mixing bowls next to him on the counter.

"I just don't want you to get lonesome. What if you pick up some stranger and we never hear from you again?"

Never hear from you again. Alyssa's face suddenly flashed through Maggie's mind.

"Magpie, what's the matter? You look like . . ."

"Steven Tate McKenzie, I've asked you a thousand times to stop calling me that ridiculous name." Maggie grabbed the bowls and plunged them into the sink, splashing water all over her.

Steve touched Maggie's cheek and gently turned her head toward him, forcing her to look him in the eye. "Is that all?"

Maggie sighed in mock exasperation. "Isn't that enough? I don't like to be compared to a noisy, raucous, endlessly chattering bird."

"Too late," Steve teased. "The similarity was all too strong in my formative years."

Maggie threw the wet dishcloth at him. Steve caught it and flipped his wet towel at her. Maggie darted from the kitchen and headed toward the stairs, announcing, "You've insulted me enough for one evening. I'm going to bed. I'll be gone before you're up in the morning so make sure Mom and Dad have a merry Christmas. I'll call Christmas morning."

"Hey, we're not through," Steve yelled after her. "Get back here."

"You're not through. I am," Maggie called from the top of the stairs. "You've driven me off with that dangerous weapon in your hands. Good night." She slammed her door and locked it, hoping Steve would leave well enough alone and not try to pursue their conversation. He'd hit closer to home with every question.

Having left the warm, sunny weather of California and preparing to head into icy, winter weather in the Midwest, Maggie retrieved a suitcase from her closet and filled it with her warmest sweaters and wool skirts and pants. She'd definitely need a different wardrobe than the one she'd packed when she headed for the West Coast—at least until she reached the sunny South and Louisiana. If she got that far.

As she tried to find sleep, her brother's words haunted her, drifting again and again through her mind: *Never see you again. Never see you again.* Just as she felt herself finally relaxing and drifting into sleep, Maggie heard a strange sound outside her window.

CHAPTER 6

Must be the wind, she thought. Then she heard it again. *Not the wind.* Maggie lay still, reluctant to leave her snug, warm bed, unwilling to jar herself completely awake by getting up to investigate. She listened, hoping the gusting winds had simply blown something against the window. It remained quiet long enough for Maggie to drift off.

It came again. *Definitely not the wind.* She tried to get out of bed and investigate but felt imprisoned under her covers by something incredibly heavy. Maggie could not free her arms from the blankets cocooned around her. The noise at the window repeated, this time louder, more distinct. It sounded like . . . what? Metal scraping on metal? Metal on glass?

Maggie peeked over the covers. The silhouette at the window was big, too big to be Steve playing pranks on her. Maggie's throat closed up in terror as she saw the man's face press against the glass, his bushy hair and big ears clearly outlined against the light from the barnyard beyond. She watched in silent horror as the locked window slid quietly open, and the bulky man put one leg inside. He ducked under the window casing, his broad shoulders filling the window, then the rest of him entered the room without a sound.

She tried to scream. Nothing came from her throat. She fought the covers, frantically watching the man come closer and closer to her bed, a blanket held before him.

Help! Help me, someone. Steve, where are you? Please help me. Just as the intruder raised the blanket over her, someone banged on her door. "Maggie! Maggie, are you all right? Your door's locked. Let me in."

Maggie shot upright up in bed, frightened out of her wits. She looked around the room. No one was there. The window was closed.

"Maggie, are you okay?" Steve shouted, pounding on the door. "Open the door. What's going on in there?"

Maggie threw off the covers and jumped out of bed, flying to the door to unlock it. She flung the door open, fell into Steve's arms, and clung to him, trembling uncontrollably.

"What's going on? You were screaming your head off." Steve held her away from him and tipped her chin up to look into her eyes. "I've never seen you so scared. What happened? Bad dream?"

He folded his arms around her again until her body stopped quivering, then he led her back into her bedroom and they sat on her bed. "Okay. Time to level with me. What was that all about? What's bugging you? I know something's not as it should be. You're holding back."

Maggie shivered again at the thought of the huge man with the bushy hair and big ears she could see so clearly outside her window. "I just had the nightmare to end all nightmares." She tried to smile up at Steve, glanced at his serious face, and quickly looked away, knowing she could never look him in the eye and say nothing happened. She told him about the noise at the window, the man in her room who came toward her with a blanket, about not being able to move or to scream.

"You were dreaming you couldn't scream. I could hear you just fine over the TV in the family room in the other end of the house. Thought someone was being murdered up here." Steve laughed, then saw Maggie's ashen face. "Sorry, Maggie. Just a dumb joke. Are you okay now?"

Maggie sat back on the bed, pulled her knees up under her chin and hugged them with her arms. She nodded, avoiding Steve's eyes.

"Want to tell me what triggered the nightmare?"

"How do I know what ever triggers dreams and nightmares? I'm probably just exhausted. Maybe Dad put my subconscious to work with all of that 'alone' business."

"The offer still stands. I'll be glad to ride shotgun or share the driving." Steve tucked a stray strand of her long, red hair behind her ear. "I promise no backseat driving when you're at the wheel. I'll let

you decide what to eat, where to eat, when to eat, and we'll go wherever you want to go. I'll just be like a fly on the wall until you need
something."

Maggie laughed. "You? A fly on the wall? More like a pesky
mosquito." She realized Steve had worked his magic once again,
soothing and calming her anxieties, pulling her out of a near panic
attack. She flashed a sincere smile and chanced a look up at him.
"Thanks, Steve. You're a superhero in my eyes. You know that." She
paused. "Well, most of the time, anyway. I appreciate the offer. But
again, no thanks. This is something I really want to do on my own."

Steve looked at her for a long minute. "Sure you don't want to
unload something?"

"Give it up, Stevie." Maggie swirled on the bed, straightened out
her legs, put both feet in Steve's back, and shoved him off the bed.
She laughed. "Go to bed." Then she paused. "But I'll tell you what.
I'll leave my door open—and you leave yours open, too. Then if I
scream again, you can come and rescue me from whoever is invading
my dreams. Okay?"

Steve grabbed the blanket she was sitting on and yanked hard,
sending Maggie rolling across the bed and almost onto the floor on
the other side. "Okay. But if you're going to scream for me, do it
before I get to sleep, please. I need my beauty rest."

As Maggie threw her pillow at him, he dodged it and darted out
the door, leaving it open as he fled to his room across the hall. Maggie
sat quietly for a minute, thinking about the dream. Where had it
come from? She'd been thinking about Alyssa as she fell asleep—and
it was apparent she had fallen asleep, even though she thought she
was awake when it happened. Thank heaven it was only a bad dream
and not for real.

But it had been for real for Alyssa, she thought as she retrieved her
pillow and turned off the light. She could hear Steve's music in his
room, low enough so it wouldn't disturb her but loud enough to
mask his noises and comfort her.

As she crawled back into bed, she wondered if that had actually
happened to Alyssa, and if so, had Alyssa felt that same terror at being
unable to move, to scream, to alert anyone? Maggie shivered, experiencing
the panic all over again. When she closed her eyes, she could still see the

man in the window, but as she opened them in the semidarkened room, Maggie suddenly knew the man in the dream with the big ears wasn't a dream at all and he hadn't come after her.

He had come after Alyssa.

Maggie lay awake a long time trying to analyze the certainty she felt about this unexpected insight into the mystery of the girl's disappearance. There was simply no way she could have any idea this was how Alyssa had vanished; no way she could know what the man looked like; *but she knew.* Was this something she was receiving from the Spirit, some revelation to help her understand what happened to Alyssa? That was a comforting thought.

She finally forced it from her mind, acknowledging that sooner or later she'd discover *how* she knew. Until then, she'd simply accept the fact that somehow she had an eerie connection to the girl who looked so very much like her, and hoped if it was the Spirit guiding her in this knowledge, she'd be receptive to further revelation and insight as she pursued this new quest.

After a night of restless sleep, Maggie awoke in the predawn hours and crept silently down the stairs to pack her computer and bag in her car. She'd heard her father come in well after midnight, so apparently there had been some problem with the birthing, and she knew her mom had waited up for him. But Maggie needed to leave as soon as possible and didn't want to wake them, so she decided she'd call at breakfast time to say her good-byes, after the fact.

As she hurried to her car, Maggie heard Pegasus calling from the corral and realized she couldn't leave without one last ride. Slipping quietly back upstairs, she changed into an old pair of jeans, slipped into her winter chores coat and carried her boots down the stairs.

Pegasus greeted her noisily, evidently as glad to see her as she was to see him. Maggie didn't bother with a bridle or saddle. She unlatched the gate, stood on the barrel next to the fence, and Pegasus stood quietly while she threw her leg over his back, grasped his long, luxurious mane, and mounted her magnificent friend. Leaning forward, she whispered in his ear, calming him until they reached the pasture, then gave him his head.

They flew to the far end of the field, stars twinkling in the royal-blue night sky above them, horse and rider moving perfectly as one.

Maggie thought, *This is the kind of joy you must feel in heaven—pure, unadulterated delight in being alive.* As they cantered back to the barn, Maggie realized wistfully it could be weeks or even months before she would be able to experience this pleasure again.

Steve met them as they returned to the barn, holding the corral gate open so Maggie didn't have to dismount until she was in the barn.

"Mornin', Magpie. I didn't think you could resist saying good-bye to Pegasus."

"Steve, I can't believe you're up so early!"

"I didn't sleep a lot last night." Steve's quiet voice and serious tone created an immediate unease in Maggie.

"Too much dessert?" Maggie laughed, trying to lighten the mood or change the subject. It wasn't like Steve to be this serious with her.

Steve caught Maggie around the waist as she jumped off the horse and gently set her on the ground, holding her in place until their eyes met. "No. I'm worried about my little sister."

"Why?"

"I think something isn't quite right. Whatever's bothering you, if you won't tell the folks because you think they'll worry, tell me."

Maggie's nervous laugh sounded shaky, even to her own ears. "Well, if you just *think* something's wrong and you can't sleep, what if something *was* wrong and I told you? Then you'd never get any sleep." She wriggled out of Steve's hands and grabbed a brush to groom Pegasus's gleaming coat.

Steve picked up another brush and started working on the other side of the horse. "Level with me, Maggie. What's got you worried?"

It *would* make her feel better to talk to somebody about it. Maggie took a deep breath. "Before I say anything, you've got to swear on your honor that you will not mention a word of this to anyone, because I promised I wouldn't tell a soul."

Steve looked down at her over the horse's back. "But it's a bigger burden than you can handle alone?"

Maggie shrugged as her eyes met his. "I just need a sounding board more than anything else. I'm feeling some strange things, and I guess I need to bounce a few ideas off somebody, but neither Mom nor Dad would be the proper ones right now, since they're sort of worried about this trip anyway."

"Aw, don't worry about Dad. He just can't see you as anything but his little girl. He wasn't really ready for you to go to California, much less get an assignment like this and take off across the country alone. The fact that he's not putting up a fuss says a lot, Maggie. He trusts you—he trusts your judgment. I promise I won't say a word, so hit me with these very weighty matters that have you so worried."

Maggie came around Pegasus to comb his mane, positioning herself so she could watch Steve's reaction to her revelation. "I have a look-alike somewhere. Her name if Alyssa; she's the daughter of my new boss, but she was kidnapped about seven years ago on her sixteenth birthday. When I walked into the office yesterday morning, the receptionist nearly dropped her teeth. That's how much we look alike. She kept staring at me. I have a picture of the girl. Steve, it could be me!"

Steve tossed the brush on the shelf and leaned against the stall, observing Maggie's expressions. "Okay, so you've got a look-alike who was kidnapped. What's that got to do with your job?"

"Lily, the office manager, didn't want my new boss, Mr. Lawson, to see me until she'd figured out a way to break the news that I'm a dead ringer for his daughter. When she saw my books and heard about my dream to write a story about the Lewis and Clark Bicentennial, she decided that would be a perfect opportunity to get me out of town until she could explain me to Mr. Lawson. As she was giving me the assignment, I suddenly—without knowing I was going to do it—asked for the files on Alyssa. Steve, I don't know why I did that."

Maggie concentrated on a tangle in Pegasus's mane, then continued. "She gave them to me, very reluctantly, and swore me to secrecy that I wouldn't tell anybody that I was actually looking for Alyssa. She even said I'd lose my job if I even mentioned Alyssa to her, unless I found her or proof that she was dead. After reading the newspaper clippings in the files Lily gave me, I started getting into Alyssa's head. I feel really close to her, and the connection is becoming spooky."

Steve retrieved the brush and continued currying Pegasus, letting Maggie's tale spill out without interjecting comments or questions.

"Then last night when you said 'never see you again,'" Maggie continued, more slowly, "I just had this incredible flash into what happened to Alyssa and when I went to bed, as I was dozing off, I dreamed about that man at the window. After you left and I thought about it, I just had the strangest feeling that man wasn't after me, as I first thought. That man was after Alyssa. He may have been the one who kidnapped her."

"Could you identify him?" Steve asked.

Maggie stopped combing Pegasus's tail to consider that. "I could give a general description. I didn't see eye color or facial features, but he's a big man with bushy hair and big ears. A bulky man."

"I suggest you write it down while you're thinking about it. Every impression you have." Steve faced Maggie. "Does it make you feel uneasy or worried about going on this trip alone?"

Maggie thought about that. "No." She paused, then answered more certainly. "No, not at all. That's the funny thing. I have no fear or reservations in any way about this trip. No qualms or apprehension about traveling alone. No hesitancy or misgivings about any part of it."

"Maggie, I'd be happy to go with you." Steve placed his hand on his little sister's shoulder. "My offer still stands."

"Thanks, Steve." Maggie was touched by Steve's genuine concern for her and the offer, which she knew meant leaving behind his friends at the height of the Christmas celebrations when he was just getting back into the social scene after being gone with the military for the previous three years. "I know you'd come, but you're registered for school. You start in a few weeks."

Maggie put the brush away, said good-bye to Pegasus, and headed back to the house as Steve continued to argue his case.

"School starts the end of January so I have seven weeks before I leave. Your assignment might be finished by then. I could go, and if it extended longer than that, I'd fly home from wherever we were."

Maggie remained silent as they trudged through the early morning cold, wondering how to answer Steve's offer without hurting his feelings—with some small part of her wondering if she should take him up on it.

Steve interrupted her thoughts as they climbed the steps to the back door. "Why do you think you feel this connection to a perfect stranger? Is it your penchant for mystery?"

Maggie reached for the doorknob, then stopped to answer his question. "I think it's more than that. I'm always fascinated by a mystery and I'm delighted to have one. I was *so* excited at the assignment to write the Lewis and Clark stories, I couldn't believe my good fortune. But the more I thought about the missing girl, the more intrigued I became about that, almost to the over-powering of the Lewis and Clark thing, which, as you know, has been my dream for a very long time."

"But it's not just the mystery," Steve said, more as a statement than a question.

"I don't know," Maggie said slowly. "I just don't know. I'm really puzzled about this closeness I feel . . ." She was interrupted as the door swung open and her mother's arm reached out to pull her inside.

"Why are you two standing out in the cold? You'll catch your death! I've got breakfast ready, so hurry and wash up." Rose bustled off to the kitchen.

Steve grabbed Maggie's hand and dragged her into the study. "I know you've got your route plotted. Show me. If you don't want me along, okay, but I want to know your exact route—where you plan on being every day."

"I can give you my plan, but I can't give you any deviations I might decide to take at the last minute, and I certainly won't promise that I won't change my plans at some point."

Steve cleared some papers to spread the road atlas on his father's mahogany desk. "That's okay. You can always let me know if that happens. I'm going to be your personal check-in point."

Maggie sat in her father's big, maroon leather desk chair and showed Steve the route she'd planned. "My first stop will be overnight in Casper, Wyoming, then on to Rapid City, South Dakota, where someone thought they'd seen Alyssa and notified her father at the paper. The next letter came from St. Joseph, Missouri, then Pine Bluff, Arkansas, another from Texarkana, Texas, and the fifth from New Iberia, Louisiana." She traced the route with her finger, clearly showing the southward progression. "There are several Lewis and Clark points of interest along the way, so I'll be doing my stories in those places as I attempt to locate the people who said they spotted the missing girl."

"Okay, here's the deal. I want you to call me on my cell phone every morning before you leave and every night when you get to wherever you're staying, and any time in between when you see or feel anything out of the ordinary. If I don't hear from you, then I start a search. I'll fly immediately to wherever you were last heard from to find you, so you need to remember to check in, because you can bet your bottom dollar I won't be alone when I come."

Maggie couldn't believe her ears. She stared up at the serious expression on her brother's face. "Steve, don't you think that's a little overkill?"

Steve sat on the corner of the desk and folded his arms across his chest. "You know what, Sis? I don't think it's overkill at all. Your instincts have always impressed me. If you're feeling anything unusual at all about this, then I think we need to put those safeguards in place."

Maggie started to argue the point when her dad called them to breakfast. Knowing there wouldn't be another chance to talk to Steve alone, she agreed as they followed their father to the breakfast nook, but she made sure he understood she didn't think it was necessary and would discuss it further on the phone after she left.

With her start already delayed nearly two hours, Maggie gulped her breakfast, barely tasting the delicious Belgian waffles with home-made blueberry syrup and whipped cream cheese. She quickly shed her jeans and changed back into traveling clothes—a heather-knit pantsuit with a black turtleneck sweater—kissed her parents good-bye, and hurried to her car before they could change their minds about her "opportunity," as her Mom called it, and her "new independence," as her Dad labeled her trip.

Steve walked her to the car. "Remember, twice a day or I come to find you, Maggie. If you look so much like this Alyssa, maybe whoever kidnapped her will try it with you. I'd like you to explore this connection you feel to her, and will you please talk to me about it? I'm curious why you feel it so strongly when you'd never met or heard of the girl before now."

Maggie slid into her seat, started the car, then looked up at Steve. "Maybe we were twins separated at birth," she teased. Then what she said in jest struck her and she became quite serious. "Did you ever think of that? Maybe that's why I'm the only redhead in the family."

"Don't think so, Magpie. We have pictures of Mom very pregnant with you and pictures of me holding you when I was barely more than a toddler. I remember thinking you were sure an ugly, wrinkled little thing for everybody to be making such a fuss over, and who needed a girl anyway with a houseful of boys already?"

"You have a real talent for making a girl feel loved and wanted! Talk to you later about this arrangement. And Merry Christmas!" Maggie slammed the door and drove off, leaving Steve waving in the driveway and calling after her, "Twice a day or I come and find you!"

We'll see about that, Stevie boy, Maggie thought as she settled in for the long drive ahead of her. *Twice a day? No way!*

CHAPTER 7

Though the mountains still hid the sun, darkness had been dispelled and the world awakened to a new day with cloudless skies and the promise of no imminent winter storms. A good thing, Maggie thought, if she was going to reach Casper, Wyoming, before dark.

Before plunging into her column for the day, Maggie relaxed and enjoyed the familiar scenes around her, waving to neighbors turning herds of dairy cows into the fields from barns where they'd just been milked. Little puffs of steam rose above the herds as the warm, moist breath of the cows met the cold morning air.

But when she left the valley, and the road climbed into the snow-covered rolling hills, Maggie began taping her column so she could transcribe it and e-mail it to Lily when she arrived in Casper. She began by introducing the key players in this important early American drama. Everyone knew President Thomas Jefferson, so she concentrated on Meriwether Lewis, a young wealthy plantation owner who joined the army during the Whiskey Rebellion and became paymaster because of his talent with figures, and his integrity. The job required Lewis to travel to all U.S. Army posts carrying large sums of money to disburse to the soldiers. As president, Jefferson made Lewis his secretary partially because of his personal acquaintance with every officer in the army.

When Jefferson began planning the exploration of the new lands to the west, Meriwether was his first choice. Previously, Lewis had served in the army for six months with William Clark, and the two had developed a mutual respect and admiration. Lewis offered the position of cocaptain to Clark, the most unusual army arrangement in the history of the United States.

Maggie included interesting details of the arrangement of the expedition and ended the column with Jefferson's formal charge to Lewis: "The object of your mission is to explore the Missouri river, & such principal stream of it as by it's [sic] course and communication with the waters of the Pacific ocean, whether the Columbia, Oregon, Colorado or any other river may offer the most direct & practicable water communication across this continent for the purposes of commerce."

Little did he know there would be no direct water route across the continent, Maggie thought. But Jefferson wasn't alone in his thinking. Everyone at that time assumed there was such a route, and the British had already established fur-trading posts throughout the Northwest in anticipation of the discovery of the waterway.

Her assignment out of the way, Maggie noted unique landmarks as she crossed the frozen wastelands of southwestern Wyoming, a landscape much improved by glistening snow covering the normally barren desert. Diamondville could have been named after the dazzling ice crystals on the snow that sparkled like diamonds in the sun.

After a long, lonely stretch of U.S. 30, where she felt like the only soul left in the world, Maggie connected with Interstate 80 heading east. She felt herself relax as she merged with huge eighteen-wheelers, SUVs, and campers, and laughed aloud when she realized she'd been tensely gripping the steering wheel for the last hour. Had she actually been afraid on that stretch of highway with no one else around? Impossible.

A glance at her gas gauge startled Maggie—it approached the empty mark. That rarely happened, as she usually paid more attention to her driving than she'd apparently done on this trip. *Must make sure that doesn't happen again,* she thought, *or I could find myself in deep trouble out on these roads in the winter.*

She exited at Little America, froze her hands in the icy wind filling the gas tank, then parked and jogged to the restaurant, the cold, bitter wind penetrating her jacket and biting her nose and ears. She ordered a plate of nachos, and while she ate, she sat in a sunny window seat people-watching, her favorite pastime.

Then her thoughts turned to Alyssa for the first time since she left home. How had Alyssa's kidnapper fed the girl? Had he dared bring her into a café, or had he left her tied up in the car, or hidden in the back of a van? Maggie could get no visual picture of the arrangement. She drew a complete blank in this area, which was interesting to her, because she had felt such insight into some other areas of this tragic affair.

Back on the road, Maggie retrieved her tape recorder and recorded some thoughts on the letter Lion Lawson had received from a woman named Doris Butler in Rapid City, listing questions she needed to ask the woman, supposing that she could actually locate her. The letter was over a year old and the detectives who'd been hired to talk to her hadn't been able to interview her. Maggie turned off the tape recorder. Why did she think she'd be able to do any better than professionals had done?

She was so deep in thought, she almost missed the turnoff to Casper. Where Interstate 80 had been clear and dry because of heavy traffic continually blasting through the snow blowing endlessly across the highway, U.S. 287 was snowpacked and icy. Maggie slowed to fifty miles per hour and concentrated on keeping her little Mustang on the road. She glanced at the temperature gauge Jeff and his family had given her for her new car—minus fifteen degrees—and said a quick prayer for her safe arrival in Casper.

The sun was low on the horizon as she neared Muddy Gap and Martin's Cove. She thought of stopping at the visitors' center for a few minutes to get the kinks out of her legs, but the road to the entrance was covered with drifts three to four feet high. What would be an interesting, even delightful stop in the summertime, had held horrors for two handcart companies of Mormon pioneers that started across the plains too late in the season and had been stranded in early, heavy storms with no food and little warm clothing.

Of the five hundred and seventy-six pioneers in the 1856 Martin Company, as many as one hundred and fifty died before they were rescued by a party sent from Salt Lake with food, clothing, horses, and wagons. The Willie Company was somewhat more fortunate, losing only sixty-seven of the five hundred emigrants trying to reach the Great Salt Lake Valley before winter.

Maggie had always felt a deep sorrow for those suffering Saints as she heard the stories, but now, looking at her thermometer and knowing firsthand how cold it was outside, and how quickly exposed flesh froze and how hungry they must have been, she felt a new empathy for those unfortunate souls. What if her car slid off the road?

She had little in the car to eat. She had no warm blankets to wrap herself in to keep from freezing. There was not enough traffic to depend on anyone coming by to help. She wouldn't be any better off than those ill-fated travelers a century and a half before. Mother Nature was no respecter of persons; all were at her mercy, even with today's modern conveniences.

She shivered as she turned the heater up in her car, remembering other stories from Church history of the incredible suffering of the pioneers as she passed Devil's Gate and Independence Rock. She felt almost guilty as she drove easily and comfortably across the North Fork of the Platte River to Casper. When she arrived at the Holiday Inn, her hands ached from gripping the steering wheel for so long. It had been an exhausting drive, emotionally as well as physically, and she was anxious to relax.

But the article to Lily came first. She quickly set up her computer, transcribed the story from her tape recorder, and barely made the five o'clock deadline to e-mail it.

There was only a one-liner from Lily when she checked her e-mail, thanking Maggie for the column she'd e-mailed from home the night before. Would this be the extent of the correspondence, or would Lily be more communicative as the articles continued coming in every day? Maggie hoped that special relationship she had felt with Lily would survive this undertaking to find Alyssa. She liked Lily. Liked her a lot.

Next on her agenda: dinner in the hotel restaurant. It had been decorated for Christmas with thousands of little white lights inter-twined in dozens of small trees scattered throughout the huge indoor courtyard. Even the balconies of the floors above that overlooked the courtyard were strung with tiny, sparkling white lights.

Maggie loved Christmas, loved the lights, the gaily trimmed trees, and the beautiful decorations that hung from nearly every street lamp and storefront. But tonight, she felt a little lonely sitting at a table for one listening to the plaintive strains of Nat King Cole singing, "I'll Be Home for Christmas." She changed seats to avoid staring at the young couple nearby holding hands and smiling into each other's eyes and the older gentleman who kept trying to catch her attention. Lonely she may be, but there was no one's company here she wanted. Only for a minute did she wonder if she should have accepted Steve's invitation to accompany her. No, she could do this alone, and she would enjoy her independence.

A pool sparkled in one corner of the courtyard with a Jacuzzi gurgling next to it. After a cup of hot soup and a huge chunk of hot sourdough bread, Maggie ran back to her room, changed into her swimsuit, and indulged her tired body in the hot tub by letting jets of hot water beat on her aching neck and back muscles to relax them.

At what kind of place would Alyssa's kidnapper have stopped, she wondered as the water bubbled around her. *Certainly not one as nice as this. Did the man with the bushy hair and big ears tie her to the bed to make sure she didn't get away? Or did they sleep in a car or van so there was no opportunity for her to escape?*

As a group of young men noisily approached with towels in hand, their coarse language and suggestive banter signaled the end of her hot tubbing. Maggie quickly slipped out of the Jacuzzi and through the white wrought-iron gate before they could enter the fenced area. Ducking into a phone booth behind a Christmas tree, she eluded the one who vaulted the gate and tried to catch her. Did he seriously think he could bring her back to the group or was he just showing off to the others?

Not tonight, guys, she thought as she closed the elevator door behind her and punched the fourth floor button. *Actually, not ever with the likes of you!*

Totally relaxed after the hot tub and a quick shower, Maggie settled down with the letters again, trying to see if she had missed anything important in her haste to get through them all. The woman who'd written from Rapid City worked at Mt. Rushmore National Monument and said the girl and her father were employed as summer help in the café.

The girl and her father! How had she missed that in her first read-through? They were masquerading as father and daughter? Was Alyssa a willing captive? Or was this a false sighting? Maybe Maggie wasn't the only one in the world who resembled the missing girl.

Mt. Rushmore would be the first stop, Maggie determined, right after she located the local visitors' center for maps and information.

She arranged her clothes for tomorrow on a chair to rid them of wrinkles acquired in her suitcase, then organized her belongings so it would take minimum preparation time to leave in the morning. As she reached to turn out her light, her cell phone jingled in her purse. Whoops. She'd forgotten to call Steve.

"Maggie, are you okay? You didn't call! I've been trying to reach you for two solid hours. I've been worried sick." Steve's accusatory words came in a rush that instantly made Maggie feel both sorry and ashamed for being so negligent.

"Oh, Steve. I'm sorry. I raced to get my article off to Lily as soon as I checked in at the hotel, then ate and hot tubbed. The drive was long and grueling, and I was so tired I forgot to call. Forgive me?"

Maggie heard Steve exhale slowly. "I'll forgive you this time, Magpie, but don't do that to me again, okay? The Weather Channel showed iced-over highways and freezing temperatures across Wyoming, and all I could think of was you sliding off those icy roads down an embankment where no one could see you, and freezing to death before you were found. Please, promise me you'll call when you check into your hotel every night before you go to dinner, okay? And be sure to keep your cell phone turned on."

"I promise. Anything else?"

"No news since this morning. How was your day?" Steve seemed in a chatty mood now that he knew everything was all right.

"Very long, and I have to get an early start tomorrow. I'm just on my way to bed, Steve. Will you give my love to Mom and Dad and tell them I'm fine? 'Night, worrywart. I love you." Maggie hung up and turned off her cell phone. Steve might have been in the mood to talk, but she definitely was not. All she wanted right now was a good night's sleep without nightmares or dreams of any kind—even good ones—and certainly no phone calls. How could she feel independent if she had to keep answering the phone to reassure her family? She really wanted to prove to them that she was capable of doing this on her own.

Alyssa had been too heavy on Maggie's mind before she fell asleep because for the second night in a row she dreamed of her. They were riding together, experiencing the joy Maggie had just felt riding Pegasus, but as they raced toward the end of the pasture, the scene faded and Maggie's heart began to beat wildly. That man, that bulky, bushy-haired man was at the window again, trying to get in. But this time she realized it was not her window. It was a different window, and he came right in.

CHAPTER 8

Maggie fought to clear her mind, to throw off her covers and turn on the light, to get out of bed and face the monster in her room, real or imagined, but once again the covers felt heavy around her, too heavy to lift, too heavy to toss aside. With mounting horror, she watched the man come through the window, walk over to unlock the balcony door and slide it open, then turn to her. She tried to scream for help, tried to wake those sleeping around her, but no sound would come from her throat.

Suddenly someone rattled the doorknob. Fully awake at last, Maggie tossed off the covers and turned on the light, illuminating the dark corners of the room. No one was there. But someone *was* outside her door. They rattled the handle, then tapped lightly on the door.

"Hey, pretty little redhead, come out and play. Come swimming with us." Then there was laughter and shuffling noises in the hall.

Maggie didn't need to check the peephole to know who was making all that noise. She punched the front-desk button on her phone.

"Front desk. How may I assist you?"

"You can send someone up to room 418 immediately. Some drunks are knocking on my door. I don't know how they got my room number, but when I find out, someone at that desk is going to lose their job!"

"I'm so sorry. Yes, ma'am. We'll have someone right up there."

Maggie knew a guest's room number was never to be given out to anyone. When someone inquired about the room number of another guest, proper procedure required the desk clerk to call the guest and ask if they wanted to see the person inquiring about their room number. That provided privacy and prevented just this type of scenario from happening. This—or worse.

The boys from the pool had probably been flirting with some cute little thing at the desk and weaseled the room number out of her. Maggie wished she had some ice water in her ice bucket. She'd open the door and douse them with it. On second thought, she wasn't going to open her door for anyone, even the bouncer they sent.

She pulled the chair in front of the door, then looked out the sliding glass doors to her balcony to check her car and make sure it was okay. While there, she double-checked to make sure the lock was still secure, then flew back to bed and pulled the covers around her shoulders. Icy wind buffeted the glass doors and flowed in around edges that weren't properly sealed. Opening those heavy curtains had let all the cold air into the room, and she shivered as she snuggled under the covers, waiting for her body heat to warm her bed.

The noise abated in the hall, and she hoped no one from the front desk would call to verify they'd handled the problem. The fact that the offenders were gone was verification enough.

Maggie didn't turn the light off. She turned her back to it and lay awake a long time thinking about the nightmare. This time she had actually seen the man come through the window, then open sliding glass doors in Alyssa's room. Was there actually a balcony with sliding glass doors in Alyssa's room? Were any of these things she saw real, or were they all simply figments of her vivid imagination?

And why on earth was she having this recurring nightmare anyway? Had she become too immersed in and intrigued by the story and her subconscious wouldn't let go of it? There was no reason to be having any insights at all into Alyssa's kidnapping, since she had not known the girl, had not even heard of her until a couple of days ago. Strange.

The questions kept coming, one after another until Maggie finally reached over and pulled her scriptures out of her bag on the night table. She began each day with scripture study and recording the previous day in her journal, but that hadn't happened this morning in her rush to get on the road. Maybe a few verses of scripture would put other things from her mind and allow her to sleep.

She let the scriptures fall open, then read the verse highlighted in red: "But whoso hearkeneth unto me shall dwell safely, and shall be quiet from fear of evil" (Prov. 1:33).

Maggie settled back on the pillow to think about that. A comforting thought, and she *was* in the habit of "hearkening" to the Lord. In Proverbs 3, just across the page, she'd highlighted verses 5 and 6 at some time during her study: "Trust in the Lord with all thine heart; and lean not unto thine own understanding. In all thy ways acknowledge him, and he shall direct thy paths."

Good idea, she thought. Turn it over to the Lord and don't worry about figuring it out, because she certainly didn't have *any* understanding of what was happening. That decided, Maggie slipped her scriptures back in her bag, turned off the light, and within minutes fell into a dreamless sleep.

Of course, the alarm went off too soon, but Maggie reluctantly dragged herself out of bed, grabbed her clothes, and dressed in the bathroom with the heater turned on high. She made a mental note to stop earlier today to e-mail her article to Lily, have dinner, then catch up her journal and read scriptures before bed. That worked well last night—after she'd had that dream. Tonight she'd read before she went to sleep, hoping it would prevent nightmares.

Quickly checking her e-mail before packing her computer—there were no messages—she gathered her bags and went downstairs. They were just spreading the continental breakfast on the buffet at six o'clock when Maggie poked her head into the dining room. She grabbed a bagel, a little round of cream cheese, a plastic knife, a small bottle of pineapple-orange juice, and a banana to eat in the car, and checked out of the hotel. She could already feel the anxiety building to get to Mt. Rushmore and discover what answers it might hold.

Casper lay far behind her, and Maggie was well on her way to Buffalo when daylight finally peeked over the horizon, revealing a fresh skiff of snow covering everything. As the sun's first rays hit the frozen crystals, they cast a soft, purple glow, then pink, then gold over the whole world. The cloudless sky was azure blue, and the air icy cold; definitely a day to be snugly ensconced in a car with a good heater.

She knew she should be taping her article as she drove north on Interstate 25, but she was intrigued by the names of rivers and creeks the highway crossed: Castle Creek, Teapot Creek, Salt Creek, Crazy Woman Creek, and the legendary Powder River. Maggie wished she could stop and discover how the waterways came by their colorful names and learn about the people who lived in this sparsely settled area of the country. Did they choose to live here, or were they born here and just never left? Questions such as these had led Maggie to write fascinating special-interest articles, which she highlighted with award-winning photography. The journalist in Maggie was always drawn to the why, when, how, and who, and when she had answered those questions to her satisfaction, she usually made her editor very happy with the result.

As she reached Buffalo and turned east on Interstate 90, she started the column on Sacajawea, the sixteen-year-old Shoshoni Indian, who, with her husband, Toussaint Charbonneau, was hired as a guide and interpreter. Because of her contributions to the exploration of the vast unknown West, Sacajawea was honored by being featured on the golden dollar coin of the new millennium in 2000.

Maggie acknowledged Kenneth Thomasma's book, *The Truth About Sacajawea*, and the Lewis and Clark journals as she told of the girl who'd been taught by her mother to find and preserve food, make clothing, construct shelters, care for children, and pack for travel to distant hunting grounds before being captured by enemy warriors and made a slave when only eleven years old.

She made a mental note to include the paragraph on page twelve of Thomasma's book for her column. There was a great deal of controversy over the spelling of Sacajawea's name and the author noted that the Hidatsa Indian Language preferred *Sakakawea*, or Bird Woman, and was preferred by North Dakotans. *Sacajawea* spelling was preferred by Sacajawea's descendants, but others felt the most correct spelling was *Sacagawea* as Lewis and Clark spelled everything the way the pronunciation sounded to them. Maggie opted for the "j" spelling since the Sacajawea Interpretive Cultural and Education Center near Salmon, Idaho, used that spelling.

In November, 1804, Lewis and Clark encountered sixteen-year-old Sacajawea as they wintered in the Mandan-Hidatsa villages above present-day Bismarck, North Dakota. One of two wives of Charbonneau, a French-Canadian trapper, and pregnant with her first child, she was chosen because of her skills with the Lemhi Shoshoni language, which the explorers would need as they entered that territory on their explorations.

On February 11, 1805, Captain Lewis recorded that Sacajawea had a tedious labor marked with violent pain. He'd been informed the rattle of a rattlesnake would hasten the birth so he ground a small portion of a rattle, mixed it with water and gave it to the young woman to drink. Ten minutes later she gave birth to a beautiful baby boy, Jean Baptiste Charbonneau.

As Maggie dictated the article, she wondered if there had been any feedback from the public on her articles, or from Lionel Lawson himself. Had Lily sent the columns to Mr. Randolph? So much depended on the reactions of those two powerful men. She'd be incredibly disappointed if they didn't like her writing and pulled her back into the office before she'd done justice to her subject, and before she'd been able to fully investigate the claims of those who had seen the kidnapped girl alive as recently as a year before.

The irony didn't escape Maggie. She was writing about a young woman who'd been kidnapped; at the same time, she was searching for another who, two hundred years later, had also been snatched from her home and family.

Maggie's curiosity tempted her to explore Devil's Tower, the nation's first national monument, so designated in 1906 by President Theodore Roosevelt. She resisted that, as well as the impulse to stop at Bear Butte State Park when she crossed into South Dakota. Anxious to find the woman who'd written the letter about Alyssa, she drove on, trying to convince herself the reason she wasn't giving in to temptation to explore these areas filled with stories was that her assignment was to write about Lewis and Clark, and they never came this far south.

With breakfast four hours behind her, she was happy to arrive in Rapid City to placate the gnawing emptiness in her stomach at the first fast-food establishment she encountered. That most important item out of the way, she located the visitors' center where she gathered brochures, maps, and information from the friendly, helpful woman at the counter.

Rapid City was a tourist mecca, she discovered, where only the hardy came in the winter, but where hordes descended in the summer to visit numerous spectacular caves, Mt. Rushmore, Crazy Horse Memorial, mines and museums, Dinosaur Park, Storybook Island, and so many other things the woman listed she couldn't remember them all. Even a portion of the Berlin Wall rested in a local city park.

But Maggie had only one destination in mind as she traveled south on U.S. 16: to seek the person who'd written the letter about Alyssa. She could scarcely contain her excitement as she wound through beautiful rock- and tree-covered hills. Definitely a tourist destination. She passed Reptile Gardens, Flying T Chuckwagon Supper and Show, Bear Country USA, Christmas Village, Old McDonald's Farm, and Sitting Bull Crystal Caverns, to name only a few. Her oldest brother, Jeff, and his family would love it, especially those kids!

At the entrance to Mt. Rushmore National Memorial, Maggie paid her parking fee with trembling hands. What if the woman wasn't there? What if no one knew how to get hold of her? She wasn't in the phone book, which Maggie had checked at the visitors' center.

She'd been so caught up in arriving and finding the restaurant that she didn't notice her surroundings. When she climbed the stairs and gazed up the colorful avenue of state flags waving above tall, white granite pillars, and the grandeur of the four presidents carved into the towering mountain above, the sight absolutely took her breath away. Of course the cold, biting wind that blew down from the mountain might have contributed, but the sight was awesome.

She spotted the restaurant, and apart from being a haven from the frigid wind, Maggie was elated at her initial opportunity to work on the mystery that had captivated her from the first moment she'd heard about it.

As she walked through the door, a middle-aged woman in a wheelchair greeted her from across the room with a heavy Irish brogue. "Katie, m'love! Me thought to never see ye again."

Maggie stood with her mouth open, surprised beyond speaking. *If I tell her I'm a reporter, she might not talk to me,* Maggie thought frantically. *What can I say that won't scare her off?*

The woman wheeled her chair swiftly across the room, stopping just short of Maggie's shins. She looked up, tilted her head to the side, and said with a slight frown, "Ye look different, lass. The same, yet a wee bit different."

"I'm not Katie. I'm her twin sister." Maggie blurted the first thing that came to her mind, crossing her fingers behind her back in a gesture from childhood that supposedly canceled the lie.

"Why, that Katie never once mentioned a twin sister," the woman said, shaking her head.

Maggie thrust out her hand. "I'm Maggie. There was a divorce. Mom took me. Dad took Katie. Now I'm trying to find her."

"Kathleen O'Sullivan," the woman said, grasping Maggie's hand firmly. "I loved that sister o' yours. Timid, quiet, rarely smiled, but when she did, she lit up the room. A great sadness, me thought, weighed her down. Maybe 'twas missin' the likes o' you, missy. She took to me daughter Jamie, when she worked here, but that father o' hers didn't like that much. He didn't want Katie makin' friends 'cause it was too hard to leave, he said, and they had to leave a lot. But a girl's just gotta have a best friend, and Jamie was hers."

"Do you have any idea where they are now?" Maggie asked, afraid to get her hopes up but doing it nevertheless.

"Ya know, lass, I don't. They were only summer help, and in the winter, when we have few tourists, we don't need extra hands. I heard they hired on up to Crazy Horse for a special celebration when they finished here, but ye can be sure they've moved on. None o' the summer help sticks around for our cold winters. Ya might check there. Someone might know something."

"Thank you so much, Kathleen. Could I possibly talk to Jamie and see if she can remember anything that might give me a clue?"

"Sorry, lass. Jamie isn't back from college for the holidays yet. Won't be home until next week."

Maggie pulled out her notebook, scribbled her cell phone number and name on it, and handed the sheet to Kathleen. "If you remember anything else, or if Jamie does, would you call me? I haven't heard from Katie for several months, and I'm worried that something might have happened to her."

"Sure, lass. I'll call Jamie tonight and talk to her."

"Can I assume you're from the beautiful Emerald Isle?" Maggie asked, insatiably curious about people and their origins.

"Sure and ye can, lass. Me tongue always gives me away." Kathleen tilted her head to the side and laughed.

"How did you end up here in the middle of this country?"

"Me man read about the Crazy Horse project, and when his job ended in the quarries in Ireland, he said he had to be a part o' this. Shaping stone into beautiful things is his life's work, so every day he carves rock out o' that everlasting mountain, helping the Korczak Ziolkowski family turn their vision into reality. I don't much expect to be around when Crazy Horse is finished, or when the university and medical training center are built, but I expect me man will chip away at that mountain until I lay him in the ground. If'n I don't go first," she added with a wink.

"Thank you so much, Kathleen. It's been a pleasure to meet you." Maggie turned to leave, then spun around. "Oh, do you know a woman by the name of Doris Butler? I think she worked here."

Kathleen's smile vanished, and her eyes went to her hands clasped tightly in her lap. She sighed, then looked up at Maggie. "Sure and I knew her. She worked in the gift shop from the time I started here in the café, nearly ten years ago. Last year she took a nasty fall down the stairs out on the overlook. After that she wasn't the same. Kept tellin' crazy stories about a killer tryin' to get her and a girl bein' kidnapped, and she was goin' to be the next headline in the paper if people didn't believe her." Kathleen stopped, and her head sagged toward her ample chest.

"What happened?" A cold chill gripped Maggie's heart.

"It appears we shoulda listened to her babblin'. They found her dead in her bed. Never did hear if the coroner decided whether she died in her sleep or was smothered by the pillow they found over her face." Kathleen paused for a long moment, then looked up at Maggie. "I wish ya God speed, lass, in findin' that pretty sister o' yours." She turned and wheeled back to the counter.

Maggie, frozen in place by the revelation of Doris Butler's death, watched Kathleen resume her task of filling catsup and mustard bottles.

CHAPTER 9

The cold chill that gripped Maggie as she left the restaurant and followed the signs to the gift shop was not caused by the wind blowing across the granite terrace. Was she following a killer as well as a kidnapper? Maggie shuddered as she slipped inside and pressed her head against the huge window that perfectly framed the faces of the four presidents on the mountain.

A child's voice penetrated her grim thoughts as he read to his mother. "This says the mountain rises five hundred feet above the valley floor and each face is sixty feet tall."

"Very good, Ethan. Can you name the presidents without reading their names from your paper?"

Maggie turned to watch the blond little boy, probably about eight years old, screw up his face in deep concentration. "George Washington, Abraham Lincoln, Thomas Jefferson, and . . ." He paused. "The Rough Rider. I can't remember his name."

"Theodore Roosevelt," his mother said, leading the boy to the exhibit area and explaining why those men were chosen for the memorial.

Chosen. The word jumped out at Maggie. Why was Alyssa chosen to be kidnapped? Why was she the one singled out from all the girls sleeping over that night? Was it a random selection, or had she been watched and stalked? Why had there been no ransom demand? That was another puzzler. Alyssa's father was a wealthy man who would have willingly paid a hefty ransom for his daughter's return. Did the kidnapper not realize which girl he had taken? Did he not know who Alyssa really was? What exactly was the motivation behind the kidnapping?

And why, after all those years, did people begin to come forth with sightings of the kidnapped girl? Had the kidnapper kept his victim hidden away the first few years, then thinking it was safe to come out, ventured out into public and been spotted? Had Doris Butler discovered who Alyssa was and confronted the man with the bushy hair and big ears? Had he shoved her down the stairs, then finished the job with a pillow when she survived and kept talking?

Maggie shuddered and left the window to find the gift shop and a change of venue to rid herself of the creepy feeling these thoughts induced. She browsed the book section looking for any information she didn't have on Lewis and Clark, but Maggie couldn't concentrate on books. Kathleen said Katie was with her father. Had the kidnapper convinced her that he was her father? Katie had to be the same girl as Alyssa. There couldn't be *three* people who looked so much alike.

What prevented Alyssa from leaving, from returning to her home in California? Had she bonded with the kidnapper? What a strange phenomenon, that a person could actually establish a bond with the person who kidnapped them, which prevented them from trying to escape, and even created an allegiance to them. Maggie didn't understand the psychology behind the phenomenon but knew from researching an article she'd written that it happened.

As she left the gift shop, she walked to the overlook and photographed the monument whose faces gleamed white against the brilliant blue sky behind them. Maggie thought about following the sidewalk that wandered down among the trees where she'd heard one of the park rangers tell that little boy, Ethan, he could get some great pictures looking straight up at each of the faces and read about each president, but her mind was too filled with finding some clue to Alyssa to consider the detour.

After all, she thought, *the story is not about the Black Hills and all it contains. The story is Lewis and Clark, who were never here.* But the bigger story—the one she felt compelled to follow—was the missing girl who looked incredibly like herself.

Tonight she'd e-mail pictures of the famous monument to Steve to show him where she was and touch base with him. But now she consulted her map and headed for the Crazy Horse Memorial on a beautiful, winding scenic drive, which in summer would be delightful. Today the road was icy and slippery and required all her concentration and skill to stay on the pavement instead of sliding off into snowbanks, as three other cars had already done.

Soon the country opened up and spread out before her, the afternoon sun melted the ice, and she turned on the road to the Crazy Horse Memorial. She stopped short of the entrance to compare the silhouette on the wrought-iron sign to the mountain ahead with its figure of the famed Indian Chief Crazy Horse taking shape in the golden granite. What a massive undertaking!

Surprised at the magnificent visitors' center and museum hidden in the Black Hills, Maggie was even more amazed at the actual dimensions of the monument. Where each president's heads at Rushmore was sixty feet high, Crazy Horse's head was more than eighty-seven feet tall—nine stories! The overall dimensions of horse and chief were five hundred and sixty-three feet high and six hundred and forty-one feet long.

While she was reading the brochure, a young man with a guide badge approached Maggie, looking anxiously around him. "Can I help you find something? I'd be happy to show you through the visitors' center."

Maggie wondered at the cause of his nervousness. She certainly wasn't an intimidating person. Then he snatched the brochure from her hand, and pretending to point out something, whispered, "How'd you ditch your old man? What are you doing back? I thought you were gone for the season."

Maggie stared up into puzzled dark eyes peering from a nice face with a frightened expression. As she appraised the tall, skinny young man with thick, straight black hair that brushed his collar, he whispered, "Gee, Katie, you look great. I like your new hairdo and I *like* your clothes. You look all grown up, sort of the same, but different."

"Maybe it's because I'm not Katie," Maggie whispered laying her hand on his arm.

He jumped as if her hand had burned him.

"I'm her twin sister and I'm trying to find her."

His jaw dropped and his eyes popped. "Honest?" he gasped.

"Don't you think we look like twins?" Maggie asked.

"Well, yeah, but Katie never said anything about having a twin sister."

Maggie repeated the fabricated story of their relationship. "I'm trying to find her. I've traced her this far, but I don't know where she went from here. Do you?"

"Come over to this window and let me show you the monument so it will look like I'm working. If we're looking at the carvings, they'll think I'm telling you about them."

He led her down a long pine hall lined with Native American artifacts, quilts, and paintings to a wall of windows overlooking the memorial. About a mile away, the mountain was slowly and laboriously being blasted into the form of the great chief on his horse.

"Where was Katie going from here?" Maggie asked while her nervous guide gestured silently out the window.

"She didn't say. Her crazy dad never told her where they were going next. They just showed up in the spring, got hired, then left, usually without telling anyone they were leaving. At least, Katie didn't know they were going. He probably collected their paychecks and then told her to pack her bag."

Maggie had a new thought. "Did they come back here every year?"

"I only knew her for two summers. I never asked if they'd been here more than that." He looked around nervously and pointed to the beautiful paintings behind them. "We need to keep moving. I'm supposed to be helping the people who come here."

Maggie glanced at his name tag. "You are helping me, Jimmy. You're giving me information on my sister so I can find her. But let's keep walking. I don't want to get you in trouble." They entered another long pine hallway lined with Native American paintings that were masterpieces of detail and color. "When did you last see her?"

Jimmy thought for a minute. "It's been over a year. They worked at Rushmore for the summer, then came up here for a celebration we had—we needed extra help—then suddenly one morning, they were gone. No good-byes, no nothing. Just gone."

"You liked her a lot, didn't you?" Maggie asked softly, seeing the pain in his face as he spoke.

He nodded, then looked over his shoulder again and hurried her into the next pine-paneled area where he paused at cases filled with precious ancient and modern artifacts. "She was so lonely. Her dad didn't want her to talk to anybody, but when he wasn't looking, she'd talk to me. She was just so . . . alone. So sad."

"What did you talk about?" Maggie asked, pretending to read about an elaborately beaded ceremonial dress displayed on the wall. Then she remembered her camera. She would never have walked through a building like this without taking copious amounts of pictures for some future article. That just showed where her mind was today!

"Mostly her dream." Jimmy steered Maggie through a set of double doors into an area with quotes from famous chiefs carved in shining metal plaques. "She wanted to go to college in the worst way. She wanted to be free from her father, to have her own life."

"Couldn't she just leave and go do that?" Maggie asked.

"And this is one of the saddest of the quotes," Jimmy said suddenly, pointing up at the plaque under which they were standing. "In 1891 Chief Red Cloud said: 'They made us many promises, more than I can remember—They never kept but one; they promised to take our land, and they took it!'" he recited.

"It is a tragic episode of American history, isn't it?" Maggie said without turning around, snapping pictures all the while of the chieftain's quotes. "You're a good guide, Jimmy. What else is there to see here?"

Jimmy pointed to a huge teepee standing in the middle of the floor, and as they moved in that direction Maggie heard the door close quietly behind them. Apparently Jimmy was either being evaluated by a superior or watched to make sure he was really working.

"I'm sorry I can't just sit and talk to you," he apologized softly. "This project is funded entirely by contributions so they can't waste money on hiring help that doesn't do their job. I need this job to pay my tuition next semester."

"I understand. I'm just grateful you'll take the time to talk to me, and I'm getting a bonus—a personal tour of this incredible facility I didn't even know existed. It really is amazing. But you started to tell me why Katie wouldn't just leave."

"She was afraid of her father. He had a terrible temper and if she left him, she knew he'd find her and hurt her. She was all he had in this world, and he was the only family she had, so they needed to stick together. No one else cared about them so they had to care for each other."

"I can't believe he'd tell her that—or that she'd believe it! She knew better." Maggie shook her head in disbelief. Suddenly she had a disturbing thought. "Jimmy, did Katie ever seem . . . drugged?"

The young man thought for a minute as he guided Maggie into the gift shop. "Now that you mention it, there were times when she had a hard time staying awake, and an even harder time speaking. She never talked when her dad was around. Only when we were alone." He stopped and looked at Maggie. "You know, I think I might be the only person around here who ever heard her speak. She was almost never out of her father's sight. When he'd get really busy, she could sometimes slip away for a few minutes and find me. I felt like I was the only friend she had in the world." Then he amended, "Except for Jamie O'Sullivan."

Jimmy picked up a video of the history behind the idea and the work at the Crazy Horse Memorial, *Dynamite and Dreams,* which Maggie quickly bought. She couldn't afford to have this informative young man taken from her at this point in their interview.

"What did they do here?" Maggie asked, realizing she had no idea how they earned their living.

Jimmy led her onto an outdoor deck area displaying a marble model of the mountain carving and explained that Chief Crazy Horse was pointing in answer to the derisive question asked by a white man, "Where are your lands now?" The chief replied, pointing, "My lands are where my dead lie buried." Maggie snapped pictures with the vibrant blue sky as a background for the gleaming white statue.

Jimmy continued quietly, "He was a cook—a pretty good cook. Katie was his helper. The arrangement was he got full pay, and if they didn't want to pay full wage for her, he settled for half salary for Katie, as long as they could work together."

Maggie peered over the edge of the balcony at the deep blue waters of man-made Arrowhead Lake. "If they were only here for the summer, do you know where they lived the rest of the time?" She stood back and captured the arrow-shaped lake that pointed at the memorial on the mountain beyond.

Jimmy steered her back along the veranda. "They didn't have a home. They just traveled from one place to another working. She said last summer they were in Missouri, then Texas and Louisiana for the winter. This is sculptor Korczak Ziolkowski's studio and family home." Answers to Maggie's questions and tour information flowed smoothly together as they walked.

"Did they come back this last summer?" Maggie wanted him to say yes.

"No. I kept hoping they would. I even had Jamie watch for her and promise to call me if they showed up. Jamie's mother worked in the restaurant with them, and Jamie tried to be her friend, but Katie's dad made a big fuss so they couldn't even talk when he was around."

Hmm, Maggie thought. *Did Kathleen know that and hadn't bothered to tell her, or had she just forgotten? It had been nearly a year and a half ago.*

Maggie gasped as they entered the rock building housing the artist Ziolkowski's studio and home. Polished hardwood floors gleamed in the soft lighting, and a beautiful grand piano graced one corner of a long room filled with antiques and fine art. Not at all what she expected to see in the hand-built rock home of the once-destitute artist who refused government help in building his dream and that of the local Indian nations. Definitely worth several pictures.

"When did you last see Katie?" Maggie asked.

"In October, a year and two months ago." Jimmy led her through the sculptor's workshop where Maggie saw a picture of the son of Gutzon Borglum, the carver of Mt. Rushmore, and the daughter of Korczak Ziolkowski, the carver of Crazy Horse, working together on projects. There was certainly a story there! She snapped pictures of the images and the printed information. Much easier than taking notes, and she'd delete them from her digital camera later when she'd copied them to her computer.

"I did have one card from her," Jimmy remembered, "postmarked from St. Joseph, Missouri, saying they were working their way south. Her dad couldn't stand the cold so they worked their way toward the warmer weather every winter."

"Jimmy, were they well paid? Did they make pretty good money?"

"Not a fortune, but enough to support themselves. Here's the Native American Educational and Cultural Center. It's two levels, built with blast fragments from the mountain."

Maggie glanced around the huge rock-and-pine room, but nothing registered. She took pictures randomly, pointing her camera automatically as she asked, "What did they spend their money on?

Did Katie have nice clothes? Or did they have to spend it all on housing while they were here?"

Jimmy shook his head. "Katie didn't have nice clothes. A couple pairs of jeans, a few shorts, and shirts. I don't think she even had a dress. She carried everything in one suitcase so when they were ready to go, she just tossed it all in there and they walked out the door. They stayed in cabins near here that most of the summer help used. Inexpensive, with a couple of beds, a bathroom, and tiny little kitchen. They always ate at the restaurant. Never cooked at home. That way they didn't have to buy groceries."

He led Maggie outside. "There is the famous fighting stallions statue, and you gotta see the Nature Gates."

Maggie slipped her coat on and wrapped her scarf around her neck to keep out the cold December wind. "I assume they owned a car. Do you know what kind it was?"

"Yeah, a battered VW van. An old clunker that Katie's dad worked on all the time to keep it running. Maybe that's where a lot of their money went. Katie said they worked all year, so they probably didn't have to have a lot of money stashed away. He never had a hard time finding a job as a cook, no matter where they went, but Katie rarely had a penny of her own, not even to get a soda from the machine. Sometimes she was able to keep some of her tips, but he usually took them from her."

As they approached the gates, Maggie could see the parking lot beyond and, with a sinking feeling, knew her interview was nearing its end.

"Jimmy, did they ever work anywhere else in the area besides Rushmore and Crazy Horse?"

The young man paused in front of the gates and thought about her question. "You know, I think they might have worked a week or so at the Alpine Inn in Hill City. I remember Mom mentioning she thought she'd seen Katie in the kitchen when they went there for dinner." He grinned. "If you want the best food in the whole area, stop at the Alpine Inn for lunch or dinner. It's the greatest!"

Then he reverted to his guide persona. "These gates are forty-six feet long and have two hundred seventy brass silhouettes of birds and animals." He smiled proudly. "Unique in all the world."

"They're beautiful." Trees, birds, flowers, and animals both big and small gleamed in the setting sun which Maggie captured with her artist's eye. Then she asked Jimmy to stand in front of the wrought-iron gates while she took a picture of him.

"Thank you, Jimmy. I appreciate the time you've spent with me and the information you've given me. You're a great guide." Maggie wrote her cell phone number in her notebook and tore the page off. She passed it to Jimmy with a twenty-dollar bill wrapped inside.

"That's a contribution for your tuition next semester, and please call me at that number if you hear from Katie or remember anything else that might help me find her." Maggie extended her hand and thanked Jimmy again as he shook it.

"I sure hope you find her. She'll be glad to know she has more family than just her mean old dad. Good luck." Jimmy turned and nearly ran back to the big pine center.

Maggie hurried to her car, elated at having received so much information, but when she realized it was over a year since Jimmy—or anyone here—had seen Katie, her elation evaporated. She took a picture of the huge complex and got into her car out of the icy wind.

Hill City. She checked the map—it was on her way back to Rapid City, just using a different route. Shadows were long as she drove out of the parking lot and down the winding driveway to the highway. She'd need a place to stay tonight. Thinking of a hotel reminded her of her column, which had to be e-mailed to Lily. Maggie glanced at her watch. Five o'clock. That should make it four o'clock in California. She didn't remember crossing a time zone so this should still be in Mountain time. She hoped.

Within fifteen minutes she entered Hill City and looked for a hotel while she kept her eyes open for the Alpine Inn. When she found it, she was delighted to discover the two-story building served as a hotel as well as a restaurant.

The minute Maggie walked through the antique doors of the inn, she felt an eerie sense of déjà vu.

CHAPTER 10

Maggie knew she'd never been to the Alpine Inn, but the hotel felt strangely familiar. She shook off the eerie feeling; this rustic place probably reminded her of somewhere else.

Fortunately, one room in the hotel was available. Holiday travelers filled the others, with the exception of two which were rented on a permanent basis to a writer and an artist. Monika, the present owner, led her up steep, narrow, blue-carpeted stairs and down solitary hallways to a simple, small room furnished in antiques. As they walked, Maggie got the whole story of Monika taking the reins from her mother, who'd owned and run the hotel since 1974.

"I'll take it," Maggie said, even after Monika explained she'd share a bathroom with other guests on that floor, just as guests had done decades ago. Maggie registered, then grabbed her computer and tape recorder from her car and raced back upstairs to transcribe the day's article and e-mail it to Lily.

Only then did she examine her room. Burgundy tapestry drapes dripping with fringe were pulled back revealing crisp white sheers. Twin pedestal lamps on antique spindle night tables flanked the brass bed covered with a simple white chenille spread. One brass ball was missing from the post on the headboard.

Maggie's rumbling stomach reminded her it had been hours since she'd eaten. Not only was she famished, she was anxious to speak to anyone with knowledge of Katie. She'd almost ceased to think of her as Alyssa. She hurried downstairs to the dining rooms and was seated by a young hostess who kept looking at her with a puzzled expression.

"I'm Jenna. I'll be your waitress. What can I get you to drink?" she asked, avoiding Maggie's eyes.

"Just water for now, thank you."

The girl whirled and almost ran to the kitchen. Maggie followed, pretending to examine the artwork lining the wallpapered walls: very nice paintings, some for sale, some not. Hidden by a wooden partition near the kitchen door, which was covered with plants, paintings, and plates, Maggie listened to the conversation generated by her appearance.

"I tell you, it's Katie."

"No, they wouldn't come back here, not after what happened."

"Come and see for yourself."

"I'll peek later. I can't leave this right now. Talk to her and make sure it's her. It's been a long time since you've seen her. Maybe you forgot what she looks like."

"Yeah, right. You don't forget something like that."

The conversation stopped and Maggie heard ice clinking in a glass. She sidled back to the dining area as the sun's last rays illuminated the stained-glass door at the end of the room. Wall sconces glowed with golden light, giving the room a warmth Maggie didn't feel after that final comment.

You don't forget something like that. What did that mean? Had Alyssa done something to draw attention to herself, or had it been her father? Did someone suspect him of killing Doris Butler? First thing tomorrow she'd check newspaper files to see if there had been any suspects in the killing, or if the coroner had deemed it accidental.

As Jenna brought her water, Maggie settled at the polished wooden table. "What do you recommend?" She hadn't had time to look at her menu, but in a charming place like this, the house specialty was usually one of the best items on the menu.

"Everyone loves our filet mignon. It's served with a side salad, house dressing, baked potato, and Texas toast. We also have great German dishes, but you need to save room for dessert. We have over thirty homemade desserts to choose from, and every one is more delicious than the last."

"The filet sounds good. I like it medium rare. And we'll see about dessert when I'm through with dinner." Maggie smiled at the young woman who seemed a little more at ease now. "Have you worked here long?"

"About four years."

"It has a very nice atmosphere. A warm, friendly, homey feeling. I felt something when I walked in the front door." She had felt something, but it wasn't exactly a coming-home-to-family feeling.

"Everyone loves working here. They treat you real good." The girl stopped, then blurted, "You know, when I first saw you, I thought you were someone else. But now that I talk to you, I can tell you're not."

Maggie leaned forward and asked softly, "Was her name Katie?"

Jenna's blue eyes widened and she stepped back, hesitating before she answered. "Yes."

"Katie is my twin sister. Mom and Dad divorced; Mom took me, Dad took Katie, and I'm trying to find her. She stopped writing a few months ago and I'm afraid something has happened to her."

Jenna looked around the still-empty dining room and slipped into the chair opposite Maggie. "They used to come here regular—about every summer—and work till the tourist season was over. But I don't think they'll be back. There was . . ."

The bell at the front desk signaled the appearance of other guests, and Jenna excused herself to seat the newly arrived patrons. She didn't come back. Maggie wondered what the girl was about to say. Why didn't she think they'd be back? What had happened?

Maggie read the back of the menu: a history of the Alpine Inn, formerly Harney Peak Hotel, built in 1886 for use by the executives of the Harney Peak Tin Mining, Milling and Manufacturing Company.

Hill City, the second town established in the Black Hills, had once been nicknamed One Mile of Hell because even though mile-long Main Street had a church on each end, more than fifteen bars with their associated rowdiness and gunfights among miners and railroad men occupied the rest of the road.

More fodder for interesting articles, Maggie thought. When she finished this assignment, South Dakota would be a fascinating place to spend time.

Jenna brought her dinner and apologized for not having more time to talk. The restaurant was filling fast and she was too busy.

"I'm staying in the hotel tonight. Maybe when you're through we can talk. I need to find my sister and I hope you can tell me something that will help me locate her."

"Enjoy your meal. I'll talk to you later."

But would she really? Maggie thought. That didn't sound like a promise, more like a pacification. But if she paid her compliments to the chef in the kitchen, maybe that would elicit some information. If Katie/Alyssa had been here, she wanted to know everything about that stay.

And she *would* pay her compliments to the chef. After tasting the first bite of the filet mignon, she decided it was the best she'd ever eaten. After finishing everything on her plate, Maggie scanned the dessert menu, but with so many delicious choices, she couldn't make up her mind, so she passed altogether.

Jenna brought Maggie's bill and said she was still too busy to visit but would try to come to her room later. Maggie headed straight for the kitchen. She poked her head around the door, saw two people working feverishly to provide food for patrons in the filled-to-capacity dining rooms, and decided this wasn't a good time to approach them.

"Just wanted to offer my compliments to the chef," Maggie called from the doorway, watching their expressions carefully as they looked up. "That was by far the best steak I've ever had. Thank you."

The plump blonde glanced up with a smile that froze on her face when she saw Maggie. The brunette nodded her head in acknowledgment and went back to chopping onions.

Maggie took advantage of the blonde's surprise. "I'm Katie's twin sister. I haven't heard from her lately and I want to find her. Do you have any idea where she might be?"

The woman shook her head then whirled to stir something in a bubbling pot on the stove. Interview over. Maggie put her dinner bill on her room tab, noting the antique safe on which the modern cash register sat, and wondered if the proceeds of the manufacturing company had been kept in that safe a century ago.

She climbed the long, narrow flight of stairs to her room. It was dark and the halls were dimly lit. *A spooky place if you had an overactive imagination,* Maggie thought, *especially when the history of the hotel had mentioned the resident ghost that wandered these very halls.*

Maggie collapsed on the bed with her cell phone and called Steve, reaching his voice mail. She left a message that she was checked into the Alpine Inn in Hill City, South Dakota, and would e-mail pictures of Mt. Rushmore and Crazy Horse Memorial. She was sure Steve had never been there and would probably be as amazed as she was at what she'd photographed.

Going online, she did some research on the local newspaper to see what she could access without having to visit the newspaper office. Unfortunately, they only had the current news available online, not archives. That would be her first stop in the morning. She needed to know the outcome of the autopsy report on Doris Butler, and whether there had been any suspects mentioned if it had been murder. Had anyone ever been arrested in the case, or had it simply been an accidental fall and smothering later? That didn't seem likely to Maggie.

Probably the wisest use of her time while she waited to see if anyone came to her room would be construction of tomorrow's column which she'd e-mail when she finished tonight. That would relieve the pressure of arriving at a destination tomorrow in time to file the story before Lily left the office. When she'd checked her e-mail, she'd found only a brief acknowledgment from Lily. Maggie hoped tomorrow there would be feedback. If not, she might have to ask Lily outright how the columns were being accepted. If she should be taking a different approach, she needed to know it before she progressed too far into the series.

Tomorrow's spotlight would be on William Clark, Lewis's cocaptain, who wasn't really a captain at all. His promotion, which Lewis had insisted he be given to help lead the Corps of Discovery, was rejected. But only Lewis and Clark were aware of the War Department's slight; the men of the corps never knew and always called him Captain Clark.

Lewis assigned Clark the responsibility of recruiting and training the men they'd need for the hazardous trip though the unknown wilderness. He chose well, "some good hunters, stout, healthy, unmarried men, accustomed to the woods and capable of bearing bodily fatigue in a pretty considerable degree." They performed admirably.

Clark's geographical genius was apparent throughout the expedition as he determined by observation and common sense which fork of a river was the correct one to follow, saving many days' unnecessary travel. His organization of the portage of the keelboat around the Great Falls of the Missouri was a remarkable achievement, as was his survey of the best route and the construction of the crude "truck" with which a few selected boats were transported over the mountain pass.

An experienced frontiersman, he was also a detailed journalist, and where Lewis had months of lapses in his journals, (whether because they were lost, or because Lewis simply was too busy with other things to write), Clark filled the void with his accounts of the expedition. His detailed maps of routes covered by the explorers were amazingly accurate, and he included sketches of animals and birds encountered along the way.

In 1807, after the successful Voyage of Discovery was completed, Clark was appointed superintendent of Indian Affairs at St. Louis, and in 1813 he became governor of the Missouri Territory. In those years, the Plains and Northwest tribes knew and venerated their red-headed chief, the white man whose "tongue was straight," as their brother. Maggie added an interesting and lesser-known fact: William was the younger brother of George Rogers Clark, a valiant soldier of Revolutionary War fame who had been approached by President Jefferson after his victories in the war to explore the West but declined.

Her column would probably be cut, since she had included so much information, but William Clark was a remarkable man. She e-mailed it to Lily and found a message from Steve asking about the pictures she'd promised. She connected her digital camera to her laptop and sent them.

Still no visitors. Maggie glanced at her watch. Nine o'clock. Maybe she should wander downstairs and see if the girls were busy or if they'd gone home already without coming up to talk to her. She slipped on her shoes and reached for the knob just as someone rapped on the door.

Without hesitation, Maggie threw open the door, expecting Jenna and hoping the cook had come with her. Instead she stared up into the scowling face of a tall, dark-haired, dark-eyed stranger. Stunned, she opened her mouth to speak, but no sound came out.

He broke the silence with an accusatory tone. "I understand you're looking for Katie."

It took Maggie a minute to recover from her surprise at the startling statement. "Yes, I am," she stammered.

His eyes narrowed as he advanced one step closer to her. "Why?" he demanded.

For some reason, she hesitated to repeat her fabrication to this stranger who literally filled her doorway. "I didn't catch your name. I'm Maggie McKenzie."

"Flynn," he said, leaning against the door frame and folding his arms. "Why are you looking for Katie?" The scowl disappeared, but his gaze remained intensely focused on Maggie.

Two could play this game, she thought. She smiled and said, "Why do you want to know?"

"Do you always answer a question with a question?"

"Frequently, if I'm puzzled as to why the question is being asked when the answer is quite obvious." *Who is this man?* Maggie thought. *How did he find out I'm looking for Katie?*

Flynn straightened. "Why won't you give me an answer?"

Maggie tilted her head as she pondered his question. The man blocking her doorway no longer seemed threatening; he was good-looking in a rugged sort of way, appeared to have a sense of humor, and he sported a decent haircut.

"I'm trying to decide why I should," she said.

"Would you like to sit down and discuss this?" He looked over her shoulder into her room. "Maybe we could go downstairs, have a drink, and overcome this impasse."

"Better than standing in the doorway." Maggie touched her pocket to make sure she still had her room key. She thought about grabbing her purse, but it was across the room, and she wasn't comfortable with the idea of leaving her stance at the door to get it. She didn't feel in any danger from this intriguing stranger—and her instincts were usually pretty good—but a female traveling alone had to be careful.

He stepped aside while she locked the door, then motioned for her to precede him down the long, narrow, dimly lit hall.

"How did you find me?" Maggie asked, over her shoulder.

"You're the only redhead in the hotel."

"And that means?"

"I knocked on every door until I found the pretty redhead who likes to ask questions."

Maggie stopped at the top of the stairs and looked up into the dark eyes of the man standing very close behind her. "Why did you need to find me?"

"To ask you why you are looking for Katie, which I think puts us right back where we started."

Maggie laughed and turned to the stairs, but her rubber-soled shoes caught on the carpet and she found herself teetering on the edge of the top step, clutching frantically for the railing to prevent a headlong plunge down the steep staircase.

Flynn grabbed her flailing arm and whirled her back from the edge, right into his arms. Maggie clutched at the wool shirt that enveloped her and clung for the briefest of moments before she realized what she was doing. She tried to step back, out of the embrace of the good-looking stranger, but he didn't release her.

She looked up, trying not to show her alarm as she pushed on his chest to put some distance between them. What had she been thinking, leaving her room with this man whom she'd never laid eyes on before, a man she knew absolutely nothing about, and who wouldn't answer any of her questions?

"If I open my arms and you step back, you'll fly backward down the stairs." He paused, then asked with a mischievous smile, "Do you still want me to let you go?"

Maggie peeked around the encircling arms down the steep staircase, then looked up into those laughing dark eyes. "On second thought, you step back instead of me. Then when you do, you can safely release me so I can breathe again."

He pretended shock. "Am I holding you too tight?"

"I have a problem breathing easily when I'm in the arms of a stranger. I usually prefer to be introduced and get to know a man before I become this intimate with him."

"But we were introduced. I'm Flynn and you're Maggie."

"Flynn, let me go." It wasn't unpleasant where she was standing; in fact, Maggie sort of enjoyed the repartee with this intriguing man, but she could imagine her parents' reaction to the situation and realized it wasn't a wise thing to allow it to continue.

"As you wish." He opened his arms and released Maggie from the embrace, but he didn't budge an inch. They still stood very close together on the edge of the stairs. She didn't take her eyes from his while she placed both hands on his chest and pushed. He stayed firmly put, his smile filled with what she interpreted as great pleasure in teasing her.

Maggie groped for the railing, her eyes never leaving his. Was there a possibility he might give her a gentle shove that would send her flying head over heels down the steep staircase? His eyes revealed nothing but humor at the situation. When her hand touched the railing, she gingerly felt her way down the top step, then continued to walk backwards down the stairs as he advanced toward her with each step, never allowing the space between them to diminish, a tango minus music. A third of the way down, she whirled and descended the rest of the stairs to wait for him at the bottom.

Flynn silently took Maggie's arm and guided her into a small room on the other side of the stairs, opposite the dining area she'd been in earlier. They were alone in the room, but Maggie could hear voices and eating noises coming from across the foyer so she knew patrons were still being served.

"What would you like? Dinner? Dessert? Drink?" Flynn led her to a table in the far corner where they couldn't be seen from the other dining room and pulled a chair out for her to be seated.

"Will you be my waiter?" Maggie asked in surprise.

"I'll take your order." He stood waiting for her answer.

"Maybe just a cup of hot chocolate. I've already had dinner."

"How about some apple strudel to go with it? They serve the best apple strudel in the world in this establishment. Waldtraut, Wally to those of us who know and love her, brought the recipe with her from Germany in 1961. It's a house favorite for good reason."

Maggie laughed. "You twisted my arm. I'll have apple strudel with my hot chocolate."

Flynn disappeared around the corner to take her order to the kitchen, Maggie assumed. She laughed aloud, delighted at the unexpected turn of events. Flynn was a very attractive man, probably in his early thirties, maybe a little older, casually sophisticated, with a self-confident air Maggie liked. His teasing nature reminded her of Steve.

Then she quickly sobered, wondering what on earth she was doing. How did she let herself get into this questionable situation? From the very pleasant sensation of being held in the arms of this likeable stranger, to having a tête-à-tête in a dark corner of a hundred-twenty-year-old hotel, this was probably the very kind of thing her father had hoped she wouldn't encounter. And the kind of encounter Maggie had never envisioned, even with her creative imagination.

CHAPTER 11

Should she discontinue this little adventure and return to her room before Flynn reappeared? No. He'd knock on her door again, and they were better off down here where there were other people than in the dimly lit hallway upstairs, or even worse, in her room, if he turned out to be less of a gentleman than he seemed.

Flynn returned, bearing two cups of steaming hot liquid. He placed a mug of hot chocolate on the table in front of Maggie and coffee on the table opposite her. "Jenna will bring our strudel in a minute. She's still pretty busy." He eased down into the wooden chair and stirred the coffee while he looked Maggie over.

Maggie ignored his obvious assessment of her. "You know your way around here very well. How is that?"

"I live here," Flynn said, leaning back in his chair and stretching his long legs into the aisle between the tables. Maggie noticed for the first time his worn jeans and boots. The man dressed for comfort but still appeared neat and polished.

"You live here?" Maggie realized what he'd said. "In the hotel?"

"Well, a few months out of the year. I come when the tourists leave and spend the winter in quiet seclusion until . . ." Flynn let his voice fall away and lifted his cup to his lips.

"Until what?" The man certainly had an intriguing manner, Maggie thought. He kept a person off tilt and on edge with his unexpected behavior and provocative comments.

"Until I hear a beautiful redhead is asking interesting questions." He looked over the cup at Maggie as he blew on the still-steaming liquid, took a tiny sip and replaced the cup in the saucer, then leaned across the table and said quietly, "Then I have to come out of seclusion and ask why."

Maggie didn't break eye contact as she leaned forward and asked just as softly, "What do you do in your seclusion?"

Flynn slapped his hand on the table. Maggie jumped back in surprise. "You are the most aggravating, vexing female I've ever encountered in my life," Flynn said quietly, emphasizing each word. "Why can't you just answer a simple, straightforward question?"

"Probably for the very same reason that you won't answer any of my questions," Maggie countered.

"And that is?"

"I want to know how you found out I was asking for Katie. I want to know why you're interested enough to come knocking on my door in the middle of the night. After I'm satisfied with the answers to my questions, I'll gladly answer yours."

Flynn settled back in his chair and the smile returned to his eyes. He picked up his fork and pointed it at her. "Okay. Peace. I'll answer one question for you, then you answer one question for me, although I don't think it's entirely fair that you go first, since I actually asked the initial question."

Maggie jumped in before he could change his mind. "How did you find out I was asking about Katie?"

"Jenna told me when I came down for dinner."

That answer threw Maggie. "And why would Jenna mention that to you?"

"Because I asked Jenna what new and exciting things had happened in her day." Flynn sat up. "You've had two answers. Now it's my turn. Why are you looking for Katie?"

For the first time, Maggie felt guilt at repeating the fabricated story of their relationship. She concentrated on stirring her hot chocolate so she wouldn't have to look Flynn in the eye when she said, "She's my twin sister, and I haven't heard from her for awhile, so I thought I'd better see if something had happened."

When he didn't say anything, Maggie looked up and found him staring at her, no, more like staring *through* her. She filled the awkward void with another question. "And your second question is— or do I get another turn?"

Flynn narrowed his eyes and said slowly, "My second question is, how do I know you're telling the truth?"

Maggie swallowed hard. She hadn't expected to be challenged in her lie. "Guess you either believe what you see, or you don't. If you knew Katie, you know what she looked like. I should think the resemblance alone would be convincing. Did you know her?"

Flynn took a minute to answer, appearing to concentrate on the designs he began drawing on the tablecloth with the fork. "Yes." The one word reply came softly. He didn't look at Maggie when he said it.

She waited for more, but Flynn continued to stare at the designs he was creating. "And?" she prompted.

"And what?" He dropped the fork and looked at her, waving his hand as if dismissing the ridiculous word. "I answered your question." He leaned toward her. "The agreement was a question for a question. No one mentioned a lengthy explanation with the answer. Now it's my turn." Flynn reached for his cup, curled one finger through the handle as he watched Maggie, raised it to his lips, then set it back down in the saucer with such force the coffee splashed out. He let loose a barrage of questions. "If you're really twins, why didn't Katie ever mention a sister? Why did she stay with that bear of a father instead of coming to you?" He picked up the fork and waved it in her face, punctuating his sentences with it. "What kind of sister are you to let her suffer that nomadic existence with a man who considered her not as his daughter, but as his slave?"

The picture came so quickly and with such vivid, violent imagery it took Maggie's breath away: Katie crying herself to sleep every night because she was so miserable, so lonely, convinced she had no where else to go, no other family, no one who loved her.

Tears stung Maggie's eyes and rolled down her cheeks. She was there, in that cold, dark place, listening to the bulky man with the bushy hair and big ears snoring on the other side of the room, unable to sleep, unable to move to another room because there was only one, covering her head with a pillow to drown out the noise of the sleeping man and to muffle the sound of her own sobbing. Maggie experienced Katie's loneliness, her desperation, then resignation, and finally the dulling of all emotion. Katie felt dead inside. She had nothing to live for, nothing to look forward to but the same pitiful, miserable existence. She'd rather die than go on like this.

"No!" Maggie cried. "No, Katie. Don't do anything. I'm coming."

"Maggie. Where are you? Maggie, can you hear me?" Flynn reached across the table and patted her face, then grabbed her hand and rubbed it vigorously.

Maggie looked around, surprised to find herself fully dressed, sitting at a table with a strange man holding her hand. Then she remembered. This was *her* life. She was Mary Margaret McKenzie who belonged to a family who loved her, spoiled her, adored her. That was Alyssa Lawson. Correction. That was Katie . . . Katie who? The beautiful, vibrant, pampered Alyssa Lawson had ceased to exist and in her place, a sad, lonely girl filled with hopelessness barely endured her miserable life.

Maggie looked across the table into the puzzled, dark eyes of the man still holding her hand, waiting for an answer to his question. Maggie wasn't even sure of the question. What could she say? How could she explain this incredible, almost out-of-body experience she'd just endured? How could she get so . . . so *into* Katie's head? How could she feel those very emotions Katie felt? It was like she had entered Katie's head, her body, and had become Katie for those few seconds.

"Maggie, what's going on? What's happening to you right now? What are you thinking, feeling?" Flynn's voice was quiet, soothing but insistent, coaxing her out of that dark world and back into the present.

Suddenly Jenna appeared, bearing two heaping plates of apple strudel, its delicious aroma bringing Maggie fully back into the world of here and now.

"Sorry it took me so long, Doc," Jenna apologized. "We're just swamped back there tonight. Can I get you anything else?"

Flynn looked at Maggie, raising one eyebrow in a questioning glance. She shook her head. "No thanks, Jenna," he said. "We're fine. Just take care of your paying patrons." He winked and Jenna laughed. Apparently this was a joke between them.

As the waitress disappeared around the corner into the foyer, Maggie asked, "Are all your meals on the house, *Doc?*" emphasizing the name Jenna had called him.

Flynn took a bite of tantalizing-smelling strudel, rendering himself unable to speak. Maggie followed suit. It was too tempting to postpone, even to quell her curiosity about the enigmatic man opposite her.

"When I first started coming here, years ago, I teased that my meals were on the house, meaning just put them on my hotel bill, which I paid by the month."

"And the *Doc* part?" Maggie asked when he neglected to address that portion of her query.

Flynn ingested another forkful and reached for his wallet, extracting a business card which he tossed across the table to Maggie.

She glanced at it, read "Flynn Ford," followed by a string of degrees an alphabet long. "I believe this first one means you're a psychiatrist." Maggie looked again. "Or is it a psychologist? I never can remember the difference."

"Psychologist. Psychology is the science of the mind; it tries to explain why people act, think, and feel as they do. Psychiatry deals with the treatment of mental and emotional disorders."

"So you study why people do what they do, then send them to a psychiatrist to treat their disorders?" Maggie looked up to find those dark eyes laughing again.

"I guess you could say that."

"I could say it, but I'd rather know what you really do, not what I think you might do."

Flynn waved his fork at Maggie's plate. "Your strudel is getting cold. It's much better when it's warm."

She took a bite and closed her eyes to savor the delightful combination of cinnamon, apples, whipped cream, and flaky pastry. When she opened them, Flynn was staring at her, all humor absent from his expression.

"What happened a few minutes ago, Maggie? You blanked out on me. Totally. You were like a hollow shell sitting there with no one home, no one inside your body."

Maggie leaned her elbows on the table and covered her face with her hands. She'd promised Lily she would not tell a soul about her quest for Alyssa, but that last experience of getting so deeply into Alyssa's mind frightened her. Could Lily forgive her for reneging on her promise of secrecy? She'd already broken the promise once, but she knew her brother would never betray that confidence.

Suddenly Maggie wondered why this quest needed to be such a secret. Was Lily only trying to protect Lionel Lawson from the emotional trauma of knowing his daughter had a look-alike who worked for him, and who was now seeking his lost daughter? Why should that be such a confidential matter? Or was it simply because it was so painful for Lily and Lawson to remember and relive the tragic memories? Maggie shook her head. It was too puzzling, and far too overwhelming to consider at the moment.

Was Flynn trustworthy? Maybe as a professional, he was just the person to confide in, now that things seemed to have gotten out of hand with this mind thing. She looked across the table at the stranger she'd known for less than an hour, his expression filled with sympathy and some anticipation. *Guide me, please, Father, in how much I should tell here.*

"Talk to me, Maggie," he said quietly. "Tell me what happened."

"Let me think about it while I finish my strudel. You're right. It's too delicious when it's warm to ignore." That would give her time to rationally analyze the situation instead of emotionally plunging in as she usually did.

They ate in silence until only empty plates remained. Maggie washed down the last bite with an equally rich swallow of chocolate, which was no longer hot or even warm.

Flynn pushed his chair back, stretched out his legs again, folded his hands across his belt, and asked, "Have you decided how much you can safely tell me and what you shouldn't reveal? I assume that was the real reason for the delay."

Maggie smiled. "Do they train you to be a mind reader as well?"

Flynn shook his head. "No. If they'd done that, I wouldn't have to sit here and ply you with questions that never get answered. I do know you have a huge problem, and that something's bothering you, and you can't decide whether or not to share it. Tell me why you're afraid to share what's so unsettling to you."

That was an easy one for Maggie to reveal. "Because I'm on a quest about which I've promised I wouldn't tell a living soul."

"Ahh, I see. That makes sense. But something happened just now, and you're frightened or worried, and it would be a great relief to talk about it. Would it help if I promised," he held up three fingers in the Scout salute, "on my honor not to tell anyone?"

Maggie laughed and relaxed. "Probably."

"Tell me about you first. Tell me where you're from and what you do, and if you like to do it, and why. Tell me . . ." He paused, then went on, "tell me about yourself."

Maggie had the impression he was going to say, tell me what you're doing in South Dakota looking for Katie, but if he'd asked that, would she have given him the rest of the story? He was smart to get her talking, she realized, because once she started unfolding her story, he could wheedle the rest out of her one bit at a time. Did she want to tell all? She remembered the terror of her nightmares, how real they were, and how strange to know so much about someone she'd never met. The episode of a few minutes ago convinced her she needed to talk to someone, and probably this man was the best qualified of any she could have found, since he was in the business of figuring out why people act and think and feel like they do.

"You asked why I was looking for Katie. You were going to ask that again just now, so I'll cut to the chase and tell you so you won't have to be bored by my life story." Maggie recited the tale of her first day on her new job, the shock Lily tried to conceal when she saw her, the delight she felt at the unexpected rapport with Lily, then the offer of the dream assignment to travel and write on Lewis and Clark's expedition. Then she told him about her missing look-alike and how she'd found herself asking for information in the files to help her find Alyssa, but promising a distraught Lily she wouldn't tell anyone she was doing it.

"What I didn't expect was to find myself suddenly projecting into Alyssa's life after I read the newspaper clippings on her kidnapping, having dreams so real they were terrifying, and then realizing it was either dreams Alyssa had, or it was insight into what happened to her. How could I know how she felt? How could I know what this man looked like, how he got into her room, how she felt when he wrapped the blanket around her and she couldn't move? But I do."

"Maggie, twins have an incredible bond that no one has really been able to explain scientifically. We just all accept that it's there."

Impatiently she looked up into expressive dark eyes that were deep wells of compassion. "Flynn, weren't you listening? I'm not Alyssa's twin. We're not related at all. We don't share the same bloodlines or the same genes. I just look amazingly like her, so I used that story to get people to feel sorry for me, looking for my lost twin, and tell me things they probably wouldn't have told just anyone looking for the girl."

"Are you sure you're not related? Could you have born to the same parents and separated at birth?"

Did he realize how his words had struck at Maggie's heart when he said them? Did it show in her face?

"That happens more often than you'd like to believe," he offered, probably to soften the blow he'd just delivered.

She took a deep breath. "I had thought of that. I even asked my brother, but he says he remembers Mom being pregnant with me, and him holding me as a newborn. We have dated pictures in the family album that I've seen, so I know it's true. And you'd have to know my family to understand Mom and Dad would never ever give up a child for any reason. Every one of us was precious and prayed into the family circle."

Flynn frowned and pulled at his ear. "Okay, we'll set that theory aside for the time being. Tell me what happened a few minutes ago when you blanked out on me."

That was harder for Maggie to put into words because she could find no logical reason for why it happened; therefore, she hesitated to enunciate something she felt was so far-fetched. But it had seemed so real. "You accused me of being a terrible sister by allowing her to remain with her bear of a father. Suddenly, I was in her mind; I could feel her loneliness, her resignation, her helplessness, but even more, I could see the bulky man with the bushy hair and big ears and hear him snoring on the other side of the room. I felt the pillow pressing on my head trying to drown him out and muffle my sobbing. I swear I was there, in her body, experiencing exactly what she was feeling and thinking." Maggie stopped. "And now I'm worried because anyone who feels that way, so totally hopeless, is contemplating ending her miserable existence. Flynn, I've got to find her before she kills herself."

"Do you have any leads? Do you know where she is now?"

"I only have the letters people wrote to her father's newspaper when he ran her picture again nearly eighteen months ago. She was spotted here, Missouri, Arkansas, Texas, and Louisiana. One of the women from the gift shop at Mt. Rushmore wrote she thought the girl and her father were working in the restaurant. So I came here, but Doris Butler is no longer with us, having suffered a serious fall down some stone steps, and then either smothering herself accidentally, or being smothered by someone."

Flynn nodded. "I suspect Katie's father did it, from some of the things Katie told me about him."

Maggie nearly jumped out of her chair. "Then you did talk to her! You did know her!" Suddenly she looked puzzled and leaned toward Flynn, speaking in a quiet but very accusatory tone, "Why didn't *you* do something about getting her away from her father if you think he killed that woman?"

"Because the morning after Katie talked to me, they disappeared. I never did find out where they went from here."

"What did she say? How was she able to talk to you if her father watched her so carefully?"

Flynn stood and paced around the table. "They were about to finish the season at Crazy Horse, but Monika asked them to stop here for a couple of days while her cook took care of some family business. He was an excellent chef. There is a network among the kitchens in the area, exchanging info on who they can grab when they need help, and Katie and her dad had been coming back here summers for a few years, so his reputation as a chef created a demand for him. He never lacked for work. Katie worked in the kitchen, but when they got really busy out here, she also helped in the dining rooms. Everyone was keenly aware of how isolated he kept his daughter."

"But no one ever did anything about it?"

"There was never any evidence of abuse, except the isolation, and you can't take a child from a parent for that, especially when she's over eighteen. Everyone figured she was old enough to leave if she wanted to."

"Did she appear to you to be on drugs?" That was the only reason Maggie could imagine the girl would stay in those miserable circumstances.

Flynn stopped pacing and looked at Maggie.

"Do you think he could have kept her on something that dulled her senses and took away her initiative to leave?" Maggie explained. "Something that left her just out of it enough to not be able to think clearly? Otherwise, I can't imagine the girl the newspapers described as Alyssa Lawson, and the vibrancy I felt in her when we were riding, staying in that situation for five minutes more than she had to."

"You just said you rode with Alyssa. What did you mean?" Flynn sat down to face Maggie across the table. "I thought you said you didn't know her."

Maggie shook her head and waved her hand as if to clear the air. "I told you the dreams feel real. I dreamed we were riding our horses together in my pasture, and I could feel the exhilaration she felt because I was feeling the same thing."

"Your horses?" Flynn looked puzzled.

"We share a number of interests; in fact, it was really eerie. That was when I secretly wondered if we could be twins. You know, you read about twins being reunited in later years and discovering that they like the same TV programs, eat the same food, drive the same model car. That's sort of the way it was as I learned about Alyssa. Except that she was a nut for marine biology and I'm more into land animals. She wanted to save the whales and the dolphins. I took in all the hurt birds and animals in the county."

Flynn pushed the dishes out of his way and leaned forward. "What else did you have in common?"

Maggie reviewed all the similarities she'd discovered in their personalities and characters and activities they liked in their teens. Exceptions being that Alyssa's parents had been very well to do, where Maggie's were simply comfortable, and Alyssa's mother had died from cancer so she'd spent a lot of time with her live-in housekeeper. Maggie's family had never had a housekeeper, even for a single day, except, of course, her mother, Maggie thought with a smile. Rose McKenzie often teased that she was the live-in housekeeper, cook, and scullery maid, and no one would miss her as their mother, but boy, would they miss her if she left those other jobs!

Flynn sat silently tugging at his right earlobe.

"Well?" Maggie said, running out of things to say. Now she just wanted some answers.

"You certainly seem bound to the girl, for whatever reason. I don't want to disturb you, but since you seem like a pretty stable individual, I think you can handle this conjecture and what it might bring." He stared into Maggie's eyes, as if plumbing the depths of her soul to make sure his diagnosis was correct and she'd be able to handle it.

"Okay, let's hear it."

"I'm puzzled by the incredible connection you seem to have to this girl. It's unusual if you're not twins. These things happen in the psychic world occasionally, but they can frequently be cleared up with logical explanations. What would you think about a DNA workup on the two of you, if we can collect specimens from Alyssa's home, supposing her father still lives there?"

CHAPTER 12

"Flynn, you actually think we're twins!" Maggie couldn't believe it. Then she remembered she'd thought about having Alyssa's DNA checked—though it had been for a different reason entirely: to compare it to that of unidentified corpses in case one of them happened to be Alyssa.

"Wouldn't you like to know whether you actually have a twin sister?" Flynn asked. "Wouldn't you like to understand why you feel such a link to this girl? Why you can get into her head so easily? Why you can feel what she's feeling? What if it leads to answers?"

"Of course I do, but what I want to know right now is where she is and if she's okay. If she's still alive. After I find her, then I'll worry about checking DNA and connecting the dots. In the meantime, I think I'll call my folks and see what they have to say about it."

Flynn studied her face for a minute before asking, "Do you really think they'd tell you if you were a twin, and the other one was with another family—after keeping something like that a secret all these years?"

"Of course," Maggie assured him, believing, knowing, with certainty that they would not keep a secret like that from her. If Rose McKenzie acknowledged she was Maggie's birth mother, and that she had no twin, that would be the whole truth and the end of the matter.

Flynn let it go with a shrug. "You must have a very unusual family."

"Oh, I do," Maggie assured him.

They remained lost in their own thoughts for a minute, then Flynn broke the silence. "What's your plan now?"

"Exactly the same as before, just with more urgency. Go to each of the cities where the letters to Lawson originated to interview the people who sent them, if possible."

"You're traveling across country alone?" Flynn asked, raising his eyebrows.

"Of course. It's my job. I always travel alone."

"Maggie, you're a very young woman to be traveling thousands of miles without . . ." He paused.

"Without what? An escort? Without someone to take care of me? Flynn, I can't believe your thinking is so old-fashioned. I can change a tire, fill my car with gas, watch the gauges on my car to know when to change the oil, check myself in and out of hotels, and even make sure that I eat properly. I've taken self-defense courses, and I have guardian angels that watch over me, including a brother I check in with every night of the world on my cell phone and with whom I'm in touch by e-mail daily. I'm hardly alone and on my own."

Flynn held up both hands in mock defense against Maggie's tirade. "Sorry. Sounds like it might be a sore point with you asserting your independence, but forget I said anything, and tell me your plan of action."

Maggie brushed aside his words, accustomed to people wondering at and questioning her strong sense of independence. "Tomorrow I plan to check the Rapid City newspaper archives to see if I can find anything on the death of Doris Butler—if the coroner ruled it was accidental, or if not, were there any suspects?" Then Maggie had a sudden thought. "You don't happen to know anything about that, do you?"

"As a matter of fact, I do. What would you like to know?"

Maggie leaned anxiously toward Flynn. "Was her death accidental?"

"The coroner's findings were inconclusive. They did a lot of investigating, simply because of the pillow over her head, but I sometimes put a pillow over my head to drown out noises, so you can see that alone wouldn't be enough to conclude she was murdered. There was no sign of struggle. No bruises or marks of violence. No forced entry into her home."

"Wait a minute. Didn't you say Katie thought her father had murdered Doris?" Maggie put her fingers to her temples. "Did you say that or was it my imagination? Yes. You did say that but you didn't tell me what Katie said that led you to believe it. And you didn't tell me how she was able to talk to you if her father watched her so zealously."

"The restaurant was seriously short of help the nights they were here so Katie was brought out of the kitchen and pressed into service as a waitress, which also happened in other places. She was a likeable girl, personable, very quiet and sad, as you said, painfully introverted, but Jenna seemed to ignite a spark in her, and she actually talked to Jenna and the patrons. Jenna introduced us, apparently told her my field of expertise, and when I asked her how she liked traveling all over with her father, she starting talking."

"Just like that? She just opened up to you, a total stranger?" Maggie found that hard to believe, thinking of the Katie she had come to know through interviews with Kathleen O'Sullivan and Jimmy, until she remembered how she had just spilled her whole story to this stranger. She laughed. "Guess I just did the same thing."

"I think the pressure of not being able to talk to anyone about her feelings had her ready to explode, and when she found out what I do, the floodgates opened and it all came spilling out—that coupled with the opportunity—which apparently came very seldom."

"Flynn, I'm seeing two totally different people in Alyssa and Katie. According to all the newspaper accounts, and even Lily, Alyssa was a brilliant, vivacious young woman, vocal, outgoing, anything but a wallflower, totally *not* introverted. She apparently made independent decisions with wisdom and intelligence. My picture of Katie is just the opposite. She's a sad, silent, cowering child who will not make independent decisions, will not stand up for herself, will not resist this man's unholy hold on her, simply will not make a better life for herself. Can being snatched from your environment do that to you? Make such an incredible change in someone who already seemed to have their character formed?"

"Oh, yes." Flynn nodded vigorously. "There are a number of methods kidnappers routinely use to control their victims. They tell them they'll kill or cripple their family or loved ones if they try to escape. Or they use drugs, as you suggested, for mind control."

Maggie interrupted Flynn. "Jimmy said Katie's father told her he was all the family she had in the world and they had to stick together, but Alyssa was sixteen years old when she was taken. Definitely old enough to know she had a father who absolutely adored her, and apparently a housekeeper who was like a mother to her. Why would she buy into a story like that?"

"The mind is a complicated thing, Maggie. It's like a computer. If you feed it erroneous information often enough, it will begin to assimilate that information as true."

"So if he lied to her and told her that *he* was her father, not Lionel Lawson, and made her believe it, she would feel betrayed by Lawson, and form an attachment to her kidnapper in lieu of her relationship with her father, Lionel Lawson." Maggie grabbed her head. "Oh, this is so confusing. I don't even know the name of this man who claims to be her father, this man I am convinced snatched her right out of her sixteenth birthday party and ruined her life."

"Cleat Wiggins is the name he goes by," Flynn offered. "I don't know if that's an alias or his real name, but that's the name on his employment records and social security card."

"Cleat Wiggins." Maggie sounded the name out slowly and thought about it. "Has a villainous sound, don't you think?"

"Only to someone with an active imagination." Flynn smiled. "Or there is the Stockholm Syndrome. Personally, I tend to think that's what might have happened to Katie, or Alyssa."

"Hmm, I've heard of that, like in the Patty Hearst case. How do you psychologists explain the phenomenon, and where does the Stockholm bit come in?"

Flynn leaned back in his chair and began, "In 1973, four Swedes held in a bank vault for six days during a robbery became attached to their captors, apparently bonding with them as a means to endure the violence during their captivity. Over time, victims can become sympathetic to their captors, initially as a defensive mechanism, out of fear violence will be conducted against them. Any small act of kindness by the captor is magnified since the victim expects only bad things to happen. Rescue attempts can also be seen as a threat by the victim since they feel it's likely they'd be injured during the attempt to release them from bondage."

"That sounds totally unreal, but if it's true, how could that apply to Katie?"

"Look at it this way—the Stockholm Syndrome is an emotional attachment, a bond of interdependence between captive and captor that develops when someone threatens to take your life, deliberates, then doesn't kill you. The relief resulting from the removal of the threat of death generates intense feelings of gratitude and fear, which combine to make the captive reluctant to display negative feelings toward the captor. The victim's need to survive is stronger than his impulse to hate the person who has created his dilemma. The victim can start to see the captor as a 'good guy' or even a savior." Flynn paused and looked at Maggie. "Have you had enough explanation?"

"If there's more, go on, please. This is fascinating. Gruesome. Unbelievable, but fascinating."

"Okay. This condition, this syndrome, occurs in response to four conditions. First, a person threatens to kill another and is perceived as having the capability to do so. Second, the captive cannot escape, so her life depends on the threatening person. Third, the threatened person is isolated from outsiders so that the only other perspective available to her is that of the threatening person. Fourth, the threatening person is perceived as showing some degree of kindness to the one being threatened."

Maggie shivered at the thought. "All Cleat Wiggins had to do was threaten to kill Alyssa, hold her hostage and isolated long enough for that bond to be made, and she was held captive by her own psychological chains." She shook her head, not wanting to believe, but realizing that must have been what happened; that had to be why Katie hadn't tried to run from the kidnapper posing as her father. "You still haven't told me what Katie said that led you to believe she thought Cleat killed Doris Butler."

"That's what she said and how she said it. 'I'm so afraid my father killed Doris Butler.' I was sitting right here." He pointed at their table. "I prefer seclusion when I'm dining, and there were only a few people up front, the overflow from the other dining rooms. Katie would swing by my table every time she came out of the kitchen with someone's dinner or to take an order and whisper another portion of her story."

"She told you her life story?" Maggie couldn't believe her ears.

"Not exactly." Flynn stood and stretched. "At the time, the investigation of Doris Butler's death was in full swing and was, of course, the only topic of conversation. Katie was worried her dad might be involved because she'd seen them arguing on the steps at Rushmore just before Doris fell."

Maggie jumped up and faced Flynn. "Kathleen O'Sullivan said Doris kept telling everyone she'd been pushed down the stairs, and when no one believed her, she said she'd be the next headline in the news. She expected the person who pushed her to come back and finish the job, but apparently no one took her seriously."

Flynn nodded and leaned against the wall, nearly knocking a picture down. He straightened it, moved over, and continued. "That all came out in the investigation, but no one had any idea why anyone would want to push her down the stairs or eventually 'finish her off.' She wasn't involved in anything controversial, she was a very likeable woman, there was simply nothing in her life that pointed to anyone wanting to murder her or any reason for anyone to do it, and no one came forth with any kind of motivation for her death, imagined or real."

"Unless she'd seen the picture in the newspaper of the missing Alyssa Lawson and connected it to Katie. That was ample reason for Cleat Wiggins to silence her." Maggie paced back and forth between the tables. "Katie should have had a recollection of the kidnapping. She should have known they were looking for her. She should have known her father, Lawson, would be frantic."

"Not necessarily," Flynn said. "She may never have known that Doris saw the picture in the paper. She may never have known anyone was searching for her. Stockholm Syndrome aside, Cleat could have filled her with all sorts of lies. He could have told her no one cared that she was gone, no one was looking for her, they were glad to be rid of her, or that she was a drain on their time, energy, money. If he could convince her he was the only one in the world who cared about her and that he would take care of her for the rest of her life, and that she had been a burden to her former family, then that's what her mind would tell her. It's easier than you think when you've got a person in a traumatic situation."

Maggie stopped pacing and looked at Flynn. "Do you really believe that?"

Flynn nodded. "It happens all the time. If you tell a person something often enough, they begin to believe it, then it becomes an established part of their makeup. If you continually tell children they are stupid, or ugly, or bad, they'll eventually believe it and become the very thing they've been labeled. The power of suggestion is incredible. So I go with the syndrome explanation for why she hasn't tried to escape."

Maggie nodded. That had to be it. But the greater problem now was how to find Katie before she became so desperate to escape her loneliness and misery that she tried to kill herself. Maggie had no doubt suicide had crossed the girl's mind many times. The hopelessness she had sensed with Katie was simply too overwhelming, too overpowering to ignore.

"I guess I've answered your questions, and you've answered mine," Maggie said, suddenly exhausted. "Tell me why, Dr. Flynn Ford, I feel so completely drained. Emotionally and physically."

"Because you've just had a very traumatic experience. Come on. I'll walk you back to your room and make sure you don't fall down the stairs." Flynn looped Maggie's arm through his and headed for the foyer.

"You never did tell me what *you're* doing here. You said you stay here part of the year. Tell me you don't use the hotel as an office."

"No. I'm writing a book." Flynn hesitated before softly adding, "I gave up my practice a few years ago."

Maggie glanced up at the pain in his voice, but his expression was blank, bland, unreadable. "What's the subject of this book?" she asked.

Flynn looked away, avoiding Maggie's eyes. "It's a technical treatment of . . ." he paused, then finished quietly, "the effects of Stockholm Syndrome on the families of those who have been kidnapped and returned."

Maggie stopped short and stared at him. "This is a very personal paper you're writing, isn't it? Did you have someone . . . ?" She couldn't finish, the anguish in his face was so apparent. "I'm sorry, Flynn. It's none of my business. I'm sorry I brought it up."

They continued up the stairs, but neither of them spoke as they strolled silently down the dimly lit hall to Maggie's room. As Maggie reached in her pocket for her key, she looked up at Flynn. "Thank you for an intriguing evening, Doc. Thank you for the delicious strudel and hot chocolate, and thanks for the information on Doris Butler. I'm going to bypass the newspaper archives in the morning and hit the road at daybreak. I have your card. Would you like to know what I find, if anything?"

Flynn nodded. "You might give me your cell phone number and your e-mail address, just in case I come across anything here."

Maggie opened the door, grabbed her notebook, scribbled the numbers in it, and tore off the page for Flynn. She handed it to him, then held out her hand. "I'm glad I met you, Flynn Ford."

He responded with a slight smile and shook her extended hand. "And I'm glad I met you, Maggie McKenzie."

But Maggie didn't let go of his hand. As she held on, she looked up into his dark eyes and said softly, "If you ever need to unload your burden, I'm not a licensed psychologist, but I am a good listener and I have a very compassionate nature. You can call me anytime."

Then she lightened the serious moment with a laugh. "Especially if you find any clues to Katie's whereabouts."

Flynn nodded. "Will do. Take care, Maggie. And promise me you won't pick up any hitchhikers."

"I promise!" Maggie waved a hand at the man in the hall, shut and locked the door, then leaned against it, wondering what tragedy had caused Flynn to give up his practice and delve into the study of the Stockholm Syndrome, and how she could find out, short of asking the man outright.

As she brushed her teeth, Maggie made a decision. She e-mailed Steve and asked him to confront their mother and ask if there was any chance she had adopted Maggie instead of giving birth to her. She then clipped her fingernails, pulled out a few strands of her long auburn hair, put them in an envelope, licked the flap to stick it shut, and addressed it to her brother, Alan, who worked in a forensics lab on Long Island. She then e-mailed him, told him to watch for the envelope, and asked him to run her DNA and compare it to his, and get the results back to her as quickly as possible, stressing the importance of her request.

She ran the envelope downstairs and left it at the desk in the outgoing mailbox. That done, she shook out the wrinkles from the outfit she planned to wear tomorrow and repacked the clothes she'd just taken off, but she couldn't stop thinking of the pained expression on Flynn's handsome face. As she settled into bed, pulled the covers up around her ears, and tried to put Flynn from her mind, another face came to haunt her: Katie's pale, thin, tear-streaked face as she contemplated the quickest and easiest way to end her life.

CHAPTER 13

The place was dark, damp, musty smelling. Maggie's skin crawled as she peered through the broken window. How could anyone be expected to stay here? Mosquitoes by the hundreds poured through the torn screens. A gap between the casing and screen door offered an open invitation to all the rats in the neighborhood, and the alligator in the swamp a hundred feet away would probably have no trouble making himself right at home in the dirty little shack.

Maggie wanted to run, as fast and as far as possible from the miserable place. Why couldn't she? She seemed to be alone. There was no one to stop her from leaving. What held her here? As she tried to turn away, she heard a frantic knocking from somewhere within. She grabbed the handle and tugged on the flimsy front door but, strangely, it wouldn't budge. The knocking grew louder and more insistent, but Maggie couldn't get in to find out who was knocking.

"Miss McKenzie! Miss McKenzie! Are you in there? We came to talk to you."

Maggie's eyes flew open. The mosquito-infested swamp was gone. The broken-down shack and alligator had disappeared. Heart beating wildly, Maggie sat up in bed and tried to figure out where she was.

The knocking came again. "Miss McKenzie. It's Jenna. Are you there?"

Jenna. The Alpine Inn. The knocking was on *her* door. Maggie jumped out of bed and hit the light switch as she unlocked the door.

Jenna and the plump blonde from the kitchen stood in the dimly lit hall, hands raised to knock again. "You *are* here," Jenna sighed with what seemed to be relief. "Doc said he left you here an hour ago and I didn't think I'd seen you go out, but we couldn't get any answer and we were afraid something might have happened to you."

Maggie stepped back and motioned the girls into her room. "Something like what?" she asked as she shut the door behind them.

Jenna stopped, her face flushed. The blonde answered for her. "When Cleat Wiggins is involved, you never know what's going to happen. It wouldn't surprise me to have him show up here and . . ."

Jenna interrupted. "What Betty means is that we were all afraid of Cleat Wiggins, and we tried to avoid having anything to do with him, tried to keep out of his line of sight whenever possible so he wouldn't take notice of us. He had such an evil presence. You could just feel it when you were in the same room with him."

"How did you work in the same kitchen then?" Maggie asked, waving the two girls to sit on the bed and taking the antique chair.

"We worked the preparation stuff in the back room," Betty explained. "Jenna took the orders and brought them to the kitchen, and Katie and I prepared all the ingredients. You know, peeled and chopped the vegetables and made the breads and salads while Cleat did the main cooking and assembled the dishes. We tried to stay completely out of his way." Then she seemed to suddenly remember that this was also supposed to be Maggie's father. "Beggin' yer pardon, but you were sure the lucky one to stay with your mom. If I was a superstitious person, which I'm not," she quickly assured Maggie, "I'd think he had the evil eye and could put a spell on you. And rest assured, it wouldn't be a good one."

"Do you think that's what he did to Katie?" Maggie asked. "Put the evil eye on her so she wouldn't leave him?"

Jenna nodded. "Why else would she stick around that horrible man? If my dad ever treated me like that, I'd have been out of there in a heartbeat."

Maggie leaned anxiously toward them, hoping they had information she needed. "How did he treat her? What did he do?"

"He ordered her around like a slave. He never had a kind word to say to her, never a 'thank you' for anything she did. He just yelled at her to be faster." Betty angrily pounded her fists on her legs. "Katie, do this! Katie, do that. And do it now."

"He called her awful names," Jenna said softly, her eyes filling with tears. "I don't know why he wanted to have her around, except to wait on him. He really didn't seem to like her at all."

"How did she feel about him?" Maggie asked, reluctant to hear more of their heartbreaking story but not daring to miss a word.

The two girls looked at each other. Betty answered first, fists still tightly clenched. "She never said a word against him. She never defended him, but she never answered our questions when we asked why she stayed with him and took his abuse."

"Do you know where they went?" Maggie asked, hardly daring to hope they could tell her what she needed to know.

Both girls shook their heads. "Katie never knew where they were going, or when they were going to leave, and she never dared ask," Jenna said.

"I only know they always headed south for the winter where it was warmer. He didn't like the cold and didn't like to pay heating bills," Betty offered.

"Did they have a home somewhere?" Maggie asked. "Did they go back to the same place every year?"

They didn't know.

"How will you find her?" Jenna asked.

"I have letters from Missouri, Texas, Arkansas, and Louisiana. I'll talk to the people who wrote them and see if they can help me find Katie."

"Then what will you do?" Betty asked, leaning forward with narrowed eyes.

"I won't know until I find her," Maggie said, knowing that she truly would not. She had no plan. She hadn't thought that far ahead. She only knew she had to find Katie before she did something desperate—something permanent that couldn't be undone. "Can you tell me anything else?"

Betty and Jenna looked at each other, then at Maggie, shook their heads, and in a soft, sincere tone, Jenna said, "I hope you find Katie and can take her away from her miserable life."

As they stood, Betty grabbed Maggie's hand. "Please get her away from that monster. He doesn't deserve to have her with him. He's horrible. And she's so sad all the time."

Maggie took the girl's hands and squeezed them. "Thanks for coming. I appreciate you staying up after your shift to talk to me. I'll do all I can to find her and take her home."

Jenna opened the door. "Will you let us know if you find her?"

"I promise I will." Maggie grabbed her notebook and scribbled her telephone and e-mail address on the page and handed it to Jenna. "And if you think of anything else that you didn't tell me, e-mail me at this address or call my cell phone at this number anytime, day or night."

The girls promised and hurried down the long, quiet, empty corridor. Maggie leaned against the door frame and watched them round the corner and disappear. She remained there, thinking of what she'd heard, picturing the man with the bushy hair and big ears verbally abusing the girl who wouldn't speak out against him or leave him. Was there more than verbal abuse? Did he beat her? Or worse?

If he'd already killed one woman, would he hesitate to kill again? With provocation—or without? Or was Doris Butler his only victim?

A small noise echoed through the profound silence, startling Maggie from her reverie. She moved quietly into the hall and peered into the gloom. What was it? The clicking of a lock? Halfway down the hall, a light suddenly glowed from underneath the door. Had someone listened at her door, then slipped back into their darkened room when the girls left, waited for them to leave the hallway, then shut the door all the way and turned on the light?

Who occupied that room? Didn't Monika say the two other rooms on this hallway were rented to an artist and a writer? Was the writer Flynn Ford? Had he listened to the girls' report? Or was it the resident ghost? Maggie almost wished she could believe it was. She wanted Flynn to stay the good guy and not go sneaking around listening at keyholes.

Once again Maggie locked her door, turned out the light, and crawled into bed, but she didn't sleep, nor did she dream. She lay awake a long time mulling over in her mind all the girls had told her about Cleat Wiggins and his treatment of Katie, and Katie's reactions. Maggie began wondering what she would do if and when she found Katie. The scenarios played over in her mind long into the night until she finally drifted into an exhausted, troubled sleep.

Maggie did not jump out of bed fresh and excited to begin her new day when the alarm went off at six o'clock in the morning. She'd loved to have rolled over and snuggled back in her blankets for a couple more hours of restful sleep, and might have, if her cell phone hadn't jolted her upright in bed.

She grabbed the offending instrument from the night table, looked at the number displayed and groaned. "Good morning, Steve," she said, trying to sound awake and alert. "You're up early this morning."

"I'm helping Dad today, and you know what an early bird he is. Thought before we left I'd better get back to you with Mom's reaction to your question, which she termed 'very strange indeed.'"

Wide awake now, Maggie was all ears. "What was her reaction, and what did she say?'"

"First she just laughed. Then when she understood it was a serious question, she was really puzzled that you would ask such a thing. I tried to explain as generally as possible, without going into real specifics, why you were asking. She informed me that, yes, she was your birth mother and that she would never forget the circumstances of your arrival because she almost lost you. And no, you weren't a twin. There was only one of you, which sometimes makes her very happy."

Maggie laughed. "You made up the last part. I've heard the story before. They had to go to California to see Dad's sister who was ill, and Mom unexpectedly went into labor. I was born in a little hospital somewhere along the beautiful California coast in a tiny hospital that had only one nurse, and they had to get the doctor from another town over the mountain to deliver me. That's not news. Did she say anything else?"

"Only that she loved you and to tell you to please finish this assignment and hurry home, in time for Christmas, if possible." Steve paused. "Is it possible or are you going to follow this all the way to the end?"

"Whatever the end is, I'm certainly going to follow it there. I'm leaving in a few minutes for St. Joseph. I should make it by nightfall and hopefully interview the letter writer from there tonight. Then, unless I find out something that changes my plan, I'll drive to

Arkansas tomorrow, Texas the next day, and on to Louisiana. Steve, I'm finding out some troubling things about the man with the bushy hair and big ears. His name is Cleat Wiggins, and everyone says he's a beast to be around. They're all quite afraid of him." Maggie was about to tell Steve he was also suspected of killing a woman who had written one of the letters but thought better of it.

"Keep in touch, Magpie. Gotta run."

"Oh, wait, Steve. I have one more favor to ask of you. Will you clip your fingernails and pull out some of that wild hair and send it to Alan? Also, don't say anything to the folks, but will you get some hair from Mom's brush and some from Dad's and send that? If you have time to do it today, it would be wonderful. Please next-day-air it to Alan. I've already sent some of mine and asked him for a comparison to his."

The silence on the other end lasted so long Maggie finally said, "Steve, are you still there?"

"What's happened, Maggie? Why isn't Mom's word enough?"

"Because I keep getting into Alyssa's mind, and last night I even felt like I actually slipped right into her skin. The connection between us is too strong to ignore. I could feel what she felt, and she's one deeply troubled girl." Maggie paused before adding one last comment, and even as she said it, she wasn't sure she should have. "I think she's contemplating suicide."

"Maggie, I don't like the sound of this. Please leave it alone and just come home."

"I can't, Steve. I may be the only lifeline she has. I've got to find her, and very soon, or I may be too late. Give Mom and Dad my love. And don't forget to send hair samples to Alan so he can compare our DNA. Thanks loads. I'll reimburse you for the postage when I get home. Love you, big brother." Maggie quickly disconnected and took a deep breath.

She felt a twinge of guilt asking Alan to use his time and energy—and his lab facilities—doing DNA profiles on her family. He'd be wasting all that effort, but at least it would resolve all those questions in that area, she thought as she slipped into her clothes. Then they could concentrate on another solution to the connection with Katie. In a scant fifteen minutes, Maggie had checked her e-mail for messages from Lily, checked out of the Alpine Inn and loaded her over-sized bag containing her computer and overnight case into her little blue convertible.

She'd looked around the dining rooms but hadn't seen Flynn Ford. Maybe he was a late sleeper. Maggie would have liked to say good-bye. She'd thoroughly enjoyed the time she'd spent with him, and as she scraped the ice and snow from her windshield in the predawn darkness, she laughed at herself. *Let some tall, dark, handsome man pay attention to you and you fall all over yourself to see him again. He's too old for you, Maggie girl. Besides,* she thought as she pulled away from the parking lot, shivering in her frigid car, *he wasn't interested in you, just in what you knew about Katie. And he has some tragic secret that will probably keep him from ever forming any lasting relationships.*

Maggie turned the heat on high and sped down the dark highway not yet illuminated by the approaching dawn. She turned on the tape recorder and dictated her thoughts and reactions to the two girls' comments the previous night, and Flynn's conversation with her, then tried to glean some additional clues from it all.

Was Cleat Wiggins a killer? Or was he such a mean, abusive man that people, including Katie, thought he must be capable of killing? What would she do if she ever confronted him? Would he see her as a threat and be a danger to her? If she did find Katie, she would most certainly meet Cleat Wiggins. Then what would she do?

CHAPTER 14

Maggie hit Interstate 90 at Rapid City as the sun peeked over the horizon, slowly lighting the frozen, undulating hills of South Dakota. She'd forgotten breakfast. Forgotten to check her gas gauge. Forgotten everything but this unwieldy puzzle that seemed, on the outside, to have nothing to do with her but which, in fact, she felt had *everything* to do with her.

Surely her mother could not be wrong about giving birth to her. And just as surely, there had only been one child born at that time to her mother. Then why did she feel this eery, strong connection to Alyssa Lawson, who during the last seven years had morphed into Katie Wiggins? Maggie simply could find no satisfactory explanation.

As she flew east down the nearly deserted highway, her gas gauge beeped and the low fuel light began flashing on the dashboard. That brought her crashing back to reality. There was very little along this seemingly barren part of the country, not even many houses. She didn't know how long it had been since she left Rapid City and got on the interstate and had no idea where she was now. As she watched for signs along the roadside, one Wall Drug advertisement after another appeared.

A profound sense of relief flooded through her when she read "Wall Drug—five miles." Her comments to Flynn echoed through her mind. "I can fill my car with gas . . ." Yes, she could. She just needed to remember to do it.

Maggie pulled off the interstate and filled her nearly empty gas tank at the first service station she saw in the tiny town of Wall, South Dakota, then, out of curiosity, followed the signs to "World

Famous Wall Drug, Home of Free Ice Water." Definitely not anything she needed this frosty morning with an icy wind blowing across the hills and right through her coat.

Wall Drug was a huge emporium, complete with traveler's chapel, western-clothing shops, jewelry store, museum, art gallery, carved post of Butch Cassidy and the Sundance Kid, Silver Dollar Bar, soda fountain and café, to name a few, but best of all, a donut factory. Maggie bought half a dozen assorted donuts and a cup of hot chocolate and headed back to her car, leaving the rest of the place, including the dinosaurs in the "back lot," to be explored another time.

Back on the highway, Maggie nibbled freshly made donuts and sipped sweet, warm Dutch chocolate as she mentally reorganized her priorities for the day. Better start another column for Lily while there was a long stretch of straight highway ahead and few distractions. Then she could "ponder and pontificate," as her dad said, on Katie and her captor.

Lewis and Clark had not traveled through western South Dakota but had entered what now constituted the southeastern point of the state near Sioux City, Iowa, then followed the Missouri River up through the central part of the state and on into North Dakota. But Maggie knew the journals by area, and without having to stop and search through her books, she knew that when she crossed the Missouri River at Chamberlain she could drive up to the bluff overlooking the area and see much the same view Captains Lewis and Clark saw two hundred years before.

In September of 1804, the expedition suffered several chilly days of persistent drizzle and rain. When they arrived in the Chamberlain area near Oacoma, they camped in what Clark described as a beautiful plain surrounded by groves of trees. They were exhausted and in desperate need of a break, having spent many days in the water dragging the keelboat through shallows and over sandbars, so they stopped to dry out soggy clothing and rearrange the cargo.

Here Lewis wrote the first descriptions of white-tailed jackrabbit, the black-billed magpie, mule deer, and coyote. They thought the coyote was a fox, then called it a small wolf. Clark shot what he called a "fleet, mysterious wild goat," actually a pronghorn. Amazed at its agility, acute sense of smell, and speed, Clark described them as

helped Maggie locate the address from her letter. They tried to look up the telephone number, but there was none listed for Nora Simons. The woman recommended the local Ramada Inn, just down the street, and suggested Maggie might drive by the home address *after* she had checked into her hotel—exactly what Maggie planned to do.

She scooped up the tourist information the woman pressed on her so she could "know what to enjoy on her stay in St. Jo." Unfortunately, Maggie wasn't staying long enough to enjoy much of anything. She checked into the Ramada Inn, took the key, raced back to her car, and followed the woman's hand-drawn map from Frederick Boulevard to a modest residential section of town with towering trees and friendly feeling streets.

The house was small and built of red brick, like most of its neighbors. Bell-shaped solar lights lit a small garden along the curved sidewalk, revealing Snow White's seven dwarfs cavorting among the snow-covered plants—or what Maggie could see of them for the skiff of snow that lightly covered everything.

She rang the bell and waited. No answer. Maggie rang again. There was a light in what she assumed might be the kitchen area of the house, and she could hear noises within, but still no one came to the door. Finally, Maggie rapped loudly on the metal screen door. A scuffle behind the door informed her she had finally been heard.

"I want to answer it!" a little girl's voice squealed.

"No, it's my turn," a boy shouted. They were apparently fighting over who would open the door, but no one did. The doorknob rattled and the scuffling continued.

Finally the dim porch light flipped on and the door opened, but the two children had been replaced by a young woman in jeans and a sweat shirt with a baby on her hip. She peered cautiously out the door. "Yes?"

"I'm Maggie McKenzie. I have a letter from Nora Simons. Is she here?"

"Nora was my mother. She passed away more than a year ago. Where did you get the letter?"

"She wrote it about sixteen months ago. Could I come in, please, and talk with you for a minute? I'm sure you don't want to flood your house with this icy outside air."

The young woman hesitated, looked Maggie over, then unlocked the screen door and moved into the room so Maggie could enter. Maggie shut the door behind her and shivered involuntarily. "It's very cold tonight," she said.

"Please sit down." The woman motioned to an overstuffed chair near the door for Maggie. As she took the sofa, the little boy and girl who appeared to be twins about four years old, reappeared and snuggled shyly next to their mother, giggling when Maggie winked at them.

"I'm sorry to intrude on your family tonight, but I'm looking for my twin sister who disappeared seven years ago. Your mother responded to an ad in the newspaper asking if anyone had seen the girl, but when the detectives came to follow up, they couldn't find anyone at home. So I'm trying now."

"My mother was killed in a hit-and-run accident more than a year ago. She lived alone and left the house to me. We were out of state but came back here when my husband was transferred last year. That's probably why they couldn't find anyone home."

"Do you remember your mother saying anything about seeing a missing girl?" Maggie pressed. *There must be some information here,* she reasoned, *and if there was, she was determined to find it.*

The young mother tucked her blonde hair behind her ear, then shook her head thoughtfully. "No, I don't. But Mom worked at the St. Jo Steakhouse in the Frontier Casino, so she could have seen many different people."

Maggie's heart triple-timed. "Was she a cook there?" she asked breathlessly.

"No, she was the hostess who seated everyone, though she knew all the cooks and waitresses. They always had a great Christmas party, and they were sort of like family, which was nice. I lived so far away, she didn't have anyone else here but the neighbors and her work family."

"Do you mind talking about the accident?"

The woman looked at the floor and shook her head.

"Will you tell me what happened?" Maggie asked softly. "You said it was hit and run?"

"Yes. She had just finished her shift and was heading home at midnight, when someone in a big old van ran a red light and smashed into her, knocking her car into the light pole, which crumpled right into her windshield. He didn't even stop. Just fled the scene. They never found him. Witnesses behind her had a pretty good description of the van, but they figured it wasn't from around here. No one got the license plate number." She paused. "Mom was killed instantly so at least she didn't have to suffer."

"I'm so sorry, but I am glad she didn't have to suffer. Death seems always hardest on those who are left behind," Maggie offered.

"Well, we're good Christians, so we believe in heaven and that's where Gramma is now, isn't it, kids? With Jesus in heaven." She put her arms around her little brood and they nodded, appropriately serious expressions on their faces.

"It is so very comforting to know that this life isn't the end. In fact, is really only the beginning of wonderful things for those who have moved on." Maggie stood. "Thank you so much for talking to me."

"I'm sorry I couldn't be any more help. I hope you find your sister."

As they moved to the door, Maggie turned. "Do you remember what kind of van hit your mother's car?"

"They said it was an old battered Volkswagen van—the kind popular with flower children and hippies in the '60s."

"Thank you. Bye, kids." Maggie smiled, and waved, and exited quickly into the dark, frigid night. It felt like snow. Maggie felt like crying. An old, battered Volkswagen van. Cleat Wiggins drove an old VW van. Cleat Wiggins was a cook, and the steakhouse at the casino probably was a place where he could have found work easily. Everyone knew each other. Nora Simons would have known the cooks and waitresses—which could have included Cleat and Katie.

Maggie shivered as she drove away from the modest red brick home. Was it Cleat who broadsided Nora's car, not just accidentally running a red light, but targeting, by design, the woman who had recognized the girl he kidnapped? Had Nora said something to him—or to Katie?

Then as Maggie drove back to the Ramada Inn, she had a new thought. If Nora—or anyone—mentioned having seen her face in the newspaper, would Katie tell Cleat? Would she mention it innocently, and then Cleat would take action? Or did she tell him purposely? And if so, did she know the consequences of her report? Something else to ponder.

Maggie lugged her ever-present tote containing her laptop computer and her overnighter to her room, turned the heat on high, and jumped in the shower to fight the chill that had seeped into her very bones. As the hot water poured over her, she wondered if the cold wind had really chilled her so thoroughly, or if her chill stemmed from thinking about the possibility that Cleat Wiggins may have killed two women, both of them having suspected he had kidnapped Alyssa Lawson.

Finally warm, Maggie suddenly remembered she hadn't sent her column to Lily. Fortunately, her foresight in getting a column ahead stood her in good stead, since it was now eight o'clock and beyond her deadline. She wrapped her hair in a towel, donned warm flannel pajamas, and curled up in bed with her laptop to transcribe the article she had constructed earlier on her tape recorder.

This time she went to the journals and provided interesting facts about the journey, describing the large peace medals given to the Indian leaders to establish friendly relations and the weapons Lewis and Clark took with them. They had fifteen modified 1792 and 1795 militia rifles obtained from the Harpers Ferry Arsenal and an air gun Lewis bought in Philadelphia that fired forty rounds before reloading. She listed the Lewis and Clark sites in the St. Joseph area, of which there were many.

Maggie reread the column before she e-mailed it to Lily and decided she must do better on the next one. She hadn't even sent photos, as she'd promised, so she immediately put her camera clip in and sent the pictures she'd taken atop the bluff overlooking the Missouri River at Chamberlain. She realized her heart was no longer in this project that had been her consuming passion for nearly two years. Now she was consumed by another obsession—the absolute need to locate Alyssa Lawson. Or Katie Wiggins.

Leaning back on her pillow, Maggie wondered which girl she would encounter, if she did find anyone. Had Alyssa's personality and character been completely eclipsed by Katie Wiggins? One more thing to occupy thoughts that never seemed to stray far from the girl who had become almost a part of her. That thought disturbed her. Maggie didn't want that close an attachment to the girl.

While online, Maggie whipped off a quick e-mail to Steve to tell him where she was and give him a report on the second letter. She left out the part about the possible connection between the hit-and-run accident and the fact that Cleat Wiggins drove a similar kind of vehicle. No sense worrying him; she was worried enough for the two of them.

She disconnected and was ready to put her computer away when she felt an urge to go one step further in her investigation, something that had entered her mind several times but that she'd never acted on. Should she do it or not? Every time she decided not to and started to slide the laptop to the floor, another argument why she should occurred to her. Finally she gave up arguing with herself and, forgetting her promise to Lily, reconnected and sent an e-mail requesting hair specimens or anything of Alyssa's from her room at home so a DNA workup could be done. As she disconnected again, she had an impression of Katie applauding her impulsive act.

Then, in a burst of energy and conscience, Maggie began work on her next column. As she opened the *Journals of Lewis and Clark,* she knew there would be little sleep in the coming hours. She couldn't turn off her thoughts, couldn't get Katie out of her mind, and she wasn't excited about the prospect of Cleat Wiggins invading her dreams. In fact, Maggie realized, she didn't want to go to sleep, tired as she might be, because she was afraid she might get even further into Katie's mind—and not be able to come back. Was that possible? A frightening premise.

She worked until long after midnight, completing several columns and forwarding them all to Lily, then turned on the TV and caught the Weather Channel forecast. Snow tonight, clearing tomorrow. Still reluctant to turn her subconscious over to sleep, Maggie read the brochures thrust upon her at the visitors' center. St. Joseph looked like a fascinating city. Not only had Lewis and Clark stopped here on their way up the Missouri River, Jesse James was killed here, and the Pony Express began its historic run in St. Joseph.

It was the home of countless interesting museums and historical sites, including the Shakespeare Chateau Bed and Breakfast which housed the largest collection of stained glass in a private home. The picture of the Queen Anne mansion intrigued Maggie with its turrets and description of extravagant contents. St. Jo was a great place for a travel article and a greater place for fascinating interviews with its citizens. But not this trip.

Maggie pulled her computer back on her lap and logged on to a site where she could plan the next day's travel. Normally she'd have chosen scenic byways rather than interstates, but she had two overriding reasons not to: first, interstates were more likely to be clear of snow; second, she had an intense desire to find Katie before she did something rash. As Maggie turned off her computer and slid it to the floor, she pondered that. What effect would it have on her, on Maggie, if Katie did commit suicide? The bond that connected them had never seemed so binding, so constricting, so smothering as it did with that thought.

Maggie turned off the light, said her prayers, and almost as an afterthought asked to be blessed with no nightmares. No time travel, no mind travel, just deep, therapeutic sleep. The clock read 1:30 A.M. when she finally snuggled under the covers. Maggie looked at it again at 2:00 A.M. She fought sleep, singing over and over in her head, "I Am a Child of God" to keep from thinking about Katie. Then she started other hymns, trying to remember all the verses to her favorites. When she finally slipped into a deep sleep, what came to her was so different from what she might have expected, even Maggie's imagination could have not conjured it.

CHAPTER 15

Maggie stood in an exquisite garden surrounded by huge, ancient oak trees dripping with Spanish moss. Bright, colorful birds dipped and whirled, darting among exotic flowers and filling the air with delightful song. White egrets stood on one leg in glassy shallow ponds that mirrored them perfectly, occasionally dipping their long, pointed beaks languidly into the water. Blue heron stretched majestically from half-submerged logs.

It was a soothing scene, thoroughly tranquil and serene. Maggie strolled under a large, red Oriental gate with beams curving gently toward the blue sky, and wandered a serpentine gravel path to a stone bridge that arched gracefully over still, green water. There the path divided. She couldn't see around the bend ahead of her, and the path across the bridge lay hidden from sight by a thick grove of trees covered with moss and ivy.

Maggie stopped at the foot of the bridge, knowing somehow that the way she chose would not just be important, it would be absolutely crucial—but she didn't know why. The sure and certain knowledge that she must choose the correct path filled her with fear, but she couldn't see where either of the two paths led, and there wasn't time to explore. She had one chance and only one, and she felt an urgency to decide that minute with no additional clue, no other information to guide her in one of the most important decisions she would make in her life. She stood, paralyzed by indecision, realizing all the while she must act quickly.

Her quandary resolved itself with the annoying ring of her alarm. Maggie dragged it off the night table, punched the Off button, and stuffed it under her pillow, then nestled back under the covers to think about the dream she'd just experienced. As she lay remembering the emotions it invoked, she felt an impression, as specific as any prompting she'd ever received, that it was important she remember every detail.

She jumped out of bed, turned the heat up in the room, snatched her laptop, and snuggled back in bed to record everything she could remember about the scene, the feelings she had, and the dilemma she felt. Even acknowledging that the quandary she felt and her elevated emotions were probably exaggerated by the dream world, she still sensed importance to its content.

When she was satisfied she'd covered everything, she said her prayers, pleading for whatever divine assistance she would need during the day, including safety as she traveled, attentive guardian angels, and that she would meet the contacts she'd need to be successful in her quest. Then she dressed quickly, checked out of her room, gassed her car, and headed for Pine Bluff, Arkansas, the origin of the third letter. The one thing she didn't do was check her e-mail before she left.

Morning had dawned crystal clear and icy cold. A thick frosting of new snow decorated everything, making the pine boughs along the road droop low with their load, turning the world into a glorious, winter wonderland. Snow plows had already cleared the roads, leaving a two-foot-high mound outlining the highway, and early morning traffic took care of what the snow plows might have left on the road.

But Maggie didn't see the beauty of the morning. She never noticed the miles and miles of power lines piled with two inches of snow along the wires or every bare branch of the leafless trees covered in a froth of white. She was single-mindedly consumed with her journey and the road in front of her, and nothing else came within her view. She beat the busy business traffic through Kansas City, and as she drove south on U.S. 71, Maggie felt better than she had for two or three days.

What made the difference? Did she feel good because she was pursuing her goal without delay or detour? She still felt the driving need to find Katie before anything happened. She still felt the strange, close connection she had before, but today it didn't seem as fatal. *Fatal.* That was a strange thing to think. Why had her mind picked that particular word? Had she subconsciously been thinking along those lines because of Cleat Wiggins?

Once again, Maggie forgot to stop for breakfast, forgot everything but her mission and its consequences—for both her and Katie. And, yes, Wiggins too, for there would be consequences for him, she was sure, if and when she found Katie. She would see that he paid for the grief he had caused Alyssa's father and their housekeeper and Lily. And Alyssa herself, though it was hard to combine Alyssa and Cleat in the same thought. It was easier to think of Cleat and Katie.

As she approached the Missouri-Arkansas border, Maggie suddenly realized she hadn't eaten yet. She was famished. The leftover donuts in the bag from Wall Drug sat untouched on the passenger seat, and she hadn't even noticed them. Maggie recognized with a start that this obsession to find Katie had caused some drastic changes in her life. Changes she didn't think she liked. She rarely went without breakfast, knowing she was sharper, thought faster, and was overall more perceptive when she ate.

And Maggie never went anywhere without noticing everything along the way, and usually making many detours to see things that interested her. That hadn't happened yet; in fact, she had bypassed places she truly wanted to visit, despite the fact she had time to stop. She suddenly realized this compulsion to find the girl that was so inextricably linked to her had changed so many things about her life.

She nibbled a stale donut as she thought about the changes that were taking place in her, that *had* taken place since she read the clippings about Alyssa's kidnapping. She'd never kept anything from her parents, had always been totally open with everything happening in her life and always sought their input. Now she was even enlisting Steve's help to go behind their backs to have their DNA profiled.

She'd always been totally aware of where she was, what she was doing, and what was happening around her, but yesterday she could have run out of gas on that long stretch of deserted highway in the freezing cold because she wasn't paying attention. That had never happened to her before. As she thought of that, she glanced at her gas gauge and realized she'd need to stop for gas soon.

Maggie didn't like these disturbing feelings she was experiencing for the first time in her life. She felt she was losing control. All she wanted to do was find Katie, and that obsession seemed to be changing the way she did things, the way she thought about things, even her eating habits.

As that thought crossed her mind, Maggie slammed on her brakes. Was the missing girl taking over her mind, or did she even know Maggie existed? Was this more than a one-way thing? Did Katie feel her emotions as keenly as she had felt Katie's? Or could Katie get into *her* mind as *she* had been delving into the girl's psyche? Was that why she couldn't think of anything but finding this stranger to whom she felt such a strong connection?

Time for a break, for some real food, fresh air, and some gas. Maggie started watching road signs and discovered she was twenty-five miles from Fayetteville, Arkansas. She must have crossed the border and not even noticed.

Time to take back her life, or at least to get it back on track. She refused to think that someone could control her way of thinking, her actions, her subconscious. She turned on a CD and started singing along with the music, but before Maggie had driven much farther, she became absorbed once more with Katie without realizing what had happened.

Would she be able to locate the young woman who had written the third letter? What if she was no longer there? What would be her next plan of action?

Maggie stopped for gas and food in Fayetteville and checked the map again. She had two choices: Interstate 40 through Little Rock to Pine Bluff, or a scenic route through the beautiful mountain and lakes region into Hot Springs. She struggled with the decision because she wanted it to be hers, not something she was being psyched into doing by Katie. She'd left the snow somewhere behind her—she couldn't say where or when—so she couldn't use that as an excuse for taking the interstate anymore.

She'd also left the Lewis and Clark Trail at Kansas City, so now her only quest was that of finding Katie. If she pursued that with the fervor and passion she had thus far demonstrated, would that be turning herself and her own will over to the girl who seemed to be crying out for her help by pulling Maggie into her thoughts?

Maggie had never had so much trouble making decisions in her life, which led her to believe that she was in serious trouble. In the end, she decided to stick with the interstate to arrive in Pine Bluff sooner rather than later and complete her quest as quickly as possible. It may not have been her own idea, but how was she to know?

The two hundred thirty-five miles from Fayetteville to Pine Bluff dissipated like so much smoke into the clear December sky, and before she knew it Maggie had arrived at her destination. She followed the signs to the local visitors' center but it was closed, and the service station on the corner had no city maps. The man who worked there told her in broken English about another visitors' center in a downtown hotel. Maggie followed his directions, parked in the parking lot the hotel shared with the public library, and asked for a map or help to find the address on the envelope from the young woman. She'd already checked the phone book for a listing for Liza Farrell, but there was none. It couldn't be that easy.

The woman at the desk gave her a map and pointed out the general area where the address should be located, but the map wasn't detailed, and she could only give Maggie very sketchy directions. She apologized that they were all out of the good maps.

Maggie walked away from the desk wondering what she would do. There was always the fire department. They had city maps and knew every address in town. She just had to find a fire station—or a service station that did carry city maps.

For some reason, Maggie didn't have much of hope of speaking to Liza Farrell. She'd been fortunate thus far to glean some little bit of information, some little piece of the puzzle from each person she'd interviewed. A nagging suspicion told her that was about to stop. And maybe she didn't want to find out any more about the letter writers. They all seemed to have come to a disastrous end. If this one was also dead—this young woman who should have had a long life ahead of her—Maggie wasn't sure she wanted to get any closer to Cleat Wiggins.

But at the thought, her heart began pounding and Katie's face, Katie's pale, sad, hopeless face, filled her mind. That frightened Maggie. Was this a two-way link, and Katie could tell what she was thinking? Stunned, Maggie dropped into a seat facing a large picture window and covered her face with her hands so no one could see the horrified expression she knew she wore.

A pleasant-looking woman approached Maggie and touched her arm, bringing her out of her shocked state. "I overheard your request for an address. I know that area. What street did you want?"

Maggie took a deep breath, steadied her emotions, and showed the woman the envelope.

The woman sat down next to her. "That's the address of a soldier who was stationed at the Pine Bluff Arsenal, but he's been transferred overseas. My husband was his commander. That young woman, Liza Farrell, lived with him for several months and they planned to marry."

"Do you know what happened?" Maggie asked, hardly believing she'd stumbled across a source of information immediately after feeling she'd find nothing this time. "Did she move with him when he left or did she stay here?"

"I honestly don't know. I do know she worked at the Snow White Grill. It's a greasy-spoon restaurant where Bill Clinton used to hang out."

Bells went off in Maggie's head when she heard another restaurant was involved. That meant cooks, waitresses, and possibly clues. "Thank you so much. I'll check with them to see if they know anything."

"Is it important that you locate this girl?" The kind voice was filled with concern.

"Actually, it's very important." Maggie repeated the lie she'd told so often she almost believed it herself, and it flowed quickly and easily from her lips. "I'm searching for the young woman who sent a letter saying she'd seen my sister here in Pine Bluff."

The woman extended her hand. "I'm Cathy. If you run into a dead end, call me and we'll try to trace her through her soldier. My husband can find out where he is now." She wrote her phone number on the top of the map Maggie held. "Do you know where the Snow White Grill is?"

Maggie shook her head. "I don't know where anything is. I almost couldn't find this place. Imagine a visitors' center being located in the lobby of a hotel next to the public library."

"The restaurant isn't far, and I'm finished with my business here. I can take you there if you want."

Maggie stared in disbelief at Cathy's offer. "Thanks, but I'm sure it would be a terrible inconvenience for you."

"Heavens no. Nothing in this town is very far from anything else. In fact, how about if I give you a little tour so you'll know where to find things?"

"Are you sure?" Maggie couldn't believe her ears.

"An in-depth tour of the whole Pine Bluff area would only take thirty minutes, so a quick spin through downtown will take a fraction of that. Why don't you leave your car in the parking lot and come with me? I'll show you around and bring you back here in less than fifteen minutes."

That seemed like an offer Maggie couldn't refuse. Cathy turned out to be a pleasant, talkative person with a quick laugh, and she was a walking encyclopedia about the city. She pointed out the historic murals painted on buildings in the downtown area, each of which told a potion of the city's story. Maggie especially like the unique architecture of the Hood Building on Main Street and the Jefferson County Courthouse, but the tangled mass of girders that was supposed to pass for artwork on one of the corners in the old part of town left her cold.

Cathy felt the same way. "What a waste of money that was." She stopped so Maggie could snap a picture of the historical signs on Barraque Street and the old homes that were still there. Barraque Street was named after a Frenchman who had served under Napoleon.

"Imagine that," Maggie said. "Makes you wonder how he ever ended up clear out here in the Midwest."

"I'm glad the official visitors' center was closed today, or I wouldn't have met you," Cathy said, pointing to the little white house that was one of the original in town. "Are you ready to check out the Snow White Grill, or do you want to ride out and see our thriving shipping lanes on the Arkansas River?"

Maggie laughed at the tone in Cathy's voice. "Thanks, but I think I'll pass on the shipping. I need to see what I can find out about Miss Farrell. If you want to just drive by the grill and show me where it is, then you can drop me off at my car and I won't detain you any longer."

Cathy laughed. "You aren't detaining me. I've enjoyed showing off our town. Makes me feel useful."

She slowed as they drove by the Snow White Grill, a plain white frame building with two big windows in front. "They said Bill Clinton loved to eat here. Of course, I understand he's big on chitlins and greasy-spoon type food, so this must have been right up his alley. Now I'll take you to your car, but before you come back here you'll want to walk over to the library and see the International Friendship Garden that commemorates Pine Bluff's relationship with her sister city in Japan. Beautiful spot for meditating—or just thinking through your problems."

Maggie looked quickly at Cathy. "Do I look like I need to think through my problems?"

"Let's just say you didn't seem to be a carefree, happy-go-lucky young woman when I first saw you." Cathy pulled up next to Maggie's car and stopped. "If you need anything, please call me. My husband is not only the base commander, but he's the bishop as well. If you need to talk to someone about what's bothering you . . ."

Maggie stared at Cathy. "How did you know I was a member of the Church?"

Cathy laughed. "I was really just guessing, but there is that something special about you that sort of sets you apart from people who spend too much time 'in the world.' Remember, if you need anything at all, please call that number. In fact, if you're going to be in town tonight, would you like to come to dinner?"

Maggie considered the generous offer only briefly. "Thanks, but I've got time to get further on down the road if what I discover at Snow White Grill doesn't keep me here for any reason. And I do need to get on with my search as quickly as possible."

Cathy reached for Maggie's hand and squeezed it. "Keep that number and use it any time of day or night, for any reason, if you have any kind of need."

Maggie's eyes filled with tears and she didn't know how to say a proper thank-you. "Cathy, you may not know it, but I think you were sent to me today. I needed you very much when you found me."

Cathy nodded. "I think you're absolutely right. I'd just finished getting some things from the library and was on my way back to my car when I suddenly decided I should check out the brochures in the visitors' center before I went home. When I saw you, I knew you were the reason I was there. Now, before you get in your car, why don't you run across the lawn to the library and wander through the garden and ask for whatever other help you need Him to send."

Maggie leaned over and kissed Cathy's cheek. "Thanks so much. I'll do just that." She left the car, then turned and waved as Cathy drove away. On the way across the lawn, Maggie started to pray, pouring out her fears, knowing they were being heard even if she wasn't on her knees.

She wandered through the beautiful garden but was so intent on her pleadings to heaven that she didn't stop to read the inscriptions on the plaque, or really even note the lovely white marble Japanese sculptures that adorned the garden. Hers was a soul tormented by the knowledge that she was not just connected to the stranger she'd never met, but by the knowledge that this person could tap into her thoughts at any time.

Maggie sat down on a cold marble bench, ignoring the late afternoon breeze that ruffled her hair and caused her to draw her coat more tightly around her. She bowed her head and begged for help to understand what was happening to her. She didn't like knowing what someone else thought and felt. She hated experiencing the frightening emotions that terrified Katie. Suddenly Maggie realized she no longer thought of the missing girl as Alyssa, and that as Katie took prominence in her mind, replacing the way Alyssa communicated with her, the tenor of the thought projections had also changed.

Suddenly Maggie felt two heavy hands on her shoulders. Terror shot through her from head to toe like an electric shock.

CHAPTER 16

Cleat Wiggins! That was Maggie's only thought and it filled her with a deep-seated fright such as she had never before experienced in her life. She jumped to her feet and whirled around, ready to run for her life.

"Whoa, Maggie. I'm sorry I scared you. I didn't mean to." Flynn Ford raised both hands and backed away a few steps. "I'm harmless, really I am."

Maggie couldn't believe her eyes. "Flynn!" She was so surprised to see him, she couldn't think of a single thing to say.

"Is that all I get? Not a 'Glad to see you, Flynn' or 'How did you find me, Flynn?' or . . .'"

Maggie finally found her voice and interrupted him. "What on earth are you doing here? How did you find me?" Then she knew. "You've been following me." She shook her head in unbelief. "Why?"

Flynn reached for her hand. "Come on. Let's get out of the cold so we can talk."

Maggie stared at him with narrowed eyes. "Why are you following me, Flynn? I want an answer before I take one step from this spot."

"Because I was worried about you."

"That's not the reason."

"Maggie, listen to me. This is a very dangerous world for a young woman alone, but it's even more dangerous when you're dealing with something you're not prepared to handle." He paused. "And I'm not talking about flat tires or muggers or hitchhikers or someone breaking into your room."

Maggie looked away. She knew very well what he was talking about. Yesterday she might not have known so quickly or so clearly, but today she knew exactly what he meant, and she had to admit she was very glad to see him, though she didn't tell him that.

"Come on. You're trembling. Let's go someplace where it's warm. I'll feed you some real food and we can talk."

"What do you mean, 'real food'? I had lunch today."

"You skipped breakfast, stopped briefly for fast food at lunchtime, and haven't even had a drink of water since. That's not only unhealthy, it weakens you."

Maggie stopped and looked up into dark eyes filled with concern. "Have you been behind me since Hill City?"

Flynn nodded and looped her arm through his, pulling her along toward the parking lot. "Every single mile. Do you have some kind of favorite food, or did you plan on dinner at the Snow White Grill?"

Maggie laughed a little uneasily. "I have no secrets at all, do I?"

"Not since I met you, at least, not while I've observed you. I haven't monitored phone calls or e-mail, which I assume you are still doing regularly with your brother."

"They usually call that stalking, Flynn. Is that part of your job? Is that how psychologists work?"

"Only when they have a deep concern for a patient who's in over her head and doesn't realize what she's dealing with."

Maggie didn't know what to say. It was true, she didn't know what she was dealing with, but she wasn't sure she liked the idea that Flynn had followed and observed everything she'd been doing without her knowledge. That was definitely disconcerting.

They reached the parking lot, and Flynn motioned to their cars parked opposite each other. "Your car or mine?" Then he thought better of his offer. "We'll take mine. I'm not as distracted at the moment as you are."

"What do you mean, distracted?" But Maggie didn't object when he opened the door and motioned for her to get into his car.

Flynn got behind the wheel before he answered. "I would have been very worried about you; in fact, I probably would have stopped you if I hadn't remembered you said guardian angels watched over you. I don't believe in angels—or at least I didn't until yesterday.

Maggie, if that's how you usually drive, you're a menace. When you slammed on your brakes in the middle of the highway, you almost caused a five-car pileup. But you've convinced me you do have guardian angels because that's the only way you could have avoided accidents. It was like you were in a trance."

Maggie thought Flynn was joking, but there was no humor in his voice, no trace of it in his eyes. She opened her mouth to rebut his accusations, but as she remembered about her obsessed condition the last two days, she was afraid the accusations were true.

Flynn noted her silence as acknowledgment that he was right and continued. "I'm assuming the woman you were riding with gave you information you needed about the letter that originated here."

Maggie nodded. "The girl worked at Snow White Grill and was living with a soldier from the arsenal, but he's moved. Cathy's husband is the base commander and can find out for me where he is now. She knew nothing about the girl except that they had been together. She had no idea if they still were."

Flynn started the car and turned up the heat. "Do you want to go to the grill now?"

Maggie thought for a minute. She did want to see if anyone knew anything about Liza Farrell, but it was such a relief to feel like she was in control of herself again, she didn't know if she was ready to delve back into that—Maggie wasn't even sure what to call it—that other world. However, she did have Flynn at her side now, and that was more comforting than she would have ever thought possible.

"Let's go to the grill," she decided. "When that's out of the way, we can go somewhere for dinner. I'm not sure I'd enjoy eating there. Cathy called it a greasy spoon. I don't do greasy spoons unless I can help it."

Flynn drove out of the parking lot, and they traveled the few blocks to the Snow White Grill in comfortable silence. When they parked at the restaurant, Flynn turned off the car and faced Maggie. "Do you want me to go in with you, or do you want to do this alone?"

Maggie pulled the letter from her purse while she considered his offer. "I'll do it, unless you feel you need to come in."

Flynn's eyes narrowed as he watched Maggie. She laughed at his expression. "You don't have to be so concerned. I'm only going to ask a few questions."

"Then I'll wait for you in the car."

"I'll only be a few minutes." Maggie left the warmth of the car and ran quickly inside. The wind off the water had begun to whip the trees, and as the sun descended across the Arkansas River, the temperature seemed to drop at the same rate.

Only one waitress and her patron were in view. When the waitress finished delivering the man's meal, Maggie approached and asked if she had a minute to talk. With a wave of her hand at the empty room the waitress acknowledged that she did.

"Liza Farrell used to work here. Did you know her?"

The waitress, whose name tag identified her as Rena Belle, led Maggie to an empty table near the kitchen. "That name is sort of familiar, but I can't find a face to go with it. Why do you ask?"

"I'm looking for my missing twin sister. When a notice appeared in the newspaper asking if anyone had seen her, Liza answered, reporting she'd seen her working in Pine Bluff. I was told Liza had been a waitress here."

Rena Belle took her glasses from her pocket and stared at Maggie through them. "Are you fraternal or identical twins?"

"Identical," Maggie blurted, having never thought of that particular aspect of the invented situation until this minute.

"You do kind of look like a girl that worked here—maybe last year. Let me think. Yeah, she helped her old man in the kitchen usually. Quiet mouse. Not very friendly. Her old man was even worse. He had a nasty temper. You stayed out of his way when he got that look in his eye."

Maggie's heart thumped wildly. "Do you know where she is? Are they still in town?"

Rena Belle thought for a minute. "No, I don't think they're still around. There aren't that many places in the area. I know 'em all and everyone who works 'em. I think they must have moved on after . . ." She stopped. Her eyes got a faraway look like she was thinking back a long time.

"After what?" Maggie asked softly, almost afraid to interrupt the girl's thoughts.

"Hmm. I'm not sure. I seem to recall something going on but I can't quite remember what it was." She came back to the present, glanced at Maggie, and shrugged her shoulders. "Sorry. Can't quite put my finger on it. Maybe 'twasn't anything after all. Cooks come and go. They can be a transient lot. Don't need much of a reason to move on except the change of season—or less."

The lone patron cleared his throat to catch Rena Belle's attention. "Sorry, love. Gotta get back to work. Anything else I can do for you?"

"Thanks, Rena Belle. Nothing I can think of right now." Maggie stood and turned to go when Katie's face filled her mind. Maggie stopped, waited for the image to fade, but it stayed, getting stronger, until all Maggie could think of was Katie's desperation and the need to keep talking to Rena Belle. Weak-kneed, she slid back into her chair and waited, hoping the impulse would disappear, hoping she could put from her mind these unwanted, uninvited thoughts.

Rena Belle came back holding a tray full of dishes. "Did you think of something else?"

"Do you remember who the girl's friends were? Surely she spoke to someone occasionally."

"Hmm. Now that you mention it, she did spend a little time with another waitress here. I never got to know her—we were on opposite shifts. I don't remember the girl's name, just that she had a soldier boyfriend that used to drop her off at work and pick her up after." Rena Belle nearly dropped the tray of dishes. "That's what I was trying to remember. That girl just up and left without telling anyone she was quitting. Left us real shorthanded for a few days until we found a replacement for her. Funny thing. She didn't even collect her last paycheck. Everybody said her soldier boy got transferred and she eloped with him, but she could have had the decency to at least give a little notice. Worked a real hardship on all of us."

Maggie had a hard time controlling her excitement. "Rena Belle, do you remember about when this was? Can you give me any dates?"

Rena Belle squeezed her eyes shut and stood motionless, apparently concentrating on the question. "Let's see. I graduated from high school, got this job the next month, had only been working a few weeks and getting used to it when that all happened. Glad she didn't leave any sooner. I couldn't have handled both shifts like I had to do when she left. And we had a lot of extra people in here about that time. Lots of sheriff's deputies and even FBI men. Kind of cute, they were."

"What were they doing here?" Maggie was almost afraid to hear the answer.

"Seems somebody fishing down by the river caught a finger on his hook. Human finger. They never did find the body that went with it, even though they dragged the river for days. All those folks came in to investigate. Never did come to anything, so they left. They figured somebody must have lost a finger somehow working near the river. 'Scuse me. I gotta get rid of these dishes. This tray is heavy."

"And the cook and the girl left about the same time?"

Rena Belle nodded as she backed through the swinging doors into the kitchen and disappeared.

"Thanks, Rena Belle," Maggie called after her. She wanted to get up and run from here, but her legs wouldn't hold her. Her knees shook and she began trembling, terrified at the thoughts that came with Rena Belle's revelation. She put her head down on the table for a minute, and suddenly felt two strong arms around her.

"Come on, Maggie girl. Let's get out of here." Flynn lifted her to her feet and put an arm around her to steady her while they walked to the car. When she'd settled in, he started the car but leaned toward her instead of driving away. "What happened in there? What did you find out?"

Maggie leaned her head back and took a deep breath. "I was going to leave because all I discovered was that they were probably here, but Katie came to me and my head was filled with questions to ask and I had to just keep looking for answers."

"Questions that led you where?" Flynn asked quietly.

"Somewhere I didn't want to go. Somewhere I didn't even know to go." Maggie turned to Flynn. "I think Liza Farrell didn't leave town with her boyfriend. I think Cleat Wiggins killed her, cut her up and threw her in the river. And Katie knew that. She led me right down that avenue until the answers came." Maggie recounted her conversation with Rena Belle.

"And the police never put two and two together?" Flynn asked incredulously.

"Apparently they assumed somebody accidentally lost a finger and everyone at the grill thought Liza had eloped with her boyfriend when he was transferred. No connection. Everyone here was furious that she left without notice and left them shorthanded. The authorities may have done a cursory check, but if the story they got about the missing girl was that she had left town with her boyfriend, maybe they didn't check further with the military, especially if he wasn't easy to get in touch with during his transfer overseas."

Flynn put the car in gear and drove out of the parking lot. "First, we have to get some nourishment into you. You have to be strong enough to fight Katie. How long has she been invading your thoughts?"

That caught Maggie by surprise. "What do you mean, invading my thoughts?"

"When did the search for this girl become an obsession? When did you begin noting changes in your normal way of doing things? For example, when did you give up something you wanted to do—had planned on doing—to pursue this 'quest' as you call it?"

Maggie stared at him with her mouth as wide open as her eyes.

Flynn glanced at her and nodded. "I thought so. When you had that experience at the table the other night, when you were just sitting there like an empty shell, knowing what was in Katie's mind so intensely, so intimately, I was afraid things might go beyond just the thought connection. You were a wide-open conduit for her stream of conscious to flow into."

"But I don't understand. I didn't even know about this girl until I read the articles. How could she connect with me when she couldn't have known about me?"

"Tell me what you did when you first heard about her?"

Maggie thought for a minute. What *had* she done when Lily first told her about her look-alike? She gasped as she remembered. "I can't believe it. Flynn, right from the first moment I knew about her, I did strange things quite out of the blue. I asked for the newspaper clippings and was surprised to hear myself requesting them. I hadn't even thought about it, had no idea those words were going to come out of my mouth. I didn't even know where the idea came from."

"Do you now?"

"I guess so, but I have no idea how it could be possible." Then Maggie sat up straight. "Wait a minute. I once had a teacher say the Holy Ghost doesn't usually give you words you don't know. Unless you study the scriptures, He can't bring them forth to your remembrance when you need them. Maybe that's what happened here. When the time was right, when I learned about Alyssa, He could prompt me to ask for the files and He could help Alyssa project what she needed me to know."

"Are you comfortable with that theory?"

"Yes, of course. If it comes from the Holy Ghost, it has to be good."

"And do you feel that same way now that it seems to be Katie who's coming to you instead of Alyssa?" Flynn asked.

Maggie thought for a minute. There was a great difference in what she felt, knowing it was Alyssa's thoughts and emotions she was experiencing, and what she now felt when Alyssa's alter ego, Katie, came to her. Had the Spirit shown her what questions to ask, prompted by Katie's projected desperation? "Oh, Flynn, I don't know. I can't think straight right now."

"It's okay, Maggie. Don't even try. Just relax. You've been through quite enough the last couple of days, I'm sure. Why did you stay up so late last night? The light was on in your room until well past midnight."

Maggie stared at Flynn. "How did you know that?"

"I told you, I was worried about you. Were you afraid to fall asleep, afraid that you'd link with Katie again?"

"Yes."

"What else happened that you haven't told me?" Flynn pulled up to a big, new hotel and stopped.

"What are we doing here?" Maggie had paid no attention to where they were driving and was surprised at Flynn's choice of destination.

"First of all, we're going to this very nice restaurant to have dinner. Then I think we'll book a room." He shot a quick glance at Maggie. "Or rooms. We'll spend the night here as it's too late to get on the road again. In case you haven't noticed, it's dark, and as far as I know, you don't have a place to stay tonight."

"No, I don't, but I promise you, it won't be with you."

Flynn smiled. "As you wish, Maggie girl. But you *are* going to eat."

CHAPTER 17

They entered through double doors into a lobby filled with gleaming walnut paneling and shiny brass fixtures. Christmas greenery with red velvet bows draped the front of the registration desk and a huge, elegantly decorated Christmas tree filled one corner of the lobby near the door to the Hearthside Dining Room. Flynn steered Maggie through the open doors into a warm, cozy café with blazing fireplace on one wall and little red candles glowing on each table.

The ambiance was subdued and intimate with tiny white Christmas lights adorning ficus trees that separated each section of the dining room. The hostess led them to a table in a dimly lit corner, but Flynn requested one next to the fire.

"Thanks for putting us near the fire," Maggie told Flynn as he held her chair for her. "I don't know if I'll ever be warm again."

Flynn slid into the chair across from Maggie and fixed her with a serious stare. "Did you know that lack of food will cause your temperature to drop several degrees? Food is the fuel your body needs, and it acts just like fuel, warming you up."

"No, I didn't know that. Is that a prelude to a lecture on eating properly?" Maggie tilted her head and looked at him, trying to decide if he was teasing her. "For some strange reason, I thought I was cold was because it's December and temperatures have hovered between twenty and thirty degrees all week. Not to mention the icy wind that keeps blowing everywhere I go."

"Minor additions to the problem," Flynn said with a wave of his hand, but seeing the humor in his eyes, Maggie relaxed. She liked this man. She felt comfortable with him. At the moment she felt safer than she had for a couple of days.

A cocktail waitress materialized at Maggie's elbow, dressed in a low-cut, green velvet dress with a short skirt and fishnet stockings that covered long, slender legs. She bent slightly toward Flynn and asked in a sultry voice, "What can I get for you tonight?" Maggie almost laughed at the blatant come-on, but Flynn never once raised his eyes to the girl.

He studied the wine list, ordered some foreign-sounding wine, and asked Maggie what she'd like to drink.

"I think I'll stick to ice water with lemon, unless you have decaffeinated herbal tea." Maggie reached for her wine glass and turned it upside down on the green linen tablecloth.

"Your waitress can bring you that. I'll be right back with your wine, sir." She turned to go, but Flynn, without raising his voice or eyes called her back. "The lady will have her tea now. Please bring it when you bring my wine."

The waitress spun on her heel and vanished toward a leather-padded swinging door.

"Thank you, kind sir," Maggie said, almost laughing. "I could have waited, you know."

Flynn dropped the wine list on the table and looked at Maggie. "Of course you could have, but it was a perfect way to tell her to buzz off. I wasn't interested in whatever she was offering." The way he stared at Maggie warmed her throughout, and she slipped her coat off, letting it hang on the back of her chair.

"I'm glad you're finally warm. I didn't even have to feed you. Just sit you next to a blazing fire and make you blush."

"You don't miss a thing, do you, Flynn?"

"Not much gets by me," he admitted, watching Maggie closely. Then he surprised her by abruptly changing the subject. "But now I want to know what you discovered in your interview with the woman in St. Joseph."

Maggie steepled her fingers and leaned forward on her elbows. "The woman who wrote the letter worked at a restaurant in a casino where all the employees worked closely together. She was killed in a hit-and-run accident by someone in an old battered Volkswagen van.

That's the kind of vehicle Cleat Wiggins drives. I'm sure he's the one who hit her."

"So the woman in South Dakota was pushed down some stairs then smothered. The woman in St. Jo was killed in a hit-and-run. The girl in Pine Bluff disappeared about the time they found a finger in the river. You think Cleat Wiggins committed three murders?"

"I think three may be a minimum. I'm not sure I want to go to Texarkana." As soon as she said it, Maggie was sorry. This time she recognized what was happening—she felt Katie coming, felt a rush of blood to her head, and then Katie's sad face appeared in her mind. Maggie felt Katie telling her, "You can't give up. Please find me. Save me."

Flynn gripped Maggie's hand and rubbed it vigorously. "Katie?" he asked when the glazed expression left her face.

Maggie looked across the table into dark, worried eyes. She wanted to lose herself in those eyes, wanted to flee from the uninvited visitor in her mind. She nodded, not moving her hand from Flynn's.

"What did she want?" he asked.

"She doesn't want me to give up. She wants me to find her, to save her."

"When you said you didn't want to go to Texarkana, is that what triggered it?"

Maggie nodded. "I think so. But this time I felt her coming."

"But you couldn't block her?"

"I'm not sure I tried. It happened so fast, she was just suddenly there."

"Have you had visitations like this you haven't told me about?"

Maggie reluctantly slid her hand from under Flynn's, leaned back in her seat and nodded. "I saw a dirty shack in a swamp and felt it was tied to Katie. This morning I dreamed something entirely different." Maggie stopped. "Maybe it wasn't so different after all." She recounted the dream in the beautiful garden and the vital decision she needed to make at the foot of the bridge.

"What do you think it meant?"

Their server arrived at that instant with menus. They went through a very ordinary conversation, debating what to have for dinner. Flynn waved the waiter back, gave their order, and they resumed their very *extra*ordinary conversation.

"I could be wrong, but I think Katie was giving me a hint, a glimpse of where I might find her. Then again, she could have been telling me that I have to hurry."

The girl in fishnet stockings appeared with Flynn's wine and Maggie's herbal tea. "Thank you," Flynn said, again without raising his eyes to look at the girl or her long legs. She didn't wait around to pour, Maggie noted with glee.

"Now, then," Flynn began again as he poured a deep burgundy wine into his glass. "Why do you think she sent you both of those dreams, or visions if you will, instead of just connecting to you with thoughts?" He reached for Maggie's glass but Maggie stopped him with her hand on his.

"Thanks, Flynn, but I don't drink wine."

"Normally you may not drink wine, but your doctor is prescribing it tonight."

Flynn didn't let go of the glass, so Maggie left her hand on Flynn's. "But you're not my doctor."

"What do you think this little exercise we've been going through is, if not a patient/doctor session?" he asked with a twinkle in his eye. He couldn't have dowsed the warmth in the air any faster with a bucket of ice water.

That comment ripped through Maggie's bosom like a dull sword slicing her heart in two jagged pieces. Of course it was a patient/doctor session. What on earth did she think it was? She quickly removed her hand from Flynn's and busied herself reading the Celestial Seasonings label on the Gingerbread Spice tea bag, then removed it from her cup and added a pouch of sweetener.

"I'm sorry, Maggie. That sounded pretty cold, didn't it? What I meant to say . . ."

Maggie leaned across the table and touched Flynn's lips with her fingertips. "Don't say anything more." She met his gaze and smiled, trying to sound sincere. "I'm glad you said what you did. It prevents any entanglements that might have been forming. You do have a wonderful bedside manner, Dr. Ford."

Flynn pressed her hand to his lips and kissed her fingers. Maggie slipped them through his hand and back to her teacup. "You asked why I thought those two instances came in dream form instead of

Katie thrusting herself and her thoughts at me as she has today. I'm not sure. Maybe it was easier to give me visual pictures than putting words into my mind. When I write, I try to form visual pictures in people's minds with my words."

Flynn sipped his wine. "What are you going to do now?"

"As soon as we finish dinner, I'm going to prevail upon you to return me to my car, then I will check into a hotel, e-mail Steve informing him that I am still in one piece, see if my employer answered a query asking if she could collect something from Alyssa's home so we could do a DNA profile on her, make sure I've e-mailed her the columns I wrote last night when I was afraid to go to sleep, and then I'm going to go to sleep."

"And tomorrow?"

Maggie paused. "I don't think the area around Texarkana has the kind of swamp I saw in both dreams. The last letter came from New Iberia, Louisiana. That sounds like a more likely spot to find what I saw."

"So you'll bypass Texarkana and go right to Louisiana?" Flynn watched the wine swirl in his goblet as he moved the glass in lazy circles.

"I think so." Maggie smiled. "Unless Katie has other plans for me."

Flynn leaned forward and said quietly, "Don't laugh about it, Maggie. This isn't anything to play with."

Maggie looked at him in surprise.

"Katie's connection to you is stronger than any I've seen before. I don't know whether you aren't trying hard enough to block her thought projections or whether she's so . . ." He stopped to find the right word.

"Desperate?" Maggie supplied.

Flynn nodded slowly. "Desperate is a good description of the state she's probably in right now. And the more desperate she becomes, the stronger she'll come to you." He stopped, though Maggie sensed he was going to say something else.

"And?" she prompted.

Flynn hesitated.

"How can I guard against what might happen if I don't know about it?" Maggie argued. "You're the doctor. You'd better tell me everything I need to know about this phenomenon. I'm a total novice. I have no idea what I'm dealing with."

"Neither do I, Maggie. Science is just beginning to recognize and study how extreme the connections can be regarding twins and telepathy. It apparently is a phenomenon common to that unique world."

Maggie shook her head. "It's not common in my world."

Flynn put his glass down and leaned forward. "Tell me about your world, Maggie. You're an unusual young woman. I'd like to know what kind of world you inhabit." His tone, soft and sincere, enticed Maggie to open up and let him glimpse her world.

"As I told you, I come from a very loving, close-knit family. Do you know anything about Mormons?"

Flynn nodded. "Something."

"Then you'll understand why I don't drink wine and why I said I wouldn't share your room."

Again Flynn nodded.

"I don't believe in fate. I don't believe in coincidence. I believe in a loving Father in Heaven who is omniscient, who controls much of what happens in our lives by blessing us through our obedience, though not all, because we do have our agency to act as we see fit, and I don't believe our meeting was accidental. I believe that you knocked on my door because God knew what was happening to me and He sent you to help me through this." Maggie smiled. "You see, He knows I'm quite a simple person and wouldn't have the slightest idea how to handle this, so He sent you to teach me."

Flynn sat quietly while the waiter brought their dinner and left. "And why do you think He would allow Alyssa Lawson to be kidnapped and abused by that heathen who has her?"

Maggie smoothed her napkin in her lap and sipped her soup. "I told you, we have our agency. All things have their opposite. If there was no evil in the world, we couldn't appreciate the good, and we wouldn't have anything to test us. This life *is* a test, a time of trial, to see whether we'll choose to be obedient to the commandments we've been given or if we'll turn our backs on the God who created us and follow Satan."

"So you believe there really is a Satan, a devil?" Flynn raised one eyebrow at Maggie as he sliced into his steak.

"Just as surely as there is a God in heaven, there is a devil to tempt and entice us to turn away from Him." Maggie knew this to be true as surely as she knew the fire next to their table burned.

"You're very young to be so sure about something as philosophically lofty as that. The great minds of the world have been debating those things for centuries and are still doing so and haven't reached conclusions with such assurance as the statements you're making."

Maggie smiled. "They're just looking in the wrong places. I can tell them exactly where to find the answers."

"So you believe that people like Alyssa Lawson and her parents have to suffer because some weirdo chose evil instead of good?" Flynn cut another piece of steak. "Doesn't seem fair to me," he said as he stuck it in his mouth.

"Flynn, life isn't fair. Didn't anyone ever tell you that?" Maggie put down her spoon and leaned across the table. "We're given challenges so we can grow. I don't know what I'm supposed to learn from this situation, but there is bound to be something good come of it. If I can find Katie before something terrible happens—something worse than she's undergoing right now—then it will have been worth it. Especially if we can put that monster behind bars for what he's done." Maggie stopped. "Actually, instead of behind bars, I'd like to have him dumped in a pit of huge, hungry alligators."

At that comment, Flynn nearly choked on his steak. His face turned red and he coughed till Maggie handed him a glass of water. When he recovered, he laughed. "I can't believe you said that. Here you are spouting good Christian Sunday School doctrine, and then you turn him over to the bloodthirsty crocs. Whatever happened to 'turn the other cheek'?"

"I didn't say I was perfect. I'm only working on it. Maybe in a thousand years I'd feel like he deserved something else. No, make that several millennia. In the meantime, he can . . ." Maggie looked up from her soup to see Flynn wiping his eyes from laughing so hard.

"What's so funny?" she demanded.

"You are, my good little Christian. I'm glad you gave me a glimpse of your world. I think I like it."

"And what about your world?" Maggie asked, setting her soup bowl aside and tackling the salad and crusty Italian bread.

"Oh, Maggie girl, it's not nearly as nice as yours." At the sudden change of tone in his voice, Maggie glanced up to see pain darken his eyes.

"I'd like to hear about it, if you want to tell me," she said softly.

He looked at her for a minute like he was actually going to share his world, then his expression changed. He shook his head. "No, Maggie. You really don't want to hear it. Will you excuse me for just a minute? I'll be right back. Finish your dinner, then we'll get your car."

Flynn left the room, was gone several minutes, then returned without saying a word. He finished his baked potato and put his napkin down. "Ready for some dessert?"

Maggie shook her head. "No. I thought I was getting a *cup* of soup instead of a bowl, but you'll notice I ate every spoonful. Now I'm too full, but please have some if you'd like."

Flynn stood and pulled Maggie's chair out, then helped her on with her coat. As they entered the foyer and headed for the front door, Maggie realized they hadn't paid the bill and called it to Flynn's attention.

"I reserved rooms and put dinner on my hotel bill." He took her arm and guided her toward the door.

Maggie stared up at him. "Maybe I didn't want to stay here." Then she added as an afterthought, "What if I *had* wanted dessert?"

Flynn escorted her out into the frigid night. "But you didn't, did you? When I saw you do away with all that soup and then salad and bread besides, I figured you wouldn't want dessert. But we can always go back . . ."

Maggie laughed. "You win. I don't. You did say 'rooms,' didn't you? As in plural?"

Flynn helped Maggie into the cold car and hurried around to the driver's side. As he slid in and started the car, he looked at her. "What if I only got one room?"

"Then I would go get another one for me."

"We could save money," he said as he turned out of the parking lot onto the highway.

Maggie laughed. "Give it up, Flynn. I know you're only pulling my leg. This is a doctor/patient relationship. You're here to help me get through whatever strange phenomenon I'm undergoing at the moment, not weaken my morals."

"Maybe I'm part of the tests and trials you're supposed to be undergoing."

"You know what they teach children in elementary school—just say no to drugs? Well, I just say no to relationships and situations like that until I kneel in the temple across the altar from my husband, if I ever get that far in this lifetime."

"What if you don't get married, Maggie? What if you become an old maid? Look what you'd have missed out on."

"What, Flynn? A guilty conscience? A child out of wedlock? Shame? Disease?"

"You sure know how to take the fun out of life."

"You know what? None of that sounds like fun to me. Anyway, I know you're only teasing me. I think you're one of the good guys and wouldn't take advantage of a girl who wasn't an active and willing participant."

"Ouch. You sure know how to hurt a guy. Don't noise that around, okay?"

"I won't let the cat out of the bag," Maggie promised with a smile.

"Are you paying attention to where we're going, or are you just going to follow me back to the hotel?"

"Both."

"Here we are. Do you want to drive my car back? It's warm. I'll drive your cold one for you."

"See, I told you you're one of the good guys. Thanks anyway, but I'll drive myself." Maggie unbuckled her seat belt as Flynn stopped next to her car. "I'm surprised you offered to let me drive your car after your comments about my driving."

"You're not distracted anymore. You're alert and in your right mind, and right now no one else is occupying it with you."

Maggie shivered at that comment and opened the door before Flynn could see her reaction. "See you at the hotel. Oh, did you get my key for me?"

"I'll give it to you when we get back."

Maggie unlocked her convertible and slid onto an icy leather seat. Maybe she should have taken Flynn up on his offer to drive the warm car. Why did this climate seem so much colder than her Idaho winters when Idaho was much farther north? She was used to the ice and snow and long winter weather, but this seemed worse.

As she turned the key to start the car, she felt the sudden rush of blood to her head and a feeling of helplessness wash through her. "No, Katie. Go away. I don't want to talk to you any more tonight.

Go away. Leave me alone." Maggie gripped the steering wheel and willed the pale, sad face to leave her mind. A battle of wills began, but Maggie wasn't winning. Katie became stronger.

"Hurry, Maggie, I need you. Come now or it will be too late."

CHAPTER 18

Maggie leaned her head back on the seat and prayed, harder than she'd ever prayed for anything in her life. Katie faded slightly, then reemerged in her mind. "Come now, Maggie. Tonight. I need you."

Maggie renewed her efforts and her prayers. Suddenly she was jerked from the car and shaken. "Maggie. Snap out of it. Look at me."

Maggie opened her eyes, looked up at Flynn, then sagged into him as he wrapped his arms around her.

"Katie again?" Flynn asked.

Maggie nodded against his coat. He stood for a minute holding her, then eased her back into her car and crouched beside her. "What did she want?"

"She wants me to come to her right now, tonight," Maggie whispered, leaning her head against the cold steering wheel.

"Did you try to fight her? Maggie, look at me. Did you try to keep her out of your mind?"

"I tried, but apparently not hard enough."

Flynn stood. "I think we'd better leave your car here tonight. Come on, get back in mine. This is a hotel parking lot. It will be safe to leave it here until morning."

"Maybe I ought to just check in here."

"I don't think your expense account can afford it. Besides, I don't want to leave you alone tonight." Flynn led Maggie to his car. He took her keys, transferred her overnighter to his trunk, locked her car, and got back into his. Maggie's eyes were closed; her head reclined against the headrest.

He leaned over and touched her cheek. "Maggie, talk to me."

"What do you want me to say?"

"Anything that comes into your mind. Keep talking to me all the way back to the hotel. Tell me about your family. What do they do? Talk to me."

"Why can't I shut her out, Flynn?"

"Possibly because you were so open to her at first. You never tried to stop her coming into your mind, did you, when you first started 'getting into her head,' as you called it?"

Maggie sat upright and turned to Flynn. "Did you hear what you just said? That sounded like two different processes. When this started, I felt like *I* was projecting into *her* life, *her* thoughts, things that had happened to *her*. I felt the blanket tight around me and couldn't get loose. I saw the bushy-haired man with big ears at the window. Not my window. It had to have been hers. She allowed me to catch these glimpses, invited me into her mind. I wasn't afraid at all when it happened, just disturbed that I could have such a connection to a person I'd never met." Maggie stopped.

"And now?" Flynn asked as they parked in front of the hotel.

"It's not the same. The thoughts have become so much stronger. That's the terrifying part. I don't know how to sever the connection and keep her thoughts from my mind, but now it's overwhelmingly Katie's thoughts, and not Alyssa's. Does that sound crazy?"

"Go on."

"Flynn, I feel ashamed that I can't control this mind thing—but more than that—I'm ashamed that my life has been so wonderful and hers has been so rotten."

"Only the last seven years, Maggie. Remember that. Come on, let's go in and get settled into our rooms. Then we'll continue this line of thought."

They went to the elevator and got off on the fifth floor. Flynn produced a single card key that opened the door to not just a hotel room, but an extensive suite that must have stretched across half the fifth floor.

Maggie stared open-mouthed as Flynn guided her into the lavish suite. "Flynn, you live very well. I certainly couldn't afford this, even with my expense account. Nice digs. May I have my key?"

Flynn handed Maggie the card key. She looked up at him, not understanding what he was trying to tell her.

"You said you got rooms. Plural. This can't be where I'm staying so it has to be yours. Where's mine?"

Flynn walked to one end of the extensive suite and opened a door that revealed an elegant bedroom with a huge, mirrored bathroom just beyond. "This is your room." He pointed to another door at the opposite end of the suite. "That's my room. This expanse in between is common area—ours. You'll note that they've lit the fireplace and turned up the heat, and the rooms are cozy warm so you won't be cold tonight."

"But . . ."

"You'll also note the lock on your door, although I'll ask you not to use it. You do have your agency." He paused for that to register. "But I'd rather you weren't alone with Katie tonight. Tomorrow we'll drive to Louisiana together, actually I'll drive," Flynn flashed a smile at Maggie and continued. "We'll find Katie, have Cleat Wiggins arrested, and everyone will live happily ever after."

Maggie stared at him, then turned and moved to the fireplace, which contained gas logs instead of real ones, but were warm, inviting and beautiful to watch nevertheless. She didn't know what to say. Flynn's logic was . . . logical. Everything he said made perfect sense. Except that Maggie could never face her parents and tell them she'd spent the night in a suite with a man she had met only two days ago—or was it longer? Time had no meaning for her anymore.

Flynn deposited his bag in his room, put Maggie's in her room, then came to stand beside her. "Okay, let's hear it."

"I can't do this, Flynn." Maggie looked up at him, hoping to make him understand. "I trust you implicitly . . ."

"As an eligible, red-blooded man, that is not a compliment. As a doctor, confidant, and friend, I thank you."

"I've been taught to avoid even the *appearance* of evil. Think how this would look to my parents, my family, to someone who didn't know our relationship. They'd think we were . . ." Maggie couldn't say the words.

"Lovers?" Flynn supplied with a smile.

"Yes," Maggie said, feeling the flush on her cheeks, hoping Flynn would think it was her proximity to the fire that caused it. She moved closer to the fire so he couldn't see her face.

"Would that be a bad thing, Maggie, if it were to happen?" She whirled around at the tone in Flynn's voice.

"Flynn Ford, you are one strange man. One minute you're the very proper, distant doctor, the next you act like you're trying to seduce me. Make up your mind. No. It doesn't matter. I'm out of here now, whatever you decide you want to be. I'll get my own room and take my chances with Katie." Maggie's declaration was tempered by the sudden realization that she didn't want to be alone with Katie's access to her mind; nevertheless, she started toward the bedroom to collect her things, determined not to be compromised in a situation that her parents wouldn't approve of and that didn't seem proper to Maggie either.

Flynn stepped in front of her and lifted her chin to make her look at him. "Just testing, Maggie. Some people talk a good line, but when temptation is placed in front of them, they don't remember how high their standards were supposed to be. I admit I was curious how really committed you were to your standards, because they seem to be *very* high indeed."

Then he stepped back and put space between them. "But I worry about you being alone tonight. Call your parents or your brother, explain the situation and see what they say. I promise I'll be the perfect gentlemen and uphold my Hippocratic oath faithfully. I'll speak with them if you'd like."

Maggie thought about that. She shook her head. "I think I need to have my own room and take my chances with a totally sleepless night."

"What if it's more than that?" Flynn asked quietly.

Maggie looked up at Flynn. The tone in his voice was solemn and unsettling. "What do you mean?"

Flynn silently stared into the fire for a moment, then took Maggie's hand and led her to the chair in front of the fire. "Sit for a few minutes and let's talk about your connection to Katie."

Maggie sat down and searched Flynn's face for some clue as to what this was all about. They'd already discussed it. For hours. What more was there to say? But she knew from his expression what he had to say wasn't a rehash of what they'd covered before. He didn't meet her eyes for what seemed a very long time, just stared intently into the fire.

"I'm listening," Maggie said softly. "What do you want to tell me that is apparently so hard to communicate?"

Flynn finally looked at her, rubbed his earlobe, and cleared his throat. "I hoped I wouldn't have to tell you this. I don't want to scare you, because the studies aren't complete—they're just that, ongoing studies. In fact, scientists are now studying every facet of the relationships between identical and fraternal twins. A Phoenix doctor is studying twins' obesity and the ability to burn calories; in Philadelphia, an expert is researching twins and multiple sclerosis. A forensic expert in Texas is doing handwriting comparison of identical twins."

Flynn paused. "In fact, there isn't much they aren't studying about twins. Sense of humor, cancer, chronic fatigue syndrome and fibromyalgia, even obsessive-compulsive disorders in identical twins, which, by the way, is higher by 90 percent than in fraternal twins. Ohio State University is doing a study on the learning style of fraternal versus identical twins. They're even studying headaches in twins."

"And your point is?" Maggie asked when he stopped.

"Among the studies on the phenomena of the connection between identical twins, one scientist in Germany is looking into the more sinister aspect of thought transference." Flynn watched Maggie's face as he began unfolding this controversial study and its results thus far.

"Thought transference? That sounds like what Katie's doing." Flynn had Maggie's full attention. "You said the more sinister aspect?"

Flynn nodded. "He began studying 'good twin-bad twin' behavior, with the hypothesis that one twin is usually more dominant than the other, and in some cases will lead the more malleable twin for good or evil. Then, coupled with his first study, he came across the incidence of thought transference, or leading the weaker twin through a telepathic connection."

"Telepathy?"

"In its simpler form, it's actually quite common between mothers and their children. A mother will hurry home from somewhere, knowing that one of her children needs her or has been in an accident. Sometimes the connection or bond is strong enough for the mother to know which child or even what happened, but rather than call it telepathy, it's usually attributed to an uneasy feeling that all is not as it should be—a special bond between mother and child."

Maggie nodded. In her world, that would have been called "promptings," and it was a fairly common occurrence.

"Take that a few steps further. Many twins acknowledge having an extraordinary bond. Throw in a magnified sense of communication, one that allows actual thought transference, and think of the possibilities for good or evil. If there was a dominant twin with a disposition toward evil, what might be the consequences?" Flynn watched as Maggie processed those new ideas.

"You think Katie is practicing thought transference on me." Maggie stood and paced the floor, mentally agreeing that it was probable. How else could she explain her knowledge of Alyssa's kidnapping and the continued deep connection with her, feeling her emotions, her fears? Except that she wasn't her twin. Maggie turned to Flynn, still watching her. "Are you also suggesting that she, if there is a twin connection, which I can't believe, may be the dominant personality? Even an 'evil' twin?"

"No. No," Flynn repeated emphatically, jumping to his feet and shaking his head. "I'm not suggesting anything of the kind. I'm simply giving you some things to think about. We know Katie is strong enough to alter your normal behavior with thought transference; we don't know exactly how strong she is or what her motives might be, therefore I suggest that you not be alone until we know more. It may be that you simply needed to understand what's happening so you can know to block her thoughts or control her transmissions, or whatever you want to call them."

Maggie resumed pacing the sculpted carpet, considering the implications of all this new information. Again she stopped and turned to Flynn. "What are the chances of finding this kind of connection between unrelated people?"

Flynn didn't answer for a minute. "Unknown. But given your incredible physical likeness and interests, I'd put my money on the belief there *is* a blood relationship, especially since the scientists who study thought transference see it as a very real and valid occurrence in twins. The only unknown, as far as I'm concerned, is what Katie has in mind. Is she simply asking for your help, or does she want something more from you?"

Again, Maggie paced and processed these new thoughts, weighing the intellectual side against the emotional viewpoint and what she ultimately felt in her heart.

"Would you like to talk to your parents?" Flynn asked. "I know this can be rather much to digest and you may want to discuss it with them."

"I haven't told them about Katie—Alyssa. They only know I'm writing articles on Lewis and Clark for the newspaper." Maggie dug in her purse for her cell phone. "That's another by-product of Katie's influence over me. I've rarely kept anything from my parents—until now."

"Why did you tell your brother?" Flynn moved back to the fire and settled into the plush lounge chair near it. He motioned to the chair opposite for Maggie.

"Steve and I have always been very close. He can pry my deepest thoughts from me. I've always gone to him with the little things I didn't think I needed to bother my parents about. I got scared the first time I had these visitations or thought projections or whatever you call them. I think I told him more as a safety factor than anything."

"How did he receive that bit of news?"

Maggie curled up in the chair by the fire. "He already knew Dad wasn't happy about this cross-country assignment, so Steve promised he'd support me as long as I checked in daily and let him know all the details as they developed. Otherwise, he'd fly out immediately to be with me. So you see, my leash may appear to be nonexistent, but it's very real and isn't very long at all."

"I think you're one lucky girl, Maggie, and I think your family must be very special and unique and love you very much."

"They are," Maggie said as she dialed Steve's cell phone. Maggie didn't notice the look on Flynn's face at that comment. "Steve, hi. Just checking in. What's going on?"

"Rick's addition to the vet clinic is almost finished. Just in time for Christmas. Oh, I got the samples sent to Alan and then had a phone call from him asking what's up. What did you tell him when you sent yours?"

"Just that it was very important and to expedite it. I didn't take time for explanations since I didn't know *what* to tell him."

"This is your little secret so I'll let you explain, but you'd better get in touch with him or the folks may find out what's going on with your look-alike. Mom's continually shaking her head now so I know it's heavy on her mind that you questioned your birth."

"Steve, I'm going to put my phone on speaker mode. I don't remember if I told you about meeting Dr. Flynn Ford at the Alpine Inn. He's a psychologist and an expert on the Stockholm Syndrome. We think that may be what happened to Alyssa when she was kidnapped. She may have bonded with her captor and not tried to escape, but now she's getting desperate. Just so you know why I'm telling you all this, those glimpses I was getting into Alyssa's life and emotions have been getting stronger and more frequent." Maggie paused, hating to continue, reluctant to reveal how scary things were getting for her, as well as Flynn's latest disclosures.

"Okay, Magpie. What's going on?" Steve asked when she hesitated too long.

Maggie took a deep breath and plunged into her story. "Katie, Alyssa's alter ego, has been practicing thought transference. Dr. Ford's helping me understand what's happening and how to cope with it until we can get to Louisiana and find her."

"You're traveling with Dr. Ford?" Steve's voice sounded incredulous.

"Actually, no. He followed me because he was worried after he saw one of my episodes with Alyssa in Hill City. But that's why I'm calling. Steve, I need your honest opinion on something I hate to even ask about."

Maggie's slight hesitation caused Steve to interject immediately. "Maggie, do I need to fly out there?"

"Let me finish, then you can talk. Dr. Flynn has rented a suite in the hotel. It has two bedrooms, one on each end of a living area. He thinks he—we . . ." Maggie simply did not know how to broach this subject that seemed more far-fetched with every word.

"Steve, this is Flynn Ford." Flynn leaned forward and Maggie held out the phone so he could clearly be heard. She was more than happy to let him take over.

"I'm observing your sister because at this point Katie is not only projecting into Maggie's mind with more frequency, but has begun to alter her behavior. Maggie hasn't learned how to block Katie's thought projections, and I'm proposing to observe her tonight, keep her awake all night if necessary to prevent Katie from doing any mischief. This is a new field, and studies are showing some dangerous things can happen, depending on the sender and the receiver. Since we don't know Katie's intent, I'd like to stay with Maggie. Your sister said that this is a very improper setting and that to avoid the appearance of evil," Flynn winked at Maggie, "she needs to have her own room. I think that would be a mistake. I'm a gentleman and a doctor with her best interests at heart, and without alarming you further I will just say that your sister will be perfectly safe with me, but left alone with Katie . . ." Even Flynn didn't know how to finish the thought.

There was no immediate answer from Steve. Just a long silence.

"Steve, are you still there?" Maggie asked.

"Magpie, you can get yourself into more interesting, awkward, implausible situations than anyone I've ever heard of. And dangerous too, it sounds like. Dr. Ford, if this is as serious as you make it sound, I can only agree to your staying with Maggie tonight. However, I do have to tell you that I will cheerfully wring your neck with my bare hands until there is not a breath of life left in your body if anything happens to her. A young, naive girl, alone, far from home . . ."

Maggie interrupted. "Okay, Steve. He got the message. I do trust him. I just hated the thought of how it would look—and how it would sound when I tell Mom and Dad this incredible story."

"So you made me an accomplice. Thanks a lot, little sister. Anything else I can do for you?" The light sarcasm in Steve's voice made Flynn smile.

"That should be sufficient for now," Maggie said.

"Magpie, be careful. I don't like what you're playing with here."

"I don't either. I'll be very happy to have this all over." The conversation was getting much too serious for Maggie. "Anything going on I should know about?"

"For your information, I have a hot date tonight with Toni Keller. Remember her? The little blonde from down the road? She grew up while I was gone and we're going caroling with the young adults, then to a movie after."

"See how much more fun you're having socializing than tagging around the country with your little sister? Tell Toni hi for me, but don't fall for her. I've got someone in mind for you that you'll like much better."

"Who?" Steve boomed through the phone.

"She's from Brigham City. Tell you about her later. Bye for now. And thanks for being there for me, Steve. Love you." Maggie hung up quickly before Steve could say anything else. This sibling interaction must have seemed quite humorous to Flynn, judging from the amused expression on his face.

"What did you find so funny?" Maggie asked, dropping the cell phone back in her purse.

"The image of your brother defending your honor by strangling the life out of me." Flynn stood. "Would you like a soda?"

"Not right now, thanks, and don't laugh too hard. Steve takes his role as my protector very seriously. It would take a half a dozen men your size to keep him from following through on his threat if—if he felt it necessary." Once again Maggie's face flamed bright crimson.

"Did you know when you're embarrassed, your face takes on the same hue as your hair?" Flynn rumpled Maggie's hair playfully as he went to the small refrigerator and pulled out a Coke.

"Did you know there is very little that makes a woman more angry than to have someone tousle her hair as if she were a two-year-old?" Maggie retrieved her computer from her voluminous bag in the bedroom and brought it to the mahogany desk to check her e-mail.

"Actually, no. I didn't know that," Flynn said, settling again by the fire. "Why?"

"Why what?" Maggie asked, concentrating on hooking her computer into the phone line.

"Why does it make a woman mad to have someone play with her hair?"

"No, you didn't understand me. I said tousle, not play. They are two entirely different things. To rumple or tousle a grown woman's hair is demeaning, not to mention how it messes it up."

Maggie's attention turned totally to her e-mail. She had a message from Lily and it was not at all what she had expected.

CHAPTER 19

Maggie frowned as she read the brief note, her heart sinking to her toes.

Dear Maggie,

What happened to our agreement? I remember asking that you not mention Alyssa to me again until you found her, or irrefutable evidence of her demise. Did you forget the consequences I imposed for breaking your promise that you would not bring her name up, or did you simply ignore that promise? In either case, I'm dreadfully sorry those consequences must now be suffered. You are hereby notified your employment has been terminated. Please immediately return the credit card. Any monies that you may not have already spent will be deducted from your salary. Please send an address where your salary owed thus far can be sent. This hurts me deeply to do this, because the columns were being very well received, and I personally found your writing educational, entertaining, and edifying. However, be that as it may, we had a verbal contract. A promise is a promise and you broke yours. It breaks my heart to do this.

Lily

Maggie sat back in her chair, stunned by Lily's letter. Fired. Fired from her very first real job. Employment terminated. That would look great on her resume when she went job hunting again. Why hadn't she remembered her promise to Lily? Why had she ever written asking Lily to help her get Alyssa's DNA in the first place? Talk about stupid. Maggie slapped her hands on the desk in frustration at her utterly witless, irresponsible behavior.

"Bad news?" Flynn asked.

Maggie turned in her chair and rested her chin on the high striped sateen back as she looked at Flynn lounging comfortably by the fireplace. "I'm currently unemployed."

Flynn came up out of the chair and strode across the room. "You're what?"

Maggie showed him the e-mail. "In all fairness, I did promise Lily I would not breathe a word of this to anyone, and I would not mention Alyssa to her again. I just wasn't thinking when I e-mailed her the other night asking if she could get samples of Alyssa's hair so we could have her DNA work done."

Flynn crouched beside Maggie. "What *were* you thinking when you sent that e-mail?"

Maggie shrugged. "How do I know what I was thinking? It was late at night. I don't even remember which night."

"Maggie, this is important. Think carefully. Remember where you were when you sent it. Remember what you'd been doing, what you'd been thinking, and what you thought about after."

Maggie was about to brush off Flynn's request, but his urgent tone and intense expression changed her mind. "Okay, let me think. How long have I been on the road? Everything is such a blur."

"Did you do it before or after you stayed at the Alpine Inn?" Flynn coached.

"After, I think."

"Then it had to be last night. The night before you were at the Alpine Inn."

Maggie stared at him. "Are you sure? It seems there has been a whole week's worth of days since then."

"Trust me, Maggie. It's only been forty-eight eventful hours since I met you. So it was last night you sent the e-mail. Last night you spoke to the woman in St. Joseph, then went back to your hotel, carried your luggage to your room, showered for a long time, then didn't turn off your light for several hours. What happened during those hours?"

Maggie stared in disbelief at the man before her. "How do you know all that?"

"I followed you, remember? I booked the room right next to yours. I could hear your shower. The hotel courtyard was built in a U-shape and by simply looking out my window, I could see your light reflected in the windows across the courtyard. What did you do after your shower? What were you thinking? Did you call Steve or e-mail him? Were you reading? Dozing?"

"Stop. Let me think. I got into bed with my tape recorder and computer . . ."

Maggie paused a moment, then continued her thought. ". . . and typed my column, then beefed it up a bit, since I wasn't happy with the way it turned out."

"And then?" Flynn dragged a chair over and sat knee to knee with Maggie.

Maggie closed her eyes and remembered that room, picturing it clearly. She'd wrapped her wet hair in a towel, and after she finished her column and e-mailed it, remorse that she'd been so lax about her assignment prompted her to send pictures as well.

"I felt guilty for losing the passion and excitement so quickly for the job that had been my only desire for two years, and for replacing it with this all-consuming passion to find Alyssa—Katie. I thought about that for awhile, realized that my thoughts were never far from her, and felt uncomfortable, disconcerted because of it. Like wanting something so much that you never think of anything else. I didn't like that happening to me."

"Keep talking, Maggie. I think we're getting somewhere."

"Let's see." Maggie concentrated on the dancing, flickering flames in the fireplace, as if the answers she sought were there. "I e-mailed Steve telling him where I was staying and that I'd talked to a lady about the second letter." Maggie glanced at Flynn. "I didn't tell him the woman who wrote it had been killed."

"Good thinking."

She had a hard time pulling her gaze from Flynn's intense dark eyes. She liked their intelligence and concern and had to force herself to look away. "Umm, then I logged off the e-mail connection and started to put my computer away when I felt this urge to send Lily an e-mail about Alyssa's DNA. I'd thought about it several times before but had never done it. I vacillated back and forth for several minutes before I finally gave in, logged back on, and sent it." Maggie stopped. "Oh."

He nodded. "What made you finally send that e-mail you'd never sent before, Maggie? Or should I ask what stopped you from sending that e-mail until then?"

Maggie shivered and hugged herself. "I don't like this, Flynn. Not even a little bit."

Flynn pushed the chair back and stood up. "Come on back by the fire. The chairs are more comfortable there."

Maggie turned to log off her e-mail connection. "Just a minute. I have another message." Her heart leaped inside her. Alan. It was too soon for the results of the profiling. Steve had said Alan wanted to know what was going on. Still, her fingers trembled as she called up the message.

Okay, sweet little sister of mine, what are you up to? Why all the secrecy and sudden interest in our family's DNA? Yes, I'm doing it. I'm setting aside some very important stuff and have made this the lab's number-one priority, only because I know you wouldn't waste my time with anything frivolous. Nevertheless, you owe me big time. But my curiosity got the best of me so I have to ask why I'm doing this at all, much less rushing it. Are you trying to prove I'm not your brother or something? I promise never to tease you unmercifully again. Steve said it was your project, so tell me, Sis, what gives?

Alan

P.S. Will send results in the morning. They should be ready by then.

"More bad news?" Flynn asked. Maggie jumped. She hadn't realized he still stood at her side.

"Not really. Alan just wants to know why I've asked him to compare our DNA. Here, you can read it." Maggie stood and stretched while Flynn bent over the computer.

"What are you going to tell him?" he asked when he'd finished.

"Nothing tonight. I'll wait until I get the results in the morning."

"Is that fair?" Flynn went back to the chair by the fire.

Maggie logged off and returned to the fire, snuggling back into her comfortable chair. "Not really, but he may not have time to read it before he finishes the profiling anyway. As soon as I have the results, I'll explain the whole thing."

Flynn raised his eyebrow. "The whole thing? Everything?"

"Why not?" she asked.

Flynn watched her for a minute, then leaned toward her and asked, "Have you given any thought to what those results might be?"

Maggie was startled by the question. "Of course. They'll prove that Alyssa and I either are or aren't related." Then she stopped and shook her head. "No, they'll prove that I'm a biological sister of my brothers or I'm not—whether I'm a biological daughter of my parents or not. I keep forgetting I have no way of getting Alyssa's DNA. My head just keeps telling me that I'm trying to prove whether or not we're really twins."

"What does your heart tell you?"

Maggie stared at the handsome face so close to hers. "You keep asking very hard questions, but I'm afraid to analyze that one. Flynn, I'm enjoying this evening very much because I feel so safe with you, but I don't want to push the envelope by delving too deeply into those issues right now and have Katie force her way back into my mind."

"What if you can't stop her?"

"Isn't that why you're here? To help me combat this?"

"I can only do so much, Maggie girl, then the rest is up to you. Consciously or not, *you* will decide whether to let her back in. Remember that when you feel her coming back. You *can* keep her out of your mind."

"How do I keep her out? I tried praying, but that only helped for a minute and then she slid right through the wall."

"Interesting way you put that. Why did you use that particular phrase?"

"Good grief, Flynn. Now you're beginning to sound like a psychologist."

"Amazing that you're just now recognizing it." Flynn flashed her a charming smile. "Answer my question."

Maggie thought for a minute. "I guess because I felt my prayer could block her, put up a defensive wall she couldn't penetrate."

"And what happened? Could you literally see a wall?"

Again Maggie thought about it before she answered. "No, I don't think so. I think I just wanted it to be there. The image of her face sort of faded in and became stronger, then when I prayed she started fading out, then came in again even stronger.

"What does she look like?"

Maggie opened her mouth to say, "Just like me, of course," but then she realized that Katie didn't look like her.

"Yes?" prompted Flynn. "You were going to say . . . ?"

"I was going to say that she looks just like me, but she doesn't. Alyssa and I looked alike seven years ago, or at least I look like Alyssa's picture did seven years ago, but the face that comes into my mind hardly resembles me."

"Describe it."

Maggie closed her eyes. "She's very pale. Her face is thin. Too thin. Her hair's short, shaggy, matted. She's dirty, hungry, sick, and she's scared." Maggie described her, curled up on a dirty cot, her clothes mere rags, a chain around one ankle. Her limbs were thin, painfully thin; she couldn't have weighed more than ninety pounds. She looked like pictures Maggie had seen from the holocaust.

"That's enough, Maggie. You've seen enough. Don't go there anymore," Flynn warned.

Maggie didn't hear him. She could only see Katie stretching out her hand and crying, "Come to me, Maggie. Hurry. You're the only one who can help me." Tears left streaks down the wan, dirty face.

Maggie's heart melted. "I'm coming, Katie. Tell me where you are."

"The garden. Come to the garden. Hurry, Maggie. He's coming back. He'll kill again. Hurry."

"That's enough, Maggie." Flynn said. He jumped to his feet and pulled Maggie from the chair. "Maggie, snap out of it. Fight her. You're stronger than she is. Make her go away."

Maggie was confused. She wanted to help Katie. She needed to help. If she didn't, who would?

"Maggie, listen to me. Tell Katie that you and I are leaving tonight to help her. We'll be there tomorrow. Do it now, Maggie." Flynn gripped her arms and shook her. "Maggie, Katie will leave your mind if you make her. You're stronger than she is. Fight her."

As Flynn fought to help Maggie overcome Katie's strong presence in her mind, he found himself doing something he hadn't done in years. He prayed. "Dear God, Maggie believes that you're all powerful. Please use some of that power in her behalf right now. Help her until she's strong enough to help herself."

CHAPTER 20

Maggie blinked her eyes, and her knees gave way. Flynn pulled her against him and held her until she stopped quivering, then he eased her back down into the chair. As he knelt beside her and turned her face gently toward his, he said thank you over and over to Maggie's Father in Heaven who'd heard the pleading of an atheist and answered his stumbling prayer.

Flynn stroked Maggie's soft cheek, brushed her auburn hair back from her beautiful face, and would have kissed her if he'd dared. Heaven only knew how much he wanted to, but this wasn't the time or the place to demonstrate his affection for this blithe spirit whose genuineness and charm had captivated his heart. What if he hadn't stopped this? Then Flynn rephrased that thought. What if God hadn't stopped this? Flynn hadn't done anything but lead Maggie to that precipice where he needed divine help to bring her back.

Finally she opened her eyes. "Hi."

One simple word, but it flooded Flynn with pleasure. He could barely speak. All his emotions clumped together in one giant lump in his throat. "Welcome back."

"Thanks." Her eyelids fluttered closed.

Frantic, Flynn grabbed Maggie's limp hand. "Maggie, are you . . . ?"

The long lashes slowly opened and Maggie looked at him. "Am I what?"

Flynn settled on the floor at her feet and leaned against his chair. He took a deep breath, fought to regain some portion of self-control and professionalism, and asked, "How do you feel?"

"Exhausted," Maggie said, forcing a smile.

He recognized the effort it took. "Are you up to a long drive into the night?"

Her silence extended for what seemed minutes. "You promised, didn't you?"

Flynn nodded. "Yes. We've got to leave as soon as you feel able so we can go find her."

"Can I just sit here by the fire for a few minutes?"

"We'll stay as long as you wish. Can I get you anything? A Coke? Sprite? Orange juice? Let me see what else there is around here." Flynn jumped to his feet and went to the mini-fridge, glad for the chance to expend his pent-up energy and emotion doing something, anything with a purpose. "There are a couple of bottles of spirits in here. Don't suppose you'd consider drinking one for medicinal purposes?"

"Not even for medicinal purposes. Thanks, Flynn, but no. I'm feeling weaker than I should. I didn't realize how much energy it would take to block Katie's thoughts, to send her completely out of my mind."

"If you're thirsty, I could . . ."

"Truly, I'm fine. Come back and sit by me so I can see you. I don't want to be alone."

Flynn sat on the floor again and took Maggie's hand. "I'm right here, Maggie girl, and I'll be here as long as you need me." He didn't quite know how to start what he wanted to say next, but he knew it had to be said.

"Maggie, forgive me, please? I took you down a very dangerous path without realizing how strong Katie was." Flynn hung his head. He couldn't look into those beautiful, trusting, blue eyes while he confessed how he'd failed her. "I'm not excusing myself, but I didn't realize how tenderhearted you are, nor did I realize how well Katie knew you. She knew you so much better than I did. But she played on your sympathy. I can't prove it until we find her, but I think she lied to you." Flynn finally looked up at Maggie. "When we find her, I don't think she'll be as she portrayed herself in your mind."

"But she was chained to a cot. She was rail thin and sick and so dirty and afraid . . ."

"That's what she wanted you to see. She wanted you to feel sorry for her, so sorry that you would do anything for her."

"Do you really believe that?" Maggie thought for a minute, then shook her head. "I can't believe it. But it's interesting that I'm not seeing things"

"It doesn't matter now. All that matters is that you were able to block Katie and whatever purpose she had, and as soon as you feel up to it, we'll go find her." Flynn intertwined his fingers with Maggie's and sat watching the color come back into her face and the sparkle return to her eyes.

"How do you fare driving all night?" she asked.

"Just fine as long as I have someone to talk to me and enough caffeine in my system to keep me alert."

Maggie smiled. "Then you'd better begin caffeinating the system. I think we should get started before any more of the night is gone. What time is it anyway? I've absolutely no sense of the hour."

Flynn glanced at his watch and was surprised to see how early it was. "Just nine o'clock." He felt like it should be dawn already. He could have sworn the emotional ordeal he'd just endured had lasted well into the wee hours of the morning. "I'll gather up our things. You sit by the fire for a few more minutes."

He packed Maggie's laptop back into its case and dropped it into Maggie's monster of a bag, which she somehow thought of as a purse, then brought his bag from his room and Maggie's overnighter from her room and put them by the door. Maggie stirred in her chair. It was the first time she'd moved more than to change expression.

"I think we're about ready," Flynn said. "Do you need to use the . . . "

"Yes, I'd better do that. Will you help me up, please? My knees don't seem to want to hold me upright."

Flynn gently pulled Maggie to her feet and, with his arm around her waist, supported her across the living room to her bedroom door. She smiled up at him with blush-tinged cheeks.

"Thanks. I think I can make it from here."

She held on to the walls, then the elegant four-poster bed and shut the door to the mirrored bathroom. Flynn paced back and forth in front of her bedroom door until she finally emerged. She walked back across the room carefully, as though she were stepping on eggs and didn't want to crush a single shell, and she made it all the way to the bedroom door before she stopped and leaned against the door frame.

She looked up at Flynn apologetically. "That last ten miles really tired me out. Maybe I'd better rest a few minutes before we make the hundred-mile trek to the car."

Flynn scooped her into his arms and deposited her back in the chair by the fire. "I have an idea." He called the desk and told them to prepare his bill. "We're checking out in about five minutes. Will you please have someone bring a luggage trolley to our suite, and do you happen to have a wheelchair in the hotel?" He paused. "No problem. We'll get by without it."

Flynn disappeared into his bedroom and came back in time to answer the door a few minutes later. While the luggage was loaded onto the trolley, he slipped into his jacket, pulled Maggie to her feet, and helped her on with her coat. The boy held the door while Flynn picked Maggie up once again.

"Flynn, put me down," Maggie whispered, totally embarrassed.

"Would you rather he carry you and I take the luggage trolley?" he asked.

"I can walk," she insisted quietly.

Flynn nodded. "Probably sometime tomorrow. But for now, we'll do it this way." He carried her out of the room, down the hall, and into the elevator while the young man studiously avoided eye contact with either of them, concentrating on the control panel as they descended to the lobby.

"Please let me down," Maggie whispered when the door opened.

"Only while I sign the bill." Maggie clung to the desk while Flynn gave his car keys to the boy, asked him to put the luggage in his car and start it, then remain there until they came out. Flynn signed the receipt, and in answer to the receptionist's questions, explained that the room had been thoroughly satisfactory but Maggie had suddenly taken ill. Then he picked her up and carried her to the car, which by now was almost warm. Not quite. Flynn tipped the fellow generously, made sure Maggie was comfortable, and pulled out of the parking lot.

"We have a decision to make," Flynn said as Maggie pulled her coat closer around her. "Will you object to leaving your car here and taking mine to Louisiana, or would you prefer that we drive yours? We can't take them both as you're in no condition to drive, and I won't leave you alone anyway."

Maggie objected. "Flynn, you can't drive me all the way to Louisiana. What about your book? Your work?"

"The book can wait. Katie can't. And you're in no condition to drive."

"My legs are just a little wobbly and weak. They'll be fine. I'll be fine," Maggie insisted. "This isn't your battle."

"And what happens if Katie decides to visit you again with the intensity of that last thought transference while you're driving down the interstate at seventy-five miles per hour? How will you handle that?"

Maggie had no answer. She knew she needed to get to Louisiana as quickly as possible to find Katie, so she couldn't wait until she felt strong enough, both physically and with the assurance she'd be able to block Katie's thoughts. Not just Katie's *thoughts*, she noted with a start. That last episode was more than thought transference, but she didn't know what to call it.

She leaned her head back on the seat. "You're right. As much as I'd like to do this on my own, it appears that I need your help. So, it doesn't matter which car we take. Whichever you prefer."

"This one."

"Can we drive by the other hotel and ask them to watch my car until I return to get it?"

"We're on our way there as we speak. Any other requests? Your wish is my command."

"A little more heat? I can't quit shivering."

"It's already on max, but it will be blasting you out in a minute or two. In the meantime, we could always pull over to the side of the road and . . ."

Maggie laughed. "Thanks, but I'll wait for the heater."

"It's so good to hear you laugh, Maggie." Flynn paused, wanting to reach over and take her hand, but he stifled the impulse. "You had me very scared for awhile tonight."

"Me too," Maggie said softly.

"Do you want to talk about it?"

"Not yet. I'm not sure I can even explain what happened."

"Then talk to me about something. Anything. Remember, you've got to keep me awake."

Maggie smiled. "Somehow I don't think you're a bit sleepy, and I can't think of anything that wouldn't bore you right to sleep. I have a better idea. Tell me about you. Where are you from? Do you have any brothers and sisters? Where do your parents live? I think you said you were eligible, which I take to mean single. Why? Do you analyze yourself out of relationships or are your female friends simply afraid of being analyzed to death?"

Flynn laughed. "Sounds like you're about back to your normal self, which is the good news. The bad news is that I'm a very dull person, and you don't want to hear that boring stuff for the next several hours. By the way, I hope you're good at map reading, which I assume you are or you wouldn't be driving across country by yourself. You'll need to check the map and get us on the right road out of town. I'm not even sure where New Iberia is."

"Just below Lafayette. Do you have a map?" Maggie asked.

"Hmm. Probably not of Louisiana."

"When we get to the hotel, we can get mine from my car."

Flynn glanced at Maggie and caught her looking at him. "Okay," she admitted with a rueful smile, "*you* can get it from my car. But I'm feeling much better now so I promise I won't be a helpless ninny much longer."

"You can stay a helpless ninny as long as it takes to get your strength back. It's my fault that happened, Maggie, and I'm so sorry I didn't realize how close Katie was to . . ."

"Flynn, stop. It wasn't your fault. I had no idea when this started it could be so exhausting. Actually, so terrifying. And I had no idea when I tried to get into Alyssa's mind at first that I'd be inviting her into mine and that it would be so invasive."

"Unfortunately, we've both learned a lot—the hard way." Flynn pulled under the arched covering at the lobby entrance of the Ramada Inn & Suites Convention Center Hotel, and left the car running while he informed the receptionist inside that they were leaving a blue convertible in the parking lot for a couple of days and would they please keep an eye on it. Then he drove around to Maggie's car in the parking lot.

"Do you want anything else from the car besides the map?" Flynn asked, opening the door and digging Maggie's car keys from his pocket.

"Not that I can think of. I have everything in my purse. But while you're out, will you bring me my purse from the trunk? I feel lost without it, and my cell phone's in it. I'm sorry to be such a bother," Maggie said apologetically. "I promise I'll do half of the driving as soon as my reflexes are restored to their normal state."

Flynn touched Maggie's cheek softly. "You're not a bother. You're . . ." Flynn was going to say a delight but thought better of it. Maggie didn't need to suspect his feelings for her just yet.

Maggie frowned. "I'm what, Flynn, besides a nuisance, a bother, a burden, and a disobedient patient?"

"Bite your tongue, Maggie girl. You're none of those things. I was looking for some descriptive terms more along the lines of challenging, fascinating, entertaining, maybe a little frustrating, and certainly instructive."

"And you talk a great line of blarney. Hurry up and shut the door. You're letting all the warm air out and the cold air in."

Flynn shut the door, found the map, and retrieved Maggie's extra-large tote from the trunk, then rejoined her in his car.

When he started to speak, Maggie said, "No jokes, please, about what I carry in my purse. I've heard them all and then some."

"But I wasn't going to say . . ."

"Good. That's points for you. My brothers could never resist the temptation to poke fun at me, and I have to tell you, it really does get tiresome."

Flynn laughed. "Maggie, I think you're well on the road to recovery." He started the car. "And speaking of road, which one do we take out of here?"

Maggie opened her road atlas to Arkansas, traced the most major highway straight south to Louisiana, and pronounced, "U.S. 425."

"And where do we connect with that?" Flynn asked.

"My guess would be two blocks north where we should run into Highway 65. From there we'll look for signs telling us where to turn and head south."

"If you're right, I'm duly impressed." Flynn followed Maggie's directions to Highway 65. She was right. "Do you stay up nights studying the atlas?"

"No, I just look at the map occasionally and remember the roads I'm supposed to be on so I won't get lost. Highway 65 is the one we came in on from Little Rock, remember?"

"No, I actually don't remember. I was just following you, so I didn't pay any attention to how we were getting there. I was so amazed at the power of your guardian angels to get you safely to your destination, I didn't notice anything else."

"Low blow, Flynn. I have no defense for that as I don't remember much of the trip except the highways."

"How long is this trip going to be, anyway? Can you look at the map and give me an estimate of mileage and travel time?" Flynn had no doubt that she could normally do it, but right now he was checking to see how completely she'd recovered from her ordeal. His experience with this kind of situation was limited, and he didn't know if that type of encounter had lasting effects of any duration. Would it affect her powers of calculation? Observation? Dull her thought processes?

Maggie studied Flynn's profile in the dim light from the dashboard. "Was that the equivalent of 'are we there yet?' and 'how much farther is it?' Are you tired of me already, before we're even ten miles down the road?"

Flynn laughed. "Truce. I'll stop teasing you if you'll stop reading something negative into everything I say. Agreed?" Their eyes met briefly before each of them quickly looked away.

"Agreed," Maggie said and turned on the overhead light to study the atlas. "As to time and distance, it appears to be about ninety miles to Louisiana." She paused while she flipped to the Louisiana map. "Then about two hundred miles into Lafayette, then another twenty or so to New Iberia. Averaging sixty miles an hour, since this isn't an interstate, we should arrive there at approximately three o'clock in the morning, allowing time for gas stops and any other stops we might make."

Flynn was impressed with Maggie's quick calculations and logged that information in his clinical data bank to add to the case study at some future point. Then he grunted. "Guess maybe we shouldn't have been so quick to vacate our comfortable premises."

"Remember, all I have to go on is the name and address of someone who wrote over a year ago. Considering the history of the letter writers thus far, our chances of locating the correspondent and actually speaking to her are very slim. Then we have to locate the swamp garden, and if we don't get any clues about its location from being able to speak to the letter writer, I think this may be a very long quest. Can you imagine how many gardens there are in that area connected in some way to a swamp?"

Flynn's first thought was that would be a very pleasant way to pass the winter months. "Guess we'd better work fast since you have no more checks coming and your expense account just disappeared. What are you going to do, Maggie? Any ideas about another job?"

Maggie was quiet for a minute, and Flynn glanced at her as the silence extended, first in fear that Katie might be visiting her again, then curious about what she might be thinking.

Maggie looked at him and smiled. "I'm okay, Flynn. That was what you were thinking, wasn't it? That Katie might have come back? I have a silly question. Do you ever stop being a doctor, or is it so ingrained in you that it's become your entire persona?"

Flynn remembered his recent clinical thoughts and laughed. "Guilty as charged on both counts. Yes, I was afraid Katie had returned, and I guess I don't ever stop thinking like a psychologist. At least, I haven't so far. Are you willing to take on the challenge and see if you can change my behavior?"

This is heading into territory that I don't want to enter right now, Maggie thought, *but at some other time and place, I'd love nothing better than the challenge of doing just that.*

CHAPTER 21

Maggie changed the subject. "Is that why you're single, Flynn? You can't stop being clinical long enough to let someone get to know the real you?"

"What makes you think this isn't the real me?"

"I've caught glimpses of a very different, very caring, more human Flynn Ford when the analytical Dr. Ford lets his guard down." Maggie wanted to say more but realized she was bringing them right back on the personal level she had been trying to avoid. She didn't want Flynn to recognize the crush this patient had on her handsome doctor.

"Hmm. Are you saying that doctors aren't human?"

"Did I say that?" Maggie blushed and was glad it was dark enough that Flynn couldn't see her face. "What I meant was . . ."

"What you meant was doctors are cold and clinical, always probing for answers when they should be spending more time listening to their patients, who can give them the answers."

Maggie tilted her head and looked at Flynn. "You make me sound profound. What else did I mean?"

"That a patient will respond much more openly to a doctor who has a caring, sensitive bedside manner." Flynn was quiet for a minute. "Which is one reason I quit practicing and started researching. My bedside manner was too abrupt, too brusque, and not nearly sympathetic enough for patients who expected me to tell them to do whatever they wanted as long as it felt good without worrying about the consequences."

"You mean people really believe they can do whatever they want and not have to pay the price for their actions?" This was a foreign concept to Maggie, who had been taught that every act was connected to a consequence. You could choose to do whatever you wanted, but the consequence of that choice could not be avoided.

"If you're surprised at that, you'd be astounded at the number of professionals who tell their patients just what they want to hear and sit back raking in big bucks. I couldn't be part of that, so my partners decided their practice would be much more lucrative without me, and I decided I'd be much happier doing research and writing about it where I didn't have to be hypocritical."

"Here's 425," Maggie pointed. "We turn south now."

"Enough about me." Flynn navigated the loop, then glanced at Maggie. "I have a question for you. If it turns out that you and Alyssa are twins, who do you think are your parents? How and why were you separated? Have you given those things any thought?"

"Yes, but I have no answers." Maggie bit her lip. "I can't believe by any stretch of my imagination that my parents would ever give away one of their children. But I also can't believe they wouldn't tell me if I weren't biologically theirs. So I'm at an impasse. I can't get beyond the first question of who could be our parents if we *are* twins, to that second question of why we were separated."

Flynn waited without comment, recognizing from the inflection in Maggie's tone that there was more to come.

"And that brings me right back to the original question. Why do we have this incredible connection if we aren't twins? How can it happen? Flynn, it's driving me crazy!"

"Don't let it drive you over the edge yet, Maggie girl." Flynn flashed her a smile. "Hang in there. We should have a lot of answers—maybe even all the answers—in the next twelve to twenty-four hours."

"What if we can't find the girl who wrote the letter from Louisiana? We'll have to backtrack to Texarkana, but there is no guarantee we'd be able to find that fellow either. So much rides on whether we can locate the person who can tell me where she saw Katie and Cleat Wiggins, or at the very least, how to find the swamp garden."

Flynn thought about it for a minute, hesitated, then said quietly, "If all else fails, you do have one other alternative to help you pinpoint the location of the garden."

Maggie looked at him curiously, but Flynn kept his eyes on the road and said nothing more. "And that is?" Maggie prompted.

"You tell me."

She thought about it, considered all the possibilities that came to her mind, then finally shook her head. "The only thing I can think of is to let Katie back in and ask her. But I don't consider that an option."

"Why?"

"There you go again with your infernal psychological questions. Don't you *know* why it's not an option for me? Yes, you do know, but you want me to say it out loud, then think about it and decide whether I'm brave enough, or smart enough, or strong enough—or all three—to ask Katie to come back into my mind."

"And now that you've voiced it and thought about it, how do you feel about it?" Flynn was curious. Was the experience Maggie had so terrifying that she would never voluntarily undergo something similar even to find Katie? Did she doubt her own strength? Didn't she believe that she could actually control the situation? Or—and Flynn hadn't considered this possibility until now—perhaps Maggie *didn't* have the strength to control Katie's thought transference, or whatever had happened in that hotel room, and she knew it. Maybe that was what terrified her. A slight shiver ran through him. If that was the case, then he would have to teach her how to block Katie and hope that it worked.

"I don't like it," she said vehemently. "I don't want to ever undergo anything like that again."

"Why?" Flynn asked quietly.

"Is that your favorite word?" Maggie looked at him impatiently. "Why do you think? All my life I've been taught not to take into my body habit-forming substances that would remove my agency, anything that would destroy or alter my ability to control my own thoughts and actions. Have you ever experienced anything like that, Flynn? Have you ever been terrified that someone was controlling you and could make you do things you didn't want to do? Do you know what it's like to feel helpless—to just know that if they wanted you to do something, you'd have to do it whether you wanted to do it or not?"

"Twice," Flynn admitted, then immediately wished he hadn't.

Maggie leaned on the console that separated the two seats and waited, but Flynn didn't offer the rest of the story. "And the circumstances of that were . . . ?"

Flynn bit his tongue hard, wishing he could take back the offhanded, facetious reply that had slipped out before he even thought about it. "Never mind, Maggie. Please continue describing your feelings."

Maggie leaned back in her seat and looked at Flynn with narrowed eyes. "No, I think I'll wait until you tell me. I'm always spilling my story, my feelings, pouring them out whether I want to or not. Now I want to hear about you. Otherwise, I may not say another thing."

"But there is a good reason you're doing that, Maggie girl. I'm the doctor here. You have to tell me your feelings and thoughts so I can process them into . . ."

"Won't work, Flynn. Not this time. Why won't you tell me? Are you afraid it will make you appear too human? Do you think it will topple you from your lofty doctor's pedestal if you let me glimpse your personal, private world for a minute?"

"Wow. I guess that states plainly what you think of doctors. All doctors, or just this particular one?"

"Depends."

"On what?"

"On whether or not you decide to open up to me as I've opened up to you." Maggie paused, took a deep breath and barreled on before she changed her mind and chickened out or thought better of it. "Flynn, I thought we had a pretty special . . ." She had to say this just right. "Patient/doctor relationship. You opened up to me a couple of times and I appreciate that. It made it easier for me to talk to you and made me trust you more because you seemed more caring and concerned about me and my problems. For heaven's sake, you even followed me halfway across the Midwest. Surely you can sit right there and finish what you started to say. Would that be so hard?"

Flynn thought about it. Not that it ever *would,* but if their relationship *could* become anything besides the doctor/patient situation it was now, he would have to tell her those things. At some point, Maggie would have to know about the darker side of his life. He sighed. Confession wasn't easy. It came near to being impossible when you wanted to keep the brighter side of your life forward and forget about the nightmares that brought you upright in the middle of the night drenched with cold sweat and the dread of going back to sleep for fear it would happen again.

He glanced at Maggie. "Are you really sure you want to hear this? You'll never again think of me as you do now. What I'm going to tell you will color your perception of me—and will affect our relationship from this point on."

"Well, if you really didn't want to tell me, you just blew it with that introduction. Now I have to hear your story. I'd die of curiosity if you didn't tell me." Maggie leaned over the console and looked closely at him. "You know, I realize you have an ulterior motive for telling me, because I don't think my threatening to not say anymore could possibly cause you to reveal something you didn't want me to know."

"Now who's playing the psychologist?"

"I'm listening, Flynn."

Flynn set the cruise control and reached forward to dim the interior dashboard lights. This would be hard enough without Maggie watching every expression that played across his face.

"You asked if I ever felt helpless, if I ever felt I had to do something that someone else wanted me to do whether I wanted to do it or not. Yes, I've experienced that in two different ways. Once for love, and once out of desperation." Flynn glanced at Maggie. He didn't want to meet her eyes, but he had to know her temperament right now. Was she jubilant that she had won this little battle of will and words? Was she sincerely interested? And most of all would she, could she, understand what he was about to tell her without judging him too harshly?

Then he started his story, speaking so softly Maggie had to strain to hear him. "The first time I went through college, I went to med school, where I fell in love with a beautiful girl. That she was interested in me, a starving medical student who never had time for anything but study, was the greatest wonder of my life. In a moment of insanity caused by my overwhelming awe that this woman would look at me twice, much less go out with me, I asked her to marry me." Flynn stopped speaking, recalling that night as he had so many times since, remembering the sound of Neapolitan mandolins from the jukebox in Pisano's Pizza Parlor, reliving the pure joy he felt when Susan said yes.

Maggie waited quietly for him to continue, sensing that he was undergoing an intensely emotional experience as he recounted his story.

"We were married, I started my practice, we bought a house with a garden, hung a swing in the backyard in a very tall, old tree, and had a little girl who loved more than anything to have me push her in that swing. Every night she'd wait at the front door for me to come home, and before we even had dinner we had to 'fly up to the sky with the birds.' I'd do anything for my girls whether I wanted to or not, simply because they desired it and it gave them pleasure. It became a compulsion for me to do whatever they wanted, give them whatever they wanted, because I loved seeing them happy."

Flynn stopped again and was quiet so long Maggie hesitantly reached out to touch his hand resting between them on the gearshift. He jumped as if her touch had been red hot, and when he glanced at her, his eyes glistened with tears. He looked quickly away, and after another long pause, resumed his story.

"I started working late. I didn't have to, but I wanted to give my girls the world. I scheduled patients when I should have been home pushing Kaitlin on her swing, reading her stories, and telling Susan how much I loved her."

This time Flynn didn't stop soon enough, and Maggie heard the catch in his voice, the crack he couldn't disguise as a cough. She didn't reach out to him, didn't move, hardly dared breathe. She wanted to melt into the seat, be absorbed like water, and disappear. Why had she insisted that he tell his story? Why had she forced him to relive this memory that seemed to cause him so much pain? They must have driven twenty miles in silence before Flynn resumed his tale.

"One night I came home late. The house was dark. I started to put my key in the door but it swung open. It wasn't shut tight, much less locked. Susan never left the doors unlocked. I called out to her, but the house echoed with emptiness. She was gone. Kaitlin was gone. My guilty conscience told me they'd left me for being such a workaholic. I was desperate to explain, to make amends. I vowed to never work late again, to spend every possible minute with my two wonderful girls. They deserved so much better than I had given them." Flynn stopped, concentrated on passing a truck, then continued.

"I called Susan's mother, but she hadn't heard from Susan in a couple of days. I called Susan's best friend, her sister, everyone I could think of, but no one knew where she might have gone, and they were surprised to think she'd packed up and left me. That was when I checked the closets. I was in such a daze I hadn't thought of that. All their clothes were there, as far as I could tell. All the suitcases were in the garage."

Maggie glanced at Flynn and wasn't surprised to see tears streaming unchecked down his cheeks.

"Then I began to think instead of react. The movies. The grocery store. The park. There were a dozen places they could be, since they had no idea when I'd be home. I went into the kitchen looking for clues. Susan usually started dinner and left it simmering on the stove. The pork chops had defrosted in the sink and a box of rice sat on the cabinet, but the table hadn't been set. That was Kaitlin's job. Susan had thought about dinner, hadn't she? So they would be home soon. I flipped on the patio light and started to take out the garbage when I saw Mittens, Kaitlin's kitten, with the life crushed out of her on the cement."

Now Flynn became like a man on a runaway toboggan flying headlong down a steep hill, telling his story in a rush of words as fast as they could pour out.

"I called the police but got a lot of garbage about having to wait twenty-four hours before I could file a missing persons report unless I had some kind of proof they had been kidnapped. No, I hadn't found a note. No, there wasn't a message on the answering machine. I just had a dead kitten on my patio, but that wasn't enough. I begged, I pleaded for them to do something, to come and search the place, but they insisted their hands were tied until the waiting period was up. Too many wives left in a huff and then came back the next morning."

Flynn swiped at his cheeks with the back of his hand. "I got a call the next day. Fifty thousand dollars and I could have my family back. I agreed to do anything he wanted. I begged and borrowed until I got the fifty thousand, then when I delivered that, he wanted another fifty. This time I called the police—who brought in the FBI. I mortgaged the house and borrowed some more. I was complying with his demands. I did everything he asked because he controlled my life, my happiness, my family. He promised he wouldn't hurt them. I could have them back as soon as we worked out the details so he could leave them and get away. I agreed to everything as long as he'd give my family back to me. After the second fifty was delivered, he didn't call to tell me where to find Susan and Kaitlin. He disappeared, slipped through the trap. The FBI had no leads, no fingerprints, no motive, except the money. The trail was dead."

Flynn fished fruitlessly in his pocket, and Maggie handed him a tissue from a little pack she always carried in her purse. He didn't say thanks, just wiped his eyes and nose and continued.

"Four excruciating months went by with no word at all. I didn't sleep. I didn't eat. All I did was beg God to bring them back to me safe and sound, and walk through my days and nights like a zombie. Then the police called and said they'd been spotted in Florida. The authorities had surrounded the shack in the Everglades where they thought he was keeping them. But instead of helping her rescuers, Susan was shooting through a window." Flynn's voice went flat. "She was defending her kidnapper, shooting at her rescuers."

Flynn blew his nose. "A gunfight ensued. A sniper got the kidnapper, but Susan came out on the porch and shot an FBI agent. Someone shot her."

That was as far as Flynn could go. He pulled off the road into someone's darkened driveway, turned off the engine, and got out of the car. Maggie could see his shoulders heaving and left him alone as long as she could. Then she opened her door, quietly walked around to where he leaned against the fender, and touched his shoulder.

"I'm so sorry, Flynn. I'm sorry it happened, and I'm sorry I forced you to tell me what you didn't want to relive. Please forgive me for being so flippant. I had no idea . . ." And then she knew. Maggie gasped.

CHAPTER 22

"Stockholm Syndrome. That's why you study the syndrome. It happened to Susan."

Flynn nodded.

Maggie stood next to Flynn, not touching him, not speaking, just being there if he needed her. Finally, Maggie had to break the silence. "Do you want to tell me what happened to Kaitlin? You don't have to if you don't want to."

Flynn turned and leaned on the car, his head bowed. "When the shooting was over, they went inside and found her. Ballistic reports took so long coming, I no longer cared which gun had taken her from me. I buried my two beautiful women and the swing, moved out of that house and never went back to the neighborhood. I left my medical practice, went back to school to study psychology, buried myself in my studies and then in my new practice until I couldn't stand the hypocrisy anymore. Then I began trying to find the answers that kept me awake every night. Why did she defend him? Could she have forgotten me and fallen in love with a slob like that so quickly? Or was she so angry at me for not being there when she needed me that she turned to him to spite me? Those questions were burning my brain out, haunting me every hour of the day and night. I had to know what happened in her head."

"And are you satisfied that you know now?"

He nodded. "At least, I think I do, but I don't like it. I've got to find a way to prevent that from happening in future kidnappings. I'm interviewing every victim I can find, trying to discover what phenomenon made them go against every sensible, normal reaction. I have to discover what happened to them and why their experience might have been different from others' who didn't succumb to the syndrome."

They stood at the side of the highway, an occasional car flying by, briefly illuminating the night around them. At last Maggie spoke. "And you've never quit blaming yourself because you weren't home to prevent the man from taking your wife and child."

Flynn's silence was all the affirmation Maggie needed.

"I'm sure someone else has already told you this, but you might have been killed yourself if you'd been there."

"I wish I had." Flynn turned and looked up at the heavens almost as if he were pleading for a release from this life.

Maggie wanted to throw her arms around him and comfort him, tell him that life was worth living and that she knew how to help him. Instead, she stood quietly, hesitating, not knowing whether it would be out of place to say anything. Finally she said quietly, "I'm glad you weren't. I think you were sent to help me through this. I truly don't know what I would have done without you. So, very self-ishly, I'm glad nothing happened to you, but I'm terribly sorry that you've had to suffer so much."

A light mist dampened the air, and Maggie realized they would be wet soon if they stayed where they were. "Flynn, it's starting to rain. We need to get in the car. Would you like me to drive for awhile? I'm feeling fine now."

Flynn turned to Maggie, reached out and touched her face. "I'm glad you're feeling better." He studied her thoughtfully for a moment, tried to plumb the depths of her sapphire eyes and reach all the way to her heart to know what secrets it held at the moment, then he took her arm and walked her around to the passenger door and opened it. "I'm afraid your guardian angels might be sleeping, so I'll drive awhile longer." When she tried to object, he smiled and assured her he was okay.

They pulled back onto the road and resumed their journey south, neither of them breaking the silence for several miles. Maggie wanted to assure him again it wasn't his fault, but she knew nothing she could ever say would change his mind until he had experienced a true healing. That healing could only come from one source, and she didn't feel this was the time to tell him about it. But she would. She promised herself that she would give him that gift.

Flynn turned on a CD and the strains of Vivaldi's *Four Seasons* filled the car. "Oh, I love that. It's one of my very favorite compositions in the whole world," Maggie said. She listened for a minute. "I don't recognize the artist."

"She's a new violinist I just discovered." He looked sheepishly at Maggie. "But for the life of me, I can't remember her name right now."

"It doesn't matter. I'll just enjoy it and find out later who gave me such pleasure."

"What else do you like to hear, Maggie? What do you listen to when you're all alone?"

"I love Bizet's *Carmen*, most everything Tchaikovsky wrote, and I adore all of Sigmund Romberg's operettas. I've cried copious tears through each of them, either because they were so beautifully sad or because they were so funny I laughed myself to tears. But my tastes are eclectic and it would take hours to name my favorites. And you?"

"Almost everything with a classical guitar, cello, or French horn, or any combination of the three, and Wynton Marsalis doing anything classical. I'm not much on jazz or blues, but I do like an occasional bluegrass sound. The noise of hard rock turns me off completely."

"Me too. How about opera?" Maggie asked.

"Hmm, I'm ambivalent. Some are great. Some are not. And a lot depends on who's singing. I do enjoy listening to a great tenor. Since you're a writer, I assume you like to read. What do you read?"

"I love history and mysteries. I enjoy biographies because I want to know what made people do what they did. I guess that's what got me excited about Lewis and Clark. I read Stephen Ambrose's *Undaunted Courage,* which set my imagination on fire and gave me a passion for the Voyage of Discovery. How about you? What do you read—for relaxation?" Maggie quickly added.

Flynn thought for a minute. "Nothing. I guess I never read for relaxation. I scan headlines in the newspaper, but that's about it. I can't remember when I last picked up a book that wasn't related to my field of study."

"When was the last time you took a vacation?"

Flynn didn't answer.

"What do you do for fun? For relaxation?"

No answer.

Maggie hesitated before asking the question that burned her tongue, until she finally had to spit it out. "What do you do to feel alive, Flynn?"

There was a long pause and Maggie thought he was going to ignore that question, too. Then finally he said softly, "Who says I do?"

Maggie was puzzled. "Do what? Feel alive?"

"Isn't that what you asked me?"

"Flynn, how long ago did . . . did it happen?"

He thought for a minute. "Six years, ten months, two weeks, and three days."

That stunned Maggie, not only that he could recite the time down to the day so quickly, but that he still clung so tenaciously to the painful memories and apparently made no attempt at a new life.

"Do you realize you're a study in contradictions? Why are these last two minutes of conversation—and silence—forming a mental picture of a workaholic stick-in-the-mud when you don't seem to me to be that way at all? That label would never occur to me from observing you since we met. What little I've learned of you in our conversations and interaction—and I admit it is scanty—has left the impression of a vital, caring, decisive individual who is deeply involved with life and passionate about his work."

Flynn shook his head. "I don't know where you came up with that personality sketch, but it certainly isn't me."

Maggie leaned on the armrest. "Know thyself."

"What do you mean?"

"That proverb, inscribed on the temple of Apollo at Delphi, was ascribed to the Seven Wise Men. It means we should search inside, and know ourselves. Correct me if I'm wrong, but the picture you're painting of yourself is a hollow shell without any feeling, a being merely existing on this sphere, independent of anyone, beating himself daily for his failures, with one aspiration only and that is to learn how to combat Stockholm Syndrome. That will be your sole contribution to mankind."

"You paint a pretty bleak picture, but yes, that's probably how I see myself."

"Now compare that to how I just described you. Which picture do you think portrays the true Flynn Ford?"

"Mine, of course. You don't know me. You know even less *about* me. Your impression comes from . . ." Flynn bit back the words. That would be too cruel and he couldn't hurt Maggie like that. Then it hit him what he was going to say and he turned to stare at Maggie.

She felt his comment coming and met his surprised gaze. "From what, Flynn? From a starry-eyed girl who has a crush on her good-looking doctor?" Maggie's face blazed with embarrassment, but she plowed on through. "First of all, I'm not that young, and I certainly don't see myself as starry-eyed." Then she could take it no further.

"And the rest?"

"A crush sounds so juvenile, so high schoolish, and I'm far beyond that." Then she realized what she had said. "I mean, I'm far beyond high school in years," she stammered. "I graduated from high school six years ago."

"You're not answering the question."

"Let me get back to you on that later," Maggie said turning away so Flynn couldn't see her face in the lights from a passing car. She waited for Flynn to say something, but he didn't press the issue, for which she was grateful. "Can I ask another question?"

"This sounds vaguely familiar. Are you getting a sense of déjà vu here?"

Maggie laughed. "That did trigger a memory or two. Seriously, if you never relax, what do you do with your time? You can't work *all* the time."

Flynn glanced at Maggie. "Why not?"

Maggie thought he was teasing her until she looked at him. There was no humor in his voice or eyes. "You're serious, aren't you?"

"Of course."

"Do you ever go water skiing or snow skiing, or to the movies, or out to dinner with friends?"

"Not for years."

"Bowling, ball games?"

"Nope."

"What do you do?"

"I get up in the morning, shower, work on research and writing or interviewing if I'm fortunate enough to do that, quit about midnight, then do it all over again."

"You have no interaction with people other than the occasional interview?"

"Sure," he said. "I battle with my agent about changes in my contract with my publisher. I call my mother every Sunday. I remember to send my nieces and nephews a ten-dollar bill for their birthdays, and at Christmas I go online and buy them presents so I won't have to fight the crowds in the stores."

"Flynn, that's not good. It's not normal to closet yourself away from life. No wonder you haven't let go of your tragedy. You keep it right in front of you every minute, like a prized possession." Suddenly Maggie realized she had gone too far. "Oh, Flynn, I'm sorry. I had no right to say that. I'm certainly no psychologist. I can't even imagine the pain it must cause you every time you think of it. Please forgive me."

Flynn didn't have to look at her to recognize the regret in her voice. "Forgiven. I think it must be time for a break. I'll stop up here and gas up, and we can get out and stretch, maybe get a drink or bite to eat if you want." He glanced at his watch. "Still at least three hours to our destination, and since we'll arrive in the middle of the night, I guess we're in no hurry, are we?"

"Guess not." Totally repentant, Maggie sat very subdued, hardly daring to speak for fear she'd blurt out some other stupid comment. If she hadn't felt so comfortable with Flynn, this wouldn't have happened, but she felt like she could tell him anything; she could open her heart and pour out the very secrets of her soul and they'd be safe with him. In the same vein, she hadn't felt a need to be guarded in her comments to him about his situation, feeling she could express her opinions honestly, but she should have been more circumspect about how she said it.

The more she thought about it, the worse she felt. It sounded so all-knowing, so judgmental. Who was she to tell him anything? A girl from the sticks who had no more experience in real-life tragedies than a newborn foal.

Flynn pulled into a huge truck stop ablaze with all the normal lights, plus strings and strings of Christmas lights and decorations. Trucks and cars were coming and going like rush hour at a major intersection in a busy city, although they seemed to be in the middle of nowhere. Maggie couldn't remember passing through towns for miles.

While Flynn filled the car with gas, Maggie wandered through the truck stop hung with festive Christmas tinsel and found the rest room, and when she was through, waited where Flynn would be sure to see her when he came in. She examined the CDs on the rack while she waited, found a Wynton Marsalis, and bought it for him. That was the least she could do, although it was a very small Christmas present for someone she'd taken away from his work and hundreds of miles out of his way.

Still, Maggie was puzzled when she thought about the life he told her he led, as opposed to the kind of person she had perceived him to be. *Never the twain shall meet,* she thought. He was personable, kind, thoughtful, caring, and fun with a unique, teasing sense of humor. Those weren't attributes she would have ascribed to a workaholic stick-in-the-mud.

Flynn came up quietly behind her and spoke right in her ear. "Hungry?" Startled, she jumped and whirled around. His roguish smile revealed his obvious amusement at surprising her. A flush of pleasure raced through Maggie. No matter what he thought about himself, this guy wasn't the stick-in-the-mud type.

"You can have your choice of Pizza Hut, Colonel Sanders' Kentucky Fried Chicken or Dairy Queen. Or if you'd rather, we can stock up on munchies and drinks to take with us in the car. It's been several hours since your bowl of soup."

"Actually, you're such fascinating company, I haven't even thought about food. How about you?" Maggie asked. "Are you hungry?"

"Like you, I haven't given it any thought till this minute." He smiled and added, "That must say something about *your* company." Flynn led her to the food counter and they looked at the menu.

Maggie breathed a sigh of relief. He really had forgiven her for her thoughtless, tasteless comment. "The pizza smells good," she said. "I think I'll have a pepperoni. How about you?"

"Decisions, decisions. Do I want a supreme or some fried chicken? Guess I'll go with the pizza tonight. Tomorrow we can have Cajun chicken, which can't be beat." Flynn placed their order and Maggie pulled her wallet from her purse to pay for their meal.

"Put it away, Maggie girl. I've got it."

Maggie objected. "No way. You paid for dinner, you bought the gas, you're driving your car, so this is my treat."

"Save your money. You don't have a job anymore, remember? You'll need every penny to get home on after we finish solving the mystery of your life."

"The mystery of my life. That sounds so dramatic." She looked up at Flynn. "I've lived such a normal, quiet, uneventful life for twenty-four years that those two words, dramatic and mystery, simply would never have been used in the same sentence with Mary Margaret McKenzie. Now I feel my life is turning upside down and will never be the same again."

They settled into a booth and waited for their pizza. "Maggie, there could be another explanation for your connection to Alyssa Lawson, or Katie Wiggins, or whoever she is. Some scientists have been studying a phenomenon called mind travel. It's not a new thing; it's been around since the Cold War. Even the CIA experimented with it for awhile, but the premise is that there are people with special psychic powers who can propel their minds into that of someone else. Maybe Alyssa did that with you. That could be the sole connection, and your family could be just as you've always thought it was—as it's always appeared—and the resemblance is just coincidence."

"I've never heard of mind travel before, except in science fiction. I wouldn't have believed you except for what I've experienced these last few days. I'll cling to that hope, Flynn, that it was just a stranger popping into my mind. I don't want my life disrupted. I don't want to think my parents have done something that they've had to keep secret all these years. What a burden that would have been for them."

"You wouldn't want changes, even if you acquired a twin sister out of the deal?" Flynn watched Maggie's thought process play across her face. Speculation. Exploration. Discovery. Decision.

She shook her head. "I wouldn't want my parents to have suffered through whatever situation happened in order to suddenly acquire a sister. And to have the secret revealed after all these years, whatever the secret would be, there would have been very unhappy circumstances connected with it, and I don't want my folks to live through that again. Does that make sense?"

"Maggie of the tender heart." Flynn wanted to reach across the table and touch her hand, to connect with this delightful, tenderhearted, innocent soul, to feel her goodness flow into his empty heart and fill it. Instead he examined the salt shaker and said, "That's an admirable quality, Maggie girl. The world would be a better place if there were more people like you, instead of so many like me."

Their number was called, and he jumped to get their food, relieved to escape from the guilt their conversation elicited.

Their remarks remained general and comfortable while they ate, and they stayed longer than necessary, enjoying the respite from heavier topics. Finally they refilled their drinks and headed for the car. It was raining now, not just misting, and they had to run to keep from getting soaked. They fell into the car laughing at having dodged small puddles only to splash through even bigger ones they hadn't seen. Maggie shook her long hair and flung drops of water all over them and the windows.

"Stop," Flynn cried. "You're as bad as a big, shaggy dog."

At that outcry, Maggie shook her head even more, just to spite him. Then she shivered. "Brrr. Turn the heat up so I can dry out. I can't believe we're going from winter wind and snow to just rain and I'm still freezing."

"Get out of your wet coat. The car will be toasty warm in a minute." Flynn reached over to help Maggie shrug out of her coat and as his fingers brushed against her soft, warm neck, he let them linger longer than he should have. While she settled back into her seat, Flynn quickly started the car and concentrated on exiting the busy parking lot to the highway. That mustn't happen again. He was her doctor; she was his patient. Nothing must change that status until this situation had been resolved and Maggie no longer needed his help. And that reminded him of something he hadn't done yet.

"Not to alarm you, but I think we're both aware that Katie will try to come back, and it may get to the point where we actually need her assistance to find her. If we can't locate your letter writer, there may be no other alternative than to enlist Katie's help to find the garden. Do you feel you'll be able to control that situation, or are you afraid of her strength?"

Maggie's fingers froze on the seat belt she was trying to buckle. She thought about the frightening question as she heard the metallic click and wished that life was as simple as that little mechanism that frequently made the difference between life and death. What if Katie was stronger than she was? What if Katie's thought transference, or whatever scientific name they wanted to give it, dominated her thoughts and caused her to do something she didn't want to do? She wished there was a seat belt-like feature in this situation. But would Katie need it to be restrained, or would Maggie need it to be protected?

CHAPTER 23

"Maggie?"

She emerged from her musings to see Flynn watching her with worry and concern written all over his face.

"To answer your question, if that was your last question, I guess I'm afraid."

Flynn passed a slow-moving truck, then glanced at Maggie. "Talk about your fears so I can help walk you through them. If you bring them out of their dark closet and shine light on them, they usually fade away to nothing very quickly. If you hide them away, they grow so large they can dominate you. What do you fear the most?"

Maggie didn't even have to stop and think about it. "That Katie will take over and I'll disappear and never be able to come back."

"Do you think that could happen?"

"You tell me. Could it? Has it ever happened before? Could it happen to me?"

"Only if you let it."

"But how do I prevent it? How do I control her when she seems to just come and fill my mind?"

"Think back on your life, Maggie. How have you taken charge of a situation when someone else wanted to have power over it?"

Maggie thought about it. "I'm drawing a blank, Flynn. I can't think of anything."

"Let's get deeper than that. You said you believe that Satan tempts you to disobey the commandments of God. What do you do when you feel tempted to do something you know you shouldn't? How do you handle Satan's attempt to turn you from the right?"

"I have to consciously recognize the temptation, that Satan is real and he's trying to make me do something wrong. I examine the situation, evaluate it for what it really is, and do whatever it takes to get out of there. Then I put him out of my mind. I sing, I read scriptures, I pray, I get with people who are strong and believe like I do that can support me, even if I don't tell them what they are doing for me. I tell him to go away, like the Savior did when He said, 'Get thee behind me, Satan.'"

"You have the keys right there, Maggie. That's exactly how you control Katie, just like you control your mind when you feel temptation. You recognize that she's coming. Then you pray for strength to control her, you conduct whatever business has to be conducted, and then you tell her to go away. You can have command of the situation from start to finish. You can banish her from your mind however it best works for you by singing, praying, or just reaching out and grabbing my hand. I'll be your support group, and I'll hang on as long as necessary."

"You make it sound so easy, Flynn." But Maggie's voice was filled with doubt. Flynn knew she wasn't ready yet. But how did he take her from this point in her doubt and help her gain the confidence she needed?

"Maggie, you seem to have a great deal of trust in your God. Do you think He would want Katie to take over your mind?"

"Of course not." Then Maggie had another thought. "But I'm not sure He'd interfere if I began fooling around with some kind of black art—not that I think *this* is black art," she hurried to add. "But if I invited her to come into my mind, now that I know how frightening it can be, then am I'm sort of giving up my agency?" She thought for a minute. "If I asked for His help to dispel her, I know I could have all the help I needed. But what if I couldn't ask for help? I guess that's what I fear most. What if she catches me off guard and I can't ask for help?"

"If you knew that I was here, holding your hand and praying for you, would that give you the confidence you need? Knowing that I would not let go no matter what and would not stop asking for help in your behalf?" Even as the words escaped his lips, Flynn couldn't imagine he had actually said them. Maggie believed in this loving, protecting God. He didn't. God hadn't been there for him, hadn't heard his frantic pleadings, hadn't answered his prayers for his wife and child. The heavens had remained tightly closed to him.

Then again, a small crack must have appeared up there a few hours ago when Maggie's God did hear his pleadings and answered his prayers for her. She must be pretty special if his prayers had been heard at all, much less answered.

Maggie smiled at him and leaned her head back on the seat. "Yes, I know you'd never let me slip away. That would get me through it."

Oh, the innocence of youth, Flynn thought. The trust of the young, untarnished by the experiences and tragedies of the world. Would that he could feel that again, instead of the heavy, ugly burden with which life had shackled him. It wasn't pleasant, this comparison of Maggie's innocent beauty and purity with his troubled and tormented life. He changed the subject.

"What are your plans when we finish this little adventure? Are you going home right away?"

"Of course. It's Christmas. Our family always gets together for the holidays, unless someone for some unavoidable reason can't make it. Then we still get to talk to them on the phone so it's almost like the whole family's together. My folks couldn't believe I wouldn't be home this year, but even if I hadn't gotten this assignment, I'm sure my new boss wouldn't have given me time off to go home, so this would be my first Christmas away from home whether I spent it in California or on the road." Then Maggie sat up. "What's today? I don't even know when Christmas is. This could be Christmas Eve for all I know."

Flynn checked the date window on his watch. "The twenty-second. If we can resolve this in the next twenty-four hours, you'll still have time to make it home if you can catch a flight."

Maggie frowned. "Not much chance of that. I think I'd rather spend my Christmas in a nice warm hotel room somewhere than stranded in a cold airport with a lot of people frantically scrambling to get on too-full flights. I've had my share of curling up in the corner waiting to be called for a standby seat that never materialized. Besides, I could never afford what they charge for a last-minute ticket, and I have to go back to Pine Bluff and get my car." Then she looked at Flynn. "What are you doing for Christmas, now that I've taken you away from your everyday world?"

"To tell the truth, I haven't given it a thought. My folks usually plead with me to come home for Christmas, but the memories are too sharp yet, so I beg off with lame excuses of nonexistent deadlines or fictional commitments."

"We may be two lost souls wandering loose with nowhere to go." Maggie glanced at Flynn. Would he even consider spending Christmas with her? Her heart beat faster just thinking about the possibility of enjoying his company instead of being alone, far from her family on that special night. Christmas Day she could live through. But spending Christmas Eve alone? That would be unimaginably difficult.

Flynn's mind raced along the same lines of thought. How many years had it been since he'd had a real Christmas? What would it be like to spend Christmas Eve with Maggie? Then ashamed, he closed his mind to those warm thoughts. Not until this was over could he even contemplate such things.

"We'll see what happens," he said, not wanting to dampen the hint of hope he'd heard in Maggie's voice. "Who knows; we may be spending the night at the police station filing charges against Cleat Wiggins for kidnapping."

"That would be a nice Christmas present for Katie. Oh, Flynn, if we do find her, we can give Lionel Lawson the best Christmas present he's probably ever had in his life."

"And you may get your job back. Would you like that?"

Maggie laughed. "I hadn't even thought of that yet. Yes, I just might get my job back at that. Then it would be a happily-ever-after ending for everyone, wouldn't it?" She suddenly remembered Flynn's circumstances and glanced up at him. Why did she continually say these inane things that were so hurtful to him? It was as though she wielded a knife that she plunged into his heart at least once an hour with her thoughtless remarks.

"I'm sorry, Flynn. I can't seem to control my mouth. Please forgive my insensitive rambling." She saw Flynn's jaw tighten. Then he managed a thin smile.

"Maggie, you can't imagine how thick-skinned I've become. I can't let my tragedies spoil everyone else's happiness. I think it would be wonderful if you got your job back and everyone had the best

Christmas ever." And just in case she didn't believe those fabrications, he knew how to distract her so she wouldn't have time to think about it. "Tell me about your family's Christmas. Do you have traditions that you celebrate year after year?"

"Oh, yes. We have the most fun. We decorate the house right after Thanksgiving. The boys hang lights all over outside—on the house and the trees and the ranch gate. Mom and I put the tree up in the family room and decorate inside the house. Every square inch of it. We start baking cookies and fruitcakes and goodies and fill the freezer. Then each year we find out which families in our little community are in need, choose a couple, depending on how many are in their families, and we do the twelve days of Christmas for them."

"Twelve days of Christmas?" Flynn said. "I guess I'm not up on those things. Explain."

"Each night of the twelve days before Christmas, we leave a present for the family on the front doorstep, ring the doorbell, and run so they don't know who left it. Then on Christmas Eve they get something special."

Flynn nodded in understanding.

"We go Christmas caroling. It's lots more fun now that my brothers have children. And Dad hooks up the horses or a tractor to an old hay wagon and we have a hay ride. That usually includes a couple of other families' wagons and the whole Church, then we go back to the cultural hall and have hot cider and donuts and sometimes a Christmas program or just a sing-along of Christmas carols."

"Sounds like a Norman Rockwell Christmas," Flynn commented. "I didn't know people actually did those things anymore."

"They probably don't most places, but you have to understand, I was born and raised in a tiny Mormon community on the Utah-Idaho border, and people have stayed pretty close to their roots there. Things change very slowly, which is not a bad thing when you think about it. Everybody is still his brother's keeper, and that's a nice feeling."

Flynn marveled there were still such innocent-sounding places left in the world. "And I suppose you know all your neighbors, and everyone gets along, and there is no crime or lawsuits or all the bad stuff that happens everywhere else."

Maggie laughed. "So far about the worst crime that's happened is when somebody steals somebody else's water on watering day. That can be high crime on a ranch that depends on irrigation water. But basically we have a pretty peaceful community, probably because there are so few of us. I guess the biggest scandal we've had—that I can remember—was when the waitress at the truck stop on I-15 got pregnant and nobody knew who the father was. Turned out she'd eloped with her high school sweetheart, but they were trying to keep their marriage a secret until they had enough money to move out of their parents' homes and get one of their own. Of course, I've been away at school for the last few years, but I don't think things have changed that much."

"Oh, Maggie, what an idyllic world you live in." Flynn couldn't keep the wistfulness from his voice. Why couldn't he have found a place like that? Maybe Susan and Kaitlin would still be alive. He shook off the melancholy and blocked his mind from what might have been and never could be.

"What else do you do that's special on Christmas?" Much as it hurt remembering that he'd been cheated out of these simple pleasures and would never have them again, he wanted to know what Maggie did that caused such delighted laughter to bubble from inside her.

"Every Christmas Eve after we deliver our twelve days of Christmas presents, we have a special dinner with all our favorite foods, then as soon as dishes are done, Dad reads the story of the Savior's birth from the Bible. When we were little we used to get all dressed up in bathrobes and Mom's fabrics and act out the Nativity. Now my nieces and nephews do it. Then we choose one present from under the tree to open. Choosing just the perfect one is a process we've spent days on. We feel each one, shake it, smell it, and finally the hour comes when we get to see if we made the right decision. Mom tries to fool us so that we'll open the new pajamas she always gives us, but we like to open Gramma's because it's usually something we really want."

Flynn could feel the excitement of Maggie's Christmas just from the exuberance of her narrative. What would it have been like to have been raised in an atmosphere like that? "And then what?" This was like a story he didn't want to end.

"Then we all go to bed so Santa Claus can come. Rick and his family and Taylor and his family live close, so they take their kids and go home. But Jeff comes with his family from Colorado, and Alan and Veronica fly in from Long Island, so they stay with us and it's a madhouse. Fun, frantic chaos." Maggie stopped.

Flynn looked at her, suddenly quiet. "Yes?" he said.

"Steve just got home from the military, and this was going to be the first Christmas we'd all be together for two years. Actually three years. Jeff was involved in a big manhunt in Colorado the year before that and couldn't get away. He's in the FBI," Maggie explained in answer to Flynn's raised eyebrow.

"And now you're going to be the one who spoils the family Christmas."

Maggie nodded.

"Well, miracles have been known to happen. Maybe you'll get one this year." Flynn hoped that platitude sounded more sincere to Maggie than it did to him. He was not a believer in miracles, magic, or almost any good thing happening that he didn't cause himself. He couldn't remember the last time in the last seven years there had been something good in his life. Before Maggie.

"What do you do on Christmas Day?" Flynn hadn't asked her that just to pull her out of the little funk she appeared to have slipped into when she thought of spoiling her family's Christmas. He truly wanted to know what made Maggie what she was. What influence had formed this unexpectedly bewitching creature, who seemed to have no guile, no agenda, no bad habits, and unbelievably high standards? He'd never encountered anyone like her before.

Maggie leaned forward, her eyes gleaming. "Nobody really sleeps that night. We're forbidden to go downstairs until Dad gives the signal, but that doesn't stop us from peeking over the balcony to see what's going on. Then we congregate in someone's bedroom and just talk. I usually got the brunt of the teasing, unless one of the boys had a new girlfriend. But that was the time, after everyone got a little tired and more serious, that we talked about what we wanted to do when we grew up. Now that the boys are married, except for Steve, we have to keep the noise down a little so the babies can sleep. But the older nieces and nephews are invited into the magic circle if they want to come."

Flynn shook his head. "I can't imagine five boys having anything in common with their younger sister. That's so far from my realm of reality it sounds like a fairy tale. My older brother used me as a punching bag until I got old enough to take him on and stop him. My sister and I had a troubled truce—I wouldn't tell on her if she wouldn't tell on me. It wasn't until we had kids that we had much in common. I'm not especially close with any of my siblings. I can only envy you, Maggie, but I can't relate to how you feel. It's just too foreign a concept to me of that kind of sibling love and companionship."

"I'm sorry, Flynn. I shouldn't babble on like I do. I keep thinking that everyone has a family like mine, because we're not unusual in my town. Most every other family's similar."

"Are they really, Maggie, or do you just think they are? Everybody puts on a Sunday face so you don't see the heartache and problems they undergo during the week. I think your family must be very unusual. In the hundreds of hours of counseling I've done, I have yet to hear of anyone else who even came close to what you've had. Most of my patients experienced some kind of abuse, either verbal, physical, mental, or sexual. They came from dysfunctional families that could have used even a little of the love you apparently have in yours. It sounds like you've had a very protected childhood, shielded from the evil of the world. Oh, that more of today's children could be raised that way."

Maggie was quiet, too quiet, and Flynn looked at her just as she reached out toward him. He grasped her hand, and she clung to it.

CHAPTER 24

Flynn looked for a place where he could pull off the road. He didn't know what might transpire in the next few minutes, but he didn't want to be distracted by driving when he needed to be concentrating on helping Maggie. He spotted a white steeple in the headlights and pulled into the darkened church parking lot.

"Maggie, what's happening?" He waited, gripping her hand, and heard himself uttering a prayer for her. He found it hard to believe that prayer came so easily where Maggie was concerned when he hadn't been able to pray for himself for years.

"We're coming, Katie," Maggie said. "Just hold on." Then she was silent. "We're on our way. Tell me where you are." More silence. "How can I find you? Katie, stop. Listen to me. Tell me where to find you. What town are you in? Where is the garden?" Silence again, for what seemed a long time. Then, "Stop, Katie. I'm sending you back if you don't stop."

Maggie's grip on his hand tightened until her fingernails were slicing into his flesh, but he held on, and prayed.

"Go back, Katie." Maggie's arm stiffened and Flynn could see her go rigid in her seat. Then she relaxed, becoming almost limp.

"Maggie, what happened?" Without releasing her hand, he reached across the seat with his other hand and tenderly touched her chin, turning her face to his. "Maggie?"

She opened her eyes, and offered a weak a smile. "You were right, Flynn," Maggie breathed softly. "I am stronger than she is. I can send her out of my mind. Thank you for hanging on to me."

Each was aware of their still-clasped hands, but neither let go.

"What did she want?"

"She said we have to come right now. Cleat's coming back and he's going to kill her like he killed all the others. She's no good to him anymore, so he's going to leave her behind, after he makes sure she can't tell anyone where to find him."

"You told Katie to stop. Stop what?"

"She was flooding my mind with images and her terrified thoughts and I was experiencing her fear, her terror. She's so afraid he's going to kill her, she wanted to make sure I knew how she felt and was coming to help. Flynn, if you hadn't been here, I'm not sure what would have happened. I don't even want to know what might have happened. Thank you. That's not sufficient, but I don't know how else to thank you."

"First of all, I didn't do anything. You did. You and prayer." Flynn brought her hand to his lips and kissed it gently. He wasn't even sorry when he realized what he'd done. It had seemed a benediction to the blessing she'd been given from her God.

Maggie reached up and touched Flynn's face, which was very close to hers. "Thank you." She wondered if there had been any meaning besides relief in Flynn's gesture.

How long they sat there basking in the warm sensations that pulsed through them, neither could have said. Suddenly the CD changed and "Jingle Bells" blared through the car, shattering the mood, sending them flying apart.

Flynn hit the Skip button, extinguishing "Jingle Bells" as quickly as it had appeared and pulled silently back onto the highway. Neither of them spoke. Flynn wondered if Maggie realized the depth of his feelings. Then *he* wondered at the depth of his feelings. He couldn't really be accused of stealing from the cradle, because she wasn't that much younger, but he felt eons older than Maggie. In life's experience, she was an innocent babe and he was a wizened, disillusioned old man.

"How do you feel?" Flynn asked, knowing how weak the other encounters had left Maggie.

"Surprisingly good. I think I could even get out and walk if I had to." She leaned forward. "I wonder if it was the fact that I felt so totally helpless when Katie came into my mind that I felt so weak after. I was expending so much energy, but in the wrong way, that it left me exhausted." Then, as if she'd just had an epiphany, Maggie exclaimed, "I think she was actually using my energy against me. Well, maybe not against me, but using my own energy to replenish hers so she could maintain contact."

Flynn nodded. "Good possibility. There have just been so few studies done on this, and each case seems to be so different. There aren't any ground rules yet. We have no foundation to build on to educate people on what to expect when something like this happens. And I'm afraid we only hear about a small fraction of the cases. People don't want anyone to know what's happening to them because they think they're losing their mind. If only they understood there is so much about the mind that we don't understand yet, so much about energy, and psyche, and mind travel, and ESP that we're just beginning to discover. If more would come forward with their experiences, think how much faster our knowledge of this field would increase."

"Then it's your job to get the word out. You can't just publish in medical journals and professional magazines; you've got to reach the mainstream public. They don't read the journals. They don't have any way of finding out about these things. Flynn, you've got to tell them. Think of how many people you might be able to help if they only knew this happened to other people and these studies were going on."

He turned up the dash lights so he could better capture the fire in Maggie's eyes that he knew must be there from the fervor in her voice. "Do you get this passionately enthusiastic about everything you encounter?"

Embarrassed, Maggie leaned back in her seat again. "To my mother's dismay, yes, almost every new exciting or interesting thing I discover." She turned to Flynn, her voice rising with enthusiasm again. "Life is just so filled with wonders that there doesn't seem nearly enough time to investigate everything as fully as it deserves. There are so many places I want to go to unearth the stories that are buried in everyday people's lives. Everybody has a story, and most are fascinating to other people who are simply in different circumstances. We could have talked to any number of people in that truck stop and found the most unusual and wonderful stories you could imagine. I passed town after town that called to me to stop and learn about them and the people who settled and inhabit them. I want to learn it all, Flynn. I want to experience it all."

"No, Maggie, you don't. Don't ever again say anything so foolish and don't think that experiencing every emotion in life is going to make you happy, or a better writer, or a better person. All it will do is give you more opportunity for heartache. Granted, you'll have good experiences too, simply because that's your nature. But I promise you, my impetuous friend, you don't want to experience it all." Flynn glanced at Maggie. That should have certainly thrown cold water on her enthusiasm, but what would it do to her spirit? He never wanted to change that quixotic spirit and hoped no one else would try to rein in her ardor in her quest for all she sought to know and do. She just needed someone to guide that enthusiasm and effervescent energy in the right direction. He stifled the question that flashed through his mind: *Do you think you're the one to do it?*

"You're right, Flynn. When you get technical about it—or clinical—I really don't want to experience everything. I don't ever want to undergo what you've had to live with. What I meant was I don't want to live in a bubble looking in on other people's lives and only feel things vicariously as I write about them. I want to stand on the top of a mountain feeling the exhilaration that comes from the climb to the top. I want to sit by the river and marvel at where it's been and where it's going, and all the lives it's impacted. I want to love someone as much as you love Susan and feel the heartbeat of my unborn child inside me and know that I'm being a cocreator with God in a wondrous miracle. Those are the kinds of things I want to experience."

Flynn opened his mouth to respond, but as they rounded a corner and headed down a hill, taillights flashed red in front of them. A truck skidded on the rain-slick road, and as they watched in horror, it careened out of control and hit a bridge. Even from a distance they could hear the brakes screech, the sickening thud as metal collided with concrete. Helplessly they saw it roll over and over, down into a ravine. Then there was an ominous silence.

Maggie's hand flew to her mouth to stifle the horrified scream that never came. Her throat closed and no sound came out. Flynn sped down the hill and pulled off to the side where the truck had disappeared, told Maggie to stay in the car, and jumped out. But Maggie shrugged into her coat, snatched the keys from the ignition, locked the car, and slipped and slid down the muddy incline after

Flynn. She could see him outlined in the truck lights, jumping, sliding, tumbling down the hill ahead of her. The truck cab hung over the edge of a precipice, its lights shining into the darkness beyond.

When she reached the truck, she found it perched precariously on the edge of a deep ravine, kept from sliding off only by a jagged rock that didn't seem big enough to hold back the weight of the huge semi. Flynn was trying to climb onto the trailer and swing over to open the crushed door of the cab that dangled out into space.

The window was smashed, and jagged glass shards poked up like sword points. He couldn't climb through the window. He couldn't get the door open because the handle had been sheared off in the roll, and as he struggled to reach inside, the truck began slipping, scraping against the rock with an ominous screeching far worse than fingernails on a blackboard.

Numb with horror, Maggie watched the tableau, knowing if she tried to help, her weight might be enough to send the truck plummeting over the edge. Then Flynn reached the handle on the inside and the door swung open. A little bundle of fur leaped into his arms, nearly knocking him off his precarious perch.

"Flynn, throw it to me," Maggie yelled, and got as close to the edge of the crevasse as she dared. Flynn grabbed the ball of fur by the scruff of the neck and tossed it. Maggie fell backwards over a rock trying to catch it and landed in a small bush, but the little animal was safe.

"The driver's breathing, but badly hurt. I don't know if I can get him out," Flynn called. "I can feel the truck shifting every time I move." As he busied himself with the driver, Maggie cuddled the frightened little animal, trying to calm it while she looked for something she could get for Flynn to help get the driver out.

A ladder that had apparently been attached to the truck lay twisted under one wheel, but she couldn't budge it. She put the pup down, for it must be a dog, she thought. It wasn't a cat. One of the truck's back doors gaped open, but it was too dark to see into the interior. Oh, for a flashlight. She felt around on the inside and her hand touched a coil of braided material. She grabbed it, tugged it from under something heavy, and dragged it through the wet grass to the edge of the precipice.

"Flynn, I've found one of those strips moving companies use to tie things down. Can you use that to get the driver from the cab?"

"We won't need it, Maggie. He's gone."

Maggie could hear sirens in the distance. Another driver must have called for help. The little bundle of fur shivered and whined where she'd left it, and she picked it up again and cuddled it against her to get it warm. Flynn climbed carefully from the cab and jumped across the gap to where Maggie stood.

"The driver was pretty torn up. He may have severed an artery or vein. There was so much blood everywhere I couldn't tell where it was coming from to stop it. He said to take care of *Kit*. I suppose that must be the pup."

Heavy sadness overcame Maggie. What family might he have who'd miss him? Were they waiting even now for him to come home for Christmas?

A police car, an ambulance, and a fire truck all arrived about that time from different directions. Maggie and Flynn waited for them down at the cliff's edge rather than climb back up and have to return to the truck, if requested to do so.

When everyone arrived at the bottom of the ravine, Flynn explained what had happened, corroborated by the driver who'd called for help. Maggie offered the animal to one of the policemen, but he said she ought to just keep it if the driver had told them to take care of it. Though she offered it to everyone involved, no one else wanted the responsibility, so when they were finished, Maggie and Flynn climbed back up the slippery, muddy hill and got in the car, joined by a third member of their party who seemed happy to be safe and warm.

Flynn turned on the overhead light. "Let's look at you, Kit, and see what kind of dog you are." Maggie held up the ball of fur that was content to stay cuddled in her arms. "Hmm, what do you think?" he asked. "Sort of looks like a husky to me."

Maggie looked him over. "His tail isn't curled like a husky, but he could be a mixed breed. It's hard to tell, he's so little. He can't be more than a few weeks old. I wonder where the driver got him. He shouldn't be away from his mother yet, unless the mother was in the truck, too."

"I don't think there was another dog in the cab. If there was, it didn't survive." Flynn turned off the light and started the car. "So it looks like you're the new owner of a bundle of fur that's going to need bottle feeding for several days."

Maggie settled back in the seat with Kit curled in her lap. Then she had a disconcerting thought. "What if the driver was on his way home with this puppy for his kids? They should have it to remember their father by—his last gift to them."

"Do you want me to give your name and address to the police so you can deliver the pup to his family?"

Maggie pulled out her notebook, scribbled her cell phone number on it, and held up the sheet. "I'll take it to them if you'll hold Kit."

Flynn laughed. "I'll do it, Maggie. He looks too comfortable to disturb. I'm sure animals suffer trauma just as humans do, and that must have been pretty traumatic, being tossed all over the place as they rolled over and over down that hill." He jumped out to deliver the phone number.

"Poor baby," Maggie murmured, gently feeling its little legs and body for bumps or broken bones. The truck driver must have cuddled it a lot, as it was very comfortable with humans. A newborn animal usually preferred its mother to anyone else, unless the driver had discovered the pup abandoned and had become the surrogate mother. This wasn't anything new to Maggie. She'd hand-raised more orphaned animals in her lifetime than she could count.

Flynn got back in the car, pulled onto the highway, and they resumed their journey to Louisiana. "I don't know about you, but I'm a muddy mess. We'd scare anyone when we knocked on their door, and they wouldn't dare let us in."

Maggie reached over and ran one finger down the side of his mud-streaked face. "Yes, you are, and I'm just as bad. Maybe we'd better stop at the next truck stop where they have showers, and we can take our bags in and change into clean clothes. I can get some food for Kit at the same time."

"Good idea."

They rode in comfortable silence for awhile, until Flynn thought of something he didn't know if Maggie had even considered. "Maggie, I know this is hard for you to imagine, but how much thought have you given to the possibility that Alyssa, or Katie as I knew her, really is your twin sister? The ramifications of that, I mean."

Maggie was puzzled. "What do you have in mind?"

"If you really are twins, what if you were the adopted one? Your parents would not technically be your parents. You would have another mother and another father. Have you given that aspect any thought?"

Maggie sat quietly for a long time, the miles whipping by unnoticed as she tried to even consider such a possibility. When she'd given it any thought at all, it had always been with the question of why her parents had given up the other twin. But the thought of that was just so preposterous she'd abandoned that premise altogether. But what if . . . ?

"There really are a lot of possibilities here, aren't there? I mean, if I do have a twin and she's Alyssa, maybe we were separated at birth and each taken by the parents who raised us. Then there is the scenario that her mother had us, and I ended up with my parents. Or my mother had us and she ended up with her parents. It all makes my head spin."

"Other than making your head spin, how do you feel about having another set of parents somewhere?" Flynn probed. "How does your heart feel about that?"

"Very uncomfortable."

"Why?"

"Well, if some young girl was raped, and we were the product of that, it gives me the creeps. What kind of genes do I have? What kind of blood flows through my veins? I've always looked at my parents and thought I'd probably grow up to be pretty much like they are, despite the obvious differences in interest and personality and circumstances of jobs and moving around. But what if I had a monster for a father?" Maggie shuddered just thinking about it.

"Would that change who you are right now? Who you're well on the way to becoming? You've been raised in a wonderful home by two people that obviously love you very much and whom you adore, and you're surrounded by family that love and support you. Why would it matter who sired you or who gave birth to you? Maggie, you're a beautiful, talented girl with a charming personality and delightful outlook on life. You've made yourself what you are. And you'll continue to mold your own character, regardless of whatever accident of birth occurred. Do you believe that?"

Maggie thought about it.

Flynn pressed on when she didn't answer. "Nothing would change, unless you decided to let it impact your life in some way. If your family is as you describe them, it certainly wouldn't affect their relationship with you in the least."

"I suppose you're right," Maggie said slowly, not sounding totally convinced. "It's just such an incredible shock to think that your world is not what you've always thought it to be! It sort of shakes your foundations, like an emotional earthquake."

"Sorry, Maggie. I just thought it might be better if you had time to think through some of these possibilities, instead of being hit with them without being psychologically prepared. As I said, nothing in your life may end up changing before the end of the day."

"If ye are prepared, ye shall not fear," Maggie quoted.

"Sounds like scripture, but I don't remember reading that in the Bible. I'm not what you'd call an avid student of the Bible, but I'm not totally unfamiliar with it either." Flynn didn't add that he had gone to that source innumerable times while seeking comfort and solace after Susan and Kaitlin disappeared.

"It's from our Doctrine and Covenants, revelations the Lord gave to Joseph Smith after he restored the Savior's true church on the earth in 1830. I find little gems from there popping into my mind often."

"Are you a student of the scriptures?"

"I try to read them every day, either in the morning before I leave my room or at night before I go to sleep. I figure if God went to all the trouble of providing instructions, the least we can do is read them, especially if we're going to be asking for His help all the time. Mom told me once when I was at college, it's like asking her for a recipe, then when she sends it, I ignore it and call her on the phone and ask how to cook the dish. We have the scriptures to tell us how to live a Christlike life and how to solve many of the problems we'll encounter, but we often ignore them and continually ask for guidance when He's already given it to us."

"Good analogy. Your mom sounds like a very wise woman." Flynn spotted a truck stop ahead. "Want to stop here and get cleaned up? According to that last sign, we'll be in Lafayette in a couple of hours and it will be daylight by then."

"Yes, I'm overdue for a hot shower and change of clothes after our trek up and down that muddy hill. I don't know what was in that mud, but I don't smell too sweet. Actually, a long, leisurely soak in a Jacuzzi with lots of bubbles would be better, but I'll settle for just being clean again and smelling decent."

They rolled down a couple of windows slightly and left Kit in the car while they carried their bags into the truck stop, found the showers, and went to become presentable again. Flynn finished before Maggie, so instead of waiting for her at the entrance to the women's area, he hit the mini-mart and bought a carton of milk and a baby bottle so Maggie could feed Kit. When a man delivered a tray of fresh hot donuts, Flynn snagged half a dozen and went back for two more small cartons of milk. By the time he finished with his purchases, Maggie emerged from the rest area looking refreshed and beautiful. The wool tweed pantsuit she wore contained hues that matched her shining auburn hair, and the sapphire blue sweater must have been purchased specifically to match her eyes. She was a vision of loveliness Flynn could have stared at and enjoyed for hours.

He quickly waved the sack of food to take her attention from his face. How could he keep from revealing these feelings stirring within him, emotions he thought he'd never again experience in this life? Maggie must not suspect how he felt until this was resolved.

"I've got milk and a bottle for Kit, donuts and milk for us. Anything else?"

Maggie thought for a minute. "How about a newspaper to put on the floor? Kit won't be housebroken yet. Too bad dogs aren't as easy to train as cats to a litter box. Hmm. I wonder if we could train him to use a litter box?"

"You can ponder that during the next phase of our journey. Let's get back to the car before Kit leaves a puddle on the floor mat." Flynn hadn't thought of that when they left him in the car. He'd just as soon Kit didn't initiate his BMW in that manner.

They hurried back through the misty night and were met by an excited little bundle of noise when they opened the door. Maggie peeled off a couple of sheets of newspaper and put Kit on top of them in the parking lot. Fortunately, he either knew what they were for, or their timing was just right. When the deed was done, Flynn found a trash can, tossed the evidence, and they resumed their journey. Maggie fed the hungry pup, who then contentedly curled up at Maggie's feet where the heat blew out, and Flynn and Maggie indulged in fresh donuts, no longer hot, but tasty and satisfying.

Maggie's thoughts were tangled webs of what-ifs. What if they couldn't find Katie? What if they did find her but they were too late? What if they found her and returned her to Lionel Lawson? Would Lily give Maggie her job back? Or had there been too much water under the bridge too quickly and Lily wouldn't be able to deal with everything that had happened? What if she really were a twin? How would that change her life?

CHAPTER 25

Flynn drove silently, understanding Maggie's quiet contemplation. He knew she might be in for some rather severe shocks before the day ended, and he wanted to be able to soften whatever blows to her emotions he could, if only by getting her to consider the ramifications of an adoption in her past. Serious psychological scars could result if one descended into the dark, murky waters of self-doubt and deprecation.

The sun approached the horizon about the time they hit New Iberia but was soon hidden by thick dark clouds.

"We need to do two things—find an Internet café so I can check my e-mail to see what Alan discovered on the DNA stuff, and find this address." Maggie waved the letter with the New Iberia post mark at Flynn.

"Which do you want to do first?"

"Logically, we should get a city map or directions to the address just in case it's on this end of town. Then we can find an Internet café."

"Done," said Flynn, whipping into a service station. He snatched the letter from Maggie's hand, jumped out of the car and hurried inside to ask directions before Maggie had a chance to put her shoes on.

"It's on the southwest end of the city," Flynn reported when he slid back into his seat and dropped the map into Maggie's lap. "Not too far."

"Now all we need is someplace to plug my laptop into a phone line." Maggie took a deep breath and tried to keep her heart from pounding out of her chest. She could feel the pressure building for the end of the quest, but this quest was unlike any on which she had ever embarked. Life-changing circumstances might loom ahead for her like those ominous dark clouds hiding the sun.

As they drove through town, an Internet café did not materialize, and finally Maggie decided to just call Alan to get the results. She'd hesitated to call because she didn't want to have to explain the whole thing until she'd resolved the mystery. Actually, as she thought about it, she was afraid to learn what Alan had discovered, so instead of calling, she decided to wait until they had talked to the girl who had written the letter, if they could locate her.

The continual wet drizzle left the streets shiny, and darkened the bark on the trees, creating stark contrasts against the gray sky. They pulled up in front of what should have been the house at the address on the envelope. All that remained was a charred and blackened ruin.

They stared at the depressing sight, neither speaking nor moving. Finally Maggie said quietly, "I think I'll go next door and ask if they know where the Armbruths are now."

The tiny house next door buzzed with activity as people moved about inside past the lighted windows. Maggie glanced at her watch and decided they were a busy family getting ready to go to work and to school. As she stepped from the car, Flynn got out, too. Surprised, she didn't say anything but was happy to have his moral support. The fire-blackened ruin had shaken her.

She stepped up on the wide concrete pad that acted as the first and only step and knocked on the door. Flynn stopped a few steps behind her. A woman, hairbrush in hand, answered the door with a puzzled look at the two strangers.

"I'm Maggie McKenzie. I'm trying to find April Armbruth." Maggie flashed the letter at the woman so she could see the return address, but carefully held her fingers over the addressee. "Do you know where the family moved after the fire?"

The woman stared, then leaned against the door frame and said, "Well, I can't rightly tell. They were a good family, so they may have gone to heaven, and then again, you never really know people, so maybe they ended up in the other place. Of course, they could have split up, some going up and some going down. That's more likely what happened to them."

Maggie staggered backward and would have fallen off the step if Flynn hadn't caught her by her elbows, holding her upright. "You mean, they all died in the fire?" She could barely get the words out.

"You're a right smart girl." The woman smiled, but it wasn't warm and sincere. "That's exactly what I meant. Excuse me, I have to get ready for work." She started to close the door but Maggie recovered and stepped forward.

"Please, can I ask one more question? Do you know where April worked?"

"Hmm. Seems to me it was one of those touristy places." She turned and called to someone in the other room, "Where did April work?"

"Avery Island," came the clear reply.

"Oh, right. The Jungle Gardens," the woman said, apparently just needing a memory jog.

"Can you tell me where that is?" Maggie asked, her heart beating wildly within her.

"Follow the signs out of town to Highway 90, cross over it, and continue toward the bay. There should be signs all along the way to Avery Island Jungle Gardens and Bird Sanctuary. It's out where they make the hot sauce."

Maggie didn't want to ask one last question, but she had to know. "How many people died in that fire?"

"All four in the family. They figured someone left a candle burning and it caught something on fire during the night. They were all asleep and never woke in time to get out."

"Thank you so much," Maggie murmured and headed numbly back to the car.

Flynn opened her door and she fell into her seat, gasping for air. She felt like someone was strangling the breath out of her.

He got in and started the car, driving down the street a short distance, where he pulled into a grocery store parking lot and stopped. "Are you okay?"

Maggie shook her head. "No. I'm terrified out of my mind. Flynn, that house didn't burn accidentally. Cleat Wiggins killed those people, just as surely as he killed every one of the other letter writers."

"Now what?" Flynn asked softly. This was Maggie's show. He was only along for the—for the what? His mind had started to say ride, but was that true? Was he along to further his clinical studies of the case, or was he along to keep a watchful eye on Maggie? Or was he there simply because she made him feel alive again and he liked that more than he dared admit?

Maggie swallowed, took a deep breath trying to calm her thudding heart, and said, not sounding quite as emphatic and strong as she'd wanted, "Let's find Avery Island."

Flynn got back on the main thoroughfare, spotted the signs to the island, and followed the direction markers. The trees got older and bigger, more covered with dripping strands of Spanish moss the farther they went. Then they turned off onto a narrow road that led past a small marina where they could see bayous and swamps in every direction.

A decrepit, rusty old pickup arrived just in front of them and stopped at a white wooden slat gate that barred the road to the gardens. The sign on the gate said: Open at 9 A.M. It was only eight o'clock. Flynn got out and walked up to the man in the pickup, who leaned his head out and looked Flynn up and down like he was fitting him for a suit of clothes. *Or a coffin*, thought Maggie as a cold chill shivered down her spine. She rolled down her window to hear the conversation.

"Good morning," Flynn said amiably as he bent over to speak to the man nose to nose.

"Mornin'," the man replied.

"Any chance of looking around the place before it opens?" Flynn asked.

"Nope," the old man answered.

"Can you tell me what's here?" Flynn asked.

"Hot pepper factory. Salt mine. Oil wells. Gift shop. Bird sanctuary. Alligator, deer, possum, armadillo, nutria, squirrels, raccoon, bobcats, rabbits." He paused. "To name just a bit."

Maggie couldn't stand it any longer and jumped out to ask questions of her own. As she approached the window of the pickup, the old man stared at her. "My goodness, Katie lady. You're lookin' real fine today. You all through feelin' puny?" Then he studied her more carefully. "Nooo," he said slowly, drawing the sound out. "You're not Katie, are you?"

"No, but I'm looking for her." Maggie bit her lip, then plunged into the lie again. Well, maybe it wasn't a lie after all. "She's my sister. Do you know where I can find her?"

The old man didn't take his eyes off Maggie, seeming to be amazed at their likeness. "'Fraid not. Her no-count old man disappeared a couple weeks ago, draggin' her off behind him; then when he showed up agin, she weren't with him."

"Did he say where she was?" Maggie's heart froze. What if he had already killed her?

"Didn't say nuthin', and a body daren't ask. He's an ornery cuss, that one."

"Did they live around here?"

"Somewhere. Don't know for sure where."

"Did they work here?" Maggie was running out of questions.

"He whipped up the food they sold in the gift shop. Wasn't much of a job, so I think he had another somewhere else. There was sumthin' 'bout this place he liked cause he kept comin' back every year. Don't know what the draw was. He didn't seem ta like anybody here and didn't let that poor sweet Katie talk to nobody neither."

Maggie was almost in tears. "How am I going to find her?"

The old man just shook his head.

Suddenly a picture flashed in Maggie's mind: the swamp garden, the curved bridge, and the red Shinto gate. "Do you have a red Japanese gate here, the kind that curves up at the ends?" Maggie asked, drawing the outline of the gate in the air with her hands.

The old man nodded.

"Is there a curved stone bridge over a pond filled with lily pads?"

Again he nodded.

Maggie could scarcely contain her excitement. "Is there a winding path under the gate that leads to the bridge and then it divides?"

Once again, he nodded in the affirmative.

Maggie whirled to Flynn. "This is it. This has to be where she is." She turned back to the old man. "Can you take me to the bridge? Katie is there somewhere, and he's going to kill her if I don't find her before he gets to her."

The old man looked at Maggie like she'd lost her mind, then glanced at the man standing just behind her. Flynn nodded solemnly. "She's serious. Can you take us in before anyone else arrives? We may be able to save Katie's life if we find her before her father comes."

Finally the understanding that they were serious spread across the tanned, wrinkled face. The old man slowly climbed out of the pickup, with shaking hands unlocked the padlock that held the chain in place, and opened the gates to the bridge. He motioned for them to follow him and drive on through, then he walked back and locked the gate again. It was the only road onto the little island as far as they could see, and if Cleat Wiggins didn't have a key, maybe the lock would keep him out until the old man returned to let him in. Of course, all Wiggins had to do was climb over the wooden gates—but then his vehicle would block the road.

The old man motioned them to follow his truck, and he led them slowly on a winding road past groves of oak trees green with moss, past marshes and swamps and ponds of water, some totally covered with green slime and some that perfectly mirrored the trees around them. They passed camellia gardens, not yet in bloom, and stopped in a small parking lot that was not much more than a wide spot in the road. Maggie immediately jumped out, and Flynn rolled down his window. The old man leaned out of his pickup window and pointed at the beginnings of a gravel path.

"That's where it is. You'll come to a fork; the gate's down one path, and the bridge leads to the Buddha. D'ya need any help?"

Flynn shook his head and thanked him, then parked the car and hurried to catch Maggie, who had taken off almost at a run up the path into the trees. Every time the path curved he lost sight of her in the lush foliage that lined the walk and, in some places, hung overhead like a dark green umbrella. At last he caught up to her standing at the foot of the bridge, looking perplexed.

"Here's the bridge, but I can't see the Shinto gate anywhere. There is the temple with the Buddha across the pond, but I didn't see that in my dream." Maggie turned slowly and surveyed the scene in all directions. Then she crossed the bridge and stood on the other side, from which point she couldn't see the temple. She turned and started back up the path on the other side of the pond, and just around a corner spotted the red Shinto gate.

Maggie hurried to the gate, walked under it and back again, and retraced her footsteps to the bridge. Flynn leaned on the cold stonework and watched her.

"I can't understand this. I feel absolutely nothing here. I was sure I'd experience the same feelings I had in my dream, but there is nothing."

"Let's look at the temple," Flynn suggested. "Maybe that will give you a different feeling and a lead."

Maggie hurried toward the temple and Flynn kept pace, worried that she'd rush into something for which she wasn't prepared. He wasn't sure what *he* expected, much less what she thought she'd find, but he wasn't armed, so he hoped Wiggins didn't appear anytime soon.

As they approached the tiny pagoda on the little winding path, they slowed their pace. He stopped to read the sign about the eight-hundred-year-old, gold-covered Buddha that rested inside the glassed temple overlooking the lily pond.

While Flynn stayed at the foot of the temple's hill, Maggie hurried up the stairs and walked around it, trying to get in; the bright red doors were locked. She peered through the windows, but all she could see was the huge figure of Buddha sitting in the lotus position in the center of a giant lotus flower. There didn't appear to be a single place where anyone could hide. She walked around it again and again, then examined the little hill on which it was perched. Nothing.

"Flynn, I don't understand. My dream was so real—the bridge is just as I saw it, as is the Shinto gate. But the feelings are not here that I had, and the temple I didn't see at all. I just don't understand what Katie was trying to tell me."

"Maybe you're trying too hard to make it literal. Maybe this was just a unique spot so that you'd know you were in the right place when you found it. Maybe she's somewhere else on Avery Island."

Maggie stared at Flynn. "You could be right. Okay, let's explore the rest of the gardens and see what we can find." Maggie ran down the path and across the bridge back to the car. Even with Flynn's long stride, he had to hurry to keep up with her. They pulled back on the winding gravel road and drove along Bayou Drive past the Grover Cleveland Oak. It must have been a big deal, an important landmark or something, but they didn't stop to check it out, though it was an incredibly old, huge spreading oak tree.

The road looped back toward Buddha's temple, through an arch covered with bare wisteria vines, past more camellia gardens, a palm garden—none of which they stopped to see, and to the sunken gardens.

"Here," Maggie said. "Let's stop here."

"Are you feeling something?" Flynn said as he pulled off the road onto a graveled area marked for parking.

"A little tingle. Maybe it's excitement. Maybe it's nerves. Or maybe . . ."

Maggie didn't fly out the door this time but waited for Flynn to walk beside her as they descended through feathery-leafed ferns down several steps made slippery because of the wet leaves that covered most of them. There were sunken ponds with large orange koi swimming in lazy circles, huge pottery jars, and delicate red flowers along the walk, but Maggie felt nothing more than she had as they left the car. She even climbed the hill at the end of walk to see what lay behind the sunken gardens, but it was a tangle of vines and trees and bushes that not only blocked her way, but also blocked her from seeing beyond.

Disappointed, they silently walked back to the car. Maggie stopped, leaned against a rock wall, held out her hand to Flynn, and when he had grasped it firmly, she opened her mind to Katie. All she got was a cold rush of damp air and the musty smell of decay. But no Katie.

"Flynn, she's not there."

"Where?"

"Anywhere. She's gone. At least, she's not coming to me."

"Let's continue through the gardens. Looks like there is still a lot we haven't seen yet. Maybe you'll get something somewhere else."

They returned to the car and drove through a section of timber bamboo to a place called Bird City which appeared to be as advertised—an island full of birds. Then the road wound around to a turnoff that said E. A. McIlhenney's House, Private Drive. Flynn slowed as Maggie craned her neck to see up the drive to a large two-story building on top of a small hill. It was completely fenced with No Trespassing signs posted at close intervals all along the fence.

"It looks like an old Southern plantation with a wide porch all around it," Maggie said. "And it looks kind of spooky, like it hasn't been inhabited by humans for a long time—but maybe something else lives there." She shivered.

"Do you believe in ghosts, Maggie?" Flynn had seen the shiver run through her.

"I believe that there are spirits that either haven't gone where they're supposed to go, or that have come back. I don't believe they can hurt us at all, unless we allow them to get close to us—like inviting them."

"Sort of like Katie getting into your mind?"

"Something like that," Maggie nodded, not realizing how close the two situations actually seemed until Flynn pointed it out.

They continued on the road that followed around the perimeter of the big house on the hill, when suddenly Maggie touched Flynn's arm. "Look." She pointed at a barely visible old shack surrounded by vines, leafless bushes, and small trees. It seemed ready to fall down at the slightest breeze. Flynn stopped the car.

Maggie's voice came out in a whisper. "Remember when I told you about the shack with the torn screens that let in the mosquitoes, and the door the alligator could enter? That looks like it." Goose bumps ran up and down Maggie's arms. She glanced at Flynn, then back at the shack. "I think this is the place where we'll find Katie."

CHAPTER 26

The dilapidated shack stood behind the fence with clearly posted No Trespassing signs, and the tangle of brush and vines seemed impenetrable. Maggie opened the car door and jumped out, examining the fence in each direction. There seemed to be no place to climb over easily, and the ground was so muddy she didn't want to crawl under. But she was determined to reach that shack.

Flynn pulled off the side of the road and parked the car. He didn't intend to let Maggie do this by herself, even if they both got arrested for trespassing. He joined her as she started to climb over the fence at one of the thin fence posts that was nothing more than a stick stuck in the ground with the square, wire fencing attached to it.

"Wait, Maggie. There's got to be a better place. That pole won't hold you up."

"Then maybe we need to just knock down this whole section of fence and walk across it. If Katie's in as bad a shape as I think, we'll have to carry her out anyway. We can't do that over the fence."

Flynn agreed they didn't have any time to lose, but knocking down the fence wasn't the same as finding a way over, under, or around it. Still, Maggie had a point. "Okay, we'll try to break off this fence post, and that other one over there that's pretty flimsy. Then the fence should just lie down so we can walk over it. It doesn't look like it's strung too tight."

"It's not like there aren't a zillion other fence posts just like this lying all over the place. All we have to do to repair it is thread one through the squares and poke it in the ground. As soggy as this ground is, I shouldn't think it would be too hard."

Flynn sized up the pole, saw a knothole about two feet off the ground, and kicked the post squarely above it. It snapped in two, but the fence stayed in place. That was good. Someone coming along wouldn't know at first glance they'd broken the fence. Then he went to the second, found a point where it seemed weaker than the others, and broke it off with a swift, powerful kick. Again, the pole snapped and the fence sagged only slightly. They bent the fence wire over in the midpoint between the two broken poles and walked across it.

Maggie's mind conjured up all sorts of wild scenarios regarding what they'd find when they opened the door to the shack, but none of those things prepared her for what she saw. Most of the roof was gone, and the dirt floor was not just muddy, there were pools of water everywhere. A little animal scurried through a missing plank in the wall. Maggie hoped it was only a mouse.

In one dark corner a wooden cot hugged the wall and seemed to be piled with old rags and refuse. There was nothing else in the tiny, decrepit shack. Maggie stepped over a puddle and jumped back when a snake slithered over her shoe. Flynn caught her, steadied her, and tried to step around her to investigate the piles on the cot. Maggie took a deep breath, grabbed Flynn's arm and pulled him back.

She needed to do this. She couldn't send someone else if this was her sister. Part of Maggie hoped that Katie wasn't here—that she was in a warm, clean room somewhere safe. Another part of her hoped this was Katie and they could grab her and escape before Wiggins found them. She didn't want to ever see the man in person; he was awful enough in her nightmares.

Together, Maggie and Flynn approached the cot. As Flynn reached out to touch the pile of rags, it moved. A mouse popped out and raced over the rags, flying off the end of the cot and out through a hole. They stopped, looked at each other, and both began pulling off the dirty, wet pile of towels, blankets, and rags one at a time.

Then they saw her. Curled up under the last blanket in a fetal position, a skinny girl lay chained to the cot. Her skin was dirty and her black hair looked like it had been chopped off with garden shears. She didn't move. Didn't even seem to be aware they were there. Maggie touched her throat to see if there was a pulse. Yes, there was a heartbeat.

Flynn grabbed the chain and found it wound around the leg of the cot but not secured to anything else. He picked it up, handed it to Maggie to carry, and bent over to lift the girl in his arms.

She didn't open her eyes, and hung limp against him when he picked her up. She remained unconscious as they made their way out of the rotting shack and across the marshy ground to the fence. Maggie pulled down the wire mesh and stood on it while Flynn carried the girl across and to the car. She ran to open the back door, and Flynn gently placed the girl on the seat. Maggie slid in on the other side and held Katie's head in her lap.

Maggie looked at the slender, dirty face she held cradled in her hands. She didn't think the girl looked like her at all. Was this really Katie? Could this actually be Alyssa Lawson, the bright, vivacious girl described in the articles she'd read?

Without a word, Flynn straightened the fence back to its former position, then drove to the front gate where the little old man waited on the other side in his pickup, looking for all the world as if he'd never moved.

When he saw them coming, he got out, unlocked the gate, and drove through out of their way, allowing them access to the bridge. Flynn stopped, and the old man approached the car. Maggie rolled down her window and asked, "Is this Katie?"

The man bent over and looked at the smudged, waiflike face outlined in black, cropped hair. "Doesn't look much like the Katie I know, but then again, I 'spect it could be if she's been mistreated by that brute of a father."

"Thanks so much for letting us in so we could find her," Maggie said. "We'll take her to the hospital if you'll tell us how to get there."

His directions sounded simple enough.

"Will you call the police to come for Cleat Wiggins?" Flynn asked. "If he shows up, try to keep him up here and away from the gardens until they arrive. But be careful. He's a dangerous man."

The old man nodded and backed away from the car so they could cross the bridge and leave the island. Then he drove across, parked his ancient pickup in front of the gate, locked it, and walked the quarter mile down to the little bait shop by the marina to call the police.

Neither Flynn nor Maggie spoke on the way to the hospital. All Maggie could think was that this might be her sister. A sister she didn't even know she'd had until—how many days ago? *Less than a week,* she thought. But as she studied the pale, dirt-streaked face of the girl, Maggie wondered if this really was the Katie she'd been connecting with. When she'd met people who had known Alyssa/Katie, they'd commented on their uncanny resemblance. Had Katie changed so drastically in the last few months? Or was this someone else? She was sure it was Katie who had told her about the swamp gardens, and Katie who had shown her the dilapidated shack, and hadn't it been Katie's face that appeared to her, pleading for her to come and save her? Or had it? This was the face that had appeared to her last night—the pale, thin, dirty face. But who did it belong to?

"Flynn."

"Yes?"

"What if this isn't Katie?"

"What do you mean? Why wouldn't it be Katie?" Flynn glanced over his shoulder into the back seat but couldn't see the face clearly.

"She doesn't look like me. Her nose isn't the same. Her chin is different. Even if she gained another twenty pounds back to what her normal weight probably was, and if her hair was normal instead of dyed, I still don't think she'd look enough like me to be my twin. Everyone I've talked to so far thinks we look alike. Everyone who knew Alyssa or Katie thought I was her when they first saw me."

"And you're thinking?" Flynn couldn't imagine what Maggie was thinking or how it could possibly be anyone besides Katie, but he was certainly willing to listen to any theories she had. This wasn't the strangest case he'd ever been involved with, but it was a close second, and it definitely wasn't over yet.

"What if this is another girl Cleat Wiggins kidnapped? What if Katie knew about her and knew Cleat planned to kill her? What if she used our connection to send me to find this girl? Do you suppose that's possible?"

"Hmm. I suppose it could be. Katie could have really developed her mental gifts if she had to go deeply inside herself to escape from her loneliness and misery."

"I think we're not through yet," Maggie said quietly. "I think we still have to find the real Katie." Neither of them spoke for a few minutes, then Maggie broke the silence.

"Flynn, what are they going to say at the hospital when we bring an unconscious girl with a chain on her leg? We should have had the old man send some police to meet us at the hospital so we could explain what happened." Then Maggie thought of the difficulty in trying to explain how she knew where to find the girl. "This is going to be difficult. Nobody will believe how she showed me where to find her."

"Wait, Maggie. Think about it. How did you find each of the people you interviewed?"

"I looked them up from the address on the letter they wrote. Boy, is my brain addled."

"You're an investigative reporter who followed the story of a kidnapping, and you simply interviewed people or their neighbors until you ended up at the suspect's place of employment."

"True," Maggie said, relieved at the simple explanation that had eluded her in her befuddled state of mind.

When they arrived at the hospital, Flynn hurried inside to alert the emergency room staff and get a gurney. Maggie stayed in the car, stroking the dirty hand of the girl laying still and quiet across her lap. The peaceful moment ended abruptly as a trauma team burst through the emergency room doors, carefully placing the girl on the gurney and disappearing back into the hospital before Maggie could brush off the worst of the mud and follow them, leaving poor Kit alone in the car, much to his great displeasure.

Maggie hadn't considered the myriad questions she and Flynn would have to answer, and didn't realize the hospital wouldn't treat the girl until someone gave permission for her to be treated. Maggie signed the permission papers for her "sister," and while she was doing this, Flynn quietly presented a credit card to cover the expenses. Maggie didn't even notice.

They hadn't finished answering all the necessary questions for the medical staff when the police arrived and they had to start all over again. All Maggie could do was thank heaven for Flynn. His years of medical and psychological experience smoothed over areas where Maggie would have been stumbling all over herself trying to explain things. He knew what kind of answers they were looking for—she had no idea. She'd never been faced with anything like this in her life.

Eventually, everyone seemed to find something else to do, and Maggie and Flynn were left alone. "Now what?" Flynn asked.

Maggie shook her head in bewilderment. "I thought this would be the end—or the beginning of the end. Instead we're right back where we started. Even if the police catch Wiggins, I suspect if he doesn't want them to find Katie, they won't, but neither will we."

"You've made up your mind this isn't Katie?"

"I guess we won't know for sure until they talk to her, but I have this . . ." Maggie stopped, not knowing how to phrase it.

"Gut feeling?" Flynn supplied.

"Exactly. Deep down, I know that girl isn't Katie. But where do we start looking for her? I expect if they pick up Wiggins, he'll abandon Katie in an instant and not tell anyone where she is or anything about her. He'd let her die rather than admit he kidnapped her."

Flynn guided Maggie to a quiet alcove near the foyer where they stood looking out the window at the rain dancing in the puddles. "What about the DNA? Are you ready to see what your brother discovered? Are you up for that yet?"

"At this point, I don't want to know. I just want everything to go back to the way it was a month ago. I don't want any of this to have ever happened." Maggie sighed and turned to look up at Flynn. "But I guess that's impossible, so I might just as well face the music." She noted the sign giving permission for cell phone use in this area of the hospital, pulled out her cell phone, and shrugged. "How can things get worse than they are right now?"

Oh, Maggie girl, thought Flynn. *Don't tempt fate by saying things like that. They could get a hundred times worse, but for your sake, I truly hope they don't.*

Maggie punched in Alan's number on Long Island and waited for it to ring. A million thoughts raced through her mind in the few seconds before Alan answered.

"Alan McKenzie speaking."

"Hi, Alan. It's Maggie."

There was a pregnant pause on the other end, and Maggie's stomach felt like it did a complete flip-flop before settling upside down inside her.

"Alan, I haven't been able to check my e-mail. You'll have to just tell me in quick, simple terms what you found." When he didn't immediately jump in with an answer, Maggie stumbled forward, talking as fast as she could.

"Are you and I related, or according to your findings was I born under a cabbage leaf somewhere?"

"Maggie, maybe there wasn't sufficient . . ." Alan mumbled something that Maggie didn't quite catch, but she knew what he'd found. His response would have been quick, to the point, and he'd have teased her for wasting his time if their DNA had matched.

Maggie's mind went numb but she heard herself say, "Thanks for setting aside all your other important work. As you can tell, this was pretty crucial to me. I appreciate your quick response, Alan."

"Maggie, wait," Alan said.

"Can't talk now, but I promise to call as soon as I solve the mystery of my birth." Maggie disconnected and sagged against the wall, stunned. She could hardly breathe, much less speak.

"It's true," she whispered, feeling like someone had just jerked her world right out from under her and sent her spinning wildly through outer space.

Flynn didn't move. He wanted to hold Maggie and offer the comfort he knew she needed, but he was afraid of his own emotions, afraid she'd feel more than just his compassion.

She looked up at Flynn with tears in her eyes, and suddenly sobs she could no longer contain racked her body. Flynn stepped forward, and she fell into his arms, clinging tightly to him, burying her face in his jacket. He wrapped his arms around her, pressed her head against his chest, and they just stood there until Maggie's sobs subsided and her body stopped shaking.

Flynn loosened his hold on her but didn't let go completely, gently tilting her chin up until her eyes met his.

"Are you okay?"

Maggie sniffled and nodded. "I thought I was prepared for the results, but I wasn't."

"What now?" Flynn asked quietly, knowing Maggie's next step would be even harder than her last phone call.

Maggie leaned her head against Flynn again, slipped her arms around him, and sighed. "I have to call Dad." Suddenly she realized what she was doing and jerked away. "Oh, I'm sorry, Flynn. I didn't mean to . . ."

Flynn shushed Maggie with a finger to her lips. "You needed a shoulder to cry on. I'm available any time you need me. That's what I'm here for, remember? Dr. Ford to the rescue."

Maggie looked up into Flynn's sincere, dark eyes and saw a tenderness that surprised and warmed her. She looked quickly away, afraid she'd get lost there and forget herself again. Flynn was Dr. Ford. That seemed to become harder and harder for her to remember.

"I guess I can't put it off any longer. I'd better call Dad before I lose my nerve."

"Do you want me to leave while you talk to him?"

Panic shot through Maggie and she grabbed Flynn's arm. "No. Please don't go. I might . . ." Her eyes frantically searched the room as if what she wanted to say could be found in some far corner, before she finally looked up at Flynn and tried to sound calm. "I'll try not to replay that last scene, but I'd like you to stay close, please, if you don't mind. I'm more of a coward than I thought."

Flynn pointed to a couple of chairs along the opposite wall. "Want to sit down in case your legs give out, or do I get to hold you again if you get weak-kneed?"

Maggie felt her cheeks flushing, and as she took a seat, Flynn settled into the chair beside her. She gazed across the room, concentrating on the rain-streaked window as she explained. "All my life my brothers have teased me because I don't look like them. Dad's retort was that the Lord knew He needed to send someone prettier than they were so He had to make a new mold instead of following the same old pattern." She looked up to see Flynn watching her closely. "All my brothers look alike. At least, you can pretty much tell they're from the same family. Now I know why I look so different."

Maggie stared at her phone for a long time before she made the second phone call. Her mother answered.

"Hi, Mom. Is Dad home?"

"Hi, Maggie. I'm so glad you called. I miss you. It's good to hear your voice. Where are you?"

Maggie had to think for a minute. "New Iberia, Louisiana. How are you, Mom? Got everything ready for Christmas?" Somehow she had to sound totally normal so her mother wouldn't ask endless questions and keep Maggie from the task she dreaded more than anything she had ever done in her life.

They finally finished their mundane conversation, and Maggie breathed a sigh of relief when her mother handed the phone to her dad. Thank heaven she hadn't mentioned Maggie questioning her birth, and since her mother's answer about her birth hadn't given Maggie any enlightenment, she hoped her father could—or would.

"Hi, Maggie. How's my girl?"

"In the middle of a mystery." Then she panicked. How on earth do you tell your dad you know he isn't your father? "Dad, I just sent my fingernails and hair to Alan for analysis and asked him to compare the results to his own DNA." She paused when she heard a sharp intake of breath on the other end of the phone. What if her dad had a heart attack over this?

"Are you there, Dad?"

"Yes, I just had to go into my office and shut the door. Go on, Margaret."

"Can you tell me why we don't share any common DNA characteristics?"

CHAPTER 27

"Maggie, this isn't going to be easy to talk about over the phone. Can you come home and let me explain it to you face-to-face?"

"I wish I could. I'd like that more than anything, but I think I have a twin sister, and she needs my help right now. I can't come home until I find her."

"You're right, Maggie. You do have a sister." He paused, then asked quietly, "Is it enough for me to tell you that and let you wait for the rest of the story until you can come home?"

Maggie could hear the deep emotion in her father's voice and wished she could be there and put her arms around him. She realized this was going to be even harder on her parents than it was on her, if that was possible, and she wished she could just make it all go away.

"Maggie, your mother knows nothing about this. I need time to tell her. She believes she gave birth to you, but our own baby died in the delivery room. Rose was under anesthetic and didn't know. Another woman had twins that very same hour. Her husband needed money to pay for their babies' delivery, and when I told him how devastated my wife would be when she woke up to empty arms one more time, he offered one of his babies to me. I got you to help save your mother's life. I think it would have literally killed her to lose the little girl—for the third time—she had tried so long to have."

Maggie didn't know how to respond. "Yes, Daddy. I can wait for the rest of the story. I'll call again as soon as I have anything to tell you about Katie." Then she added softly, "I love you, Daddy."

Her father's voice cracked and he waited until he could speak. "I love you, Maggie, more than you will ever know. Say a prayer for me.

I've been trying to tell your mother for twenty-four years, and the time just never seemed right. Guess it is now." Her father paused. "Maggie, you said your sister needs help. What kind? Are you okay? Can I do anything for you?"

"Thanks, Dad, but I do have help and I'm okay. We just have to find Katie as soon as possible. I'll tell you about it later." Maggie's control was at its end. "Bye, Daddy," she whispered and disconnected before she totally lost it. This time there were no sobs, just tears that streamed endlessly down her face. She didn't notice when Flynn offered his hand, but when her fingers began to ache, she discovered she'd been clutching his tightly.

She released her grip. "Sorry," she said. "You must think I'm a real basket case."

"No," Flynn smiled, and hoped it was perceived as warm but professional. "Just a young woman experiencing a traumatic period in her life. I'm glad I'm here to help you through it." All the time his heart was breaking for Maggie. Flynn recognized the depth of his emotions and was surprised at the revelation. He did have a heart after all, not just a cold, hard lump in his chest that ached continually.

Maggie leaned on the arm of the chair, cupped her chin in her hand, looked Flynn squarely in those fathomless eyes, and said softly, "Not nearly as glad as I am. I don't know what I would have done if you hadn't been here every step of the way."

"Dr. Ford," a voice called from down the hall.

Flynn jumped to his feet with Maggie right behind.

"Dr. Ford, I'm Dr. Passey. I'm afraid I have some bad news." Maggie could tell it was really bad news and that the doctor wasn't used to doing this. He swallowed a couple of times, wrung his hands, and finally stumbled through the words, "The girl you brought in has just died. She never regained consciousness."

"Do you have any idea of the cause of death?" Flynn asked. He thought he knew from looking at the girl, but it was never a good idea medically to assume anything.

"No, I can't say yet. There will, of course, be an autopsy."

Flynn pressed. "My guess from how little she weighed and her appearance was that she starved to death."

Dr. Passey nodded in agreement. "That would be my first thought, too. I'm sorry to have to relay the news." With that hasty apology, he escaped as quickly as he could back down the long hall from whence he came.

Maggie looked at Flynn. "I hope you take this right, but she's probably better off where she is now than having to live with whatever she's been through. I mean, death has to be better than mortality when . . ." She didn't know how to explain to Flynn what she meant, so she just quit. Maggie had no tears left in her to shed for the girl. She'd never been afraid of death, because it was just another step in God's plan, and she knew that she had loving grandparents and two other sisters waiting for her in heaven.

That brought her quickly back to the present. She also had one sister still on earth who needed her help. How would they ever find her?

"I think we've done all we need to do here," Flynn said. "Shall we go back to Avery Island and see if they've caught Cleat Wiggins yet?"

Maggie shuddered. "Yes, we need to find out, but no, I don't want to ever see him in person. He's far too awful in my nightmares already. I suppose he's the only lead we have to Katie, isn't he?"

Flynn took Maggie's arm and guided her down the hall while he thought about it. "Yes, I'm afraid he *is* our only lead, unless when he's captured he gives the police her location, and I wouldn't bet a nickel on that happening."

"Maybe if Katie saw it on TV she'd come forward," Maggie said. "But she could just as easily get lost somewhere and never be found. If I were her, I'd be afraid of that horrible man getting out of jail and coming for me, so I think I'd run as far and as fast as I could and bury myself in some dark place where he'd never think to look for me."

It was still raining as they left the hospital. The gray, miserable weather perfectly reflected Maggie's mood.

"Before we head back to Avery Island, would you like to stop somewhere for lunch?" Flynn offered as they got in the car. "We haven't eaten since donuts several hours ago."

They were greeted by a pup who was very happy to see them. When Maggie picked up the wiggling little bundle of fur, he tried to lick her face to show her just *how* happy.

"I'm not sure I have much of an appetite," Maggie said, snuggling the puppy. "But I do have an idea. Instead of going back to Avery Island, why don't we call and see if we can talk to the old man and ask if they caught Wiggins. If they haven't, we don't want to go back there. If they have, we can talk to the police. I'm sure he wouldn't volunteer information about Katie, but if we tell them he kidnapped her, they might be able to get something out of him."

"Good thinking," Flynn said. "I'm impressed that you can come up with such good ideas on an empty stomach."

Maggie dialed information and had them connect her with the Avery Island Jungle Gardens, then handed the phone to Flynn to talk. Surprised at Maggie's action, Flynn took the phone and asked to speak to the old man who appeared to be the gatekeeper. The woman said he wasn't there now. Flynn asked if there had been any excitement at the gardens this morning. The woman said a couple of police cars had cruised through the area, but then left when they failed to find anyone suspicious hanging around. "Nothing else out of the ordinary happened?" he asked. Again she said no. Flynn thanked her and hung up. Maggie and Flynn looked at each other without speaking.

Maggie was first to voice the questions they both were thinking. "So, he got suspicious and didn't come to work? They came, saw us and left town? Or he left town with Katie earlier because he figured the girl he left in the shack was as good as dead?"

"I have no answers, Maggie. Only more questions. What's next? Where do you want to go from here?"

Maggie sat quietly thinking. "Okay, let me bounce this off you. Cleat Wiggins is probably employed for a few hours at Avery Island, plus the old man thought he had another job somewhere else. He wouldn't want it to be too far from the gardens—too much time lost between jobs, too much gas used. So he's probably working in a restaurant somewhere nearby." She put Kit on the floor at her feet and picked up the map. "We need to draw a circle around the gardens and start checking every café and restaurant in this perimeter. How does that sound?"

"Sound like your investigative intuition just kicked into gear." Flynn started the car. "So I assume my first assignment is to find those eating establishments closest to the gardens."

"You're a quick study, Dr. Ford," Maggie smiled, buckling her seat belt. As Flynn pulled onto the street, Maggie dug a pen from her purse and drew a small circle around the Avery Island Jungle Gardens and Bird Sanctuary. "We can first check these places inside the circle, and if we don't find anything, we'll widen the search area."

Flynn groaned. "This is only one street, and look at all these eateries. If you multiply that by all the streets just in this part of town alone, we'll be here for the rest of the year! And we haven't even reached your circled area."

"Would you feel better with something under your belt besides an empty stomach?" Maggie asked, remembering how often her brothers wanted to eat compared to the smaller appetite she had.

Flynn flashed her a grateful smile. "I wouldn't turn lunch down, if that's what you're offering."

"Pick your poison, doctor. Pull into whatever looks good to you. I have no druthers right now. I'll eat anything." *If I can muster an appetite,* Maggie thought.

Flynn scanned the restaurants as he drove by, looking for something Cajun, something local, something out of the ordinary. Fast food wasn't his normal fare, despite living alone, and he'd had more than his share of culinary catastrophes this week. He wasn't sure how Maggie had survived on the meager rations he'd observed her eating while he'd been following her.

Maggie, too, looked out the window at the numerous food establishments they were passing, wondering what kind of place Cleat Wiggins would be cooking for in New Iberia. The Alpine Inn had been much higher class than most of the joints along this strip of road, but this wasn't exactly a high-class neighborhood.

Then she saw it. Her squeal caught in her throat and one hand pulled at Flynn's while the other pointed at the old, run-down VW van partially hidden behind the building on the corner. Flynn immediately changed lanes and turned in to the street next to the café.

"What did you see?" He kept looking where Maggie pointed but obviously didn't see what had her so excited.

"Didn't I tell you what kind of vehicle Cleat Wiggins drove?" Maggie gasped.

"A van?"

"Flynn, how many '60s Volkswagen vans do you think are still on the streets today?"

"Probably a few hundred. As long as people can still get engines or rebuild them, they can almost wire the car together to keep it running. They've been known to get a million miles."

"See that one? That's what Jimmy, the boy at Crazy Horse, said it looked like. What if he's in there? More important, what if Katie's in there? Everyone I've talked to said she's always with him. In fact, she's almost always at his side in the kitchen, unless she's waiting tables."

Flynn thought about that. "This might be a good time to call the police."

"But what if he isn't there? Then we've wasted their time." Maggie bit her lip. Did she dare ask Flynn to check it out? "Flynn, if I go in and he sees me, he could run. If you go in, he probably won't recognize you since you'd be totally out of context down here. You could look for Katie, and if she's there, bring her out, and then we'll call the police."

Flynn thought through all the possible scenarios for something to go tragically wrong, thinking about Maggie and Katie. He didn't want them hurt, and where Wiggins was concerned, Flynn feared that if he could harm either or both of them, he would. And probably enjoy it. The man must be evil through and through. He'd certainly had that aura the few times Flynn had seen Wiggins at the Alpine Inn.

"Okay, I'll do it. In the meantime, what will you be doing?"

Puzzled, Maggie asked, "What do you mean?"

"Will you be sitting quietly, anticipating my return or doing hands-on investigating while I'm scouting the interior?"

Maggie laughed nervously. "That sounds like something from a detective novel. Actually, I thought I'd disable the van so he couldn't escape, supposing it belongs to him, and supposing he's in there."

"And how were you going to disable it?" Flynn never ceased to be amazed at the way Maggie's mind worked.

"At first I thought about pulling a few wires, then decided a flat tire would slow him down without damaging anything, just in case it isn't his."

"I'll tell you what, Maggie girl. I'll let the air out of one of the tires, then go see if they're there. I want you at the wheel with the motor running, ready to get out of here immediately if I come out with Katie or if I send her out. I want you both away from here as soon as possible."

Maggie panicked at the thought. "Flynn, I won't leave without you. How would we connect again? You have to come with Katie if she's in there. I don't want you playing hero and getting hurt." Maggie looked at him with pleading eyes. "Please, promise me you won't take any chances if they're in there. You know how many people he's killed already."

"Correction—how many we *think* he's killed. People are innocent until proven guilty, not the other way around, remember?"

Maggie nodded, figuring it was only a matter of time before the police would prove he'd killed all the letter writers. Heaven only knew how many others might have become his victims.

"Ready?" Flynn asked, his hand on the door handle. Maggie flashed a shaky thumbs-up and opened her door. Kit decided he wanted out, and Maggie barely caught him before he landed in a puddle.

"We might have to get him a leash when this is over," Maggie said, snuggling the wiggling pup as she climbed behind the wheel. She retrieved Kit's bottle from Flynn's cooler and started to feed the hungry pooch as Flynn bent down and cautioned, "Watch the door and be ready to go." Then he left.

Maggie leaned her head on the headrest and thought about Katie, picturing her sweating in a hot kitchen beside that monster of a man. Without realizing it, she began talking to Katie, sending messages, urging her to get away from Wiggins, to look for Dr. Flynn Ford to come through the front door of the café.

While she was doing this, Flynn walked nonchalantly across puddles accumulating in the uneven dirt driveway to the car half hidden by a tree near the end of the building. The rain kept pedestrians off the street, and traffic was light in the parking lot, so Flynn flattened the tire without being seen. Then he retraced his steps to the front of the building, winked at Maggie watching him, and disappeared into the Kajun Kousine Kafé.

That made Maggie nervous. *Katie, are you in there? If you are, please come out so we can take you safely away.* As suddenly as Maggie realized what she had been doing, it dawned on her there had been no answer, no communication from Katie at all since she banished her from her mind last night. Had that severed their connection? Or was Katie . . . ?

Maggie couldn't bring herself to finish the thought. It would be too horrible to finally discover she had a sister, a twin at that, and then lose her before they even met. But maybe there was another reason Katie wasn't responding. Maggie suspected that even if Katie had succumbed to the Stockholm Syndrome, Cleat must have been keeping her lightly sedated. She didn't think the syndrome alone could have made that much difference in the personality of vivacious, extroverted Alyssa, turning her into subdued, introverted Katie. Then again, maybe it could. But what if she were now so heavily sedated she couldn't hear Maggie, or respond to her?

Maggie clutched the steering wheel. If he had drugged her, where would he leave her? He always kept her near him. Maggie gasped. The van.

CHAPTER 28

She looked at the front door of the restaurant. No Flynn. She looked at the van, maybe twenty-five yards from where she sat. Should she leave the car running where it was so Flynn could make a hasty escape if he came flying out of the restaurant with Cleat Wiggins in hot pursuit? Or should she drive up to the van so she could . . . ?

But what if all these what-ifs were simply her imagination? Should she go in and get Flynn and tell him her latest thoughts or sit here and wait for him to come out? Another what-if crossed her mind. What if Cleat saw Flynn before Flynn saw him and tried to escape out the back door, and finding his tire flat, took out his rage on Katie?

That did it. Maggie had to know if Katie was in that van. Everything hinged on that, every other what-if. Maggie took one more look at the front door, put Kit on the floor on the passenger side, slipped the car in gear, and eased slowly onto the side street to the alley, turned in, and parked on the opposite side of the tree from the van.

Then she opened her door, left the engine running and the door ajar, ducked under a low tree limb, and jumped a puddle to peer into the van's darkly tinted window. She couldn't see a thing. She tried looking through the front window but couldn't see into the back of the van. Maggie checked the rear door. Locked. She hurried around to the passenger door, expecting to find it locked, too. It was, but the window had a large crack from top to bottom that had been repaired with duct tape.

Maggie looked around before she stuck her fingernails under the edge of the silver tape and ripped it from the window, then pushed on the broken portion. It came loose and flopped into the van, held in place by the duct tape on the inside. Maggie peered into the darkened interior and at first her eyes couldn't distinguish anything more than lumpy bundles behind the seats.

Maggie's heartbeat echoed so loudly in her ears she couldn't have heard anyone approaching if they'd come up right behind her. She looked nervously around again, then reached inside and pulled on the handle. The door lock released. Throwing caution to the wind, Maggie flung the door wide open and jumped inside, squeezing between the seats to see what was in the back under the blanket.

She grabbed one corner, flipped it off, and gasped. It was Katie— Alyssa—could even have been Maggie herself. She was curled up on top of a lumpy, ragged sleeping bag with a dirty pillow under her head like she was sound asleep. Maggie grabbed her shoulder and shook her, but she didn't stir.

Terrified, Maggie felt her neck for a pulse, found one, and grabbed the unconscious girl under her arms. If Katie couldn't get out on her own power, Maggie would have to get her out, but she had to work fast.

She dragged Katie between the seats, draped her over the passenger seat and jumped out of the van. This was going to be hard, getting Katie from the van into the BMW.

Then she remembered something she'd learned at girl's camp years before. Maggie turned her back to Katie, reached over her shoulders and grabbed the girl's arms, wrapped them around her neck from behind, and pulled her from the van in what they'd called a fire safety save or a backward hug.

Katie's weight nearly knocked Maggie over when she slumped forward, and Maggie staggered to regain her balance. Then, hanging on to Katie's arms, she half carried, half dragged the girl around the end of the van to the car, and bent over so Katie wouldn't slide off her back while she let go with one hand to open the rear door. Then Maggie turned around with her back to the car and leaned into the opening, letting Katie fall gently onto the leather seats.

Maggie ran to the other side, pulled Katie all the way in, shut the rear doors, and jumped in the driver's seat. As she shut her door, she saw movement in her rearview mirror. The man with the bushy hair and big ears from her dream! Right there, right by the BMW's tail-lights, moving for her door.

Her mouth went dry as she hit the door locks with her left hand, jerked the car in gear with the other, and slammed down on the accelerator. She spun her tires, covering the furious man with a thick coating of mud and dirty water. Heart pounding, Maggie drove to the front of the eatery, hoping Flynn was on his way out, but there was no sign of him. She circled around so she could see where Cleat Wiggins had gone and was horrified to see him driving away despite the flat tire.

How could she stop him? He only needed to leave the immediate area, abandon the disabled vehicle, and disappear in some ramshackle housing tract. Then they might never find him. Maggie couldn't let that happen.

She didn't know how, but she had to prevent him from escaping, even if it meant smashing into the van with Flynn's car. She shuddered. Flynn would never forgive her if she did that, but she couldn't let this killer escape.

Maggie glanced at oncoming traffic, whipped out in the street, turned the corner on the side street where they'd originally parked, and faced Wiggins head-on as he tried to take that avenue of escape. She gripped the steering wheel so tight her knuckles were white. As the two vehicles drew near enough so the drivers could clearly see each other, Cleat stared at Maggie, unbelief evident in his expression. A sensation of satisfaction shimmered through her.

As nanoseconds passed, Maggie's thoughts raced to the impending crash. She hadn't had time to buckle her seat belt. Katie was sprawled in the back seat without any protection. She couldn't do it. She couldn't take a chance on injuring Katie.

At the last second, Maggie swerved right, narrowly missing a garbage bin parked just off the curb, allowing Cleat to escape. Then she heard the sweetest sounds she'd ever heard in her life: police sirens. Lots of police sirens. Her head swam with the noise. Maggie slammed on the brakes, looked over her shoulder, and was ecstatic to see Cleat Wiggins's van blocked by three patrol cars as two more screeched to a halt in the parking lot of the Kajun Kousine Kafé.

Uniformed officers swarmed over the van, pulled the big brute of a man from behind the wheel, and wrestled him to the ground where they cuffed his hands behind his back. Flynn raced across the muddy parking lot to the car. Maggie unlocked the doors and leaned back on the headrest, shaking all over. The energy that galvanized her during the last five wild minutes suddenly dissipated and her limbs turned to jelly.

As Flynn opened the door, Kit lunged for freedom from his confinement, scrambling to get out. Flynn grabbed him before he escaped, then, still holding the wriggling pup, eased down into the passenger seat to look at Maggie. "Are you okay?" he asked, fearing she'd been hurt.

Maggie didn't answer, didn't trust her voice. She just pointed into the back seat. Flynn turned, looked, and gasped, his mouth hanging open for a split second before he jumped out and waved a police officer over.

"This is Alyssa Lawson, the girl Wiggins kidnapped seven years ago," Flynn explained, opening the rear door to allow the officer to look inside.

Maggie turned to the officer examining Katie. "We need to call an ambulance, or just take her to the hospital ourselves right now. I think Cleat drugged her, has been drugging her for years."

The officer looked at Maggie, back at the girl on the seat, and called for an ambulance, then squatted on his haunches to listen to their conversation as Flynn sat down with a dazed look on his face. "Where did you find her? Is she okay? How did you get her in the back seat?"

Maggie explained how she'd come to the conclusion Katie must be in the van and drugged, as she hadn't responded to Maggie's thoughts. While she spoke, Maggie reached into the back seat and took the girl's limp hand, holding it gently, feeling reassured by the pulse beating in Katie's fingers.

"How did you get the police here so fast?" Maggie asked Flynn, who still hadn't quite regained his equilibrium.

"As I walked in the front door, I saw Wiggins heading back into the kitchen, but I didn't think he saw me. I immediately called the police, then asked the cashier about Katie. She said she hadn't seen the girl for a couple of days, though wherever the cook was, his daughter was always by his side. I was afraid we were going to have to force him to tell us where they lived before we'd find Katie. Apparently he did see me, either then or as I talked to the cashier, and he hightailed it out the back door."

The policeman interrupted. "I thought you said her name was Alyssa Lawson."

"It was, is," Maggie corrected. "But everyone who's known her since the kidnapping calls her Katie. She's Alyssa-slash-Katie in my mind."

"I take it you're twins," he said.

Maggie nodded, realizing the lie she'd told all week to glean information on Alyssa hadn't been a lie after all. Then she thought of what her father must be going through. Knowing her mother's deep compassion, Maggie knew there would be no question of forgiveness for the deception. Just deep sorrow that he had borne the burden of the secret all those years.

She grabbed her cell phone and speed-dialed her home. Flynn realized what she was doing and reached for her hand, squeezing it gently in a gesture of support. Maggie squeezed back, excited to tell her father the news and pleased to have Flynn with her, sharing this happy moment. The phone rang; someone picked it up, then hung up. Maggie tried again. A busy signal this time. She dialed Steve's cell phone.

"Steve here," he answered.

"Maggie here. Where are you?"

"In Idaho, silly girl."

"Be serious with me, Steve. Are you at home?"

"I'm in the barn, taking care of Pegasus for you."

"Thanks loads. Give him a love for me. Where are Mom and Dad?

"In the house last time I checked. Why?"

"They aren't answering the phone and I wanted to talk to them." Should she tell him? Probably, so he could better deal with whatever fallout came from this incredible revelation.

"Steve, Alyssa Lawson is my twin sister. We've found her, and her kidnapper's in custody. Right now I think Dad is telling Mom that she didn't give birth to me, that their baby died and a man gave them one of his twins so Mom would have a little girl to take home. They're in the middle of an intensely emotional upheaval, I'm sure.

That's just to prepare you for what's happening in the house. But I wanted them to know we found Alyssa. Dad probably took the phone off the hook, so when they emerge from his study, will you tell them? We're going to the hospital with Alyssa to make sure she's okay. The beast drugged her and she's out cold."

"Maggie, if you hadn't confided in me all the details from the beginning, I wouldn't believe this wild tale. I'd accuse you of hallucinating. It sounds like something from a far-out chick flick."

"Steve, I don't think you can even imagine the rest of the story. You know the letters those people wrote saying they'd spotted the missing girl? I think Cleat Wiggins killed every one of the correspondents. Oh, gotta go. The ambulance just arrived. Later." Maggie hung up and turned to the policeman. "Do you think I could ride in the ambulance with her?"

He looked up from the notepad on which he'd been scribbling notes as fast as he could from Maggie's conversation and nodded. She reached for the door, then turned back to Flynn. "Is that okay?"

Flynn touched her cheek. "Of course, Maggie. She's your sister."

Maggie sat for a minute thinking about what he'd said. "My sister," she whispered almost reverently. "All my life I've wanted a sister." Tears welled up in her eyes. "I thought my brothers' wives would be the only sisters I'd ever have."

"I guess you're just lucky. Few people discover siblings they didn't know they had, much less a twin. Go ahead," Flynn urged. "Keep her company. What a nice surprise it will be for her to have your face be the first she sees when she wakes up."

Fear flash flooded through Maggie. What if Wiggins had overdosed her sister? What if she didn't wake up? That would be too cruel, too horrible, to discover a sister she didn't know she had, only to lose her before they'd had a chance to really meet.

Maggie was allowed to ride in the ambulance with Katie while Flynn followed in the car. She'd have to get used to thinking of her sister as Alyssa. Lately, Katie had become dominant in her mind. Maggie's head was awhirl with all the possibilities of their relationship, then she remembered that Alyssa wouldn't be going home with her to live as her sister; she'd be going home to her own father. Wouldn't she?

What changes had taken place inside Alyssa during the last seven years? Could she actually resume her life as she had known it before her sixteenth birthday? Absolutely nothing would ever be the same for her again. Maggie squeezed Alyssa's hand. *Sister, I hope your adjustment is easier than I'm afraid it will be. What traumas will you have to overcome? What nightmares will disturb your sleep for years to come?*

Flynn was waiting when the ambulance doors opened at the hospital. How had he arrived before the ambulance? He helped her down, and they moved aside for the same emergency room personnel who had helped them with the black-haired, rail-thin girl earlier that morning. Maggie wondered what they thought about these two mud-spattered people who kept bringing in unconscious women.

When Maggie and Flynn finished the seemingly endless reams of paperwork to have Alyssa admitted for treatment, she still hadn't regained consciousness. That frightened Maggie. What if they couldn't discover what Cleat Wiggins had given her? What if she needed an antidote rather than just letting the drug wear off? What if . . . ?

Maggie's what-ifs were as endless as the questions the police asked. Now Maggie was truly hungry. She glanced at her watch. Noon had long since passed. Poor Kit hadn't been fed either, and Flynn was probably perishing from hunger, since he'd been ready for lunch hours ago.

"Do you suppose there is any possibility of getting something to eat?" Maggie asked the officer who seemed to come up with ten questions for every answer they gave him. "We've been a little busy today and missed breakfast as well as lunch. Now it's dinnertime and I'm starving."

"Sure," the man said with an amiable smile. "Do you want to go to the hospital cafeteria or run out and get something?"

That was easy, Maggie thought. *Why didn't I think of that before? My stomach wouldn't be shrunk to the size of a marble and screaming in protest.*

Flynn answered for them both. "We'll go out."

Maggie looked through the glass where a doctor and a nurse still hovered over Alyssa. "Let me see what's going on in here first." She didn't really want to leave Alyssa, but if they were going to let her sleep off the drugs, it could be hours before she woke up.

"I'll talk to them for you," the officer said, going to speak to the doctor. He returned with good news. "They think it's just a matter of letting the drugs wear off. All her vital signs are good, and they don't think she's in any danger, but she'll probably be asleep for a few hours, so go ahead and grab a bite."

"Thanks," Maggie said. "I do want to be here when she wakes up, so we won't be long." They started out, then Maggie turned back to the officer. "Have you heard anything about the kidnapper? He is in custody, isn't he?"

The officer nodded. "And he won't be out anytime soon, so don't worry about him."

Maggie shivered as she thought about the evil man. "He's such a fiend. I think if there was the slightest possibility of escape, he'd find it, and I'm afraid he'd come directly here for Alyssa." Maggie paused. "Either to take her back or to silence her. Please watch her carefully. Don't let anything happen to her."

The officer nodded solemnly, and Maggie and Flynn left the hospital. The rain had stopped, and the sun was setting somewhere behind a thick, dark cloud. It was a gray, colorless world, except for Christmas lights flickering on as twilight fell. Kit was overjoyed to see them and even happier to have something to eat.

Maggie held him up when he finished inhaling his bottle's contents. "What do you think? Care to take a guess at his parentage?"

Flynn laughed. "Definitely a Heinz 57. And most vets will tell you they make the finest pets since they usually bring the best characteristics of all those assorted genes. I think you've got a real winner there."

"But what am I going to do with a dog? I have no place to live, no job."

"Just a pair of homeless waifs, parentage unknown," Flynn said, pulling into a parking lot filled with pick-ups. Theirs was the only passenger car in the lot. The sign above the long, low, white, nondescript building read R & M's Boiling Point.

"What's this?" Maggie said, puzzled at Flynn's choice of restaurant, if that's what this could be called.

"Supposedly the best hangout for fresh Cajun-type seafood. You probably won't find any tourists here, but the locals say it can't be beat."

Maggie had a hard time believing him. "Who told you that?"

"The ambulance driver, a couple of the police, and one of the emergency room technicians. And I asked them independently of each other. They weren't collaborating on their answer," Flynn assured her.

"I hope they weren't pulling your leg." Maggie tried to make herself look presentable by running a brush through her hair and applying some lipstick, but there was nothing she could do about the dirt on her pantsuit and her mud-stained shoes. She sighed and got out when Flynn opened the door for her. "I hope you're not ashamed to be seen with me. I've looked better after cleaning out the barn, although I probably smell better."

Flynn shut the door and swung Maggie around to face him. She looked up in surprise as he placed his hands on her shoulders and leaned toward her.

"I would never be ashamed to be seen with you anywhere, no matter how you looked, and you're even more beautiful with dirt on your face." Then, to cover the serious tone he'd allowed to creep into his voice, he wrinkled his nose and hastened to add, "It's not like I just stepped out of the pages of *GQ* or something. Haven't you noticed I'm even muddier than you?"

Maggie stared at Flynn. What had she detected in his voice? Was there a different warmth there? Or was it just wishful thinking? Could he ever think of her as anything but another patient? She could certainly imagine him as much more than a psychologist. She searched his eyes, and his met hers for a long moment. Then someone burst from the door of the café laughing loudly, and the moment vanished.

Maggie and Flynn simultaneously turned to see what caused the raucous laughter, and without looking at each other again, simply moved toward the entrance. The opportunity to explore feelings may have passed, but the feelings themselves had only been heightened.

CHAPTER 29

The place was plain, down-home, with paneling on a couple of walls and lattice trim painted in deep turquoise. Every eye turned to them when they walked in the door, appraised, then ignored them. Patrons had huge platters piled high with bright red crawdaddies or plates of steaming shrimp and rice.

A friendly waitress with a deep Southern accent seated them, presented menus, recited the specials of the day, and left to get their drinks.

"Flynn, I wouldn't have any idea what to order. Those little red things look terrible." Maggie had been watching someone at another table break the back on a crawdaddy and dig out the meat. "That's far too much work for me, even if they're delicious." But she doubted seriously anything that ugly could taste good enough to be worth the effort it took to extract that little bit of meat.

"Do you like shrimp?" Flynn asked.

"Yes, if I don't have to shell them."

The look Flynn gave her over his menu caused her to hastily explain. "You have to remember, I'm an Idaho girl—as inland—no seacoast," she emphasized. "Seafood wasn't something we ate more than once a month, if then. My father raised cattle, we had chickens, sheep, and the boys brought home pheasants and sage hen from the hills. We had an occasional rainbow trout they caught, but that was the extent of my seafood experience, except canned tuna. I'm not used to dealing with those ugly creatures and all their claws and legs."

"Then I guess I'll just have to introduce you to the finer things of life. Ever had a shrimp po' boy?"

Maggie shook her head.

Flynn lowered his menu. "Can I order for you? Do you feel adventurous?"

"If that equates with hungry, yes."

The waitress returned with coffee for Flynn and ice water for Maggie. Flynn ordered her a shrimp po' boy and for himself, boiled crabs with dirty rice.

"That doesn't even *sound* good," Maggie gasped. "Why do they call it dirty rice?"

"You'll understand when you see it—with all the spices, it looks dirty, but it's delicious."

The people at the table next to them had been listening to Maggie's comments, and one older fellow spoke up. "Have ya ever tried frog legs, Missie?"

Maggie shook her head. "Our frogs don't get big enough in Idaho to eat."

"I've pulled frogs out of my pond that had legs near a foot and a half long. Bigger'n these little things by far." He held up one that looked like a plump chicken thigh except three times longer. "Here, try this." He put it on a plate with some deep-fried potatoes and passed it to Maggie.

As she bit into the succulent white meat, he said, "I'd trade a hundred pounds of chicken any day for good frog legs." Maggie had to agree they were delicious. Then he told her how to make the potatoes. Peel, slice lengthwise, boil, then dip in a mixture of flour, milk, and cayenne pepper and deep fry. Fantastic. *And full of calories,* Maggie thought.

The friendly couple finished their dinner and left. Maggie enjoyed talking to them, but she had a lot on her mind that didn't include frog legs and recipes for deep-fried potatoes.

"Do you think I should call Lily and tell her we've found Alyssa, or should I wait until I've seen and talked to Alyssa before I break the good news?"

Flynn thought about it for a minute. "Maybe you should talk to Alyssa before you call Lily."

Maggie looked up at the tone in Flynn's voice. "You mean, wait until I talk to Alyssa to call Lily, or maybe Alyssa won't want me to call Lily at all?"

"Yes."

"That's not an answer. Which do you mean?"

"Both. Have you considered Alyssa may not want to be found? That she may not want to go home? I'm sure she'll have to undergo a lot of counseling to be able to deal with all she's gone through, and she may not be ready to face her old life, her father, everyone she knew."

"Does that happen a lot?"

"More than you can imagine. Many times the victims think of themselves as being the guilty ones. They shouldn't have allowed themselves to be taken; they should have been able to escape; they should have been able to prevent whatever occurred. And after the guilt, there is the shame of what happened to them. After that there is remorse for the unhappiness they've caused their family. It's a very complicated emotional process, and some people can never work through it."

Maggie slumped back in her chair. "Sure takes the joy out of the rescue, doesn't it? You work so hard to find them and try to give them their life back, but they don't want it anymore." Her eyes filled with tears. "Oh, Flynn. What will I do if she doesn't want anything to do with me? What if she doesn't want anything to do with her father either?" Maggie couldn't imagine anyone not wanting to go home. "Even knowing I'm not related by blood to my family, they're still my family and they still love me—and I love them. An accident of birth won't change what we've been through together."

Flynn looked thoughtfully at Maggie. His heart always wrenched inside him when she talked of her home life and relationships. "I'd like to meet your family someday, Maggie. It's hard for me to fathom the rapport you have with them. It's so foreign to what I had growing up."

"But it's not foreign to what you had with Susan and Kaitlin, is it? Didn't you have that kind of total, unconditional love?" Maggie asked.

Flynn leaned forward on his elbows. "I think we did. Sometimes it's hard to remember the good times, when . . ." He stopped, knowing he couldn't control the emotion in his voice.

"When what, Flynn?" Maggie reached across the table and touched his hand. "You can't keep it bottled up forever. And you need to remember the good times more often so you can put the bad times from your mind."

Flynn smiled, but his eyes remained sad. "I thought I was the psychologist here."

"Sometimes the biggest problems don't require any degrees to be solved, only a sympathetic, listening ear."

Flynn took Maggie's hand in his. He looked down at it, and ran his thumb along her long slender fingers. "What if I don't want your sympathy, Maggie?" He waited, hardly daring to look at her. He'd promised himself he wouldn't reveal his feelings until this was over, until she didn't need him any more. That time hadn't come quite yet, but Flynn feared things might escalate and he needed to tell her how he felt before she slipped away from him.

Maggie's heart took a dive. She watched Flynn's face, but she could read nothing there to reveal what he meant. Did he mean he didn't want her to feel sorry for him? Did he mean he didn't need her sympathy or her listening ear? *Or her?* What did he mean? Finally his eyes met hers, and she knew.

"What if I want more than that, Maggie?"

Both elated and stunned, Maggie chose her words with care. "How much more, Flynn?" she asked softly.

The warmth in Maggie's eyes and voice encouraged him to continue. "I've been intrigued by you since the moment you opened your hotel-room door and looked up at me with those incredible sapphire blue eyes, and I've enjoyed every minute we've been together since. Maggie, I thought I had literally died inside, that I could never experience love, or wonder, or feel emotion of any kind again, but you've rekindled all that in me. I started to say, it's hard to remember the good times when there is so much pain left from the bad times. But I've actually gone hours, even a whole day since I met you without feeling the debilitating pain of losing Susan and Kaitlin."

Flynn stopped, not knowing if he'd said too much or not enough or how Maggie had taken what he'd blurted out. He felt nervous as a schoolboy asking for a date to the prom.

"Thank you, Flynn. That's the nicest compliment you could ever give me." Now it was Maggie who didn't quite know what to say. She'd hoped Flynn liked her, that he would see her not just as a patient, but as a woman. He seemed to be saying that. And for some reason, it terrified her.

"I wasn't just complimenting you, Maggie. I was trying to say that . . ."

Why did the waitress choose the worst possible time to deliver their meal? As hungry as Maggie had been, her appetite abruptly disappeared. She needed to hear what else Flynn had to say. But as she looked in his eyes, they told her. Words were no longer necessary.

The waitress asked if there was anything else they needed, then finally left them alone, and Flynn finished his statement. "I'm falling in love with you, Maggie." He shook his head. "I am in love with you. I didn't want you to know about my feelings until you could think of me as something other than your doctor, but now that most of this has been resolved, you could fly out of here tonight and I might never see you again." Flynn stopped and waited for Maggie to say something, anything, in response to his confession.

"I'm sure you've guessed how I feel about you, and it has nothing to do with a patient/doctor relationship." Maggie blushed, remembering their conversation in the car. "But I have one tremendous problem we need to discuss, and as soon as you've eaten your dinner, I think we need to talk about it. Right now, don't let your dirty rice get cold."

Flynn's relief at Maggie's admission was palpable. Whatever problem she had could be worked out, as long as she felt something for him. He felt like kissing her right across the table, but he laughed with relief instead. "You're charming. Here. Taste this. I think you'll like it." He put a spoonful of dirty rice on her plate, and she did like it.

"Hmm, it might not even be too bad cold." Then she tried her shrimp po' boy and loved it, but with her mouth full, all she could do was wave it at Flynn and nod. They set aside their discussion to finish dinner with comments confined to the meal. But they didn't linger, and as soon as Flynn paid the bill, they hurried to the car.

"Now, what's this tremendous problem you have?" he said as he settled into his seat. He watched Maggie trying to get the excited pup calmed down so she could answer him, then he said, "No, before you tell me, I have to do something I've wanted to do for days." He leaned over, turned her face to his, and gently kissed her lips. He would have moved away, hardly daring to prolong it, but Maggie leaned closer and returned the kiss. Kit interrupted, jumping up on Maggie, wanting attention.

They parted, slightly breathless. "Flynn, you don't fight fair. I was all prepared to give you all the reasons why this wouldn't work, and I think you just shot them out of the sky."

"Good." He leaned over to do it again, but she laughed and held Kit up instead.

"Can we discuss this on the way back to the hospital? I hate to be gone too long in case Alyssa wakes up. I want to be there for her."

Flynn scratched Kit's head, leaned over to kiss Maggie's cheek, and started the car. "Okay, we're on our way to the hospital. Now, will you tell me about this tremendous problem you have?"

As they drove out of the parking lot, Maggie took a deep breath and prayed she'd be able to say just the right thing in the right way. "You know I'm Mormon."

"Yes."

"And you know about Mormon temples?"

"I've seen some."

"When we get married, we go to those temples to be sealed for time and eternity, for this life and the next."

"Sounds like a good idea."

Maggie paused, not quite knowing how to present the next part. "In order to enter the temple, you have to be a member of the Church in good standing and get a recommend from your bishop."

Flynn glanced at Maggie, knowing what was coming. He could read in her eyes her hesitancy at saying it.

"I can't marry anyone who isn't a member of the Church and who can't take me to the temple." Their eyes met, and hers pleaded with him to understand her heart.

"Can't—or—won't?" he asked, knowing the answer to that question, too. Maggie's standards were high because of her religion and her belief in God. This would be an integral part of those beliefs and helped make Maggie who and what she was. That was part of what had attracted Flynn to her in the first place, along with her fresh radiance, her luminescent personality, her forthright goodness.

"I won't. It's too important. I could fall in love with you, and love you for the rest of my life, but if you aren't a member of the Church, you can't hold the priesthood, you can't give me and our children the blessings we need. And one of those blessings is a covenant with God made as we kneel across a sacred altar in the temple." Maggie shut her eyes to keep the tears from running down her cheeks. Had she just closed the door on one of the kindest, most fascinating, most wonderful men she had ever met in her life?

Flynn drove silently into the hospital parking lot and turned off the car. Maggie opened her eyes, and he held out his hand to her. She took it, not knowing whether it was a farewell gesture or something else. He leaned over and kissed her cheek. "Let's see if Alyssa's awake."

They walked without speaking to Alyssa's room in the hospital that had become so familiar. They spoke to the uniformed officer posted outside the door, then peeked in. Alyssa was still sleeping, so they went around the corner to the observation window to watch her and be out of the busy corridor.

Maggie's heart was breaking, fearing she'd just turned Flynn away. Even knowing it was the right thing to do didn't lessen the ache she felt thinking about how their life together might have been.

Flynn's mind overflowed with questions. What did this religion of Maggie's entail? All he really knew about it was that it seemed to be very restrictive. Could he embrace it with everything it might require just to be with Maggie? He couldn't even guess until he knew more, and that wouldn't happen anytime in the next few hours. This would be a very long day indeed. His greatest fear was that he'd be consigned back to the dark world he'd inhabited before Maggie's brightness came into his life.

They stood side by side at the window, watching the girl who looked so much like Maggie, sleeping off the drugs, her strawberry-roan hair spread across the white pillow. The friendly comradery they'd enjoyed had vanished, overridden by tension, doubt, and their unknown future. It was like a dark cloud hanging over them.

"You know what?" Flynn said. "I'd never let her hear me because she'd just feel bad, but did you know you're the more beautiful twin?" He looked down at Maggie, then back at Alyssa. "Yes, definitely the pretty one." Flynn brushed a wispy strand of red hair from Maggie's forehead. "I wonder which of you is the oldest? You must be, since you got all the looks, and Alyssa had to make do with what was left over after you were created. A smidgen of this, a tad of that, not quite as much of the other."

Maggie laughed at the ridiculous thought, and the black cloud on their relationship dispelled. Though not the same as before, their friendship returned from the brink of capsizing. Flynn longingly touched her cheek but refrained from kissing her, understanding there were concerns to be discussed before they could progress along the road on which he had already embarked—and from which he was afraid, for him, there was no turning back.

As Maggie watched Alyssa, she thought she saw some movement in Alyssa's hand. "Look, Flynn. Is she coming out of it?" Maggie hurried around the corner into Alyssa's room and took her hand. "Alyssa, can you hear me? Alyssa, it's Maggie. Open your eyes and look at me."

On the opposite side of the bed, Flynn took Alyssa's other hand, rubbing it gently. Human touch was one of the best medicines in a doctor's repertoire of remedies; it needed to be used more often.

"Do you think she knows we're twins?" Maggie asked.

"I couldn't even guess." Flynn was quiet for a minute. "Maggie, you said Alyssa was raised by her father, Lionel Lawson, a newspaper editor. I've been thinking about that. I suppose he could have risen from the point of having nothing, not even enough money to pay for the hospital when you were born, to his current position in sixteen years, but that raises some serious questions in my mind."

Maggie looked at Flynn. "So you're suggesting we have a different father somewhere?" All this mystery over her origins left Maggie's head spinning. Then she felt Alyssa move again and gripped her sister's hand. "Alyssa, open your eyes. If you can hear me, squeeze my hand."

Alyssa squeezed Maggie's hand. Maggie repeated her request, and Alyssa again returned the pressure. "Flynn, she's responding. Oh, Alyssa, I have so many questions for you. I'm so excited to have a sister and I hope you are, too." Maggie had to bite her tongue to keep from babbling on, but she kept a tight hold on Alyssa's hand.

Finally Alyssa stirred in the bed, moved her head gently back and forth as if to loosen the cobwebs from her mind, and slowly opened her eyes. The first thing she saw was Maggie's face bending over her. And the second was Cleat Wiggins's ugly face outside the observation window.

CHAPTER 30

Alyssa let out a piercing scream. Maggie jumped back. As Flynn turned to the door to call the nurse, he saw what terrified the girl. Cleat Wiggins, blood dripping from a head wound down his face onto his dirty clothes, stood directly on the other side of the window.

When she saw the monster's face just feet from them, Maggie flung herself across Alyssa and held her tight to protect her. Flynn headed for the door to take him on, but the policeman standing outside the door and two who raced down the corridor with guns drawn were there before him. Ignoring the officers' shouts to freeze and surrender, Cleat raised his handcuffed fists and smashed them into the window, shattering the glass. He tried to vault through it to reach Alyssa, but was stopped halfway by shots that echoed down the corridors. He fell, limp and lifeless, on the jagged glass, hanging half in, half out of Alyssa's room.

Flynn turned back to the girls huddled together on the bed. "It's okay. He can't hurt you anymore." He stroked Maggie's hair and bent over to whisper, "He'll never hurt anyone, ever again."

Maggie slid off the bed and looked at Alyssa who was wide-eyed with terror. She held both of her hands and said softly, "Alyssa, look at me. Do you know who I am?"

Alyssa looked at Maggie. She nodded. The two sisters just stared at what might have been their own reflection in the mirror. Flynn strode to the end of the bed, blocking their view of the gruesome sight at the window, granting them as much privacy as they could have at the moment. Police immediately ordered Alyssa's bed removed from the room, which Flynn thought was the next best thing that had happened in the last two minutes.

Well, maybe the third best thing. The first was that the State of California had been saved the trouble and expense of extraditing and trying to bring to trial the man called Cleat Wiggins; he'd never be able to terrorize anybody again. The second was that Alyssa appeared to have survived the drugs and was coherent. The third was removing the sisters from having to see the corpse until the coroner and detectives could take care of it. Flynn knew that would not happen soon. He asked how Cleat Wiggins, supposedly in police custody, came to be at the hospital.

"Simple," the officer said. "We cuffed him, took him to the station to book him, and as he was getting out of the car at the station, he fell. We'd cuffed his hands behind his back, and he wrenched his shoulder in the fall and bloodied his head when it hit the gravel. So we brought him here to be treated, cuffing his hands in front so it wouldn't hurt his shoulder any more. I think it was all a ruse to get here. He was moaning and groaning and could hardly walk, until suddenly, when we came in the front door, he bolted."

"Did he say anything about the kidnapping? Any reason for doing it? Apparently there was never a ransom demand."

"He swore he was innocent," the officer said. "The girl was his daughter, and he was getting even with his wife for running away with her when she was a baby. Of course, they all have some kind of story. We'll just have to see if his was really true."

"I'm glad his reign of terror is over," Flynn said. "Wonder if we'll ever know how many people he killed?" He started to walk away, then turned back. "I'm sure you've got this angle covered already, but make sure they get some DNA samples. *He* won't be making any confessions, but his DNA can do it for him. Then we'll know if his story about Alyssa being his daughter was true."

The attendants wheeled Alyssa's bed into another room down the hall, and Maggie held her hand all the way. When they were finally alone, with Flynn their self-appointed guardian just outside the room, Maggie ignored the horror they'd both just witnessed, ignored the terror still tingling through her, tried to overcome the adrenalin rush still flushing through her, and gave free rein to the questions demanding answers.

"Did you know you had a sister? How did you know about me? How did you know to contact me?"

Alyssa's tongue was not working quite as it should, but she said slowly, "I felt a connection to something or someone when I was a little girl playing alone, but I didn't know what it meant. Kind of like part of me was missing and I needed to find it. When I was in high school, I started reading articles in journals where people recorded their research on thought projection, ESP, that kind of stuff. I suspected I must have a twin somewhere, because that was the most logical connecting factor they discovered."

She paused, still looking at Maggie in wonder. "You look just like me. Almost."

Maggie laughed. "I can't believe this. It's just like getting the biggest, best Christmas present in the whole world!" Then she stopped. "Christmas. It's Christmas tomorrow. I got a sister for Christmas!" Maggie whirled ecstatically around the room, then hugged Alyssa again.

Flynn, standing outside the door, heard Maggie's excited exclamation, and quietly went into action.

"Do you celebrate Christmas?" Alyssa asked.

Maggie was suddenly sobered. "Yes. Don't you?"

"Not since . . ." Tears filled Alyssa's eyes. Maggie leaned over and kissed Alyssa's cheek. "It's okay. Just cry it out. Tears are great cleansers." Maggie's sympathetic tears joined Alyssa's tears of anguish and heartache for the wasted years of suffering and loneliness and terror she'd spent. Maggie found a box of tissues, and they used almost the whole box as they got acquainted.

"Tell me about your parents and your home," Alyssa said.

This was territory Maggie wasn't ready to enter just yet, knowing how much happier her home had been than Alyssa's for the last seven years.

"First, I want to know all the things we have in common. I know you love horses and you have one." Then she stopped. "Alyssa, did you project into my head riding your horse? I feel we've ridden together in our minds."

Alyssa nodded. "That's when I really started connecting to you and felt you were finally aware of me."

"So how much do you know about me? Could you tell what I was doing? Could you read my mind? Did you know what was going on in my life? I didn't know anything about you until just this week, when I felt you connecting to me."

"No, I could never read your mind or tell what you were thinking. I had to concentrate to even send you a message."

"Did you know I was looking for you?"

Alyssa nodded. "I remember the moment I sensed you had finally discovered I existed. I don't remember how I knew, just that you were aware of me for the first time. I was so excited because I felt you might be the link I needed to get away from . . ." Alyssa couldn't even talk about it. Couldn't say his name.

Maggie stared at her sister. "Did you get me to ask for the clippings of your kidnapping? Is that where that thought came from?"

"Maybe. I just kept trying to project into your mind: find me, find me. I don't know whether that was what did it, but whenever I had time to think of you, I tried to project something to you, some image or information that would help you find me. He was so careful to never let anyone get close, so I knew I'd never be able to . . ." Alyssa shivered and turned from Maggie to look out the window. She was quiet for a long time, but Maggie waited for her to speak again.

When Maggie could concentrate on something else, it was easier to block Cleat Wiggins and those terrifying, frightful images of the last few minutes from her mind. Time seemed endless before Alyssa spoke again and Maggie could dismiss the horror she feared would be etched in her memory forever.

"I'd run out of hope. I considered killing myself because I was so miserable. Every time I thought someone might help me escape, that man stopped them." Alyssa turned to Maggie with tears running down her face. "I think he killed a lot of people to keep from getting caught. I thought if I was dead, then he wouldn't kill anyone else. You were my last hope, Maggie. If I hadn't finally connected with you, and you hadn't come to find me, I'd already be dead. I'd figured out how I could do it."

"Oh, Alyssa, I'm so glad you didn't. It's never the answer."

"When your existence becomes so unbearable, so hopeless, so miserable, there don't seem to be many options," Alyssa said quietly.

Maggie couldn't argue with that statement, but as she stroked the hand of her twin sister, she thought how wonderful it was going to be to share with her the truths she possessed that would give her sister reasons to live and to love life.

"Alyssa, do you want me to call your father and tell him you're okay?"

There was profound silence in the room for several minutes. Maggie didn't say a word, giving Alyssa time to consider her question.

"I don't know," she said slowly. "I don't know if I'm ready to face Dad and Lily yet."

"Lily?" Maggie had a funny feeling in the pit of her stomach.

"Our housekeeper. Well, she was more than that. She was like a mother to me, especially after my mother died of cancer. Then when I got older and didn't need her constantly at my beck and call, she went to work at the newspaper office." Alyssa looked at Maggie. "I think she and my father really liked each other. I kind of thought after I went to college, Dad and Lily might get married. I hoped they would. That would have given me a mother and father together as a real family, instead of me and Dad, and, the housekeeper, whenever it looked okay." She was quiet. "Maybe they're married now."

"No, I don't think so. That's interesting. I didn't know Lily was the housekeeper spoken of in the newspaper articles. No wonder she looked so shocked when she first saw me. It must have been like having you walk in the door. I almost gave her a heart attack when I asked for the files so I could look for you. Poor Lily."

Flynn knocked softly on the door. "May I interrupt this happy family reunion?"

"Please come in. I know you two met at the Alpine Inn, but Flynn, I want to formally introduce you to my sister, Alyssa." Maggie turned to Alyssa. "This is Flynn, my friend, protector, and . . ." Maggie blushed slightly, "much more, besides the greatest psychologist of his time. He's probably the only reason I was able to find you, so you can thank him as much as me that we finally got together. May I present Dr. Flynn Ford."

Flynn grasped Alyssa's hand and looked into eyes a slightly lighter shade of blue than Maggie's. "I'm delighted to meet you in your happier persona of Alyssa instead of Katie, and happy to see you looking so perky. How does your head feel?"

"Heavy. Aching, but not as bad as usual."

He turned to Maggie. "Could I have a word alone with Alyssa? I promise this won't take long."

Maggie should have expected this. Flynn was the one who should have been with her this whole time, walking her through the psychological baggage she must be carrying. She jumped to her feet. "Good timing. I'll find the rest room, then check to make sure Kit hasn't chewed up the floor mats yet, maybe even give him some fresh newspaper to work on, then I'll be back." She felt a twinge of apprehension leaving Flynn alone with Alyssa. What if he decided he liked her sister better than her? She shook off the unworthy thought and hurried down the hall.

Flynn settled on the edge of Alyssa's bed. "I have a proposition for you, Alyssa, if you feel up to it. And the decision is entirely yours."

When she looked sufficiently puzzled, Flynn continued. "I've made arrangements to fly Maggie home tomorrow for Christmas. She doesn't know about it yet. My question is, would you like to spend Christmas with Maggie's family, or stay here in the hospital, or would you like to go home to California to be with your dad?"

Seeing Alyssa's frightened expression, Flynn continued in a quiet, soothing voice. "I have to confess, Christmas at Maggie's house would almost certainly be something like a three-ring circus. The house will be filled with people and kids and noise and fun, but more than that, I think there will be more love than you can imagine. You and Maggie will have time to get acquainted, and it will give you time to get your equilibrium back again."

Alyssa looked less apprehensive, but Flynn knew she wasn't sure she could face anyone yet, wasn't sure she could be in normal situations with normal people when she wasn't yet feeling normal at all. At least, that was the usual mind-set of people who have just endured these situations, so Flynn went on speaking calmly, trying to convince Alyssa this would be the best thing she could do.

"I don't know if you and Maggie have talked about this, but Maggie didn't find out until today that her mother is not her birth mother, nor did her mother even know until today. Mrs. McKenzie was under anesthetic when her baby died, and a man in the waiting room who didn't have any money to pay the hospital bill offered one of his twins to Mr. McKenzie. Maggie's dad never told his wife her baby had died, so everyone thought Maggie was their natural child. The family knew nothing about you until a few hours ago, and if what Maggie told me is true, you will be welcomed with open arms."

"I don't know," Alyssa murmured. "I'm really not sure I could face anyone just yet."

Flynn opened the night table drawer, pulled out the mirror he was sure he'd find there, and held it so she had to look at it.

"Tell me what you see," he said gently. She didn't understand what he wanted.

"Then I'll tell you what I see. A beautiful face, lovely blue eyes, strawberry-roan hair, and someone who very much needs some normalcy in her life. Someone who needs a bunch of older brothers who will give no quarter in a fair fight, who will not make a fuss over you, but *will* offer any support you need. I see a girl who needs some unconditional love, but more importantly, one who needs to give some in return."

Alyssa tried to laugh, but it came out a little shaky. "And what else do you see, Dr. Ford? That's more than I see. Lot's more."

"I see someone who has a fighting and resilient spirit, someone who's come through perdition and back again, and survived. Someone who's going to need time to heal, but I'll help you through that healing if you'll let me. And my first prescription would be Christmas in the McKenzie household."

"Can I think about it?" Alyssa asked quietly, not convinced at all, and terrified just thinking about facing strangers. Especially a lot of them.

"You can, but I have to remind you, you're going to have to face the world sooner or later, and sooner is better. This will be an environment free from reporters and publicity, free from poking and prying into your feelings. It'll be just Maggie's family, no outsiders, and they won't ask questions if that's the way you want it. You'll be able to ease back into a normal world."

Flynn stopped and laughed. "Well, if Maggie described it accurately, it's not exactly a normal world as most people know it, but it is a safe and loving world, and I recommend it as a giant first step in your recovery from the last traumatic seven years."

"Will you be coming?" Alyssa thought she might be able to face something of this magnitude only if she had Dr. Ford's calming comfort in which to retreat.

"I wouldn't miss it for the world. I haven't been to the circus for years, and I think this will be therapeutic for everyone concerned. You see, the McKenzie family will also be dealing with this new discovery in their lives, and I think having you there in person will be good for everyone. One more thing. You need to consider calling your father as soon as possible. Can you imagine how he's felt all these years, not knowing if you were dead or alive? Think about it, Alyssa."

"I will, Dr. Ford. I promise I'll call just as soon as I have a little time to prepare myself. I've both looked forward to it—and dreaded it—for years."

Maggie rapped on the door, then peeked her head in. "Am I too soon?"

Flynn stood and looked at Alyssa. She smiled tentatively up at Flynn, then slowly stretched out her hand to Maggie. "Just in time. In fact," she said slowly, "I think we have some news that might make you quite happy."

"Me? What could possibly make me happier than getting to spend Christmas with my sister?" Then she looked at Flynn. "And my . . ." Maggie's cheeks flushed slightly. "My dearest friend," she added softly. That wasn't quite the right terminology for what her heart felt, but it would do until there had been a resolution to other things.

"What *could* be better, Maggie?" Flynn asked, trying to keep the elation and excitement out of his voice.

Maggie stared at Flynn, then at the smile on Alyssa's face. Dare she say it? Especially in front of Alyssa? What one thing in the whole world would be better than having Christmas right here with these two people? "The only thing I can think of that could possibly be better is to spend Christmas . . ." she took a deep breath and concentrated on Flynn's face, on his dark eyes that seemed to sparkle at this minute. She didn't dare to look at Alyssa, fearing she might see hurt or anguish or fear in her sister's face. ". . . in Idaho with my family, or the rest of my family," she amended. "But only if you two would go with me."

Flynn couldn't keep from smiling. "What do you think, Alyssa? Would you be willing to spend a few days in what Maggie describes as happy chaos?"

Alyssa nodded. Just watching the joy, the wonder, the excitement play across Maggie's face gave her more happiness than she'd felt in years.

"Flynn, are you serious?" Maggie asked breathlessly, ready to explode with delight.

Flynn nodded, totally unprepared for Maggie's enthusiastic thank you. She flew across the room, threw her arms around his neck and kissed him. But as Flynn's arms automatically encircled her and he felt her warmth against him as he'd so often imagined it, he brought her closer, and the kiss that started out as a quick, excited response to his offer became much more.

Maggie lost herself in that kiss. Never before had she experienced the warmth and fire it sent through her. It was intoxicating. Addicting. And frightening. When they stepped apart, Maggie looked up at Flynn and knew he'd felt the same wonderful sensations.

"I, ah, didn't mean for that to happen," Maggie murmured, backing away, and wishing with every step she could fly back into his arms and stay there.

Flynn perched casually back on the foot of the bed and winked at Alyssa. "What other surprises do you think we can concoct? I rather liked Maggie's reaction to that last one."

Alyssa smiled. "I didn't know you two were . . ."

Maggie interrupted her. "We're not," she said quickly. Then she glanced up at Flynn's laughing eyes. "At least, not yet." Her cheeks flamed with embarrassment. "I mean," she stammered, looking at Alyssa who was enjoying this very much. "I mean, we're working through some very serious matters."

Alyssa nodded. "I can see how serious they are."

Flynn took charge, as much to save Maggie's feelings as to get things rolling. "Alyssa, the FBI wants your statement and has agreed to give you time for Christmas after they interview you tonight. They'll be here shortly to do that. You'll spend the night in the hospital to make sure the drugs wear off completely. They want to make sure you have no immediate aftereffects, and that you're physically able to make the trip tomorrow. We'll check you out of the hospital first thing in the morning. I've chartered a plane to take us to the airport closest to your little community, Maggie. Pocatello, Idaho, and Brigham City, Utah, were the two closest air fields I found to the Utah-Idaho border."

"Probably Brigham City, but what about your car? And my car? And whose airplane? And . . . you can't be serious." Maggie was in a daze.

A nurse bustled in and recommended that Maggie and Flynn come back in the morning as she had to take Alyssa's vitals before she had to undergo a battery of other tests and physicals. Having been dismissed by the nurse who promised to keep away any of the press who might have discovered a story, Flynn and Maggie said good night to Alyssa, promised to return first thing in the morning, and left.

Maggie faced Flynn in the hall. "I happen to know that chartering a private plane costs a small fortune. Actually, it would probably be a large fortune to me. Can I ask if you have that kind of money?" She put her hand over mouth. "No, that's not what I meant to say. How can you afford it?" She grabbed her head. "Oh, Flynn, it's not coming out right."

"It's okay, Maggie," he said, gently caressing her cheek. "I know what you mean. I received a settlement on a life insurance policy I had on Susan. I've never touched a penny of it. Didn't want it, but my lawyer made sure it was in an accessible account if I ever changed my mind." Flynn twisted an errant strand of red hair around his finger, then looked into Maggie's sapphire blue eyes. "I think Susan would be happy to have me use it to get you and your sister home for Christmas."

Maggie was nearly speechless with wonder. "I'll never be able to thank you enough, Flynn."

"I'm sure I'll think of some way you can repay me," he said, leaning closer.

Maggie put her hands on his chest and stepped back. "You know, you keep me off balance all the time. I just start thinking you're this warm, wonderful friend, then you suddenly send me reeling by kissing me, then you act like a rake. Which is the real you?"

"All of the above," he smiled. "Do you want to call and tell your folks we're coming or do you want to surprise them?"

Maggie laughed. "I'd love to just pop in and surprise them, but I couldn't do that to Mom. She'd have a nervous breakdown trying to change her dinner plans." Then she had an idea. "But we could tell Steve, and he could concoct some kind of story about having additional people in the house—maybe some old missionary companions or military buddies or something. Oh, Flynn, this is wonderful! I'm so excited and happy I feel like my heart is just going to explode." Maggie threw her hands in the air and felt like shouting *Hallelujah!*

"And that makes me happier than you can imagine, Maggie." Flynn couldn't remember the last time he'd felt so good, unless it had been just a few minutes before with Maggie in his arms. How had he existed without this bright ray of sunshine to illuminate all the dark, dusty corners of his heart and soul?

CHAPTER 31

Maggie yawned. "What now?" she asked as they left the hospital.

"Get you to bed before you fall asleep on your feet," Flynn said, opening her door and catching Kit as he tried to escape.

Maggie sank into the cold leather seat and took the frisky puppy on her lap, trying to keep it from washing her face with enthusiastic kisses.

Flynn slid under the wheel and started the car. "You haven't had any sleep for two days, so tonight you're going to get a good night's rest so you'll be up to Christmas at your home tomorrow."

Maggie leaned her head back on the seat. "Oh, just the thought of a hot shower and clean, fresh sheets is enough to send me into rapture." It had been a long, busy, very emotional day; correction—two days—and she was delighted at the thought of just tuning out the world and going to sleep.

Flynn pulled into the first reputable-looking motel he saw. When he'd registered, he drove around to the side by their rooms and parked. He opened the door to her room, flipped on the light, put her bags on the floor, and turned on the heat.

"Sorry, it's not quite what we left the other night, but it's clean and will be warm in a minute. I'm right next door, so if you need anything, knock on the door and I'll be right here." He unlocked the door that joined their rooms.

"Thanks, but I'm so tired I may go to sleep in the shower."

"That wouldn't be a good idea. If I hear the shower running too long, I may have to come and keep you from drowning." Flynn smiled that rakish smile that always sent a blush to Maggie's cheeks.

She quickly said good night and pushed Flynn toward the door. As he reached it, he turned and looked down at her. "Good night, Maggie." He tried to look away, tried to leave, but he stayed too long, lost in her eyes, and in spite of his best intentions, he leaned down and kissed her gently on the lips. It was the hardest thing he'd ever done to not fold her in his arms and stay. Mustering all the self-discipline he had, he backed away, turned quickly to his door, opened it, and disappeared inside. Maggie closed her door, locked it, then leaned against it, weak-kneed, her heart beating so wildly she was afraid it would leap from her chest.

When she heard Flynn's door open again, she looked out the window and saw him taking Kit inside. Maggie would have to remember to thank him in the morning, but she wondered how much sleep he'd actually get with the puppy in his room.

She lost no time in showering and falling into bed. No scriptures tonight, only a quick prayer of heartfelt gratitude, then complete and total oblivion. Not even any dreams to disturb the sleep of the pure and innocent.

Flynn, on the other hand, tired as he was, lay awake a long time wondering where these events were leading. He had no answers and finally fell asleep, only to dream of Maggie bending over to kiss him. He woke to find Kit licking his face.

Morning came too soon for Maggie, who could have slept till noon; it came none too soon for Flynn, who had slept fitfully all night, partly because of Kit and partly because of the unknown territory in which he found himself and the uncertainty of his relationship with Maggie.

Kit's yapping woke Maggie and she hurried to dress, then knocked on the door that joined their rooms. "I assume you're awake in there. No one could sleep through Kit's noise."

Flynn opened the door and Kit rushed through, jumping up on Maggie. "Well, I'm glad to see you, too," she said, picking up the happy little bundle of fur. When Maggie glanced up at Flynn, the look on his face was not one of joy and gladness. "Merry Christmas," she said, "although you look like, 'Bah, humbug' instead. Did Kit keep you awake all night?"

Flynn nodded. "That, and other things."

Maggie looked up at Flynn. "I won't ask what other things, but when we get to my house, will you talk to Steve and ask him all the questions I know you have about my church and our beliefs?"

Flynn nodded glumly and collected their bags while she carried the wriggling pup to the car.

"Do I get breakfast this morning? Any little thing will do, just something to keep my stomach from growling. And Kit will need something else to eat. He's finished all his milk." Maggie looked at Flynn. "Did you get any sleep at all last night?"

"I'll survive, but tonight, you get the dog."

"Tonight he'll sleep in the barn where he'll only keep the horses awake. I'm sorry, Flynn. I was going to thank you this morning for thinking of him and not leaving him in the car. Now I'm sorry that you didn't leave him out there all night."

"And have him chew up the leather seats?" Flynn was clearly not in a good mood this morning.

Maggie sat quietly for a minute, determined not to disturb Flynn, but as she thought of picking up Alyssa at the hospital and their arrival in Idaho before the end of the day, she couldn't keep from bubbling over with excitement and happiness.

"Oh, Flynn, I can't believe this is actually happening. It seems just a dream that I suddenly have a sister, and that we'll really be in Idaho tonight with all my family. And you've made it all possible. Thank you so much."

Flynn looked at Maggie's face, radiant with anticipation. How could he remain in a foul mood with that vision of loveliness next to him? "Merry Christmas, Maggie. I'm sorry I'm such a grump this morning. Guess I just need a cup of wake-me-up to start my motor."

"Oh." Maggie let out a little exclamation, then fell silent.

"What is it?" Flynn asked as he pulled into a McDonald's so they could grab a quick bite before going to the hospital.

"Remind me to stop at a grocery store on the way home and pick up some coffee. Nobody at my house drinks coffee, so we don't keep any around, and we don't have a coffee machine. You do drink instant, I hope."

Flynn stared at her. "Nobody drinks coffee at your house? Nobody?"

"We're Mormons, remember? We don't do coffee."

"Do you want to go inside?" Flynn asked, wondering what other little surprises he was in for.

"The drive-through window is fine. I'll have a sausage and biscuit and large orange juice. Can I pay for it this time?"

"You don't have a job, remember? Besides, I think I can afford breakfast at McDonald's."

"Well, the whole Christmas vacation is on me, once we get to Idaho. I want you to know I'm not really a mooch, although I'm sure your wallet feels like I am. Flynn, I'd like to reimburse you for whatever part of this trip I can. I'll never be able to pay for the airplane, but I can give you some money for gas, and I think I can even scrape together enough to pay for the rooms. Will you let me do that, please?"

Flynn looked at Maggie's pleading sapphire eyes and he fell in love all over again. "Maggie, you're too good to be true." He reached for her hand, brought it to his lips, and gently kissed it. "Will you please accept the fact that I can never do enough for you for making me feel alive again? Thank you. And if it's possible, I'm sure Susan is thanking you too, happy that I'm finally putting that money to good use. There is more money than you could spend if you went on a shopping spree all day, every day for the next year. It needs to be used, so don't worry for a minute if there is enough."

Flynn placed their order, handed Maggie her bag and one for Kit, and put his on the floor next to his door while he drove on through. "You think he should eat this?" Maggie asked, looking in the bag.

"It's either that or ours, so suit yourself. I did get him some milk to go with his scrambled eggs. We'll need to find a place to get some puppy food. I think he hasn't been getting enough to eat. He started chewing everything in sight last night."

"That's because he's a dog. Dogs do that." Maggie looked at Flynn. "Did you ever have a dog?"

"No."

Maggie didn't pursue the subject. She tore open the bag and let Kit eat his scrambled eggs while she ate her sausage and biscuit and drank her juice. Then she gave him his bottle.

"I think you're right. I think we haven't been feeding him enough. But my dad and one of my brothers are vets, so we'll just turn his diet over to them. Maybe we can turn *him* over to them too," she added. "He's far more trouble that I thought he'd be for such a little guy. It was very different having a dog at home on the ranch."

When they arrived at the hospital, the nurse was just leaving Alyssa's room. She informed them release papers were waiting at the desk for Dr. Ford to sign her out. She'd bring a wheelchair around in just a minute and they could take Alyssa with them.

Maggie hurried in to help Alyssa get ready, and found her sitting on the edge of the bed in her hospital gown, clinging to the railing, bare feet dangling above the little step stool. "Oh, I'm dizzy," she said, waiting for the room to stop spinning.

Suddenly Maggie realized Alyssa had no shoes, and the clothes she'd worn in were little more than rags. "Is there anything at your house you want to get?"

A frown crossed Alyssa's face. "No. It's not a house, and I never want to go there again, and as soon as I find something else to wear, I'm going to burn everything I had on."

Maggie had a thought. "Can you stand up? On the floor next to me?"

She helped Alyssa to the stool, then to the floor, and they stood together. "I think you can wear my clothes." Maggie opened the bathroom door. "There is a shower in here. If you want to shower and get cleaned up, I'll have Flynn bring in my bag and we'll find something for you to wear."

"I can't tell you how good that would feel," Alyssa said, and the tone she used made Maggie wonder when was the last time was that she'd had a hot shower. Or was it the possibility of some decent clothes?

Maggie sent Flynn to the car for her bag while she helped Alyssa into the shower, staying just outside the door in case Alyssa got dizzy again. When Flynn brought Maggie's clothes, the twins found an outfit that just fit Alyssa.

Flynn returned with the nurse and the wheelchair and was surprised to find the two sisters dressed, looking beautiful, and chatting animatedly. Even Alyssa had some sparkle in her eyes and a smile on her face.

"Are my two girls ready?" he said, wondering what Maggie's family would say when they saw the two sisters together.

"We're ready for anything," Maggie blurted, overflowing with so much pure happiness she could scarcely contain it. They'd be home for Christmas, and nothing could be beat that.

"Then I guess we'd better get this show on the road, as we have some very important stops to make before we hit the airport, and that only gives us three hours."

Puzzled, Maggie asked, "What important stops?"

Flynn smiled. "You'll just have to wait and see."

The first important stop was a department store where Flynn bought Alyssa everything that made her eyes light up: a tailored, royal blue suit with a white lacy blouse; a long, black velvet skirt and beaded sweater; a hunter-green knit pantsuit with a pale green cashmere turtleneck; and assorted jeans, T-shirts, pajamas, robe and slippers, shoes, and all the accessories from the skin out, including boots and a warm coat when Maggie reminded them they'd be in Idaho in the wintertime.

When Alyssa held up the velvet skirt, she ran her hand over the lush fabric and cuddled it next to her face. As Maggie watched her, she explained, "I haven't had on a dress for seven years. I haven't had anything nice for so long."

Maggie thought she was going to cry, but after a quick hug, the fun returned to the shopping, and Alyssa got back into the spirit of the occasion.

It was pure pleasure for Flynn to watch the girls picking out things for Alyssa. They were as excited as a couple of five-year-olds in a toy store. He watched with interest the way they seemed to reach for the same item, even when they weren't looking. Their taste was as similar as their looks, and they even wore their hair in a similar style.

When Alyssa caught their reflection in the mirror, she was so amazed, she suggested they buy matching outfits to see if Maggie's family could tell them apart.

At the second stop they bought Christmas presents for everyone in Maggie's family. Alyssa was doing her best to keep up with Maggie, but Flynn sensed her energy level was still much lower than it should be, and probably would be until she had fully recovered from the drugs in her system. But her enthusiasm matched Maggie's exactly. These two were a pair of fireballs and were having the time of their lives buying presents for everyone else. He kept one little Girl Scout busy running boxes to their courtesy booth for gift wrapping.

He noted that Maggie never once looked at anything for herself. She was so excited to be making sure that Alyssa had something to give everyone in her family and that there would be plenty of packages for Alyssa to open, over and above what they had already purchased for her wardrobe. *Add total unselfishness to that long list of Maggie's incredible qualities,* he thought.

While the girls had their heads together choosing things for Maggie's family, Flynn was busy choosing gifts of his own to give, so the trunk was filled to overflowing when they finished.

The third stop was a pet store to get a carrier and some puppy food for Kit, then a pizza shop just outside the small airport where Flynn picked up two large pizzas and drinks he'd ordered ahead of time.

Then he drove to the pad where the little private jet waited, settled the excited girls and the pup into the plane, and with the pilot's help, unloaded all the bags and packages from the car. He parked his car behind the hangar and they were off.

The three of them sat facing each other in cream-colored leather swivel seats with individual serving tables. Pizza and drinks were spread out so everyone could eat as much as they wanted.

"I would have bought some champagne, but Maggie wouldn't imbibe, so we'll toast with Sprite. It's just as bubbly." Flynn realized nobody on the flight needed champagne to get high—they were already intoxicated with the Christmas spirit and just plain happiness.

He raised his glass of Sprite. "To Maggie and Alyssa, the most beautiful twins I've ever seen."

Then it was Maggie's turn. "To Flynn, who's providing the most amazing Christmas I could ever imagine, and to Alyssa who is the best present I ever got."

Alyssa was quiet for a minute. Neither Maggie nor Flynn could imagine the thoughts going through her mind. "To the adventure of the quest, the thrill of discovery, and satisfaction at the end of the day." They drank to Alyssa's strange but poetic toast. Maggie pondered it, trying to figure out a hidden meaning, but Flynn, as curious as Maggie and suddenly more vocal, asked the question.

"What's the quest, Alyssa?"

"Surely you've been on one to find me," she said softly.

Maggie nodded in agreement, but Flynn pressed to know more. "That's been our quest, and you are our discovery, and we're both more than satisfied with the way things turned out, but what is *your* quest? What are *you* trying to discover?"

Alyssa sat quietly for a minute, steepling her fingers in a gesture both Flynn and Maggie recognized as one Maggie frequently used. "Who my parents are." She looked at Maggie. "And yours."

Maggie leaned forward. "Lionel Lawson isn't your father? Our father?" she corrected, not used to thinking in terms of *we* instead of *me*. "And your mother?" Maggie said. "You don't think the woman who raised you was your birth mother?"

Alyssa silently shook her head. "I'm not sure. When Mother was dying of cancer, she had days during her chemotherapy when she was in incredible pain. Lily would sit by her side and try to soothe her. Once as I came home from school, I was trying to be so very quiet and not disturb her in case she was sleeping, and I heard Lily say something like, "'You don't have to worry about Alyssa. After all, she is my . . . '" Then she leaned over my mother and said it so quietly I couldn't hear the rest of the sentence."

Alyssa looked at Maggie. "I tried to fill in that blank so often. I even tried to trick Lily into revealing what she'd said. I'd ask, 'What am I to you, Lily?' and she'd give me some flippant answer, or she'd tell me how much she loved me and that I was the light of her eye."

"And you think she might be your mother?" Flynn asked.

"I don't know. I truly don't. I have memories of when I was very little and it was just Lily and me and we weren't in the big house, but maybe it was when she was my nanny and I remembered being some-where other than at home." Alyssa sat quietly for a long time; Maggie and Flynn didn't interrupt her. Then she said something that sent cold chills through Maggie.

"That man kept telling me he was my father. He said my mother had run away with me when I was a baby and he couldn't find me for a long time; then one day he saw my picture in the paper and knew I was his daughter, so he came to get me. He said she didn't dare come after me because she knew he was supposed to have custody of me after their divorce. He told me she used to beat me, leave bruises all over me, so the judge gave me to him. He said she didn't really love me or want me but took me just to spite him. When he kidnapped me, he was just claiming his right as my father to have his daughter."

Maggie gasped. "Cleat Wiggins said that?"

Alyssa nodded. "But I don't remember my mother ever beating me. I don't remember ever even being spanked or punished physically in any way, so I thought he was lying to me. He lied about everything all the time so I never knew when to believe him. If ever."

Flynn leaned forward. "Alyssa, they probably already asked you this last night, but will you answer it for me right now?"

Again Alyssa nodded.

"Did Cleat Wiggins ever touch you sexually?"

Alyssa looked down at her hands clasped tightly in her lap. "No. I was terrified that's why he'd kidnapped me, but he never did." Tears filled her blue eyes, overflowed and rolled down her face. "That's when I began to believe him a little. I hoped after awhile that he just wanted a slave to help him make more money and wait on him. I couldn't stand the thought of that dirty, horrid pig actually being my father."

Maggie felt like someone had just socked her in the stomach and knocked the breath right out of her. She couldn't speak; could barely get her lungs functioning again. That had been *her* greatest fear when Flynn proposed all the possibilities of her parenthood, but even that conjecture then hadn't prepared her for the eventuality it might be true.

Flynn spoke softly, addressing both twins. "He may have sired you but that doesn't make him your father. Lionel Lawson was your father in every other sense of the word, Alyssa, as was Scott McKenzie to Maggie. Your allegiance is not to who provided the gene pool, but to the person who loved and nurtured you and provided the necessities of life. Neither of you ever need dwell for a minute on that man, because you have both been raised by parents who thought of you as their own, treated you as their own, and loved you as though they had given birth to you."

Flynn reached for another piece of pizza and leaned back in his seat. "We may be getting a bit premature here anyway. Until we have DNA matches to prove it, we don't need to assume anything."

The dog carrier was even more confining than the floor of the car, and Kit was ready for some freedom. He yipped and begged until Maggie finally let him out. Then she had an idea.

"Alyssa, would you hold Kit for a minute while I call Steve and let him know we're coming?" Maggie dropped the excited, wiggly puppy in Alyssa's lap and turned to her purse for her cell phone. Kit jumped up to lick Alyssa's face and immediately stole her heart.

Maggie's eyes met Flynn's and he nodded his approval. Animal therapy, used extensively for treatment of so many ills, might be the best therapy Alyssa could have to help her return to her normal self and resume a normal life.

Maggie settled into her chair, thought happily that she had to be the luckiest person in the whole world as the earth whizzed beneath them, and called her brother.

"Steve here."

"Hi, Steve. It's Maggie. Are you where you can talk?"

"Go ahead. I'm on my way to the store for Mom. She's baking up a storm and keeps adding dishes to the menu, so I'm the gofer. She's preparing so much food we'll be eating leftovers well into the new year. What fun and exciting news do you have for me this time?"

"First, tell me how Mom is. How did she take the news that I'm not . . . that she's not . . ." Maggie couldn't bring herself to say the words. It sounded so cruel to verbalize such an outlandish idea—that she wasn't her mother's daughter.

Steve jumped in to bridge the gap. "She was totally stunned. Her first reaction was to feel hurt that Dad had kept the truth from her, then regret that he'd had to bear the burden of that secret all those years. Then in our sweet mother's usual manner, she brushed off the whole thing with, 'Well, that certainly doesn't make any difference in the eternal scheme of things. Of course, she's our daughter. And no one is going to take my girl away, so you'd better just do whatever you have to do to make sure it doesn't happen, or I will. And if they think a mother bear is protective of her cubs, they'll wish they were tangling with a grizzly instead of me.'"

Maggie recognized her mother's fierce protectiveness in Steve's recitation. Delight at that reaction left Maggie laughing at the same time she was crying tears of gratitude and love.

"So what new developments are happening in your incredible world, Sis?"

"I'm coming home for Christmas and bringing two very special people, but I want to surprise Mom and Dad, so I need you to concoct some sort of story about three additional guests for dinner so Mom will be prepared for us."

"I take it you're bringing Alyssa. And your doctor friend?"

"Yes. I can't wait for you to meet them—or for them to meet our family. Is everyone there yet?"

"Jeff and his entourage arrived last night from Denver. Alan and Veronica are flying in from Long Island in a couple of hours. Dad's gone to Salt Lake to meet their flight. So how are you coming?"

"We're in this incredibly beautiful little private jet. How's the weather there?"

"A big storm just dumped another half foot of snow everywhere, and the wind is piling it up. The main roads are barely staying cleared. Tell me when and I'll meet you in Brigham City."

Maggie turned to Flynn. "Do you have any idea what time we'll arrive so Steve can meet us?"

Flynn glanced at his watch. "When Jim checked the weather in that area, he said three hours and ten minutes from takeoff, so we should arrive at 2:10 mountain time. Tell him he'd better come in a truck to haul all this stuff we're bringing."

Maggie relayed the message, and Steve promised to meet them at the appointed hour as well as have their mother primed for additional guests.

"Oh," Maggie added, "make sure no one has taken over my room. Alyssa and I will need it. I know Jeff's girls always get dibs on it when I'm not home, so if they're in there, quietly get them to vacate and move them somewhere else when Mom's not looking, and swear them to secrecy so they don't tell her. And Steve, if Mom and Dad haven't said anything to anyone else, and they don't know about Alyssa, don't tell them. Let us surprise them."

"Will do. What a Christmas *this* will be! Fly safe." Steve hung up. Maggie leaned back, as contented as a kitten in a warm lap, and at the same time, as excited as Kit, who was getting personal attention from Alyssa. Could it really be this easy? Or were there going to be blips in the pure happiness she was experiencing at the moment? She knew there would be no problem with her family's acceptance of Alyssa. It was a given that Alyssa would be welcomed with open arms. But what was on the horizon? What would her sister's plans be after Christmas?

Then Maggie looked at Flynn and saw him watching her with what seemed wistful amusement. Where would this lead? She'd never felt about anyone before like she did about Flynn, but Maggie knew she could never let her heart lead her away from all she'd valued her whole life. If Flynn wasn't interested in sharing her beliefs and her religion, their relationship had no future. That would absolutely break her heart, and she knew it would not be a happy time for Flynn, either. Well, one thing at a time. Get home, introduce Alyssa, help her adjust to her new family, then see if she'd call Lionel Lawson. Beyond that, Maggie didn't dare speculate.

They still had one major problem needing resolution. Even with her own wonderful family surrounding her, Maggie knew she'd never be truly content until she knew who her birth parents were. She suspected Alyssa felt the same way. That would be the next big mystery, or as Alyssa had put it, the next big quest.

Would her father be able to answer that question? Maggie tried to imagine the scene at the hospital, tried to fathom the depth of the emotion the two men were experiencing with each of their traumatic problems. Would they have exchanged names? Would they have tried to stay in touch to keep the sisters connected in some way through the years? Or would the father of the twins insist on anonymity so his deed would never come to light?

So many questions. Such important, unknown answers.

CHAPTER 32

"What are you thinking, Maggie?" Flynn asked, though he thought it fairly easy to guess.

She shook her head. "So many things it would take the next two hours to tell you."

"I've got a spare couple of hours," he said.

"I was wondering where we start looking for answers to our parentage problem."

Flynn poured another glass of Sprite. "I'm sure the police have collected blood samples for DNA testing from Cleat Wiggins. That will answer the question of whether or not he was telling Alyssa the truth or if he just made it up to keep her close to him. What do you think, Alyssa? Do you have any ideas on how to find out who your birth mother really was?"

"I think Lily has the key to my mother's identity," Alyssa said thoughtfully. "She's in my earliest memories, so I'm sure she knows who it was, if it wasn't Eleanor Lawson."

"Then we need to go to San Buenaventura and talk to Lily as soon as you feel up to seeing her and your father," Maggie said. Then she stood and paced up and down the open area. "I want all the answers now, tonight. I want someone to say: 'this is how it was,' so I can say, 'that's nice,' then file it all away and get on with my life. I hate not knowing something so—so big, so earth-shattering as who my parents are."

Neither Flynn nor Alyssa spoke as Maggie vented her frustration. Then she turned to Alyssa. "I'm sorry. I'm sure you're just as frustrated."

Alyssa nodded. "Except that I've had seven years to ponder and fret, and finally I decided it didn't matter if the president of the

United States was my father. My situation wasn't going to change, so why even think about it."

"And you just put it out of your mind, just like that?" Maggie asked, amazed at Alyssa's ability to deal with the mystery in such a manner.

"Maggie, when you have no hope, you stop dealing with what-ifs. You even stop thinking. It's easier to become a zombie, just moving through life with someone telling you what to do and where to go. You stop seeing things around you. You stop living. Your body just goes through its functions without any thought on your part. You get so you don't notice pain, because that's all there is. The only happiness I've known in the last seven years has been when I've been able to steal away and talk to someone for a few minutes and forget the ache in my heart."

Tears filled Alyssa's blue eyes and spilled down her cheeks. "I had a chance to make a friend at the grill where we worked, but that man was afraid I'd told her something about him kidnapping me, so he chained her to the cot in the shack at Avery Island." Suddenly Alyssa looked up. "Maggie, did you find her? Is she okay?"

Maggie glanced at Flynn, not wanting to answer, but knowing Alyssa would find out sooner or later. "We found her and took her to the hospital, but she didn't make it."

"The doctor thought she might have starved to death, Alyssa," Flynn added. "Did Cleat forget to feed her or did he starve her on purpose?"

Alyssa swivelled her chair around to face the window. "I tried to project to you so you'd think it was me, Maggie, and you could find her in time. He said he'd make sure she'd never be able to talk, but he promised me he wouldn't kill her." She paused, then added bitterly, "So much for believing anything that man ever said."

A chill ran down Maggie's back. "Alyssa, did you know about the people who wrote letters to your father's newspaper telling him they'd seen you?"

"Not at first. I suspected a few years ago he might have done something to someone who looked at me funny after my picture was in the newspapers and on TV, but it was only after I saw him push that woman down the stairs in South Dakota that he got really mean and warned me not to ever talk to anyone again. He said that every time he found out I'd talked to anyone, he'd kill them and punish me."

Maggie stood speechless with horror.

"How did he punish you?" Flynn asked.

Alyssa didn't answer for a minute. "He gave me drugs. Held me down and shot something into my arm that made me drowsy, then he wouldn't let me have anything to eat for a few days."

"Did he give you drugs at any other time?" Flynn asked.

"I think he was putting something into my drinks from the beginning. He always forced me to drink every drop of whatever he gave me. At first I thought it was because I refused to eat and he was afraid I'd get dehydrated, then I decided it had to be more than that when I didn't feel like myself anymore."

Flynn pursued this. "How did you feel?"

"Sort of peaceful, dreamy, floating. I didn't really care about anything. No matter what happened, it just didn't matter. Then I started feeling less like that—I'm not sure how to explain it. It wasn't a peaceful feeling anymore. It was sort of . . . gray. The world lost its color."

"Did that ever change?" Flynn asked.

"Only to get worse. Then I stopped feeling anything at all." Alyssa turned around and faced them. "Until I knew that you were aware of me. Before that I just wanted to die."

"Tell me how you felt when you were able to project into Maggie's mind," Flynn said.

Alyssa thought for a minute. "The best description, I guess, is that a spark ignited inside me and I felt there was a chance for me to live. I *wanted* to live for the first time in years."

"So desperate to live that you would have taken over Maggie's mind to do it?" Flynn asked quietly.

Alyssa looked up at Maggie. "I'm so sorry. I found a book someone had left when I was clearing tables. I had to hide it because that man didn't want me reading anything. It was about mind control, the first thing I'd read in seven years. It told me how I could control your mind instead of just projecting my thoughts or images to you."

"That's when it became frightening because I didn't feel in control any more," Maggie said softly. "You became so strong, I didn't think I could shut you out." Maggie shuddered and Alyssa jumped up and put her arms around her sister.

"Please forgive me. I was so desperate. I'd lived for nearly seven years with no hope, no possibility of ever having any kind of life but pure misery with that man, and suddenly I could feel again. I wasn't thinking about what it might do to you." She stared at Maggie. "I'd forgotten that I had blue eyes; I hadn't seen any color in them for so long. Then again, I guess I hadn't really looked in a mirror for a long time. It really is so funny, looking at you and seeing me."

Maggie laughed. "I know exactly how you feel. It will be so fun walking in on my family and seeing their faces." Maggie whirled Alyssa around. "I haven't been this excited forever. I truly can't remember the last time I was so happy."

Maggie's happiness was contagious, and the twins spent the next couple of hours filling in the gaps of the missing twenty-four years.

Flynn watched in fascination as Alyssa became more animated, as life and vitality seemed to flow back into her. He'd expected it would take days at the very least, probably weeks, for her to feel like Alyssa Lawson again instead of Katie Wiggins. The transformation was amazing to watch. She seemed to draw on Maggie's energy, but Maggie didn't act any less energized. If possible, she appeared to possess even more than before. Flynn found some writing paper in the desk at the front of the cabin and began taking notes. The girls didn't even notice.

When it neared time for them to land, Flynn went into the cockpit while the girls changed into matching outfits.

"I don't think we'll be able to fool Steve or Mom, but we could probably keep everybody else guessing for awhile, if we don't say anything. Our accents aren't quite the same. We pronounce some words differently, so we'll have to keep quiet until everyone guesses which is which."

Alyssa shook her head. "I won't have any problem with that. I'm scared to death and I probably won't be able to say a word the whole time. I just hope I can face your family and not run and hide."

"Please don't let their noise and numbers overwhelm you. Just think of it as a family reunion with lots of cousins and aunts and uncles."

"You forget I was raised as an only child, Maggie. My mother had one sister who lived back East, and my dad was an only child. I had two cousins but we never saw each other. This will be the first time I've ever been in a gathering this large except for school."

For the first time, Maggie had nothing to say. She'd always been surrounded by family, large numbers of family: uncles and aunts and cousins and two sets of grandparents. She couldn't relate to Alyssa's discomfort at so many people, and Alyssa couldn't relate to Maggie's excitement at being surrounded by so much family.

Flynn rejoined them to buckle in for landing as they were having this discussion and had to admit he could certainly identify with Alyssa's point of view instead of Maggie's.

The little jet landed without a bounce and taxied to its assigned arrival gate. Light snow flurries filled the sky, and gusty winds swirled the snow around corners and along the ground. Steve waited as they came through the doors. The twins stopped so he could get the full impact of two identically dressed, blue-eyed redheads who had everyone in the terminal staring as well.

He rushed toward them, grabbed Alyssa first, then Maggie, then hugged them both. "Okay, you two. Enough with the games. Are you Maggie? No, you must be Alyssa."

Maggie could tell he was teasing them, but she didn't think Alyssa knew, so she played along. "I'm Alyssa," she said.

Alyssa followed suit. "I'm Maggie."

"Whoops, that gave you away." He grabbed Maggie in a bear hug. "You're Maggie." Then he bowed to Alyssa. "Welcome to our crazy family," and he gave her a hug and kiss on the cheek.

Flynn came straggling behind pulling two luggage racks piled high with suitcases and packages.

"Steve, this is Dr. Flynn Ford. Flynn to you." Maggie linked her arms through theirs as they shook hands and each took the measure of the other. "Flynn, this is my favorite brother, Steve, but if either of you mention that I've said such a thing, I'll deny it." She turned to Flynn. "The reason he's my favorite is that he was about the only one at home while I was in high school so I felt like he was my only brother. And I have to admit, he used to get me out of all kinds of scrapes."

"Thanks for keeping track of your little sister. I'm glad she had someone to touch base with and to fall back on for advice," Flynn said.

"Likewise, thank you for watching over her when she got in over her head." Steve was watching Maggie and Flynn, noting that Maggie didn't let go of the doctor's arm as soon as he'd have expected, and though Flynn tried to appear on a professional level, that was not a professional look he bestowed on Maggie when he thought Steve wasn't looking. *Oh, little sister, I hope you know what you're doing,* he thought.

After all the introductions, they followed Steve to his pickup, loaded luggage and presents in the back, covered them with a tarp, and tied them down so nothing would blow out or get wet from the snow. Flynn's legs were too long for the back seat of the pickup, so he sat in the front with Steve. Maggie liked that arrangement. She hoped it would give her two favorite men a chance to get acquainted and even like each other. At the moment she sensed a male rivalry or antagonism. And it would give her and Alyssa a chance to talk further.

"Steve, did Mom and Dad tell everyone yet about our big secret?"

"You mean Alyssa, or that you're adopted?"

Maggie had never thought about it until this minute, but she wasn't adopted. At least she didn't think that she was. Had there ever been any legal paperwork filed? But there were so many other eternal implications because of that. Apparently Steve hadn't thought about it either. "I meant that Mom didn't give birth to me."

"Actually, things have been so busy and chaotic with everyone arriving and getting settled in, I don't think the folks have even had much time to think about it. So I imagine your secret will be safe until we walk in the door." Steve laughed. "The look on their faces will be something to see."

"Who did you tell Mom was coming to stay?"

Steve was quiet for a minute. "Ah, I hope you don't mind, but I couldn't lie to Mom, so I told her a member of the Church I knew was bringing a couple of people for me to teach." He glanced at Flynn, then back at Alyssa.

"Steve, you're a genius!" Maggie exclaimed.

"Teach?" Flynn asked, wondering if he'd done the right thing in convincing Alyssa to come.

Maggie leaned forward and put her hand on Flynn's shoulder. "Before Steve was in the military, he was on a mission for our Church where he spent two years teaching people who wanted to know more about The Church of Jesus Christ of Latter-day Saints. That's why I told you I hoped you and Steve would find time to talk, because he can answer all the questions you have. Oh, and that reminds me, Steve, we have to stop at a grocery store on the way home. I know Mom never keeps coffee around, and Flynn usually has coffee with his meals."

Flynn turned to Maggie. "No. I can get by without it. I don't want to add any more to your mom's burdens since she'll have three extra people included in her holiday preparations."

Steve laughed. "You don't know our mom—or our crazy family. There were eight of us—five boys, Maggie and our folks—but there were always at least a dozen people for nearly every meal. Mom always said she didn't know where we found all the strays we brought to eat with us, but she was happy to serve them, because 'Inasmuch as ye have done it unto the least of these, ye have done it unto me.' You will never know how many times the miracle of the loaves and the fishes was duplicated at our table."

Flynn looked at Steve. "Since you seem to have a lot of experience in this area, teach me about your beliefs. You have a captive audience."

Steve turned the volume down on the Christmas carols playing on the radio, and songs of the birth of the Savior became background as Steve taught about the restored Church of Jesus Christ. Maggie planned to tell Alyssa about each member of her family so she'd feel like she knew a little about them when they met, but Alyssa leaned forward and was listening intently to Steve's comments.

Flynn had some good questions, which Steve answered immediately, most to Flynn's satisfaction. Suddenly they pulled off Interstate 15, onto a snow-covered road, and soon into the McKenzie driveway.

Alyssa looked terrified. Maggie could scarcely contain her excitement, and Flynn's curiosity had been even more piqued by the things he'd been taught. How could someone who believed so strongly in good Christian principles—and to Flynn they seemed very strict, almost painfully restrictive—have so much fun and love life so much? It seemed to him having to obey all those commandments, not just the Ten Commandments which were pretty basic and which he pretty much kept anyway, but all those Word of Wisdom restrictions, and the higher laws they kept must bear mightily on them and take all the fun out of life. Instead, they seemed to react just the opposite. Puzzling. His psychological observations should be very interesting.

"Now remember," Maggie whispered to Alyssa, "don't say anything, and let them all guess which of us is the one they think they know so well."

Steve opened the door, and the twins walked in on small children playing with Lincoln Logs on the floor, adults wrapping presents, Christmas carols blaring from the stereo, and delicious smells flowing through the house. A couple of boys were chasing each other up and down the stairs, but everything stopped when the girls walked in the door.

"May I have your attention please?" Steve called. That wasn't necessary, because every eye was already on the twins. "Someone please get Mom out of the kitchen and Dad out of his study so I can introduce you to Maggie and Alyssa."

The girls held hands tightly, and Maggie tried to remember to look just a little shy and uncertain, as Alyssa looked at the moment. It was so hard to contain her excitement. She wanted to shout and throw her arms around everyone and say, "Look! I finally have my sister!"

Everyone was quiet until Rose McKenzie entered, took one look at the girls, and flew across the room to embrace them. She kissed their cheeks and hugged them, not caring which twin she had at the moment. Then she backed away and looked at them. "Oh, my goodness. Just look at you." Tears were streaming down her face as she turned to her family and said, "Look at them. Aren't they beautiful? We're twice blessed today."

Scott McKenzie strode across the room, looked at the girls, and whispered to Alyssa as he hugged her and kissed her cheek, "Welcome to our family." To Maggie he whispered, "We need to talk at the first opportunity. Welcome home, pumpkin. I love you."

Flynn, who waited on the front porch with the dog carrier while the girls had their moment in the spotlight, was spotted by one of the boys still standing on the stairs. "More company coming. And look, he's got a dog."

Steve pulled him inside and introduced him. "Dr. Flynn Ford, Maggie's . . . friend."

Maggie could have killed him for the emphasis he put on that word, but she didn't look at him or at Flynn. She was enjoying the consternation of everyone in trying to decide which girl was Maggie. One by one they came closer to see if they could tell. Finally Maggie couldn't stand it any longer.

"Isn't it wonderful! Can you believe it? I have a twin sister." She hugged Alyssa, who was about ready to have a nervous breakdown standing there on display. She pulled Alyssa to the stairs and they sat down where everyone could see them. She motioned Flynn to the only chair not occupied by something or someone, and started her explanation.

"We still have lots of mysteries to solve because we were separated at birth. I'm the lucky one because I inherited all of you, but now we have to find out who our birth parents really were, and Alyssa has been through a very traumatic seven years and she's recovering from that, so I want you all to be especially nice to her. You can treat me just like you always do." She glanced at Flynn. "Well, maybe you'd better to be nice to me too. I told Flynn you were the greatest family in the world so you have a reputation to uphold."

Maggie's brother Jeff and his wife Doreen came to welcome Alyssa to the family. They pointed out their four children who were captivated by the bouncy little puppy.

"Jeff's with the FBI in Denver, and Doreen was until she decided it was more important to be home raising her children," Maggie told Alyssa. She put her arm around Alyssa's shoulder and squeezed it. "We just rescued Alyssa from her kidnapper who held her for seven years," she said, looking up at Jeff, knowing that would totally pique his interest.

As Alan and Veronica approached to introduce themselves, Maggie directed Jeff to Flynn. "Flynn can give you all the gory details I can see you're just dying to ask about, Jeff."

Alan kissed Alyssa's cheek and said, "So this is what all that DNA mystery was about. Welcome to our family, Alyssa. You'll probably think we're a wild bunch, but bear with us. We grow on you."

Veronica testified to that. "When I first met Alan, I couldn't believe this family. They were always playing pranks on each other.

Sometimes I thought they'd kill each other in the process, but you'll never feel such love anywhere." She smiled and winked. "That is, if you survive their pranks." She bent and kissed Alyssa's cheek, squeezed her hand and whispered. "I know how overwhelmed you feel, but just relax and let it sort of flow over you and you'll get to enjoy it."

Alyssa looked around. "You said you had five brothers. That's only three."

Maggie laughed. "*We* have five brothers, and fortunately, Rick and Taylor live near here with their families, so the entire clan isn't usually in the house at the same time. Although it's getting close to dinner, so they'll be coming soon." Maggie looked at the grandmother clock on the mantle. "Speaking of dinner, we'd better go see if Mom needs any help in the kitchen. As zero hour approaches, things get rather frantic in there for her, especially with a dozen grandchildren sneaking in to get snacks."

Maggie pulled Alyssa to her feet, looked at Flynn to see how he was faring, and was happy to see him and Jeff deeply engrossed in conversation. Steve and her dad had disappeared into the study, though the door was ajar so that meant that they could be interrupted if necessary, and everyone else had returned to what they were doing when Maggie and entourage entered. Maggie's nieces and nephews were still a little hesitant to approach, but Maggie knew that wouldn't last.

As she gave Alyssa a quick tour of the house on the way to the kitchen, Alyssa stopped to gaze at the huge table set in the dining room. "This is just like a restaurant," she said, amazed not only at the size of the table, but the beauty of the place settings and centerpiece. Two smaller tables nestled in corners for the children.

"How many people will be here for dinner?" she asked as Maggie pulled her toward the kitchen.

Rose McKenzie turned from forming yeast rolls to answer. "Five sons, four wives, two daughters, eight grandchildren, one guest, and your father and me. Twenty-two."

"And you do this all the time?"

Rose laughed. "Not often enough. Unfortunately, we don't get our whole family together except for major holidays, usually only Christmas. The rest of the year, we have to settle for whoever can make it home."

"Alyssa's sort of overwhelmed by our numbers, Mom. She was raised an only child." Maggie put her arms around her mother from the back and hugged her. "I love you. I'm so glad you got to be my mom."

Rose turned and wrapped her arms around Maggie, trying to keep the flour on her hands from getting all over. "I love you, too." She wiped the tears from her eyes with the back of her hand. "Come here, Alyssa." Rose hugged Alyssa, then looked at her closely. "Your eyes are a little lighter color, your hair a bit darker, and you don't have quite as many freckles, but other than that, it's amazing how very much alike you are. Welcome to our family, my dear." She returned to forming rolls, and Maggie washed her hands to help.

"What can I do?" Alyssa asked, wanting to be part of the kitchen crew. She felt very much at home in kitchens.

"The potatoes need to be peeled. I was saving that for Steve, but he's disappeared. Would you like to do that for me, dear?"

Maggie got out the potatoes, the pan, and the peeler, and Alyssa set to work.

Rose kept up a running commentary all the while they worked. "Steve told us how you came to look for Alyssa. I wish you had told us when you stopped at home that night before you headed for South Dakota." Whatever else she was going to say was forgotten forever. They heard a scream, a crash, a sickening thud, and then total silence from the family room.

CHAPTER 33

Everyone dropped what they were doing and rushed to the family room. Three-year-old Derrick lay on the floor, shattered pieces of a Nativity set surrounding him, a nasty gash on his head that bled profusely, and his arm twisted at an unnatural angle beneath him.

Doreen was the first to reach him, with Jeff close behind. As they knelt beside their little boy, Rose offered the towel she held in her hands to use as a compress to stop the bleeding, but Maggie could see it would require more than that. She ran to the kitchen for ice cubes and a clean towel.

"Get Dad here with his oil," Jeff called over his shoulder. "Flynn, what kind of doctor are you?"

Flynn bent over the couple kneeling on the floor beside their unconscious son. "I'm afraid you need more than a doctor. You need an emergency room. Fast."

Maggie's father hurried from the study, a small vial of oil in his hand. Doreen took Maggie's proffered ice cubes wrapped in a clean towel and held them in place. Scott, Steve, Jeff, and Alan, knelt as Scott anointed his ashen-faced grandson with oil, and Jeff pronounced a blessing upon his son that he would regain consciousness and be healed properly and completely.

Scott McKenzie, an experienced veterinarian, tenderly probed the limp body, the little shoulder, legs and ribs, felt Derrick's head, then carefully, gently straightened the crooked arm. "It's broken, but it's not a compound fracture. We can be thankful for that. Bring me the ironing board. We'll use that as a stretcher."

Rose went for the ironing board, and Steve ran upstairs to get more blankets. Alyssa, trembling all over, slipped her arm through Maggie's. Maggie put her arm around her worried sister. "It's okay. He'll be fine."

"But he's still unconscious," Alyssa whispered. "That's not good, is it?"

Flynn appeared at their side. "No, and the longer he stays out, the more worrisome it is."

Maggie looked up at Flynn with the utmost confidence in her blue eyes. "He'll be okay. He just had a priesthood blessing. He'll survive this without any problem."

Flynn thought Maggie was being far too optimistic for the apparent extent of his injuries, but maybe she was doing it for Alyssa's sake. The girl looked completely shaken. Then as they carefully slid the little boy onto the ironing board, he opened his big brown eyes and looked at all the faces surrounding him.

He screwed up his little face and started to cry. "Oh, Gramma, I dropped Baby Jesus. I broke him."

Rose knelt by her grandson and kissed his tears away. "It's okay, Derrick, we'll just glue him back together again. But I think you're broken, too, so they're going to take you to the doctor so they can put you back together."

Doreen ran to get their coats, and Steve backed Jeff's SUV up to the front door. Scott McKenzie called the clinic, reported what had happened and said they were on their way. "Don't let everyone leave for Christmas dinner just yet," he told them. Rose ran to the kitchen and fetched a plate of Christmas goodies to send with them.

"Some of the staff will spend the night at the clinic," Rose explained at Flynn's questioning stare, "and they'll need a little Christmas cheer to get them through. Tonight, believe it or not, can be a busy night, even at our tiny little clinic. Frank and Linda are on duty tonight. They volunteer because they don't have kids at home anymore, so I'll just send a little something along as a 'thank-you' for serving."

When everyone else went to the door to watch the whimpering child being loaded into the car, Maggie knelt on the floor to pick up the shattered figurines of the creche, and Alyssa stooped to help her. Flynn squatted down to retrieve a couple of pieces from under a chair.

"This was Mom's favorite. She put it high on that shelf so little fingers couldn't get to it. Jeff brought it to her from his mission in Italy. He saved every extra penny for six months so he'd have enough money to buy it. I think he even went without food for a couple of days."

Alyssa looked at the pieces in her hands that were beyond repair. "What will they do to him?"

Maggie looked up at her. "To who? Derrick?" *What a strange question,* she thought. "Nothing. He's a little boy. Little boys climb on things, and they break things, and they fall and hurt themselves. That's what little boys do. He'll be taught that what he did was wrong, and that because of the choice he made to disobey the rule that you don't play with Gramma's precious things, he had to pay the consequences of his disobedience."

Then she sat back on the floor and laughed. "Unfortunately, having his arm in a cast and stitches in his head may seem like more of a reward than punishment. Little boys look at things differently than girls do, but hopefully he'll hurt enough to remember the pain and not the bragging rights over the cast and think before he does something like that again."

"He won't be punished?" Alyssa couldn't fathom this concept. Even as much as her mother adored her, if she ever broke something her mother loved, she had been sent to her room without dinner, denied some privilege for an extended amount of time, and she always felt she had to work extra hard to earn her mother's love all over again.

"I think it will be punishment enough not to get to join in with the other kids' activities tonight for Christmas Eve."

"Maggie, why didn't your family just call the ambulance?" Flynn asked. "Don't they worry about trauma on the way to the hospital?"

Maggie stood and carefully placed all the fragments she'd gathered on a shelf on the bookcase. "We don't have an ambulance near. It would take an hour to send an ambulance from Pocatello or about the same from Brigham City. By driving him, they'll be at our little clinic in ten minutes, have him treated, and be home within the hour. We don't have a hospital or an emergency room here. We're lucky to have any kind of medical care at all. Wait until you see how very small this little community is. You won't believe it."

From the picture window in the family room, they watched the black SUV drive away, and Rose returned to the kitchen with Steve in tow to help. Alan and Veronica gathered Jeff and Doreen's remaining three children, who were wide-eyed at what they'd seen, and sat with them on the floor underneath the Christmas tree with the puppy, first to alleviate their fears about what had happened and what was going to happen, then to play some games.

Flynn watched the family work together like a smoothly oiled machine and marveled. His mother would have freaked out at something like this and everything would have ground to a complete halt.

"Do you two want to bring in the things from the pickup while it's relatively quiet?" Maggie asked. "You can put all those beautifully wrapped packages under the tree. By the time you finish, I'll have this mess vacuumed up and I'll show you to your rooms." She looked at Alyssa and corrected herself. "Our room. You get to bunk with me. Then maybe we'll have time before everyone arrives for dinner to go out so I can introduce you to Pegasus, my special friend in the barn."

The peace and quiet Alan and Veronica established was shattered when Flynn and Alyssa staggered in carrying stacks of presents. The older two boys were allowed to run out into the cold to help. The air was charged with excitement as load after load of presents was deposited under the tree. Finally when there was room for no more, Flynn brought in their luggage. Maggie took them upstairs and opened the door to her room, noting that her nieces had been playing paper dolls on her bed and had left them spread all over it.

Maggie turned to Flynn. "Do you mind if you don't get your own room? Steve has an extra bed in his room, and I think everywhere else is already spoken for. Any other time you could take the hide-a-bed in the family room, or one of the two guest rooms, but on Christmas, they're filled already. You can put your bags over in the corner, here in Steve's room. The bathroom's down the hall, and we'll go check with the kitchen and see if we can get a pass to go to the barn."

"A pass?" Alyssa questioned.

Maggie laughed. "Just a manner of speaking. If Mom doesn't have something for us to do, we're free, but if she does, we'll help."

While Flynn deposited his bags in Steve's room and took in the room with a psychologist's eye, Maggie threw open drawers and closets to give Alyssa room to unpack her new clothes from her new suitcase. Then she stopped. "I guess this is a little spare compared to what you were used to. I saw your room—you projected that to me, didn't you, when he came into your room and wrapped the blanket around you and took you away?"

Alyssa nodded. "But I wouldn't trade all the closets and clothes and big room and pretty things I had for this. I love your little room, Maggie. It's perfect. And you have to remember, I haven't been alone in a room for seven years." She shuddered. "He was always there."

Maggie shared her reaction to that thought. "Let's go see Pegasus, if Mom doesn't have a job for us." Maggie retrieved a couple of old coats from the back of her closet and her boots while Alyssa pulled on her new boots.

They were given thirty minutes, then were told to report back, as all available hands would be needed to make final preparations for the special Christmas dinner Rose had worked all day to prepare.

The three followed the shoveled path to the barn, but with the wind blowing, portions of it were already filling in. And Maggie didn't think all that snow swirling through the air was being picked up by the wind. It was snowing. A perfect Christmas Eve.

"Pegasus," Maggie called as she opened the barn door. The horse whinnied a greeting in return and tossed his head and stomped his feet.

Flynn shut the door behind them, then leaned on the stall to watch the animal respond to Maggie's touch. He knew just how the magnificent horse felt at her attention and wished Maggie were stroking his face and whispering in his ear instead. Pegasus seemed to sense that Alyssa was special too, and he nuzzled Alyssa's hand.

"Oh, I long to ride again," Alyssa said. "That was my happiest time, when I was out with my own horse flying through the pasture."

"Tomorrow," Maggie said. "Tomorrow we'll go riding. Do you ride, Flynn?"

"Not like the two of you do, I'm sure, but I can stay on the back of a horse without falling off, if that's good enough."

"Good enough." Maggie handed Alyssa a brush and the two girls gave Pegasus a vigorous grooming while they talked horses. Maggie watched Flynn out of the corner of her eye, wondering what he was thinking, wondering how he was reacting to her family.

Wondering how he felt about all he had heard from Steve on the way from the airport.

Then she remembered they hadn't called California yet. "Alyssa, when we go in, don't you want to call your father and tell him that you're alive? Think how wonderful that would make his Christmas Eve."

Alyssa looked panic-stricken. She bit her lip, seemed to think through all the scenarios that phone call could instigate and, hesitating, finally said, "Would you think I'm terrible if I don't call today? I don't know what to say, and I'm so afraid there will be reporters everywhere and it will spoil our perfect, quiet Christmas. I know it's so selfish, but I'm just not ready to face that yet, and I'm afraid there would be no keeping it from the press as soon as my father gets the news. They seem to know when there is a story, even if it isn't announced."

"You can call whenever you're ready," Flynn assured her. "We'll do this on your time-table so you're ready for each step of reemergence into your life."

Too soon their thirty minutes passed, and they hurried back to the kitchen to find that Rick and Rachel had arrived with their two little boys, and Taylor and Ashley with their two girls. Maggie introduced her brothers to Alyssa and Flynn: Rick, a vet in practice with their father, and Taylor, a policeman on the local force. They found her brothers' wives and children in the other room. With the briefest of introductions made, they hurried back to the kitchen to help.

"Flynn, will you do ice and water? The pitcher is there. Alyssa, will you find room on the table for these hors d'oeuvres while Steve fills the dishes? Rick, I need you to take the turkey out of the oven and pour the drippings in this pan so I can make gravy. Taylor, you're the ham carver. Maggie, will you mash the potatoes?" Rose McKenzie directed the kitchen staff like a well-organized drill sergeant.

The kitchen chatter included many questions for Maggie, Alyssa, and Flynn as they came and went fulfilling their duties. Rachel and Ashley joined the crew now that their children were settled near the Christmas tree with the puppy, under their aunt and uncle's supervision.

Flynn watched Maggie's mother check the time, and commence giving orders. "Rick, the stuffing can come out of the turkey. Steve, call your father and see how things are going there and when they'll be home. Alyssa, would you like to go out on the porch and start cutting pies? Flynn, maybe you can help her."

Maggie collected the pie servers and dessert plates and led Alyssa and Flynn to the glass-enclosed back porch, a wide area that ran the length of the large kitchen and then some. Long tables had been set up and seemed to be groaning under their load of pies and cakes. The place looked like a bakery window with Christmas cookies and nut bars stacked everywhere.

"Your mother did all of this?" Flynn asked in wonder.

"Most of it," Maggie laughed. "Rachel and Ashley contributed, but Mom loves to cook and this is her favorite holiday, so she outdoes herself. Don't bother the ones on the far table. Those will be delivered tonight for the twelve days of Christmas. We keep those separate so no one will accidentally eat them. Ordinarily, they'd already be gone, but Derrick's little accident changed the plans."

"How do you know?" Flynn asked. "You haven't been here."

"It's the same every year. If everything is always in the same place, she can send any one of us to do anything and we know where it is because it's always been there. Saves her a lot of steps and us a lot of grief trying to find what we've been sent for. My mother is an organization freak, but when you have six active children and that many friends in the house at any given time, it pays to have order. We were taught to always put things back in their proper place, then we'd know where they were."

Maggie lowered her voice. "And Mom went through a period when her mental and physical health were very fragile. It was especially important to her to have order in her life. 'A place for everything, and everything in its place,' she always said. I think it helped her cope with her deep feelings of inadequacy at the time."

"Makes sense," Flynn murmured, wondering why every home wasn't like that. He would have been saved many a scolding growing up if things had always been where they were supposed to be.

"Dad says they're five minutes from home," Steve announced loudly. "You can put the food on the table."

"Taylor, direct the kids to the bathrooms to wash their hands, and then you can get them up to their little tables," Rose directed. "Let them find their place mats telling them where to sit."

Maggie scooped up Kit and put him back into his carrier and took him up to her bedroom where his begging wouldn't distract the children. Then the food, dish after dish, was placed on the table until there was no more room, and the buffet had to accommodate the overflow. Just as all was ready, the black SUV drove up, and Derrick was carried in on the ironing board like a king being borne by his servants.

"Look! I got a green cast, just like the Christmas tree. And I got six stitches in my head."

"You look wonderful, dear," Rose said, kissing her grandson and examining the cast he held up proudly. "Now find your place at the little table, and we'll all sign your cast after dinner."

No one needed urging to get to the table. Maggie managed to seat Flynn on one side of her and Alyssa on the other. Scott McKenzie, patriarch of the family, offered a blessing on the food and one of gratitude for the Savior's birth, as well as asking for Derrick's quick recovery and giving thanks for Alyssa's deliverance, and for Maggie's safe arrival and that of her friend.

Then for the next hour, everyone enjoyed the feast. Flynn had never eaten so much good food, and Alyssa couldn't praise Rose's cooking enough. "I thought that man was a good cook, but this beats everything he ever made."

Maggie laughed. "Ambience, atmosphere, attitude, and presentation have a lot to do with how food tastes. Have you ever noticed that, Flynn?"

Flynn remembered two dinners with Maggie and how extra-delicious the food had seemed. "I think you're right. I've never thought about it before."

With dinner finished, dishes done, the twelve days' deliveries made, dessert eaten and cleaned up, it was time for Grandpa Scott to read the Christmas story and the for grandchildren to act it out. Clearly it was a tradition much loved in this household, as everyone crowded into the living room and found a place to sit. Christmas lights on the tree, mantle, windows, and up the staircase, and the fire crackling in the fireplace were the only lights as the children filed in dressed in bathrobes, towels for headdresses, and sticks for shepherd staffs. Scott read the story from the Bible, using a candle as his reading lamp. Both Flynn and Alyssa marveled at the feeling of warmth, love, and togetherness that was present.

Then everyone chose a present to open from under the tree. "This is the most exciting part for the little ones," Maggie whispered, sitting on the floor next to Flynn. She'd never been happier in her life. With Flynn on one side and Alyssa on the other and surrounded by her family, life was complete. She looked up at Flynn, caught him watching her, and felt a rush of warmth flow through her when she saw the raw emotion in his eyes. She caught her breath and tried to look away, but couldn't drag her eyes from those dark pools filled with love.

"Maggie, it's your turn," someone shouted. She looked up to see everyone watching them and her face flushed bright red.

"You choose for me. I haven't had time to squeeze and shake any of them."

Someone grabbed one with Maggie's name on it and passed it over to her. "Now find one for Flynn and one for Alyssa, and we'll open them together."

Flynn was surprised he had anything under the tree but realized Maggie had been busy shopping for him as well as Alyssa. He held up a cashmere scarf and fur-lined leather gloves. "Thank you, Maggie. I'll certainly need these up here."

Alyssa's present was a necklace and earrings to go with her black velvet skirt and beaded sweater. She was delighted. Maggie's, from Steve, was a large book filled with glorious pictures of the Lewis and Clark Trail. She blew him a kiss from across the room. "Thank you so much. You're forgiven for all the rotten things you've ever done to me."

When each had opened a present, children were shuttled off to bed. Alyssa, whose energy had been completely exhausted by this time, said her good nights and many thanks to everyone, and Maggie took her up to get her settled. Alyssa was asleep almost immediately.

Flynn, Jeff, and Alan were head to head in some serious discussion when she came downstairs, and her father signaled he'd like to talk with her. She slipped quietly into the study and sat across the desk from him in the big leather chair. The interview chair, they all called it.

"Maggie, I can't tell you how glad I am you're home safe and sound. Steve told me something of what you've been going through. I'm sorry you didn't feel you could tell me about it when you were here."

"I'm sorry too, Daddy, but I promised Lily I wouldn't breathe a word to anyone about my search. I wouldn't have told Steve, but he wheedled it out of me after he had to wake me up screaming from a nightmare."

"Tell me about Flynn Ford."

Maggie tried not to let her emotions show as she told her father how she'd met him at the Alpine Inn, then recited the story from there. "I'm glad he was there. I didn't know how to handle the mind thing that was happening between me and Alyssa, and he helped me through it so we could find her."

"Tell me how you feel about him, Maggie."

Maggie sighed. She'd never been able to keep her feelings from showing. "I like him very much. More than anyone I've ever met." Maggie stared down at her hands. She couldn't look into her father's gray eyes because she felt like he was searching her very soul. "If he isn't interested in the gospel, it will be so hard not to see him again, but no matter how I feel about him, I won't break the promise I made to myself to marry in the temple." Just thinking about having to walk away from Flynn broke her heart and brought tears to her eyes.

"He's in love with you, Maggie."

Maggie looked up and blinked back tears. "I know. He told me."

"You've been through some very emotional times with him, and you've spent a lot of time alone together. That's a recipe for . . ."

"Trouble," Maggie finished. "I know, Dad. But you have to know that he's been a perfect gentleman. He could probably have taken advantage of me if he'd been so inclined, but he didn't."

Scott McKenzie watched the flush on his daughter's cheeks, saw the brightness in her eyes, and his heart ached for her. "Maggie, I want you to know that Alyssa has a home here with us as long as she wants to stay. And as for your mother and me, nothing will ever change in our feelings for you."

"Oh, Daddy, I know that." Maggie rushed around the desk and threw her arms around her father who rose and met her with open arms. "It won't matter what we find out about our birth parents. You'll always be my only parents." Maggie drew away and looked at him. "But you do understand that we have to know?"

He nodded. "I understand, and we'll do whatever we can to help you. When this has all been settled, we have to make a date at the temple to have you sealed to our family. That has been my biggest concern for twenty-four years—that our family wasn't complete. That's been the hardest part of the lie I've had to live with all this time."

"I'm so glad it's over, Daddy." Maggie kissed her father's cheek and found it moist with tears.

"Not nearly as glad as I am." Scott McKenzie sat at his desk in the semidarkness long after his daughter left, mulling over the events of the day and praying for his daughter and her newfound sister. And Dr. Flynn Ford.

Flynn would have excused himself and gone up to Steve's room, leaving Maggie and her siblings alone around the Christmas tree as was their tradition, but none of them would hear of it. Maggie's parents said good night about eleven-thirty, but the rest talked long past midnight of everything that had happened to Maggie, got acquainted with Flynn and his line of work, and had to hear all about Alyssa's ordeal and her life before that. Then Jeff and Doreen left to get their whispering, giggling children to sleep, and soon Alan and Veronica went to bed. Steve excused himself, leaving Maggie and Flynn alone in the living room with only the Christmas lights burning. Even the fire had died down to just glowing embers.

"We'd probably better turn in too. Christmas comes at our house very early in the morning," Maggie said, getting up to turn off the stereo.

"Come and sit by me for a few minutes first," Flynn said quietly, tossing a pillow in front of the fire and sprawling out comfortably on the floor.

Maggie brought a pillow from the sofa and stretched out on her stomach beside him, her chin in her hands watching the glowing embers snap and pop.

"This is always my favorite part of Christmas Eve," Maggie sighed contentedly. "Not that I don't enjoy *everything* we've always done, but after everyone goes to bed, I always steal back downstairs to watch the fire die out and just enjoy the lights on the tree. It's so peaceful, and there is always such a strong feeling of love left in the room. I think it might be the closest thing to heaven on earth."

Flynn agreed. *This is the closest thing to heaven on earth,* he thought, *and, yes, there is a wonderful spirit here, but wherever Maggie was, it would be the same.*

"I want you to know this has been the best Christmas of my life," Flynn said, turning on his side to face Maggie. "If it were to end this minute, I'd still be the most fortunate man alive for having had a glimpse of a world I didn't know existed." He watched Maggie's face in the fire-light as a blissful smile spread across it.

"I told you my family was the best," Maggie said. "I don't think you believed me, but I'm more than happy to share them with you." She didn't dare look at Flynn. Just being this close to him and feeling his warmth made her almost dizzy.

He rolled over on his stomach to watch the fire. When he held out his hand, she put hers in it, and as he caressed her fingers tenderly, Maggie tingled from head to toe. They lay side-by-side silently watching the embers die, listening to Christmas carols playing softly in the background. Without turning to Maggie, Flynn said softly, "You said you wouldn't marry anyone who couldn't bless you and your children. Was that the kind of blessing they gave Derrick today?"

"Yes," she answered, almost in a whisper. "It's a priesthood blessing. All of the men in our family hold the priesthood of God, and as long as they're worthy, they can call down the blessings of heaven in behalf of the sick. Of course, faith plays a great part in that, but Derrick was surrounded by the faith of his family, so though he was unconscious and couldn't exercise faith himself, we could do it for him."

They fell silent again. Maggie wondered what Flynn was thinking but didn't dare ask him. Maybe he was still working through all the things he'd seen and learned that day. She had to let him discover his way on his own.

Flynn *was* thinking of all he'd seen and learned, but he was also thinking something else that would probably have kept Maggie awake all night if he'd told her.

The grandmother clock on the mantle chimed one o'clock and broke the spell. Maggie sat up abruptly. "Oh! I turn into a pumpkin in five minutes. I need to get to bed."

Flynn got to his feet and pulled Maggie up to face him. "Then by all means, hurry. I like you better as you are than as a pumpkin." He held her hands against his chest to keep from taking her in his arms and holding her the rest of the night. "Good night, Maggie girl. Thank you for inviting me into your world." He bent and brushed a kiss across her lips, then let her go, backing away so she was free to leave the room.

Maggie stood, unable to move for a moment, unable to make her legs turn and walk up the stairs when they only wanted to go toward Flynn. Finally she looked away from his mesmerizing gaze, breathed a quiet "Good night," and hurried up the stairs.

She didn't hear soft footsteps retreating in the hall in front of her, nor a sigh of relief downstairs in the vicinity of her parents' room. Maggie's heart was pounding so hard she wouldn't have heard reindeer hooves dancing on the roof if they'd been there.

Flynn sat down in front of the fire again, wondering if he could do the thing he knew had to be done.

CHAPTER 34

Maggie crept quietly into the bedroom so she wouldn't wake Alyssa, but she needn't have worried. Alyssa was curled up on the far side of the bed sleeping soundly, Kit snuggled in her arms. Neither stirred when Maggie came in, nor did they wake as Maggie brushed her teeth and got ready for bed. She turned off the night light she'd left on for Alyssa and stood at the window watching the snow flurries through the light from the barn. A perfect Christmas.

Morning came too early. She awoke to the happy shouts of children; then Kit took up the chorus and all rest ended. She wondered whether or not she should wake Alyssa, decided she shouldn't let her miss this spectacle, and shook her shoulder.

At first, Alyssa nearly panicked at the noise, then when she sat up, frightened and confused, she saw Maggie. "Oh, now I know where I am. I didn't remember." She looked at the clock. "But it's only six o'clock in the morning."

"That's almost late in this household. Grab your robe and slippers and let's go downstairs to watch the fun. I promise you've never seen anything like it in your life." Maggie slipped into her robe, drew a brush quickly through her hair, and the sisters skipped down the stairs hand in hand.

They were greeted with shouts of "Merry Christmas" from every side, children running through boxes and wrapping paper and squealing with delight when they opened a present, and Christmas carols playing loudly on the stereo. Alyssa's head swam with the noise and confusion. How could so few children make so much noise?

Maggie ran to the kitchen to fetch the hot chocolate and eggnog she knew would be waiting for them, and some cinnamon-apple tea ring straight from the oven. How her mother managed this miracle so early every Christmas morning she didn't know, just that it appeared fresh, hot, and delicious. She took a tray back to Alyssa and they watched the joyous pandemonium until the kids had no more presents and started handing out gaily wrapped gifts for the adults.

It wasn't until one of them called "Flynn" that Maggie realized he wasn't there. She'd been so caught up in the fun, she'd forgotten she had one more houseguest. Before she could get to her feet to go find him, Steve handed her a letter and a small box. When she looked in Steve's eyes, she knew she didn't want to read what was written in the letter.

Steve offered his hand and helped her to her feet. "Will you get me some hot chocolate and tea ring, Maggie?" he asked, loud enough for everyone to hear. *Bless his heart.* Maggie stumbled into the kitchen currently occupied by her two oldest nephews, Nathan and Jake, who were finishing up a carton of eggnog.

She opened the door to the back porch, refreshingly cold since no heat had been flowing into it from the kitchen yet. Her cheeks were flushed, so hot they felt sunburned, and she didn't want anyone to see her as she opened the note. She slipped into the corner where she used to curl up with a book when she didn't want to be found, and read the note Flynn had left.

My Dearest Maggie,

You'll think me an ungrateful coward for leaving in the middle of the night like this, but until I can feel worthy of you and your family, learn what I need to know, and make an intelligent decision not based on my need to be with you, I must be away from you. I'm doing you a favor, too, although it may not seem like it as you read this. I can't cause you any more heartache than I have already, if this is not meant to be for us. I'm not sorry I've fallen in love with you. You've given me my life back, and I'll be forever grateful to you for rekindling feelings I thought were long since dead. I am sorry, though, because I fear you may love me in return and I would not have you hurt for anything in the world if I could help it. Discover the secret of your birth, help Alyssa find herself again, and her way through this.

Flynn.

Maggie choked back the tears as long as she could, then they burst forth in a torrent that couldn't be stopped. *Why?* she asked, again and again. *Why?* And her answer came softly into her mind and heart. *Because he loves you so much he wouldn't let you make an emotional decision now that you'd regret later.*

Maggie pulled her legs up and hugged her knees. He was right. Her resolve to only marry in the temple might have crumbled because of her desire for him. That increasing need to be with him might have overcome every other decision she'd made for her life. She dropped her head onto her knees and prayed for him, that he'd find his answers, and for her, that she could accept, "Thy will, not mine, be done."

Rose McKenzie found Maggie where she knew her daughter would be. She waited until Maggie had read the note and worked through her emotions before she went to her. "Need a shoulder or a listening ear?" she asked, curling up at Maggie's feet.

"You know he's gone?"

Rose nodded.

"Who took him? Where did they take him?"

"He left quietly in the night, apparently on foot. He left a note in the study on the desk thanking us for allowing him to experience what a real family was like, and for raising such a remarkable daughter. He apologized for any hurt he might have caused you and asked for our forgiveness."

"He walked? Mom, it was snowing last night. And blowing. He could have frozen to death . . ."

"He didn't, Maggie. Your dad called the truck stop as soon as he found the note this morning, described Flynn, and asked Martin if he'd seen someone during the night who looked like him. Flynn had been there and hitched a ride with a trucker going to Salt Lake."

"Oh."

They sat quietly for a minute. "Do you want to read the note?" Maggie said, handing it to her mother.

Rose read it, then asked, "What else was in the envelope besides the note?"

Maggie looked at the envelope in her lap. There was something else there. She pulled out a bundle of crisp, new hundred-dollar bills wrapped with a rubber band. Stuck inside the band was a smaller note, folded in half. Maggie handed the money to her mother to count while she read the note aloud.

Please take this money and fly back to get your car. Or if you're in San Buenaventura with Alyssa, maybe Steve would like to go. I'm sorry for the inconvenience.

Love,

Flynn

"There's five thousand dollars here," Rose gasped. "Does he always throw money around like this? Is he rich?"

Maggie explained about Susan and Kaitlin, and the insurance money that Flynn had never touched until now, when he felt Susan would be happy to know he'd used it to help Alyssa and Maggie.

"What was the present?" her mother asked.

Maggie had even forgotten about the present. She retrieved it from the floor where the little box had fallen. It was wrapped in gold foil with a tiny gold bow on top, and taped to the bottom of the box was a folded piece of paper.

She unfolded it and read it aloud to her mother.

Dear Maggie:

I selfishly intended to ask your father for your hand in marriage and give you this ring tonight, but after spending the evening with your family, I realized I could not do that to you. When I have resolved all of my concerns, and when you have been distanced from me long enough to see clearly again, if we discover that we are meant to be, I will be privileged to give you the ring and all my love forever. Until then, I hope you won't mind my leaving it with you for safekeeping.

Maggie carefully undid the gold paper and, with trembling fingers, opened the white cardboard gift box to find a white velvet ring box inside. Opening the hinged lid, she stared at a deep blue marquis-cut sapphire surrounded by glittering diamonds.

"I guess Flynn was busy doing some shopping on his own while Alyssa and I were buying presents for everyone," Maggie said quietly. She'd been having so much fun shopping with Alyssa she hadn't paid any attention to what Flynn was doing all that time.

"What are you going to do with it?" Maggie's mother asked quietly.

"Just what he said. Keep it in a safe place until I see him again."

"Is it an engagement ring?"

Maggie looked at the exquisite sapphire nestled among the diamonds. "I don't know. They're using other stones besides diamonds for everything now." Maggie slipped it on the finger of her right hand and held it up for her mother to see. "It's beautiful." Then she took it off and carefully placed it back in the white velvet box. "But I won't wear it at all, not even on my right hand, until we've determined what's going to happen between us."

She stood and stretched and helped her mother to her feet. "I guess we'd better go rescue Alyssa. She's probably wondering what happened to me, and feeling totally overwhelmed by all the chaos around here."

They linked arms as they entered the bright warmth of the big kitchen. "Flynn was right to leave, though it creates a huge, empty hole in my heart," Maggie said. "I want to be with him more than anything else in the world. When I look into those warm, dark eyes, and I've never felt so safe, and so . . ."

"Desired?" her mother finished.

Maggie's face flushed. "Yes, I guess that's it." She nibbled on a piece of cranberry bread someone had put on a plate. "I thought I was so in love with Brad before he left on his mission, but that was nothing compared to what I've felt for Flynn. Mom, do you realize I've only known the man five days, six counting today? How can someone make such an indelible impression and change your life so quickly and completely?"

"You went through a lot together, and you've barely left his side during those very emotional times. That can create a strong bond. I'm glad Flynn was such an honorable man. I know this was a hard thing for him to do. He couldn't look at you without revealing to everyone in the room how he felt about you." Rose McKenzie put her arm around her daughter's shoulder and leaned her head against Maggie's. "You weren't doing so well at hiding your feelings either. I hope you're prepared for your brothers' teasing. It would be too kind of them to bite their tongues, and even if this is the season of brotherly love and kindness, I can't imagine them passing up an opportunity to do what they've done so well all their lives."

Maggie laughed. "You're right. I'll be a prime target today. Guess Alyssa and I will just have to stay out of their way. Any reason we can't go riding this morning?"

"None at all. Your grandparents will drop in about one o'clock when we spread out the buffet and last night's leftovers, but the morning is yours."

Maggie started to leave the kitchen, then turned back to her mother. "Mom, how do you feel about Dad deceiving you about my birth and keeping it a secret all these years?"

"How do I feel?" Rose reached for her daughter's hand and led her to the breakfast nook. "Many different emotions," she said as they sat opposite each other. "My heart aches for the burden he carried needlessly. He could have told me, should have told me. But I guess I can understand how much harder it became as the years passed, and I understand why he didn't tell me at first. I had my hands more than full with five active boys who were born close together, then had two difficult pregnancies and lost my two other little girls. It nearly destroyed me, physically and mentally, I'm ashamed to say."

Maggie protested. "Why should you be ashamed? You couldn't help it."

Rose shook her head. "I've always thought I should have been stronger. I hated feeling so helpless, so useless."

Maggie slid out of her seat and sat next to her mother. She put her arm around Rose and kissed her cheek. "You know we're given trials and challenges in this life, and those were certainly major ones for you, but you came through with flying colors. Look how all your children turned out. I'm so glad you're my mother."

Rose squeezed Maggie's hand. "Not nearly as glad as I am that you're my daughter. I can only love your father all the more because of what he did the day you were born in giving you to me. You've been one of the great delights of my life." She wiped away a tear that rolled down her cheek. "But if you don't hurry, you won't get your riding in this morning."

Maggie hugged her Mom, and wasted no time in rescuing Alyssa from the questions of all the little nieces and nephews, thanked Steve for being so great, and then the twins disappeared upstairs to prepare for a morning of riding. Alyssa saddled Maggie's second-favorite horse, Belle, while Maggie saddled Pegasus. They rode into the pasture and turned the horses loose to run as fast as they wanted, racing to the far end through newly fallen snow that sparkled like diamonds in the bright morning sun.

Then Maggie took Alyssa through the gate out of the pasture onto the snow-packed road, and the girls rode side-by-side down the country lane, oblivious to the Currier and Ives scenes surrounding them, oblivious to the glory of the morning, the dazzling sun, the nip in the air that reddened their cheeks. They had so much catching up to do on their past and so much planning to do for their future.

"Do you feel up to calling Lily and your father today?" Maggie asked, hoping that Alyssa would be ready to face that portion of her past very soon. "They still don't know whether you're dead or alive."

Alyssa hesitated. "It's cowardly, I know, but I could stay here with your family forever. They've made me feel so loved and welcome, and I haven't felt a shred of pity from anyone, though I did feel their compassion. No one stared at me like I was some kind of freak. That's what I've dreaded, even when I wanted nothing more than to escape—people looking at me funny and wondering where I'd been and what I'd done and what had been done to me."

"Did you ever try to escape, Alyssa?" *This was one question Flynn would have wanted to ask,* Maggie thought with a twinge, missing him all over again.

Alyssa nodded. "Several times in the first few weeks, until he gave me so much more of the drugs that I didn't care whether I escaped or not."

"Have you ever heard of the Stockholm Syndrome?" Maggie asked.

Alyssa shook her head. "No, what's that?"

Maggie explained, and asked Alyssa if she had ever felt any allegiance to Cleat Wiggins, any interdependence with him.

"No, never," Alyssa said emphatically. "Even when I felt so . . . floating, so peaceful, not caring about anything, there was still an irritation—no, more than that. A repugnance, and it became a hatred of the man. He was horrible, dirty. I think the only reason he ever bathed was so that he could pass kitchen inspection. When he wasn't working, he never went near a shower."

"I still find it so hard to understand why he kidnapped you. He never asked for ransom money, never wrote taunting letters to your dad, and if he kept you so drugged you couldn't carry on an intelligent conversation, what did he want with you?"

Alyssa thought about that. "I've wondered that a lot. Of course, I didn't know whether he got ransom money, but you know how some people keep dogs, and never really play with them? They just have them for show? I think maybe I was like that for him."

"Sort of a legitimacy thing?" Maggie asked. "Hmm. People would look at a man alone—especially a big brute of a man with a bad temper and bad hygiene habits, and he could be blamed for anything that went wrong around him. But with a daughter along, he wasn't just a man, he appeared as a father." Maggie nodded. "Yes, I can see him thinking along those lines."

They rode in silence for awhile, just enjoying each other's companionship and the joy of sisterhood, something neither had ever experienced.

"I guess I really should call my father and Lily. It isn't fair to keep them wondering if I'm still alive, or mourning because I'm dead. You know, I had really hoped they had gotten married because I didn't want them to be alone in their grief. I knew what it would do to my father to have me gone, and though Lily is so strong, she really did love me like a daughter, and I knew she'd be devastated." Alyssa looked at Maggie. "Did I tell you she was my nanny? I can't remember what I've told you and what I haven't."

"Alyssa, is there any possibility that she could be our birth mother?"

Alyssa thought about it. "I don't know. I'd be happy if she was, but why would I be raised as the Lawsons' daughter instead of hers when she was right there with me? That's the part that never made sense to me, so I just supposed it was my wild imagination making something more out of it than was there when I heard Lily say what she did to my mother."

"Are you ready to call now?" Maggie asked. "Can you think of a better Christmas present than to hear from you today?"

Alyssa reined in Belle and looked at Maggie. "I guess you're right. Why put it off?"

"I'll race you back to the house," Maggie said, giving Pegasus his head. That was all he needed and they flew like the wind down the snow-packed country lane, horse and rider moving as one. Belle was no match for Pegasus, but Alyssa's riding skills hadn't diminished much and she got the best the smaller horse had to give, arriving at the McKenzies' only seconds behind Maggie.

The twins took care of their horses, then arrived rosy cheeked at the backdoor where they shed boots and coats before hurrying to the living room to warm up by the fire. Rose brought hot chocolate and cranberry nut bread to them on a tray as soon as they sat down.

"I saw you coming and knew you'd be cold all the way through and hungry besides," she explained at Alyssa's amazed look. "Everyone in here has been eating all morning, so the hot chocolate was ready."

"Thank you so much." Alyssa couldn't believe how Rose McKenzie anticipated everyone's needs and took care of them.

Maggie laughed. "Even if it hadn't been ready, she would have made some just for us. She can see the road from her kitchen window, and I'm sure she had the hot chocolate timed for our return. That's my mom. She gets more kick out of doing nice things for people than anything else. I think she likes it even better than shopping." Maggie stopped. "But when she does shop, she never buys anything for herself; it's always for everyone else. She's just totally selfless."

Alyssa hated to compare Rose McKenzie to her own mother, because she loved her mother, but maybe it had been the cancer that made such a difference in the two women.

While Maggie ran up to her room for her purse and cell phone, Alyssa listened to the happy sounds coming from the family room where everyone was playing one of the games someone had received for Christmas. When Maggie sat back by the fire, Alyssa was snuggling Kit in her lap and talking to the puppy. "He likes you," Maggie noted.

"I like him, too," Alyssa said, laughing at the impetuous pup's attempts to lick her face.

"Then he's yours. I have no need for a dog, and he likes you better than me, anyway. Merry Christmas, Alyssa." She reached over and ruffled the puppy's fur. "Merry Christmas to you, Kit." Maggie looked at the dog. "I think he needs a new name. The trucker said to take care of Kit, so apparently that's what he called him, but I don't think it fits, do you?"

Alyssa looked at the squirming, playful puppy. "I think you're right," she agreed. "We'll have to come up with something more fitting." She thought for a minute. "How about Hope?"

"Perfect," Maggie beamed.

She pulled out her cell phone, then realized she only had the number of the newspaper office, and there was probably no one at the phones on Christmas Day. "Do you remember the number at your house?" Then she stopped. "Did Lily live with you?"

"She lived on the estate, but she had her own little cottage on the other side of the garden. I assume my father's still in the big house. Hmm. No. I can't remember the number. I didn't think I'd ever forget it. I even tried to call a couple of times, but that man caught me and knocked me down the first time, and nearly broke my arm the next. Then after he drugged me, I didn't care whether they knew I was still alive or not."

"Let's see, it's ten o'clock our time, nine o'clock in California. Maybe I'll call the paper anyway. There might be an answering machine or something." Eventually Maggie tracked down both numbers through San Buenaventura information. "Who do you want to call first?"

Alyssa's face paled at the thought of answering the questions all over again that she'd already answered. Or was she just afraid they wouldn't be as loving and accepting as Maggie's family had been? Would they somehow blame her for their heartache of the past seven years?

"Lily," Alyssa whispered, hardly able to speak for the apprehension that choked her. "But will you talk to her first?"

Maggie nodded and dialed the number of Lily's cottage. Maybe Lily was at the big house having dinner with Mr. Lawson. Maybe she had family somewhere and wasn't in town. The phone rang four times, and Maggie was about to give up when suddenly she heard Lily's voice on the other end.

CHAPTER 35

"Lily Noble speaking."

"Merry Christmas, Lily. This is Maggie. M. M. McKenzie. Remember me?"

There was a pause on the other end. "Yes, Maggie, of course I remember you. Merry Christmas." She took a deep breath. "What can I do for you?"

"You can sit down," Maggie said slowly, giving instructions she hoped Lily would follow as she spoke, "compose yourself, and then say hello to Alyssa. She's sitting right here beside me and she's safe and sound."

There was an audible gasp on the other end of the line, and Maggie handed the phone to Alyssa, squeezed her hand in encouragement, and quietly left the room. She scooped up the puppy, and motioned to Heather and Emily playing with their new dolls in the corner by the Christmas tree to come with her. She corralled Jake and Nathan, who had been chasing each other through the house, and took everyone into the family room.

Explaining that Alyssa needed some quiet time on the phone, she got them in a circle on the floor and invented a game with Hope in the center. Much as she'd love to hear Alyssa's end of the conversation, it was, after all, Alyssa's family and she needed the privacy to come to terms with her return to them.

Suddenly Alyssa appeared in the doorway looking shaken, but smiling. "Maggie, can you tell Lily how to get here from Salt Lake? If they can get a flight, they're going to fly in today, rent a car and they'll drive up—if that's okay."

Maggie jumped to her feet. "Of course it's okay!" She took the phone. "Lily, I'm so glad you're coming. That will make Alyssa's Christmas complete."

A weeping Lily tried to speak. "Maggie, I don't know how you did it, but I'll never be able to thank you enough. The job is still yours. I guess I couldn't fire you since you're Mr. Randolph's employee."

"Thank you." *Merry Christmas to me,* Maggie thought gleefully. "Now, when you get your rental car in Salt Lake, they'll give you a map of the area. Get on I-215 going north. You'll merge into I-15; just stay on that until you cross the Utah-Idaho border. Watch for the exit after the big truck stop and turn right. Stay on that little country road for two miles, and we're the first house on the right. Actually, the only house you'll see." Maggie gave Lily her cell phone number and told her to call as they were leaving Salt Lake so she'd know about what time to expect them.

"Would it be too much trouble for you to reserve us a room at a hotel near you?" Lily asked.

Maggie laughed. "We'll have a room reserved for you." She didn't bother to tell Lily that there wasn't a hotel within seventy-five miles.

Maggie and Alyssa just stood and looked at each other after Maggie disconnected. Then they threw their arms around each other and laughed.

"That wasn't so hard, was it?" Maggie asked.

"Yes," Alyssa said, clutching her heart. "It was horrible, until Lily got over her shock and finally believed it was me."

"I didn't even think she might not believe it was really you." Maggie grabbed Alyssa's hand and began pulling her toward the kitchen. "What did you say to convince her?"

"I just sang a little song she'd made up for me when I was little. I even talked to my father. He was at the cottage for breakfast. He couldn't talk much; he was too choked up, but he promised to get them here at the first possible minute."

As they burst into the kitchen, Maggie blurted with excitement, "Mom, Alyssa's father and Lily are coming."

Rose McKenzie, in the process of giving her youngest grand-daughter a drink, smiled broadly. "I'm so glad you talked to them, Alyssa. How are you feeling?" She held out her arms to Alyssa.

"Shaky. Excited. Scared." Alyssa went to Rose and hugged her. "Thanks for making this so easy for me to . . ." Alyssa paused, not knowing the words to say. "To come back," she finished. "I was so afraid to face anyone. I know there will be lots of reporters and that will be hard, but your family has made this so much more do-able than I ever thought it would be."

Rose kissed Alyssa's cheek. "You'll do just fine. And you never have to answer any reporters' questions that you don't want to. If they get out of hand, just look them in the eye and say, 'Why would you ask such a question?' Do you have any idea when your family will arrive?"

Maggie laughed. "No, and neither do they. They're going to catch the first flight they can get, but on Christmas Day that could be a real problem. It might be tomorrow or the next day before they can get here."

"Unless they call Mr. Randolph and use his private plane. They've done that before." Alyssa paused. "I wonder how much has changed while I've been gone. I suppose my father is still editor of the newspaper and Lily still works there. Is Mr. Randolph still playing tricks on my father, or is he even still alive?"

"I can answer those questions right now," Maggie said. "Your father is editor, Lily runs the office and much of the newspaper, it seems, and Mr. Randolph is still playing tricks on your father. He hired me and sent me to the San Buenaventura newspaper without even telling your father. Just sent a letter of introduction with me. Talk about disconcerting for a new employee to be introduced that way!"

"So we don't really have any idea when they'll arrive?" Rose asked, getting back to her first concern. "No problem. I'll just alert Rick and Rachel that Alan and Veronica may be moving over to their house for a night or two, and Steve can throw a sleeping bag down anywhere. We'll let you two curl up in front of the fireplace in the family room. That will leave your room and Steve's available for Mr. Lawson and Lily."

"See how easy Mom makes everything seem?" Maggie said. "Throw two additional guests at her and she's solved the sleeping problem in less time than I've been able to get a piece of pie out of this pan. Which kind do you want, Alyssa, pumpkin or mincemeat?"

"Can I have that French apple with a little bit of ice cream on top?"

"Sure. Help yourself to anything that looks good. By the way, where is everyone, Mom? It's unnaturally quiet around here for Christmas Day. Not that I mind the peace and quiet," she quickly added.

"Jeff and Doreen ran to Taylor and Ashley's for some quiet conversation without all the kids. Alan and Veronica are at Aunt Maurine and Uncle Clyde's. Did I tell you he's not doing too well? Rick's tending a sick cow, and your father tagged along with him."

Maggie's grandparents arrived at noon, an hour earlier than expected, and the story had to be told all over again of how Maggie and her twin were separated at birth and how they'd been reunited, minus a lot of the details. The family returned at various times during the afternoon, another dinner was consumed, much less formal than the day before, and even Steve made an appearance before the afternoon was over.

"Where have you been all day?" Maggie asked.

"Visiting," was his noncommittal reply.

"Visiting who?"

"Friends."

"What friends, Steve?"

Taylor spoke up. "Tell her, Steve, or I will. I saw your car parked in front of Jackie's house all afternoon."

Steve ducked out and disappeared as Maggie's cell phone rang. She dug it out of her jeans pocket and headed for the kitchen where it was a little quieter.

"Hello?"

"Maggie, this is Lily. Mr. Randolph was in Ojai for Christmas, just over the mountain, so he sent his plane for us. We're leaving Salt Lake now. How long will it take us to drive to your house?"

"About an hour and a half with clear roads and little traffic. Do you have the instructions I gave you?"

"Yes, dear, I do. Thank you, Maggie." Lily's voice caught. "I'm so looking forward to seeing you and Alyssa."

"Drive safe." Maggie disconnected and stood in the quiet kitchen, looking out on the long shadows creeping across the open fields. The snow didn't sparkle in the sunlight anymore. It was tinged with the blue of approaching twilight. Lily and Mr. Lawson wouldn't arrive until after dark. Maggie took a deep breath. How could she wait that long? The suspense was killing her. Did Lily truly hold the key to the mystery of their birth as Alyssa thought? Or would they have to wait longer and search further to find the truth?

She thought of Flynn, and the pain in her heart brought tears to her eyes. What if he decided her faith was not for him? Maggie had to admit many people looked at it as too hard, but she didn't think Flynn was one to turn away from a challenge—or a blessing. What would she do if she didn't hear from him soon? Go back to San Buenaventura and her job at the newspaper? She knew he could find her—if he wanted to. But what if he didn't want to?

Maggie leaned over and picked up the puppy, who had followed her to the kitchen. "No, Hope. He's too honorable to never show up again. But what if he only comes back to tell me he's not interested in continuing the relationship?" She held up the wiggly little dog and looked at him. "How on earth could I tell him good-bye again? Just saying good night last night was hard enough."

"You could do it, Maggie. It wouldn't be easy, but you could do it."

Maggie whirled around to find Steve leaning against the door to the back porch, pie plate in hand. He held it up. "I wasn't spying on you, just getting another piece of pumpkin pie." He brought the whole pie in and picked up a piece, treating it like finger food. "How are you holding up through all of this, Sis?"

"Great." Maggie smiled ruefully. "That is, until I think of Flynn." She tried to keep the tears from flowing, but wasn't having much success. "Sorry to be such a boob," she said, putting the pup down and reaching for a handful of tissues.

"You really fell for the big guy, didn't you?" Steve said, sliding into the breakfast nook and motioning Maggie to join him.

Maggie nodded, wiping her nose and her eyes. "I didn't realize it was happening. I thought I just had a great big crush on my doctor. I don't know when it turned into . . . whatever. Oh, Steve, I just want him here with me. Or I want to be with him, wherever he is." Maggie held up her hands to stop Steve from saying what he started to say. "I know. I know. If he isn't interested in joining the Church because of what he finds there, I don't want him joining just for me. That rarely works out. And I honestly can't see myself without the blessings of the temple and the priesthood in my home, but . . ."

"Isn't it funny how that little 'but' can play such a big part in our lives? You can't imagine yourself without the blessings of the Church, and yet you can't imagine life without Flynn. Guess you've got a lot of work to do, Maggie."

"Work?" The word puzzled Maggie. She could have guessed at a dozen other words he could have used, but work?

"Testimony-building stuff: study, fasting and prayer, getting closer to the Spirit. Those are the only things I know of that will combat this physical need you're feeling."

Maggie looked at her older brother through new eyes. "How did you get to be so wise?"

Steve's face pinked up a bit. "Remember Brittany Blake, the girl I was dating when I left on my mission?"

Maggie nodded.

Steve looked away, snapped his fingers at Hope and pretended to be caught up in playing with the dog. Maggie suspected he was stalling.

"We talked about getting married when I got home from my mission." Steve looked up, finally meeting Maggie's eyes. "I loved her, Maggie. I think I know how you feel about Flynn and how he feels about you because I watched you look at each other. I watched your hand linger on his, not wanting to break that connection. That's how I felt about Brittany. I wanted to be with her every second. I wanted to be connected, to be touching her every hour of the day and night. And I thought she felt that way about me." Steve stopped.

"What happened?"

He reached down and picked up the puppy begging at his knee to be held. "I got a 'Dear John' six months into my mission. She's married now and has a baby. So much for loving me forever."

"I'm so sorry, Steve." Maggie reached across the table and touched his hand. "Is that how you got over her? Testimony-building stuff?"

"That's the formula. Of course, lots of hard work with your mind on other things helps a lot, and in your case, probably dating a few other guys."

Alyssa peeked around the kitchen door. "Is this a private party or . . ." She hesitated slightly before she finished, "can a sister join you?"

Maggie beamed at her and held out her hand. She was so pleased that Alyssa hadn't been a shrinking violet and had become a part of the family so quickly. "Come on in, sister." Then she had a thought. "I wonder if you're my little sister or my big sister? I wonder if we'll ever know. By the way, that phone call was Lily. They've landed in Salt Lake and will be here in about an hour and a half."

Steve raised an eyebrow.

"Alyssa talked to her father and Lily this morning, and they flew to Salt Lake on Mr. Randolph's private plane. They'll be spending the night. Oh, that reminds me, we have some beds to change. Mr. Lawson will be in your room, Steve, and Lily will be in ours. You have your choice of wherever you'd like to throw your sleeping bag."

"Did you break the news to the folks they have more company coming?" Steve asked.

"Yes, Mom knows, but I'm not going to say anything in front of anyone else. I'd just as soon Grandma and Grandpa left and everyone else drift off so we don't have this huge audience when they get here."

"I can take care of that. We were talking about doing a movie and popcorn at Rick and Rachel's. Did you hear Rachel got him that new big-screen TV he's been hinting at for a year?"

"Oh, Steve, that would be wonderful if we didn't have thirty people running in and out when they get here."

"Done deal. I'll go make the arrangements. I might have to raid Mom's pantry as I'm not sure how well stocked Rachel's is after all they spent on Christmas and the addition to the vet clinic."

"Tell me what you want and I'll gather it up right now. You go change the linen on your bed and straighten up your room a little, will you? Mr. Lawson doesn't have to see you at your worst." Maggie laughed and ducked when Steve tossed a dish towel at her.

"Just make sure we have plenty of popcorn, soda pop, and chocolate. Oh, and if there is any of that spinach-artichoke dip left, we'll take that and the chips."

"If you'll tell me where to find clean linen, I'll get our room ready for Lily," Alyssa offered. Maggie directed her to the upstairs hall closet, and Alyssa left to change linen and put away the clothes they'd scattered around since their arrival.

Maggie loaded all the items Steve requested in grocery bags, then added a plate of brownies. Better they consume these calorie-laden goodies at Rachel's tonight than leave them for her to nibble. She also packed a goodie tray one of the neighbors had brought them that was piled high with fruitcake and nut breads and fancy Christmas cookies. Maggie ate the single piece of fudge remaining on the plate. No sense sending only one piece for people to fight over.

As her grandma and grandpa were getting ready to go home, Maggie promised to come and visit them before she left again for her job. She loved these two old dears, but tonight all she wanted was a bit of privacy when Lily and Mr. Lawson arrived. She prayed that Lily would have the answers she needed—correction: the answers she and Alyssa needed.

Maggie flew around straightening the living room, recovering lost toys from underneath pillows and chairs, picking up Christmas bows that had evaded her mother's eye, and gathering scattered newspapers and discarded jackets and shoes.

Steve had managed to get everyone out of the house except their parents, and as the hour approached, Maggie and Alyssa added logs to the fire, prepared heavy snacks in case Lily and Mr. Lawson were hungry, then paced the house looking for things to do while they waited. Rose had disappeared into her bedroom, and Maggie suspected she was on her knees instead of refreshing her appearance, as she'd said. It would be so like her mother to pray for blessings upon this emotional meeting.

Scott McKenzie had withdrawn into his study, and Maggie knew he would be praying. She knew he was very repentant about the secrecy he'd imposed on Maggie's birth story. Maggie didn't blame him. She knew her mother's health had been fragile for years, and that her father had always done whatever he could for the wife he adored more than anything else in this life.

And her father had a portion of the story no one else knew about, except the girls' birth father. Even their birth mother had not known.

Flynn invaded Maggie's thoughts again as she climbed the stairs to change clothes. He would so have loved to have been here, she knew, to find out the rest of the story. Maggie only hoped that's what Lily could provide. The rest of the story.

CHAPTER 40

Alyssa was as nervous as a bride waiting at the altar for a late groom, and Maggie wasn't much better. They both jumped and raced for the door when the doorbell rang. Suddenly Alyssa hung back, wanting to see them, yet afraid to face them.

Maggie threw open the door, welcoming the two into her parents' home. Lily introduced her to Mr. Lawson, the boss she had never met, though she had been in his employ just short of a week. She stepped aside quickly and ushered them into the living room where Alyssa stood, unable to move. Maggie shut the door, wanting to slip out the front and come in the back so she wouldn't be an intruder in this long-hoped-for reunion.

Scott and Rose McKenzie appeared and Maggie made introductions, asked for coats, and finally Alyssa moved. She flew to her father and he held her tight, tears streaming down his face. Then Lily held her and could hardly let go.

Rose took charge, placing everyone in the room: Mr. Lawson and Lily on the sofa, she and Scott across the room from them in the big leather chairs, and Maggie and Alyssa in the love seat between the couples.

"I can't believe my eyes. Two of you." Lily could do nothing but stare at the twins and shake her head, genuinely puzzled.

Maggie's heart sank. Above everything else this meeting needed to accomplish, she had hoped that Lily could tell them who actually *was* their birth mother. It appeared that would not happen.

No one seemed able to begin the conversation. The atmosphere was tense until Maggie finally broke the uncomfortable silence that appeared to drag on for minutes, when in fact, it was only a matter of seconds.

"You're the parents who raised us, respectively, but we don't know who our birth parents are. Lily, do you?"

Lily glanced nervously at Lionel Lawson, who nodded almost imperceptibly. "I guess we don't need to keep secrets any longer. You're my child, Alyssa." She looked relieved from an immense burden.

Alyssa jumped up and ran to embrace her mother on the sofa. The two couldn't have looked happier.

Then Lily looked at Maggie. "But how can you look so much like Alyssa? I don't understand."

Scott McKenzie cleared his throat. "I have that answer. My wife suddenly went into labor while we were visiting on the California coast in the little town of Red Cliffs. She had some serious problems with the pregnancy, and they put her under anesthetic to do an emergency C-section, but our baby girl died. Rose had already lost two other infant girls, and her health, both mental and physical, was extremely fragile. I was afraid the knowledge that she would have to go home with empty arms one more time would be more than she could handle."

He reached for his wife's hand and held it while he continued. "One other couple was in the little hospital that night. I talked with the man in the waiting room while our wives were in labor. His wife had just delivered twin girls, but he had no money. He was out of work, heavily in debt, and knew of no way he'd ever be able to pay the hospital bill. He worried how he'd feed one more hungry mouth. His wife was still under anesthetic in the recovery room, so she didn't know that she'd delivered two babies instead of one. That had been a great surprise to him. Since they had no money, this was her first visit to medical personnel of any kind. They'd only come to the hospital because she'd lost several babies when they were delivered at home by midwives."

Maggie glanced at Lily, whose face was ashen. She looked like she would faint at any moment. Lionel Lawson touched her shoulder and left his hand resting there as if to let his strength flow into her.

Scott continued, "To make a long story short, he arranged with the nurse to alter the birth certificates, I gave him a check for five thousand dollars, a few hundred for the nurse, and both mothers left the hospital without knowing what we'd done. So that his wife would never know, he refused to tell me his name and asked me to never reveal our secret. I left the check blank, he filled in his name, and when I got the canceled check, the name written there was illegible." He hung his head for a minute to collect himself. Then he looked up at Lily. "If you're Alyssa's birth mother, you're also Maggie's."

Lily's hand went to her mouth, but the cry escaped anyway. Maggie went to her, knelt in front of her, and held her hands while Alyssa's arm went around her mother's shaking shoulders. Lily wept unashamedly, letting the grief and frustration of past years flow out of her.

"No wonder I liked you so much when I first met you," Maggie said. "Imagine being interviewed for a job by my birth mother, and neither of us had any idea!"

Lily still couldn't speak, though she clasped Maggie in her arms and hugged her tight. Finally she whispered, "I thought you were a pretty special person when I met you. Little did I know how special."

"I'm so sorry, Lily," Scott McKenzie said. "I didn't think at the time what it might do to you or the girls. I could only think of Rose and how much I needed her to be strong and well enough to raise our five boys. I didn't think beyond putting that baby in her arms. The fact that I could help out a man who seemed down and out at the same time seemed nothing but a blessing to me. But not being able to tell anyone—not knowing how to tell even my wife later . . ." He stopped, reached for his handkerchief, and blew his nose loudly.

Rose put her arms around her husband. "It's okay, Scott. We'll work it out, if Lily doesn't have any objections to us adopting our—her—daughter so that Maggie can be sealed to us." Lily was too distraught to hear or understand, so Rose let the matter drop for the time being and passed around a box of tissues since there wasn't a dry eye in the room, leaving them with Maggie to administer to Lily as needed.

"I hate that man. I'll hate him to my dying day," she murmured, but everyone in the silent room heard her clearly.

"Lily, who was he?" Maggie asked. "Who was our father?"

She didn't answer for a minute, and Maggie almost repeated the question. Then slowly, quietly, Lily told her story.

"I was very young and fell in love with a man who came through our little town. He was a few years older, from San Francisco, and seemed so urbane, so suave and sophisticated. I suppose you could call us flower children. He swept me off my feet, promising me the world. We married ourselves in the spring on top of a hill overlooking the ocean. The two of us constituted the entire wedding party. My wedding dress was my Sunday dress, my veil borrowed from an old hat, held in place by a wreath of wild flowers I'd woven. Our celebration dinner was an experimental drug he said was harmless but wonderful and would open this new world to me."

Lily stopped and wiped her tears and nose. No one in the room moved, no one made a sound, held captive by Lily's revelations. When she regained control, she continued.

"I dabbled in his drugs with him occasionally, but I didn't think it was something we needed to be spending our hard-earned money on. He was nothing that he pretended to be when I met him. He had no skills, no job, and no ambition. We lived in a tenant shack some farmer let us use while we worked for him, but we barely made enough money for food, much less drugs. When I got pregnant, I quit using his drugs, which gave him more for himself, but then he accused me of thinking I was better than him, so we argued a lot. When it was time to deliver the baby, he gave me something for the pain, acted as midwife, and when I woke up, he was gone and I had no baby. When he returned, he said it had died and he buried it. He said it was all deformed, probably from the drugs. I never found the grave."

Lily's voice caught, but she stifled the sobs that threatened to overcome her as she revived those painful memories.

"The second time I got pregnant, I insisted on a real midwife to deliver the baby. He came home from town one day and said he found a good one, so when it was time for the baby to come, he went for her. She made me take something that put me out, and when I woke up, the woman was there, my husband was gone, and again I had no baby. She said the cord had been wrapped around its neck and it was born dead. He'd gone to bury it. Again, I never found the grave."

Maggie handed Lily more tissues and waited.

"Things just got worse between us, and I decided I'd leave him, though he told me if I did he'd find me and bring me back. Then I discovered I was expecting again, so I didn't go. Nobody wanted to hire someone who was pregnant, and I had no training, so I was stuck. This time I wanted to go to the hospital where they'd be able to handle any problems. We fought about it for weeks, but I went anyway and he followed. I guess you know the rest of that part of the story. When I woke up, I had a beautiful little baby girl. Finally, the third time was the charm, and I didn't have empty arms."

Lily looked at Rose. "I know how you felt. There is nothing more terrible than to carry a baby for nine months and have nothing to show for it but an aching, longing heart. I'm glad you didn't have to go home without a baby." Lily stroked Maggie's hair. "You were the lucky one, I think, because things just went from bad to worse, and finally I had to take Alyssa and run away. He was using drugs a lot more and becoming more abusive. His temper was totally out of control, and I feared he'd hurt my baby if I stayed. There was no love left between us anyway.

"So I hitchhiked down the coast, with no money, no job skills, nothing but a hungry baby in my arms that I was desperate to support. I was lucky to find a job as a cleaning lady for the Lawsons. They'd been married a long time and hadn't been able to have any children, so we entered into an agreement. They'd adopt Alyssa and raise her as their own; I could stay in the guest house on their estate and be a nanny to my own daughter. I'd keep her with me as I cleaned that big house, and they'd pay her medical bills and her schooling, and raise her like a lady. It seemed the perfect solution to someone who had no possibilities for a future."

Alyssa leaned her head on her mother's shoulder, and Maggie handed her more tissues to wipe the tears that flowed unchecked down her cheeks.

"Mr. and Mrs. Lawson paid for me to go to school at night, then when Alyssa was in school, he gave me a job at the newspaper in addition to keeping up their house. I helped Mrs. Lawson through her battle with cancer, and we were just getting over the pain of her loss when we lost Alyssa."

Lily wiped her tears and looked around the room. "So now you know my whole sordid story."

Maggie waited, but Alyssa didn't ask the question. Maggie didn't want to, but she had to know. "Lily, what was your husband's name?"

Alyssa and Maggie, eyes locked on each other, held their breath, hoping it wasn't the name they both feared it would be.

Lily looked surprised, then shook her head a little. "Oh, I thought I told you. His name was Cleat Wiggins."

Maggie waited for the roof to fall on them or something equally as drastic to occur at that catastrophic revelation. But nothing happened, except that Maggie and Alyssa couldn't look at each other as they silently coped with the news in their own way. Neither girl could speak for a minute. Maggie had hoped, had even prayed not to hear that name spoken in the same breath as *father*.

Not realizing she had just dropped a bombshell on the twins, Lily added, "And if I ever lay eyes on him again, I think I could actually kill the man for putting me through such pain and misery, and for separating you two."

"You don't have to worry, Lily," Maggie said quietly. "He's dead. We watched him die a couple of days ago, shot by the police as he tried to get to Alyssa after we'd rescued her." She shuddered at the memory and forced the awful scene from her mind. Then Maggie dropped her own bombshell. "He's the one who kidnapped Alyssa."

Lily gasped and looked at Alyssa as if needing corroboration. Alyssa nodded.

"He always said if I left him he'd get even with me," Lily said quietly, her hand at her throat. "We couldn't imagine why there were never ransom demands. Now I know. It was revenge—sadistic revenge. He was getting even with me by taking you. Oh, Lyssie, I'm so sorry."

Then Maggie remembered Flynn's encouraging words to her when she'd been horrified at even the thought of Cleat being her father, and looked up at Lily. "But after you left him, your life was good, wasn't it, and you were with Alyssa all the time, even if you couldn't claim her as your own. Although he didn't turn out to be what you wanted, you were happy with him once and loved him, and my life with my family was wonderful. Actually, all of our lives were happy and fulfilling, except for the last seven years when your family was ripped apart and you had to endure so much suffering because of it. It all can be good again, now that he's dead and can't disrupt anyone's lives any more."

Maggie's heart was near breaking as she thought of Flynn missing out on the final details of this tragic twist of fate, and she wished more than anything he was here with her now. He would know the right things to say to everyone to soothe their troubled hearts and point them to the things that would help them heal.

No one spoke. What was there to say? Then Lily quietly broke the silence, her voice filled with anguish. "If he sold one of my twins, did he—could he have also sold my other two babies?" Her voice caught and she paused, took a deep breath, then continued. "Was that why I never found their burial places? Was that where the money came from that he suddenly had after I gave birth? He said he won it gambling and selling drugs." Lily looked around the room, as if to find someone who could answer her questions. "Could he possibly have done such a horrible thing not once, nor twice, but three times?" Lily covered her face with her hands. "Could I have two more children somewhere that I've never seen? That I don't know about?"

Maggie and Alyssa stared at each other. Was it possible there were two more siblings?

Lion Lawson was first to break the stunned silence. "We'll look into it, Lily. I promise we'll do all we can to find out." He slipped his arm around her shoulder and pulled her next to him. "We'll do this together, the three of us, as a family." Then he looked down at Maggie. "How about the four of us? Our crack new investigative reporter may just have a new assignment. Would you like that, M. M. McKenzie?"

Maggie's mouth dropped open, but she didn't know what to say, still stunned by the possibility that there was more family that no one knew anything about.

Suddenly from under the love seat a bundle of fur appeared, stretched, yawned, then bounced playfully over to Maggie and jumped up to kiss her face. She promptly boosted the pup onto Alyssa's lap and got to her feet.

"I think this calls for refreshments," Maggie said, breaking the silence. She turned to Lily and Mr. Lawson. "You probably haven't had time to eat anything since you landed. You got here so fast, you probably missed meals all day."

"We were fortunate Mr. Randolph was in Ojai for Christmas, just a few minutes' flight over the mountains from San Buenaventura. But when I called, he sent his private plane for us so fast we barely had time to throw clothes in a suitcase and get to the airport." Mr. Lawson stood and faced Maggie. "I understand, M. M. McKenzie, that you are only on loan to me until he needs you somewhere else."

Maggie looked up at him. "Yes, sir. I believe that's how the contract was written."

"I'd be happy to hear how a cub reporter could locate my daughter when half a dozen experienced detectives, the FBI, and police all over the United States couldn't."

"I had heavenly help, sir, something I think the others were probably lacking."

He took Maggie's hands in his, bent down and kissed her check and tried to say thank you, but his emotions choked the words for a minute. Then he continued, "And if you had any leftover turkey from dinner that I could eat while you tell me the whole story, that would make me even happier."

That was all it took to break the ice. The six adjourned to the kitchen and Rose put out all the leftovers from dinner, including the refreshments Maggie and Alyssa had prepared. Everyone fixed his or her own plate, which they carried to the dining room to eat, all talking at once. Just one big happy family.

Almost. Maggie wished Flynn could be with them. She missed him more than she thought possible. Maybe he would still call to see how things turned out, to see if Alyssa had found the courage to contact her father and Lily. Or maybe he'd stay away for months until he discovered all he needed to know, and do what he needed to do. Maybe he'd returned to Louisiana already to pick up his car and was heading back to South Dakota.

Maggie realized she didn't even know where he lived, just that he spent a few months in the winter at the Alpine Inn writing and researching. Well, he certainly had some good material for his next publication.

It turned out to be a wonderful evening, with stories exchanged from Alyssa and Maggie's childhood by the twins and their parents. Twenty-four years worth of events meant a lot of catching up to do, and when the rest of the family returned at ten o'clock from their movie evening at Rick and Rachel's, they found the reunited group were still gathered around the dining-room table talking.

Maggie slipped quietly away while introductions were being made and headed for her back-porch retreat. *Oh, Flynn,* she thought as she hugged her knees in her private little corner. *I wish you could have waited just twenty-four more hours so you'd have all these answers we worked so hard together to find.*

Just then Maggie's cell phone rang. She jumped to her feet to dig it out of her jeans pocket. "Hello," she said breathlessly, hoping, praying it was Flynn. It was.

"Hi, Maggie." He paused. "Are you still speaking to me?"

"Oh, Flynn, of course. Where are you? Are you okay?"

"No, I'm not okay, because I'm not with you, but I'm safe, if that's what you meant."

"I missed you today, Flynn. So much happened, and I kept wishing you were here to see the resolution to all the questions." Maggie curled back in her well-worn chair and recited the events of the day.

"I had a pretty good day, with a resolution to a lot of my questions, too," he said quietly when she'd finished.

"Yes?" Maggie held her breath.

"Right now I'm in a room overlooking Temple Square and a million Christmas lights. It's one of the most breathtaking views I've ever seen. I wish . . ." Flynn left his sentence dangling and started another. "Maggie, I've been with several beautiful young women today, all of whom wear name tags with the first name of Sister."

Maggie laughed. "The sister missionaries."

"Yes. Basically, I've spent the entire day at the Visitors' Center on Temple Square, where they've shown me so many films my head's swimming and taught me why you believe like you do, and why those beliefs are so important to you."

There was a very long silence and finally Maggie said, "And . . . ?"

"Do you remember an old movie, *An Affair to Remember*?"

"Yes, with Deborah Kerr and Cary Grant. I've never been able to watch it without crying." Suddenly she knew what he was going to say.

"It was on TV tonight. As I watched it, I felt that might be a wise thing for us to do, too. This is going to be so hard for me to say, and even harder for me to actually do, but Maggie, I think we need to give ourselves a year. I'll continue studying your faith, and of course,

I'll have to go back to work, but you'll go on with your life as well. I promise not to call you or contact you, though it will be unbearable to not hear your voice during that time. If we still feel about each other in one year as we do at this moment, we'll meet at the foot of the *Christus* statue in the Visitors' Center on Temple Square at five o'clock on Christmas Day."

Flynn stopped speaking, but Maggie couldn't find her voice. She pictured Cary Grant standing alone at the top of the Empire State Building waiting for Deborah Kerr, who never came, and had a new understanding of his character's heartbreak and anguish. What if Flynn wasn't there when she got there? But the movie had a happy ending. Deborah Kerr wasn't there because her character had been in an accident, and Cary Grant finally found her and they lived happily ever after. And Maggie cried.

"Maggie?"

"Yes, Flynn. I'm sure you're right. We need to give ourselves time and space and perspective. If . . ." she faltered at the word ". . . if we still feel the same way as now, we'll meet at the *Christus* statue on Christmas Day next year."

Flynn didn't want the conversation to end any more than Maggie did. "I suppose you're going back to work for the San Buenaventura paper?"

"Yes," Maggie whispered, hardly able to speak.

"Good luck on your job, Maggie girl. Be happy and be safe."

"Thanks. Good luck to you, Flynn. Oh, where can I send the rest of the money? You left too much just to fly to Pine Bluff to get my car."

"Take Alyssa or Steve with you, or your mom. Make it a fun trip. Finish your Lewis and Clark story. Follow your dreams, Maggie, wherever they take you."

There was a pause, then a click on the line, and the phone went dead. Flynn was gone. Gone for at least a year. Maybe forever.

Maggie sat in the dark for a long time, remembering every moment she'd spent with Flynn. Then, when she realized she was freezing. She went to the kitchen, sat at her mother's desk, and began planning her new year.

Tomorrow was Sunday. Alyssa and her parents would go to church with her family, and she'd make reservations for a flight to

Arkansas. Then, Maggie thought, she would backtrack along the Lewis and Clark Trail, stopping at all those little towns that had beckoned her to find the wonderful stories waiting to be written.

She had a relationship to develop with a new sister, the job of her dreams, and a whole year of unknown possibilities ahead of her. Life would be good. Maggie would make it that way, and her continual prayer for the next year would be, "Thy will, not mine, be done."

ABOUT THE AUTHOR

LYNN GARDNER is an avid storyteller who does careful research to back up the high-adventure romantic thrillers that have made her a popular writer in the LDS market, enabling her to weave historical fact and authentic locations with intriguing fictional characters and exciting stories.

Lynn was born and raised in Idaho, attended Rigby and Blackfoot High Schools, and married her high-school sweetheart, Glenn Gardner.

Lynn and Glenn make their home in Quartz Hill, California, and recently celebrated their 50th anniversary with a long-awaited trip to China.

Lynn has visited England and Wales to research family history. And of course, Maggie's next adventure is sure to take place among the quaint villages and mysterious ruins she finds there.

Lynn enjoys corresponding with her readers, who can write to her in care of Covenant Communications, P.O. Box 416, American Fork, UT 84003–0416, or e-mail her via Covenant at info@covenant-lds.com.